Breathe You

A *Pieces of Broken* Novel

Celeste Grande

Cover Designed by:
Sommer Stein of Perfect Pear Creative Covers

Cover Photography by:
Lauren Perry of Perrywinkle Photography

Interior Design and Formatting by:
Christine Borgford, Type A Formatting

Dedication

To the women who are scared to use their voices, the teenagers who fear the repercussions of speaking up, and the children who question whether or not this evil is normal.

It's not.

Point your shaking finger.

Find your voice.

Speak your truth.

"Learn from yesterday, live for today, hope for tomorrow."

~ Albert Einstein

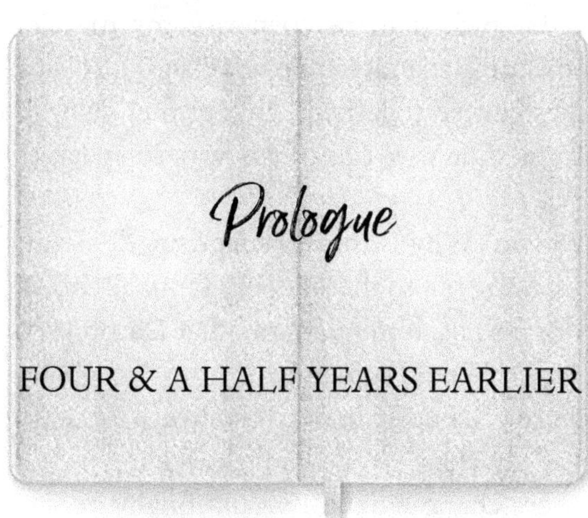

Prologue

FOUR & A HALF YEARS EARLIER

"I THINK YOUR SISTER IS narcoleptic."

My sister's boyfriend's voice broke my train of thought, but any distraction from these incoming freshman assignments for high school was welcomed. I pulled the pen cap from where it was clenched between my teeth.

"Abby fell asleep again?" I sat up straighter on the bed and moved the books off my lap. Cupping my fingers into my neckline, I tugged up, adjusting my shirt that—thanks to late puberty—didn't quite sit the same anymore.

Damon's eyes flicked to the swell of my newly blossomed breasts. I squirmed a little, blushing, unsure of how to handle that kind of attention. Deciding to pretend like I didn't notice, I pressed my palms behind me and leaned back, my legs still crisscrossed in front of me.

Damon walked farther into my room, stretching his arms above his head. "She falls asleep every damn afternoon."

I rolled my eyes. "So go wake her up." I laughed through my words.

Damon stood at the foot of my bed, eyeing me—his brown hair tousled and lying lazily over his forehead, his thumb hooked into the belt loop of his khakis. Lately, I had been noticing a change in the way he looked at me—like he was finally seeing me for the first time. I knew he was off limits, but being noticed by someone older—and not in that kid-sister type of way—made my blood pump a little faster.

Damon placed his knee on the edge of the bed before his full weight dipped it down. He picked at the corner of my marble notebook. "It's okay. I've been meaning to talk to you anyway."

My eyebrows knitted together. "Talk to me?" Not that Damon ever ignored me, but he didn't go out of his way to speak to me, especially not privately.

"Yes, talk to you. Why is that so surprising?" He nudged his shoulder with mine, rocking me to the side. His familiar chocolate-brown eyes smiled along with his lips, reminding me that Damon was almost family, around for as long as I could remember.

"Well, because . . . I don't know. I'm always forcing you guys to pay attention to me." My chest swelled a little, feeling as though maybe the hands of time were changing and I would finally be included with him and my sister more.

"Trust me, beautiful, I've been paying attention." He licked his lips, and his smile faltered, bringing a strange sense of insecurity with it which swiped away some of that short-lived pride that I was feeling.

Something in his eyes, or his glance below my neck for the second time, sent warmth to my cheeks. I covered them, not wanting him to see the change in color, and he laughed again.

"You're cute." He paused, studying my face some more before sitting up straighter, becoming serious. "That's what I wanted to talk to you about."

I stared at him, totally confused.

He scooted closer to me on the bed, his eyes looking as though he were genuinely worried about something. "You're starting high school, Eva. A small fish. Sure, Abby and I are there, but we're upperclassmen. We have important things going on, planning for college and all. We won't always be there to protect you." The corner of his lip puckered in sympathy as his eyes softened.

I didn't need a reminder of what next week would bring. I was dreading walking through those doors, getting knocked off the pedestal I had stood on all last year, being the 'big fish' as he called it. *Just one more thing to worry about.*

I expelled a nervous half-laugh, trying to conceal my budding anxiety. "Protect me? From what?"

Damon merely studied me once again, then ignored my question.

"You ever been kissed, beautiful?"

He'd been calling me that a lot recently. Last week after Abby had gone inside, he had called me that when he'd kissed me goodbye. He'd misdirected his lips, and they'd landed at the corner of my mouth rather than my cheek. When my breath caught, he'd left them there for a second before he pulled back with a wolfish grin, floating an apology my way.

"Sure," I scoffed with a wave. "Jace kisses me all the time."

Damon leaned a little closer. "I know he's gay, Eva." His whisper whisked over my flesh, and I sat up straighter, pinpricks erupting along my suddenly sensitized skin. His gaze flicked to my lips before returning to my eyes. "I'm not talking about a best friend's kiss."

I didn't know what his deal was, but I was starting to feel uncomfortable. I swallowed, trying to figure out how to go about this. I knew what he meant, and no, I hadn't kissed anyone yet, but I wouldn't admit it. I mean, who went to high school never having been kissed? Losers, that was who. "I know what you're talking about. I'm not a prude."

His voice was soft but deliberate. "That's just it. I think you are." His eyes dragged up to mine slowly, showcasing humor rather than empathy for his rude statement.

"Real nice, Damon." I scrunched up my face and reached for my pen.

His hand landed on my knee, and I halted, my eyes following it. *He's acting so strange.*

Another nervous laugh escaped my lips as I watched his index finger stroke in a tight circle. He kept touching me in these ways lately—ways that felt so different from before. When we were younger, he would put me in headlocks and rub noogies into my scalp with his knuckles. Lately, his touches were softer, lingered a little longer.

He tilted his head, his face pulled into the center. "I just keep thinking how you're gonna be around all these older guys now. I don't want you to be taken advantage of." He straightened, focusing on my face. "It would kill me to know they were saying things behind your back because you didn't know what you were doing. Making fun of you." He preached his truth, speaking to my fears. "Kids can be cruel, Eva."

My eyes widened. I opened my mouth, then closed it, heat slicing my face with blooming embarrassment. Not wanting to admit to my insecurities, I frowned instead, crossing my arms over my chest. "Thanks for the pep talk."

The corner of his mouth quirked, a twitch so slight I almost missed it. Softening, he took my wrists and lowered them to my lap, his hands resting on my upper thighs. My gaze fell to the gesture. "I'm just being honest." He shrugged. "Jeez, Eva—I've known you since I can remember. It's only right I look out for you."

"I'm sure I'll be all right." I shrugged him off, my cheeks glowing with humiliation. I just wanted him to drop this whole topic and get out of my room.

"Really?" He settled closer to me once again and moved his lips to my ear, lowering his voice. "So if I kissed you right now, you would know what to do? How to reciprocate?"

Hot waves flooded my belly, churning and rolling as my heart rate sped to a rapid little tapping beneath my ribs. *What the hell is his deal?*

"Damon, back off of me." I laughed, playing off my jitters and nudging him on the shoulder. That didn't work, though, because it only rocked him back into me, his chuckle landing on my cheek.

"See how immature you are? Playing baby games when I'm trying to be serious?"

I straightened my spine, determined to prove to him that I wasn't, but he was so close—too close—and I could barely think. "I'm not playing games."

He sobered. "Then show me." His face was stoic, as though he was talking about the weather when he spoke the next two words that would change my life. "Kiss me."

I blinked once, twice, three times. *He can't be serious.* When I didn't respond, he reached over and cleaned a dab of lint from my thigh. He studied my face and moved closer so our knees were touching, then placed his palm on the left side of my leg, leaning into my ear.

"Sometimes friends do favors for other friends, but they don't ever say anything." He pulled his head back and stared at my lips. "Get what I'm saying?"

I wanted to say yes. I searched my mind for what he could mean, but I had no clue what he was talking about. *He couldn't possibly be implying . . .*

Embarrassed, I tucked my hair behind my ear and looked down at my lap, fiddling with my fingers.

"I didn't think so." He lifted my chin. "Everyone experiments—uses their closest friend as somewhat of a trial before the real thing. Abby had me, but who do you have? Jace? We all know which way he swings." He trailed a finger along my jaw. "You need me, beautiful."

I jerked my chin away, suddenly back in the moment. "Damon, I can't do that. You're like my brother."

His face sharpened, and I thought I might've hurt his feelings. I opened my mouth to apologize when his chin lifted, and a nonchalance settled over his features. "I'm not really your brother, Eva." He rolled his eyes, making me feel small again. When they came back to find me once more, his gaze lacked its usual friendly banter. An irritation bloomed there instead, and a hot film coated my insides.

"And don't act like I'm ugly or something. You could do far worse."

I lowered my voice, feeling young and insecure all over again, confusion swarming my brain, clouding my reasoning. "I didn't say you were ugly, but it's still kind of gross." I scrunched up my nose, not understanding why he didn't get how weird that would be.

Regaining his calm composure, he brushed my lower lip with the pad of his thumb, making the warm heat return, and lowered his voice as his eyes trained on his finger. "I promise, I won't make it gross. Just enjoy it. Relax. Let me do this for you." His brown eyes flicked back to mine, and he seemed anxious for my response as he took my chin between his fingers and tipped my head back.

My eyes widened. I was nervous enough about high school. The thought of being laughed at made me feel all hot inside, and not in a good way. "But you're Abby's boyfriend."

He paused. "Then don't tell her."

My line of sight snapped up to meet his matter-of-fact tone. His head was cocked to the side, his face unfazed. My forehead puckered, anger crawling up my neck. Abby was my sister. We didn't have secrets. No way was I going behind her back like this. I scooted away from him.

"It's just a kiss, Eva." He rolled his eyes. "Do you really think she'd care about a kiss?" His scoff was enough to label me a baby once again.

Wouldn't she? I picked at the edges of my hair, my mind reeling with different scenarios. *Do I go through with this and see what it was like with someone I trusted? Do I tell Abby? Keep it from her?* Damon inched closer again, and anxiety pumped heavy in my veins. He was too close to me, pushing too hard. I needed time to think. Space.

I fidgeted, suddenly able to *feel* my sister's absence.

But Damon relaxed once again, peeling back some of the pressure I felt constricting my bed that suddenly felt smaller than a double. A reassuring smile slid across his face. "I was just saying, if it makes you feel better, I'll agree not to tell her as long as you do." His eyes sparkled with an excitement I couldn't quite place before he rushed to add, "I mean, you wouldn't want to go to school without *any* experience, would you? And you trust me, right? You know I would never hurt you. It would be our little secret." He bopped me on the nose as though this were any other run-of-the-mill question.

Suddenly it didn't feel like such a ludicrous idea. What could be the harm in a kiss? She would never know, and I wouldn't have to feel like an inexperienced child anymore. Something continued to tug at me, telling me this was wrong, but the bands of constraint that I originally felt at his proposition were loosening. Besides, I believed him. I knew he wouldn't hurt me.

"Wha—what do I have to do?" I swallowed, feeling nervous.

The corner of his mouth hitched into a smirk. "Good girl. First, I need you to say you want it. You want this, right? I'm not forcing you or anything?" He dipped his head and looked up at me, trying to will the correct answer from my lips.

No. Not really. But if everyone does this . . .

I wrapped my finger around one of my curls, toying with it to ease my nerves. Then . . .

I nodded.

His smile widened, distracting me as his hand snaked around my hip, tugging me to him, forcing our noses to nearly collide. "Just don't forget." His eyes sparkled, alight with excitement the way a cat regards a mouse. "This is our little secret. I won't tell anyone you wanted it if you don't tell anyone it happened." It was the first time someone's face had been so close to mine that I could actually smell their breath. His smelled of the grilled cheese sandwich Abby had made him. And cream soda.

My heart rate took off as his gaze dropped to my lips as though he was coveting them. The muscles in my belly sucked in, bringing with it a gulp of air.

What am I doing?

He brought his hand around the back of my neck, securing me so I couldn't change my mind. Everything became real in an instant, and I was paralyzed, staring into salivating brown eyes.

A protest rose in my throat—my mind changing as a prickly sheath slithered over my skin at having him so close. His eyelids closed just as the first brush of his lips met my own, stealing my objection, and I shivered, noticing each pant that left my dry mouth.

Fairy tales.

Bedtime stories.

From the very beginning, we're read stories of princes and of love's first kiss. The meaningful connection and the heartfelt pitter-patter of being swept off your feet and finding your happily ever after. When you picture it, the skip of your heart is coated with anticipation and curiosity. With butterflies and a giddy-anxiousness that rises in a wave and floods in a gentle heat, warming your belly.

This didn't feel like that.

I had always imagined my first kiss would be special. *Beautiful.* There was that word again—the irony of it not lost on me.

A dirty sensation crawled over me as he licked my bottom lip—probing, urging mine to part and something inside me triggered, warning bells cautioning me that this was wrong. I tried to relax, will it away, but I just couldn't concentrate. Not when his squishy, slimy tongue was invading me. It was a weird softness that I wasn't sure I could get used to, and it was complicated, trying to figure out how to breathe through my nose with someone sharing my air.

He moaned into my mouth and rubbed his tongue along mine, going deeper as his fingers tightened on the back of my neck, and then I felt the edges of his fingertips softly exploring my collarbone. Nervous queasiness bloomed inside of me. I wanted to tell him to stop, but I didn't want to seem like a baby.

But then—

His hands dropped lower.

With a quick twist of his fingers, he popped open the few buttons at the top of my shirt, exposing the delicate satin of my bra. Instinctively, I grabbed the two edges and fastened it closed as best as I could, but I still seemed to be spilling out of the center.

"Hey!" I protested, feeling embarrassed. My chest heaved, relieved to be flooded with clean air but also straining through the narrow entryway caused by the onslaught of nerves.

Staring at my chest, he swallowed hard, and I got the feeling this wasn't entirely for *my* benefit. But he played it cool, bringing his gaze back to my face with a laugh, covering my hand with his.

I twisted my shoulder back, flicking him off. "What's with unbuttoning my shirt?" I struggled hastily to fit the buttons back into their holes.

Damon took my fingers in his and moved my hands to my lap, leaving me bare and self-conscious. "Do you really think people just make out all day long?" He laughed through his nose, clearly jabbing fun at me.

Yes? I thought, but all I could manage was a blinking stare.

Damon huffed. "See, this is what I mean." The tenderness was back in his voice, his eyes coaxing me to see the error of my reaction. "You're too nice. Too naïve. Would I ever do anything to hurt you?" His eyebrows pulled in, and he looked offended.

I gulped. *Would he?* An unease that I couldn't place sat heavy over me, but this was Damon. "No, I guess not." I relaxed a little.

"You need to accept how beautiful you are, Eva. Whoever you wind up with is going to want to enjoy you. They're not going to want to be with a squeamish child." He rolled his eyes, and I shrunk a bit more, feeling stupid and inexperienced. I couldn't stand it.

"Now, come on. Judging by that last kiss, you're going to need lots of practice." He knotted his fingers into the hair at the back of my head and pulled me toward him once again. The dominance in his grip was unmistakable, even though I'd never experienced anything like that before. It stopped me cold, taking away my ability to make my own choices. He lingered inches from my face, his domineering eyes conveying a message to give in to what was happening, before he covered my mouth with his, more demanding than before.

On instinct, my lips puckered and he bit them, squeezing my hair a bit harder. Then he licked my lips, gentler, coercing me to open them. I just wanted this to be over, even if it meant being labeled a prude. I was starting to feel like my skin was too tight having him this close to me. It was hard to breathe, but I forced my tongue to try and follow his movements.

Until his strokes became more desperate.

Grazing down, his fingers explored until my breast was covered by a foreign hand for the first time in my life. I broke the kiss again, and my lips parted with a gasp.

"Damon, what're you—"

He slipped his thumb inside my mouth, its taste a bit dirty as it rested on my tongue. "Shhh . . . So beautiful," he whispered on a moan, securing my neck once again and bringing me back to him.

This time, when the circle of his mouth covered mine, it felt different. There was no room for my breath in the tiny sliver of space, and I could feel my lips object beneath his, the terse lines of mine as my tongue stopped trying to keep up and started trying to figure out how to make him stop and still save face. Helplessness began to funnel into my core like an hourglass, the first few grains that would add up and bury me if it trickled in long enough.

His weight crept up on me, forcing my back to the mattress. "You said kiss, Damon. I didn't say yes to this," I spoke around his mouth, panic creeping up my throat, closing it off.

Fully blanketing me, his hardness made itself known on my thigh.

I'm gonna be sick.

"Say yes, Eva. Let me show you." He pushed a soft kiss to my mouth, still trying to portray sincerity through his actions, but he was having trouble holding back.

That kiss was the last gentle gesture he would offer that afternoon.

"But . . ." The word was garbled under the pressure of his lips, and I knew his request was merely rhetorical. He didn't care about my response, the vibrations coming off him told me so.

"You said you wanted this. Don't be a *tease*," he spat. "That's worse than being labeled a *slut*." The glisten of my saliva on his lips, the lips I agreed to kiss, stopped me cold.

Tease? Slut? Is that what I am? I did say yes. I said yes. And now I can't say no.

My mind raced with what that would mean, but I didn't have time to make sense of it. His finger slid to the edge of my bra and then tugged down, causing my breast to tumble out of the thin material. I tried to grab for it, but he was quick to push further, bearing his weight onto my chest.

I shoved up, wanting this to end, needing him to stop like I needed air. Realization that he had no intention of ceasing swept in hard and fast, taking my breath away at the same speed and I struggled to gain oxygen. "Get off of me," I objected, trying to knock him side to side, but he grabbed both of my much smaller wrists and pinned them above my head, pushing them into the mattress.

His whole demeanor had changed. He looked starved for my skin, and the spirals in his irises, the promise beneath them that he wasn't leaving unsatisfied freaked me into silence, tunneling me into shock.

When he lifted for a moment to shift, I found one more protest buried deep inside my body which felt as though it were drifting away from me. "Da—" But his thumb slid back into my mouth, silencing my tongue, pulling down my jaw.

His wet thumb dragged along my cheek as he hovered over the shell of my ear, his breath settling over it on a light whisper. "Shhh. She'll hear you."

My blood ran cold, prickling through my veins.

Fear.

I drew my bottom lip between my teeth and bit down as hard as I could, my nostrils flaring, trying to keep the hot flood of tears from my eyes. One thousand thoughts spiraled in a confusing cyclone as I tried to make sense of what was happening.

Shhh. She'll hear you.

I cringed, feeling as though a thousand tiny insect legs were scampering over me.

Help me.

Pinching my eyes shut, I felt the pool of water sitting between my lashes as I buried the bad feeling I had. *I don't want to do this.* My soul cried, spurts of air entered and exited my parted lips on anxious puffs.

But I was helpless. And too far gone. My sister's boyfriend was on top of me. Kissing me. Touching me in places that no one had ever seen. The breasts that, until this moment I'd been so proud of, felt dirty and cheap as he squeezed and poked at them, drooling over their weight, and it was my fault it was happening. I couldn't say a word. *She'll hear you.*

Gone was the boy next door, the one I knew so well. That had helped me grow up.

Helped me grow up. I almost laughed at that irony. The person on top of me right now was totally foreign to me. Pushy and demanding. I didn't like anything he was doing, but for some reason, I couldn't tell him. I couldn't speak. Unable to watch, I looked up at the ceiling blinking away my emotions and gnawing my bottom lip.

I've already gone too far.

They would all be so mad at me. *Just get through it and then it'll be over.* I would never think about it again. Never talk about it—ever.

His weight dragged down my body, my shorts and underwear gliding down my legs, taking with it an exposed shiver. An uninhibited smile adorned his sly features as he shook the buckle of his belt loose, a jingle that I would hear in my nightmares for the rest of my life. His face pinched with longing, and I wondered briefly what he was thinking, but his next words pinned me down, slamming what remained of my adolescence into the coiled springs beneath me.

"Hold on tight, beautiful. You're about to become a woman."

No. No, no, no.

How had so much changed so fast? My body was jostled beneath his efforts, and all I did was flop around like a fish out of water. His prey, ripe for the taking.

But still, I didn't say a word.

Blackness crept in, washing away the light of the room. My body felt light and airy even though the pressure on top of it was all consuming—the sounds, the moans, the rustling and rubbing, drifting into a muffled fog. His movements seemed to be coming from some far off place, but I couldn't focus on them completely—his tongue swiping at random points to my breasts and torso, but I was shutting down. Going outside myself somewhere.

"Beautiful," he dragged out on a whisper, and I shuddered at the first breach of my virgin barrier.

Inside, I wept as Damon obliterated any hopes for a happily ever after. Or a Prince Charming. Each push was like an ice pick, shattering the young girl I was. Tears of anger, grief, guilt, fear, they all streamed down my face in a silent parade. And when it became too much, the final pieces of me shut down completely.

I turned my face away from his to find Mary, the stuffed lamb Abby had given me to keep me safe. To take away bad thoughts. I focused harder on her fleecy fur, turning what was left of my reality to a grayed-out darkness. I started chanting, wishing she could take me away, back to a time of innocence.

Mary had a little lamb, little lamb, little lamb . . .

~ And in the darkness, the dust buries the fallen.

DAY ONE.

DAY TWO.

DAY THREE.

I ROLLED OVER.

The sadness of my disarray fell in cascading waves around me. The physical pains of being assaulted and having my insides ejected from my body were nothing compared to the pain of losing my heart. Losing my soul.

One would think that, without a heart, you'd feel less. But I'd have to rebut that argument. I now knew it to be a falsity because I felt much, much more. I was feeling . . . everything.

Live me.

The words rang in my head on a constant loop. If I thought I was broken before, I was only a piece of a shattered person now. The rest was missing. My *light*—gone. A sliver of my soul had been carved out and had evaporated into thin air. *He* was gone.

Live me. Live me. Live me.

And there it replayed again, torturing me from the inside.

The disappointment in his eyes would never leave me. The hurt. The anguish in his blue diamonds as they sparkled their last dying light.

I rolled to the other side and tucked the sheet into the crook of my neck, wincing when even the softness of the pillow grazed my tender cheek. I gritted my teeth. Served me right for thinking my life would ever be anything other than this, engulfed in suffocating loneliness. I had needed the wakeup call.

As promised, Blake had walked away without even a text. I knew it was for the best, but the hurt I felt each time I checked the screen of my cell phone was insurmountable. There was no clinical term for what I had. I had death, plain and simple. When your heart no longer beat but for the simple passage of blood through your needy veins, you were no longer alive.

Live me.

I fisted the pillow and slammed it over my head, groaning.

Live me.

Live me.

Live me.

"Go away!" I screamed into the cotton-covered feathers.

But it never left.

I wanted to open the top of my head and take a hard piece of pink rubber to it, erasing all the words Blake had ever put there. Un-remember all of the feeling, all of the love, and the raw emotion. I'd never known a real love like that existed. That shit was for the movies.

But it wasn't.

It was a real, living, breathing, tangible thing.

An entity.

It swam through you and pulsated beyond your body. It reached out toward the one it yearned for and pulled them back inside, tucking them away into the little broken crevices of you that needed them.

It was real. It was true. And it was alive.

Live.

Me.

I did. That was why I was dying.

A LIGHT CLINKING SOUNDED IN the room as the door opened, and the smell of food drifted through the air. Toasted bread—jelly, maybe? Fruit?—and the unmistakable scent of freshly brewed coffee.

I felt so fragile beneath the covers as if their gentle fluffiness could snap my bones. The corner of the comforter lifted, sending new air in, replacing what my lungs had been recycling with fresh oxygen.

Jace's face pulled in with disgust. "You stink." He dropped a tray on my nightstand.

"Go away. I'm not in the mood." I replaced the cover over my matted mane. This time, the comforter was ripped aside with less patience. I folded the bend of my arm over my eyes.

"Well, that's not happening." He waved his hand in front of his face. "The least you could've done was hose yourself off. Sprayed some juniper on your stank or something."

I dropped my arm and glared at him. "Did you come here to make me feel worse?"

He crossed his arms, lifting his chin. "No. Time's up. Today you get out of bed, you eat, and for the love of God, you shower."

"Why are you doing this to me?" I rolled to my side and shoved my hands under my cheek facing him.

He put his hand to his chest. "Why am I . . ." Without another word,

Jace left the room.

I closed my eyes, content that I had succeeded in getting rid of his pesky, meddling ass. All I wanted to do was lie here and rot until I disintegrated.

Two seconds later, the swoosh of metal sliding across metal shrieked, and bright light pooled in as Jace tore open my curtains. I squeezed my eyes so tight, they ached. "Jace, what the hell!"

There was a hard tapping on my head. I grabbed for the assault weapon and only opened my eyes when I couldn't find it. A familiar shade of green looked back at me, albeit slightly duller than I remembered and lackluster. I pushed at the mirror propped between Jace's hands and clutched the comforter to my chest, trying to shrink smaller.

"*That*, my dear, is why I'm doing this. This place is going to be condemned soon." He threw the mirror beside me on the bed.

"You're being dramatic," I huffed.

"Sweetheart, I *am* drama." He swept his fingertips along his blond highlighted hairline. "But I'm not being dramatic this time. You smell like the zoo . . . at a circus . . . held in a dumpster. Shall we take a poll? Call in for opinions?" He straightened and looked around.

"Fine! Just shut up." I flung the sheet off my body and swung my legs off the side of the bed, wincing as I clutched a rib that was still sore. Jace swallowed through his frown as his eyes roamed over me briefly before he caught himself. He quickly replaced the melancholy expression with a smile that didn't reach his eyes.

Self-conscious, I jacked up the hem of my tank and tried to smooth down my hair. My fingers rolled over what felt like hard cotton, and I realized I'd never washed out the hospital.

How many days has it been?

I looked at the ceiling, mentally trying to tick off my time spent in this room when my sights rested on a delicate rose poking out of a petite, white vase in the corner of the tray. My heart wound back and punched me in the gut. I knew Jace had meant well, but that flower brought back too many painful memories of Blake, my only love.

"Get that out of here." My voice shook, the prickling of tears stinging my ducts.

Jace followed my eyes and then winced. "Sorry, love. I forgot." He disappeared with the flower. He really was cute. He'd thought of everything down to the vitamins and Tylenol lying beside a glass of orange juice. My heart warmed. He was forgiven for the flower.

The bed dipped down, and Jace's arm slid over my shoulder. He reached past me with the other arm and held a bagel with cream cheese and grape jelly in front of my mouth. "Bite."

I did as he commanded, and the food landed like a lump in my empty belly, but the sweetness on my lips was divine. I opened again, and the corner of Jace's mouth lifted in a genuine smile for the first time. His eyes lightened as he pushed a new bite into my mouth.

I ate half of it before he handed me the pills and the orange juice, ordering me to swallow. Already feeling a little better, I grabbed the mug of coffee and squeezed his leg, moving in for a kiss.

Jace's head snapped back. "Don't you dare. I was in diapers the last time you brushed those teeth. That mouth's not coming near me."

My jaw dropped open, and I quickly put a palm in front of it to blow and smell.

Jace stood and pointed toward the door. "Bathroom. Now."

I knew when not to argue with Jace. And truth be told, I wouldn't have had the strength in me to do so if I wanted to. On feeble legs I wobbled, not having used them a whole bunch in the last few days, my pajama bottoms hanging from my hips and dragging across the hardwood.

I flicked the switch on the wall and walked into the bathroom. The cool tile shocked my bare feet, and I rubbed my arms as a chill raced through me.

Jace took my hips and maneuvered me aside so he could make his way over to the tub, which forced a broken girl to stand in the reflection in front of me. I wasn't ready to see her. But now that I did, I couldn't take my eyes off her.

She looked so empty. So shattered. Her eyes were a slimy shade of grayish green, surrounded by red vines, encased in shallow purple shells. Right below, a yellowish patch was splayed over a cheekbone which was more pronounced than I remembered. Atop her head sat a matted nest.

After turning on the water to the shower, Jace came and stood behind me. He put his hands on my shoulders and stared with me, not saying a word—not having to speak. Although he had no trouble reading my mind, I knew this was one time he wanted to stay out of my head. I closed my eyes and turned away.

Jace dug around in my hair, trying to find the elastic band knotted around it. He pushed and pulled before my mane came tumbling down my back, brushing the band of my sleep pants. He tucked his fingers into the hem of my tank, and I raised my arms letting him peel it away. I was never shy in front of my best friend, but for some reason, my arms automatically crossed in front of my chest to cover myself.

Jace lowered my pants to the floor next. I felt so open and vulnerable, even with him, and it killed me that I was so weak.

Jace took my face between his hands and tilted my head to kiss my forehead. "This, too, shall pass, sugar. You'll be strong again."

I sucked my lips into my mouth, puckering the skin between my eyes to keep from breaking down. He helped me into the tub, and I pressed my back against the porcelain, staring at the barrage of water tumbling down. I was scared it would hurt, even though I knew how illogical that sounded. My hands shook, and I tried catching one with the other to still them. When I looked down, my breath caught. A red swell covered my breast, and random bruises lay scattered over my skin. Leaning forward, I discovered between my thighs were also discolored and sore. It was the first time I'd seen the extent of what Damon had done.

Quiet sobs hitched my chest up and down. Unable to carry the burden any longer, I was about to drop, my shoulders falling forward when sturdy hands caught me. Jace stepped into the tub with glassy eyes, his jaw so tight it could snap glass. Though he didn't speak, his eyes spoke volumes. I could see all of his questions, his concerns, his rage.

"Come here, munchkin." He pulled my back to his chest, and his underwear brushed my backside. He'd kept them on, and I felt relieved even though I'd seen him plenty of times without them.

The relief broke me.

He was my best friend. The one person I could *always* count on to be there for me. I wasn't supposed to think twice about being afraid of him. I cried harder. I'd lost me. All of me.

Jace bent his knees, bringing us both to sit on the tub floor. He spun us so our backs were to the water, but it was his skin it beat against. He didn't say a word the rest of the time, and I was thankful because I didn't think I could have answered. He just held me between his legs, hugging me from all angles, and rocked until he felt my movements cease.

When I had finally calmed, he reached up and grabbed the shampoo before massaging suds into my hair. I winced, clutching at a tender spot as a flashback of Damon dragging me to the couch bolted through my mind.

"I'm sorry." Jace put his hand on mine.

I shook my head. "It's not your fault. I just didn't expect it. Go ahead. It feels nice."

"I'll be gentle."

He continued to wash more gingerly, tilting my head back to wash out the suds, then repeating the process with conditioner. Leaving it there to set, he worked soap over every inch of me, careful of the amount of pressure he applied. When I was clean, he handed me the soap and backed away to give me privacy so I could wash the parts he shouldn't touch, though I didn't think they'd ever feel clean again.

With tentative hands, I felt around between my legs with the soap, scared I would hit a sore spot like the one on my head. My pubic bone was tender. I squeezed my eyes shut as tears leaked through the edges, and I moved my fingers through my folds, knowing I needed to get through this to wipe away any trace of that bastard. As I washed, my mind flashed images in quick succession, each one jolting my body as they slammed into me—

His hands.

His teeth.

Damon mounting himself on top of me, moving between my legs.

I wailed, my body bucking as it remembered it all. Remembered the feel of his hands—those fucking hands—*everywhere.*

I wept louder, faintly registering Jace's soft "shhh . . ." from behind me, and I was thankful he refrained from touching me.

I took the soap in my clutches, brought it to my arm and scrubbed, raking my nails over my skin, trying to remove as many layers as possible, feeling like someone had let an ant farm loose inside of me. Vibrant red streaks emerged over each area that I moved to, but it felt good. Like a release. Crunching down hard on my molars, I curled my lip over my teeth, picking up the pace as the hot burn sliced through me.

Unable to take it any longer, Jace grabbed my wrists and hugged me to him, whispering soothing hushes into my ear and telling me he loved me—that it would all be okay—until I was calm enough to settle. He washed out the conditioner and stood, scooping me up and placing me on the floor mat.

With delicate strokes, he patted me dry. I stepped into a clean pair of underwear, and he pulled a T-shirt over my head. I waited as he changed into dry clothes, then stood behind me, combing my hair with a careful, delicate finesse. He always loved to do that, and I always loved when he did. It made me feel protected, and taken care of. This time I could tell that he was doing it with purpose rather than enjoyment. I knew he wanted to take care of me, but I could tell he would be happy when this task was over and behind us.

When he finished, he draped my hair over one shoulder and set the brush on the counter. His hands rested on my shoulders, and I could feel the weight of his eyes on my reflection. "You don't have to tell me what happened 'till you're ready, but I do want you to see someone you can talk to."

"Jace . . ."

"Don't." His sharp tone made me look at his mirrored image. "Don't, Eva. When you finally came to me with this, it was because you knew I would help you any way I could. You couldn't take it anymore. Remember?"

I nodded.

"When I pleaded with you to tell someone, and you refused, I didn't push, did I?"

"No." My voice shrunk.

"So I did the next best thing. I got you the hell out of there and figured we'd sort it out later. Well, it's later." His eyebrows shot together in a deep V. "It's escalated. Look at you!" He threw his hand out toward my reflection.

I recoiled, looking away again, unable to bear the truth of it. He reached his arm around the front of my face and forced my chin in the direction of the mirror.

"Look. At. You." Intensity grew in his eyes as they glittered with a fresh set of tears. His lips quivered as his fingers dug into my jaw. "He's *taken* you. *Destroyed* you. Where are you? Do you even see yourself anymore?" His voice cracked with fury, with pain, giving away that he, too, was suffering through this. I had never considered what witnessing all of this for so long was doing to *him*.

My lips trembled.

"Cry, love. Get it the fuck out of you already." His voice broke and then so did he. He wrapped his arms around me, his chest heaving into my back, hot tears raining down on my shoulder.

I crumbled forward, leaning my body on the counter, taking him with me. We both bucked and swayed and cried until there was nothing left. Sniffling, Jace picked me up so my legs dangled over his forearm and walked me back to my bedroom, laying me down. He sat beside me.

"Eva, I love you so much. I only want what's best for you, so you have to listen. You have to trust me."

I stared into his amber eyes, and all I saw was adoration, laced with a tinge of what looked like regret. I knew part of him shouldered the blame for not forcing me to come clean sooner, and it was becoming harder and harder for him to live with.

"You need to—" He cleared his throat and strengthened his shoulders. "You *will* see someone. And when you're stronger, you're going to tell your family."

"Jace—"

His hand waved sharply. "Shh! You can't let Abby marry that monster. It's not right. He's progressing, Eva." He steadied his gaze on me. "He *took* you. Forcefully and against your will. You're going to tell them, and you're going to end it. No more!"

I knew he had reached his breaking point as well. I swallowed hard and nodded once, though I still wasn't convinced I'd do it. He kissed my forehead and rose from the bed. I sat up and tucked a leg beneath me, watching him move around my room, attempting to tidy.

"Jace?"

"Yeah, love?" He picked up an old pair of yoga pants, inspecting them with his face scrunched up before exhaling a puff of air, rolling his eyes, and tossing them into the hamper.

Blake's electric blue gaze twinkled before me before falling in front of me like scattered ash. "Have you seen him?" I squeezed the sheet, needing to hold onto something in anticipation of his answer.

Jace looked away.

I swallowed. "Is he okay? Tell me, Jace," I asked quietly, attempting to seem unaffected despite the knocking in my chest.

He knotted the tank he'd been folding and dropped his hands with a sigh. "How do you think he is, Eva?" He paused, looking me over before going back to his task. "Let's just concentrate on you for now. You have enough to deal with for the time being."

"But—"

His eyes sharpened. "I'm serious."

I paused, clarity taking shape for the first time in days. "We need to protect him."

Jace stopped what he was doing and fisted his hip, a white tank dangling from his clutches. "Sweetheart, forgive me if I'm missing something, but I'm pretty sure you're in no position to be protecting anybody."

The answer was clear to me now, and I needed for him to understand. "We need to protect him *from me*." When Jace's eyes narrowed, I continued. "And himself."

"I'm not following. You're going to have to decode this one."

I spoke rapidly, still trying to get a hold of my thought process. "Jace, if he were to find out—if he were to know who did this . . ." my eyes dragged up to meet his. "He'd kill him." I shuddered, knowing beyond a shadow of a doubt that was the truth. "He'd kill him and his life would be over. I can't let that happen to him. I need to do this right."

"What does that mean?" Jace questioned.

"It means it has to be me that fixes this. On my own. I just don't know how I'm going to do it yet." My heart broke, knowing full-well that meant Blake and I were really over. This was the only piece of me left to give to him.

Jace nodded, and I knew I had the word of my best friend that he would do as I asked. "Let's just concentrate on getting you better. He can't be with half a girl anyway. We need you whole, darling."

My gaze dropped to a bruise on my arm, and I looked away, feeling more like a morsel than a half.

Chapter 2

THE SHELL THAT HOUSED WHAT was left of me was thinning quickly. The bruises on the outside were turning a musty shade of yellow, ready to disappear, but I was certain the marks on the inside would remain forever. They were deeper than ever this time.

Jace told Sandra and Jessie, my closest friends here, that I'd decided to take a vacation to clear my head of the breakup with Blake and they bought it. Other than Jace, I had spent my days alone, but those days were limited. I needed to start my new semester. It was bad enough I'd missed the first week.

Every day, I asked how Blake was, and every day Jace would look away and change the topic. I was beginning to think there was something he didn't want me to know. My insides ached for Blake in a way I never could have imagined possible. If I thought I was the walking dead before, now I truly was, as I drifted without a soul. With nothing to live for.

When Damon tried to take my body that day, he'd taken everything inside of me with it. Made every memory meaningless, all of my growth pointless. Like a vacuum, he'd siphoned it all out, leaving me *this*. Whatever *this* was.

I rolled from the bed, scrubbing my face. I needed to purge some of the venom from my system. Walking to my desk, I pulled open the drawer. Two books stared back at me. One holding love, the other—misery. My heart crumpled a little as I took the journal Blake had given me in my hands, careful not to open it, not wanting to be reminded of what I'd lost.

With a loud shriek, I whipped my arm, throwing Blake's journal. It skidded across the floor, burying itself under my bed. Tears pooled in my eyes, and I pulled my *real* journal from where it had been hiding for the last month. This was the real me—tattered and fraying edges, worn and abused. Not the imposter I was gifted in the hopes I could be, pristine and sparkling. New and shiny. Mirroring an angel when it was the devil coursing through my veins.

Who asks for this fate? Who betrays their flesh and blood?

I had taken what didn't belong to me all those years ago, and now *he* would repeatedly take what didn't belong to him. And I'd pay. Forever. But that's what I deserved. I'd take my punishment for betraying the person who mattered to me the most.

Sitting on the couch, I drew one leg beneath me. My fingers flicked the worn pages, moving to the first blank one. I stared down at it for a moment, knowing how quickly my heart would fill the pristine white college-ruled lines with a glimpse of what was inside. And then my hand took over.

Pieces of Broken

Broken
On the inside
I bend and scoop up the shards
Pricking my finger they leave streaks of crimson in their wake
Pieces
Shattered Pieces
Jagged and strewn about without rhyme or reason
I look around and try to make sense of it
Pieces of me
Whoever me is.
Is there a me? Was there ever?
Pieces upon pieces
Broken little pieces

Hurting little bits, crying out in pain
I listen to their screaming cries and tears fall, knowing I can't fix them
I am the broken
I am the pieces
All sorts of pieces of broken
Scattered and ashamed
Lifeless and mourning
Trapped and unfixable
Broken
Pieces
Of
Me
If there is a me

I tossed that book, too, and fell to my side, letting my tears bleed into the cushions.

Clarity swam somewhere within me, wading through my tears, begging for me to notice it, but despair drowned out its voice. Subtle, yet probing, it tugged at me, the beginning of a battle brewing inside. I knew I needed to pull out of this, but I didn't have the strength. I didn't have it in me yet to choose who would rise to the top.

I cried until the blackness came to collect me once again.

"HOW IS HE, JACE?" I tucked my knees under my chin and stared at my best friend.

He opened the refrigerator and ducked his head inside, avoiding my question. "Have you called that number on the card I left you?"

I lifted my head, dropping my feet to the floor, finally putting force behind my voice. "Stop avoiding my question."

Jace slammed the refrigerator shut and spun around with fire in his eyes. "Stop avoiding mine!"

The doctor's card had taunted me for days, right where he had dropped it on my kitchen bar. My gaze would move to it every time I walked by, but I never actually touched it even though I kept feeling like it was reaching out and grabbing at me. It was annoying.

We had a staring standoff before I spoke, choosing my words carefully. "I will. When I'm ready."

"*Eeenh!*" He made the sound of a buzzer, signaling the wrong answer.

Without even looking at it, he swiped his hand to the side as he walked by, lifting the hard paper from the counter. He marched over to me and plucked my phone from the table. His thumbs worked furiously over the buttons as he programmed the number in, his finger hovering over the send button.

"You wanna call, or should I?"

I stood, grabbing the phone from him. "Stop pressuring me!"

"Evangelina, you're really trying my patience. I'm trying really, *really* hard to be gentle with you. And I don't do gentle. Ask around." He wagged a finger in my face. "I let you fester in your own filth for two whole weeks while you beat yourself up, and even agreed not to tell your family you'd been hospitalized! I did what you asked and gave you time. Well, time's up, sweetheart. I'm done. Make the fucking appointment, or I'm walking away from you."

It felt like his open palm had left a stinging mark on my cheek. In all our years as best friends, Jace had never given up on me. I couldn't lose him, too. My lips began to tremble, and I wanted to kick myself for showing weakness.

He took me by my shoulders with a squeezing tug. "You need to talk to someone. Someone besides me who can help you. Period. Now are you calling, or am I?"

"I'll do it," I whispered, not trusting my eyes to hold back the tears.

Jace loosened his grip. "There's my Eva." The creases around his eyes smoothed out as a warm smile coated his face.

I sat, worrying a piece of hair across my lips as a soft voice answered the line. I made the appointment. Pushing end, I placed the phone beside me and looked up at Jace. With a smile, he blew me a kiss. I didn't return his smile. I wrapped my arms around my knees and focused on his eyes.

"How is he, Jace?"

The upturn of his lips melted to a frown, dulling the brightness in his eyes. He fingered a small cut by his jaw that I hadn't noticed before and looked away, leaving my question unanswered . . .

Again.

Chapter 3

"WHAT DO YOU MEAN IT'S too late to drop the class?" I fisted my hips and narrowed my eyes at the balding man behind the registrar's counter of Columbia University.

He dropped the mouse and folded his hands. "I'm sorry, but we're already a week into the semester. All of the classes you need are either full or are offered at a conflicting time. And if you drop this class, you'll lose your full-time status."

I can't let that happen. I've worked too hard to get my grades where they needed to be last semester.

Softening my stance, I picked at the slip of paper in front of him. "You sure you can't squeeze in one more tiny little person?" I squished my fingers together for effect.

A sorry expression washed over his face. "I'm sorry, miss. I wish I could, but there's nothing I can do."

I swiped the paper from the counter, stuffing it into my bag. "Fine."

I can't see him. I just can't!

I bit at the skin surrounding my nail as I made the short walk to the English department. Blake and I had made sure to take the class together when we'd registered for the spring semester. Now, as I sat with the weight of that decision on my shoulders, I regretted not keeping my personal life separate from my academic career.

If I dropped the class, I'd be flushing everything I'd worked for down the drain. I was supposed to be on the fast track to a successful career. I couldn't jeopardize that. Now more than ever, I needed to solidify my independence and learn to stand on my own two feet. The way my brain had been since the *incident*—I wouldn't say the other word—it was going to be the biggest struggle of my life to focus and retain information, but I had to make it happen.

I checked my watch. I was five minutes late.

Perfect.

I curled my hand on the door handle and tugged, the loose hairs around my face moving to the side from the blow of air. The professor regarded me, and I nodded in acknowledgment before averting my gaze to the floor and slipping into the first seat in the first row, careful not to peek at the *VIP section* in the back.

Tingles prickled the raised hairs lining the back of my neck, and I knew he was in the room. My body always knew when he was around. Feeling as though my discomfort was visible, I rubbed at the traitorous skin, willing it to relax.

Flipping my notebook open, I put my pen cap between my teeth and tugged, exposing the tip. I scrawled down as much as I could as quickly as possible, hoping my hand would make up for my brain's lack of retention. I did this the entire class and as the hour closed in and the class was about to end, I was physically and mentally exhausted.

But then my body reacted.

Anxiety raced up my spine as my skin pebbled. My fingers circled around the college-ruled pages, my head itching to turn around and steal a glance behind me. It took all my strength not to.

He's close.

A clump of paper folded in quarters dropped on my desk just as a familiar scent floated past me on a breeze. *His* scent. A mix of soap and musk and something else entirely unique to him. Closing my eyes, I sucked it in and allowed it to simmer into my pores. I'd missed that smell and the warm tingle it always spread throughout my veins.

I didn't look up. I couldn't. I kept my chin tucked low to hide the pool that had gathered in my lower lids. My nostrils burned, my senses on high alert.

The professor dismissed class, but I didn't dare move for fear my weak and tingling limbs wouldn't carry me. I slid a shaky hand to the paper and curled my fist around it. I picked at the edges, unsure I wanted to see what was inside. Then I peeled it open, knowing I could never deny myself of even that small piece of him. At the sight of his neatly scrawled, familiar penmanship, my heart skipped a beat and prickles raged across my scalp, remembering all of the sweet words and notes he had written me in the past. But this one hit me much harder.

One word. So meaningful it punched me in the gut.

Unicorn.

Fucking unicorn. It was the best and worst thing he could have written. His words all those months ago came barreling back, shooting to my brain in a head rush.

"A unicorn is a fabled creature, a myth. They're impossible to catch. When I was younger, I thought if I looked hard enough that one day I'd find one. I guess I was right. I finally found my unicorn. That's probably why I feel like I always need to keep my hands on you. I feel like one day I'll turn around and you'll be gone."

Another promise I'd broken.

This guy would always be the death *and* the life of me.

My heart smacked against my chest cavity. I wasn't ready to face him. I looked toward the door, wiping my hand along my nose. Bunches of people rushed back and forth, but no Blake. I pushed my books into my bag and opened the front zipper, to tuck away Blake's note so it wouldn't get ruined. It might be the last I ever heard from him.

Slinging my bag over my shoulder, I exited the room. Though every sense I had ached to find Blake and be close to him, I knew it was best that I didn't. It was a battle of wills.

I pulled the edges of my wool coat together, bearing down against the cold as I stepped into the cool air. New York in January could be brutal. Tucking my head low to block the wind, I moved at a swift pace down the steps. My skin buzzed as the hairs stood at attention, but it felt different. It didn't feel like a chill from the cold. It felt like . . .

"Angel." His crisp voice cut through the nip in the air, stopping me in my tracks.

Though my legs ceased movement, I didn't look up. I couldn't meet those blue-diamond eyes. Hurt and shame barreled into me, slamming into my chest, into my heart. Showing me with its quickened state, it was still capable of pumping. Letting me feel each erratic pass of blood through it. Each beat pummeling me further.

Silence ballooned like a cloud, but I felt his approach. It felt like my skin was lifting from my bones, aching to draw him underneath. Lips slightly parted to calm my ragged breaths, I tucked my jaw into my collarbone and waited for the blow. For the feel of him this close, his voice, his . . .

"Angel?"

The familiarity of that sound was directly behind me that time, laced with heartbreak, drenched in uncertainty. If I rocked back on my heels, I knew I'd fall into his arms. God, just one rock was all it would take to feel his comfort, and I swore my heels swayed on their own accord.

But I couldn't answer.

I was so ashamed knowing someone else had touched me after I'd told him I was his. Guilt that I hadn't been strong enough to stop Damon—strong enough to be the woman Blake needed—raced rampantly through my veins. I hadn't been strong enough to open my mouth and say what was happening to me. Not just for me. But . . . for him. I wasn't strong enough for *him*.

He didn't even know why I had pushed him away. Why I had cut him off. I'd just dismissed his feelings as though they didn't matter. His love. That had probably hurt him most.

"Angel." And there was that crack in his voice I couldn't bear to hear.

Blake's chest brushed against my back, and his hands enveloped my shoulders, sending a wave of heat through my chilled body, despite my thick coat. The connection between us could never be lost. It was like a living, breathing entity, fueled when we were together. The feeling of it was so overwhelming that it swallowed me whole and made me lightheaded. Made it impossible to withstand him, and for his sake, I had to. I wouldn't drag him back into my nightmare, couldn't jeopardize his well-being anymore. I knew I needed to get out of here, or I'd give in. God, all I wanted to do was give in and let him hold me. I'd missed those hands, his warmth and his support. His voice and—my body caved further—those eyes.

I couldn't turn around and face those eyes.

"I can't do this," I whispered before pulling away from him and taking off as quickly as I could. I hoisted my bag onto my shoulder and bore down, the balls of my feet digging into the pavement. My hair whipped me in the face as my head swung left, then right, looking for an escape. I knew he was right behind me, felt the pull on my back, but I kept on.

I continued into the subway, hearing the screeching train approach. I hung onto the railing, taking the stairs two at a time, just as the train puffed to a stop in front of me. Scooting into the car, I went to the door opposite me and slammed my heaving back against it as Blake emerged at the bottom of the same steps I'd just run down. The sight of him for the first time in weeks sent the heart that was already racing in my chest, pumping in overdrive. I'd forgotten how beautiful he was, though he now wore a heavy patch of facial hair and eyes that almost seemed as though they had died and were merely used for seeing. They used to be so full of life. I once thought they could tell a whole story themselves.

He looked around before spotting me and making his way to the door.

Please close. Please close. Please close.

My knees knocked front and back as my nails dug into the flesh of my palm. In a short jog, he hurried toward me, his focus caging me to the very wall I was bound to. Right before the last stride that would have put him inside the same subway car as me, the glass and metal plates of the door closed with a familiar chime in front of him, placing a barrier between us.

He looked to the right, to the conductor. "Hey!" He pounded his fist on the Plexiglas.

The doors remained closed, and he looked back to me, hurt and angst bleeding through his eyes, begging me to come to him. He smacked his open palm against the glass, and his lips parted. Focusing on my eyes, he mouthed the three unmistakable words before the train hissed, whisking me away.

My head dropped forward, my hair creating a veiled shield as the speckled pattern of the floor bled into a kaleidoscope of tears.

"I love you, too."

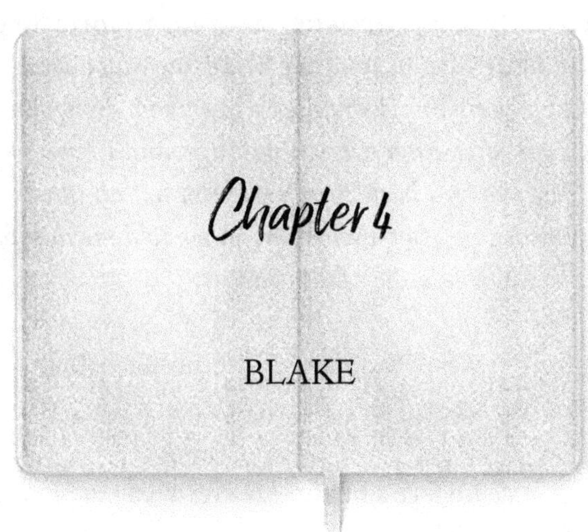

Chapter 4

BLAKE

SHE LOOKED TERRIBLE.

Seeing her walk through those doors sent a wave crashing through me. I used to ride that wave on a high, but now I was being drowned by it. I couldn't breathe as I continued the endless spirals beneath the water, trying with everything to swim to the surface. My lungs were heavy, collapsing, useless.

I tried to will her to look at me the whole class. I stared at every strand on her head, burning a hole in them, hoping she'd turn around even just once. See me. Want me. But she didn't. And the need to be near her clawed at my skin.

Even with her head low and her hair hanging in her face, I could see how bad she looked. Pale and like she hadn't eaten in days, maybe weeks. And through her thick coat, I could feel the boniness beneath my fingers. My broken angel. I didn't know what she didn't understand. Why she couldn't trust me enough to let me in, to let me fix her.

I'd kept quiet tabs on her through Jace in the hopes she'd return to me one day . . .

If there was anything left of me when she did.

"Tell me," I demand.

"I already told you, sugar. I won't betray Eva's secrets. She'll tell you on her own. When she's ready,*" Jace whips back at me.*

I shove a hand through my hair, ripping at the ends. "Listen, I did what she asked. I haven't contacted her. But, how do you expect me to help her if I don't know all the facts?" My tone is escalating, my patience dwindling.

*Jace doesn't flinch. "*I'm *helping her. The same way I always have."*

The cool assuredness in his voice boils my blood. How can he act so aloof when I'm dying over here? After everything Angel and I have been through, I'm being shunned. Thrown to a back burner like I'm not an important part of her life. From the moment I met her, everything in me told me to protect her. I don't know how to sit idly by while she's falling apart.

That's it.

I straighten my spine. "Fine then. If you won't tell me . . ." I dig deep, finding the words I'm sure will set off my girl's best friend, "then I'm sure Abby will."

Red splotches race up Jace's throat, his eyes widening before narrowing at me. "Stay away from Abby."

Good, I struck a nerve. I slowly turn to leave. "I'm sorry, I would love to. But I think it's in Eva's best interest if—"

"Don't you dare!"

Jace grabs my wrist, yanking me back and on instinct, I swing, my fist landing on his tightened jaw. Thankfully, as unhinged as I am, something in me holds back so the blow to his face is only enough to stun him, but it still feels crappy. We're on the same side. I shouldn't be fighting with the one person who knows what I'm going through—what she *is going through. He's my only gateway to her, and I can't afford to burn that bridge.*

"Jace. I'm sorry, man." I take one step forward, and he takes one step back. That makes me stop. His back straightens as he drops his hand, the glow of my mark becoming darker and darker.

Jace jabs me in the chest. "I'm going to let that slide . . . once,*" he annunciates the last word. "I know this isn't you and that's the only reason you're still standing. But even though I like it rough, if you hit me anywhere above my belt from this moment on, you will have no hand left. We on the same page?"*

"Yes," I concede. "I'm just—"

*"I know what you are. And I told you I sympathize. But don't push my buttons." Jace steps in closer, crowding me. "And if you ever—*ever*—mention any of this to Eva's family, I will hunt you down. Got me? That's for her to do."*

I swallow hard, knowing I have to agree, but not happy about it. Without responding, I pull a card from my back pocket. I stare down at it and glide my thumb along the raised print. "Listen, I found a doctor. I did a lot of research, and she's the best at what she does. I think Eva should talk to her. Do you think you can get her to go?"

Jace flicks his fingers at me, motioning for me to pass it to him. He examines it, before asking in a low voice. "You did this? After how she treated you?"

"I love her, man. And she needs help."

Jace's eyes mist as he stares at me, seeming to see more inside of me now that the anger is dissipating. He clears his throat. "I'll make sure she goes."

I relax with relief. "Thank you." If I couldn't help her, I hoped someone else could. "Please, keep me updated at least. Let me know how she's doing."

"I will."

It was fucking killing me to stand along the sidelines and not know firsthand what was happening. To not hear her voice or feel her skin, comfort her when I knew she was falling apart. It was gutting me to not know what had happened to her, though inside I was sure I already did. How could I not? If I ever found out who the bastard was that took my angel, I'd end his life. Extinguish him, so help me God.

I'd give anything for her. Any-fucking-thing. But I couldn't do this. I wouldn't survive it. I loved her, and as much as it was killing me, it was driving me. She lived in me—still. And it fucking hurt. Her life in me felt like death. And maybe it would be the death of me.

Because I felt like I couldn't fucking breathe.

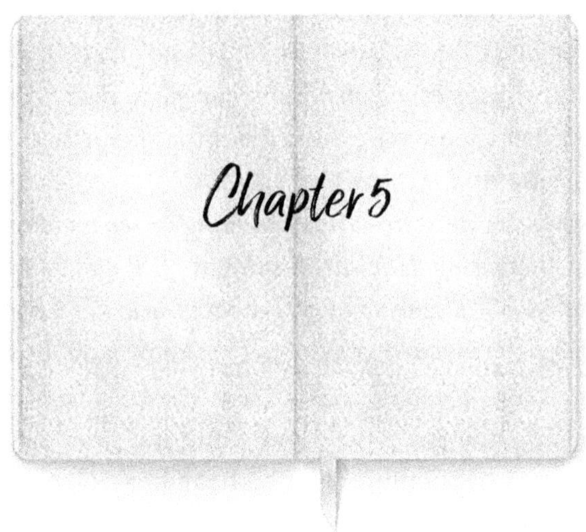

MY FIRST DOCTOR'S APPOINTMENT WAS supposed to be this afternoon.

I didn't go.

I wasn't ready to air my shit, and certainly not to a stranger. The encounter with Blake had left me shaken and confused. Even though I knew he'd be in class and I'd have to face him eventually, I wasn't prepared for the turmoil it would wreak within me.

The pity I'd heard in his voice hurt worst of all. It was a new sound. He'd never had that before. I don't think he'd ever really grasped the extent of my fucked-up-ness. Well, he had a front row seat this time, and there was no coming back from any of this.

I couldn't handle being around him. I didn't know what to do about that. I'd worked too hard to get into this school and establish my grades. I couldn't withdraw. I needed to find a way to co-exist, but . . . how? *How?*

I expelled a heavy breath, pulling open the door to The Backdoor. I hadn't seen Rick since the incident, and it was time to face the next set of my fuck-ups. Tears welled in my eyes at the sight of his back as he counted the money in the register. Much like the first time I'd walked into this place, his head bobbed to a beat, this time from the eighties, and seeing him rock out built warmth in my heart. But I would need more than music to help the jittering knock in my chest right now. Seeing him so carefree, enjoying the music he loved so much made me realize the extent of how much I cared for him. How much I appreciated the way he'd welcomed me into his *home* and made me feel like family. My conscience sunk with revulsion, looking down at me for my poor judgements and what I had done to this man and his place of business. I valued his opinion of me, and I hoped I hadn't shot it to shit.

"Hey." I glanced at him from the corner of my eye, removing my coat with a prayer he would forgive me.

His fingers stopped moving, and he tensed at my voice, sending a cringe over my skin. "Hi." He didn't look at me and my hopes sunk further. But I was prepared to grovel, to show him how sorry I truly was.

"I'm, um, sorry I haven't called." I'd been a coward and texted him the other day, asking if I could be put back on the schedule. I nearly chewed my fingers off waiting for his reply, praying that I would get one. When he had responded to come in today, I wasn't sure if I felt relief or dread, knowing I would have to face the music for what I had done.

"You left this place in quite a state, Eva."

The sharpness of his tone stabbed me in the heart. Rick was such a happy guy most of the time that I'd forgotten he even had a bone in his body capable of anger. The fact that it was being directed at me crept some extra pain into my heart.

"You're lucky you're back at all. I warned you about that when we first met."

"I know." *Shit.* I gulped, hating myself for trampling all over his kindness. "I'm so sorry. I don't know what to say. I didn't mean to disrespect you, Rick. You know how much I love this place. And you." I placed my hand on his forearm, wishing he would forgive me. The warmth of his skin did nothing to thaw the chill I felt at his cold shoulder.

The force of him slamming the drawer shut ricocheted through me. He turned to face me, crossing his arms over his broad chest. "Do you? Because I don't make a habit of giving people a key to my *home.*" He narrowed his eyes at me, distrust and anger laced through their narrowing glare.

I hated seeing the easy-going Rick this way. He was always so warm and inviting. I wanted to grab my things and run out of here, but I owed him an explanation. He had trusted me, given me a chance, and I'd let him down.

"Rick, you'll never know how sorry I am. I'm sure you can tell I have some . . . issues." I downplayed a little, not ready to fully lay all of my cards on the table. "But I never want that to be your problem. I should've thought better—not come here, but I didn't know where else to go. I just wasn't thinking, I—" My voice wept, a sting slicing through the pull of my eyebrows. "It'll never happen again. I swear it." I palmed my heart. "But if you want me to leave—" My shoulders sagged as I began to turn.

His stance softened, and he dropped a hand on my shoulder, stopping me. When our eyes met again, the anger was gone from his. In its place rested something bordering defeat. Like he was trying so hard to be strong; to show how upset he was, but his love for me outgrew all of those negative emotions.

"Of course I don't want you to leave, Eva. I care about *you*, more than these four walls. It hurt me to think you thought as little of me that you would wreck my place and take off—bottles and puke everywhere, money thrown all over the place. I felt disrespected. Dirty even." His eyes drifted from mine as his shoulders sagged forward.

I knew the feeling of having your space invaded, and it made me sick to know I'd caused someone I cared about to feel that way. I was such a piece of shit. "I get it. I can't take it back. I wish I could, but I can't. I can only make it better. You've become like family to me. Please don't think I don't care about your feelings. About this place. I'll make it better, I promise I'll earn back your trust. I'll—"

"C'mere." Any remaining tension he held floated off him as he wrapped his arms around me and pulled me to his chest to kiss the top of my head. His breath puffed into my hair on his exhale, his relief evident. "I'm just glad you're okay." His voice shook slightly around his lips in my hair. He paused before stepping to my side and securing his arm around my shoulder. "I asked Jessie about you, but she seemed as clueless as the rest of us. All she knew was that you and Blake had broken up." He shook his head. "You know you have good friends, don't you, girl? We're all worried about you." The tenderness in his voice built a lump in my throat.

A tear sparked in the corner of my eye, and I fought to push it down. It was hard to let anyone in. I'd let them all get closer than I'd intended and I was grateful for them, but, at the same time, unsure how to handle it.

I backed away and tucked a strand of hair behind my ear. "I do. I just clam up sometimes. I'm working on it."

Rick nudged my shoulder with his own. "Well, work harder. If you were my kid, I'd put you over my knee for the stunt you pulled. Don't make me call Big Joe and tell him to handle you." His mood finally turned playful, but the muscles in my belly tightened at the mention of my dad. The last thing I needed was anyone tipping off my family that something was going on with me.

I tried to mirror his spirit and make light of his threat. I jabbed a finger at him. "No one likes a tattletale. Didn't your mom teach you anything? What's the matter, no siblings to teach you a lesson?" I crossed my arms with a smile.

Something washed over Rick's expression, and his demeanor changed. He squared his stance and turned back to the stack of cash. "Nope. I guess no one ever taught me proper etiquette."

I cleared my throat, feeling uncomfortable. "I'm sorry. Did I say something wrong?"

Rick seemed to have caught himself and relaxed once again. "Huh? No. I just need to get this drawer right before we open is all." He hooked an arm around my neck and kissed my forehead.

"Okay," I replied, unconvinced he was being sincere, but it was none of my business. I had my own skeletons to deal with. I raked my hands through my hair, fastening it back, ready to slice up fruit.

"I hope you don't mind," Rick spoke over his shoulder, "but I called Angie in to work with us. Since we lost you, I've been bringing her in more. It's been a while, and I didn't know how you'd be coming back."

That caught me off guard. It was a weeknight. Normally the two of us could handle the crowd just fine. "Yeah, sure." My voice didn't mask my disappointment. I loved Angie. She was spunky as all hell and always a blast to work with, but I hated the reminder of my shortcomings.

"Nothing personal, Eva. It was just a precaution. Promise." He tapped the edge of my nose.

I waved my hand in front of my face. "Pssh, no—yeah—fine." I tugged the elastic band tighter around my hair and went to work, cradling my bruised ego.

The place started filling up. I'd thought I was ready for this, but now, with all these people around, I was feeling claustrophobic and under a microscope. I was usually able to ward off advances from the opposite sex, but the latest incident with Damon had left me feeling so broken down that the flirting was fucking with my head. I found myself unable to come up with the usual brush-offs. I felt like they were looking at me like I'd sprouted a third head when I just stared back at them, mute, unsure of how to even respond to a simple, "What's up?"

I wanted to have a drink so badly to even myself out and loosen up, but I didn't want to do that my first night back. Not after everything that had happened with Rick. I didn't deserve the second chance he was giving me. *Remember in life, there are second chances.* Blake's forget-me-not number one.

Fuck. I couldn't let myself go there.

He still hadn't shown and, at this point, I doubted he would. His seat sat barren, mocking me. Somehow, it was the loudest thing in the room. I felt it on my skin, begging me to look over. I could picture him sitting there—hair damp from a recent shower, his skin shiny and bright, a red hue to his defined cheekbones as he watched me intently, the beauty in his bright blue irises electrifying me, his long fingers wrapped around a rock's glass. I tried to think of what wise-ass sexual drink he might have ordered, and my lip twitched, recalling his sharp-witted mouth. My view focused, and he melted away like a mirage, taking another beat of my heart with it.

"Miss, your drink is overflowing."

My head snapped back in front of me as liquid pooled on the bar. *Crap.* I quickly turned the bottle upright and discarded it, grabbing a towel. "Thanks."

"No problem. You all right?"

I looked up. The guy's face was kind, handsome, and somehow familiar. Dirty blond hair was cut choppy and styled in haphazard directions, but I could tell he meant for it to be that way. And truth be told, it worked for him. Even in the dimmer light, I could see the flecks of gold sprinkled in his green eyes. The corners crinkled, inviting me to answer his concerned question.

"Yes, fine. I just got distracted." I returned to the puddle in front of me.

"You don't remember me, do you?" I could hear the smirk in his voice, and possibly, disappointment.

I studied his face again, searching my memory.

He gave me a soft smile, raising his eyebrows, trying to will a trigger. "Drew? We met at the pizzeria up the block once upon a time. When you shot me down so nicely."

Ah, the runway model from when I first arrived here. I knew there was something familiar about his face. So much had changed since then, it felt like a lifetime ago.

"Right. Drew. Sorry. I'm scatterbrained tonight. Obviously." I motioned to the mess in front of me.

"That's cool. I always hoped I'd run into you again. I was beginning to think you were something I'd conjured up." A lopsided smirk slid across his face.

My skin prickled. I didn't need anyone else poking around in my personal life.

"How's your friend? Jace was it?" A short laugh spurted from his lips. "He's a cock-blocker that one."

Though I was a bit taken aback by his sudden crassness, a chuckle escaped, because, well, Jace was. Drew's smile was inviting, and I couldn't help but smile back. "Yes, I've trained him well. And you have a very good memory."

"I thought that whole thing seemed rehearsed." He relaxed forward, his features softening.

"Yeah, sorry about that. Can I get you something to drink? It's on the house for being such a good sport." I draped the bar towel over my shoulder.

He clapped his hands together and dipped his head toward the row of bottles behind me. "Tanqueray and tonic with a lime, please."

A normal request. My heart sighed, remembering all of the drinks Blake had ordered trying to get a rise out of me. No one would ever compare to him.

"Sure thing."

I turned away to grab the named label from the back shelf. When I turned back around, Drew's eyes were in the midst of wandering my body. My cheeks grew warm at the attention. Depositing the glass in front of me, I pretended not to notice as I poured the liquor with one hand, grabbing the soda spout with the other. I dropped the lime inside and pushed the glass toward him with my fingertips.

He clasped his hands together. "So, you still with that boyfriend?" His eyes twinkled, and his smile was hopeful.

Pang.

My heart rate spiked. For the first time, I'd floundered trying to come up with a reply. I wasn't prepared for that question anymore. Blake had turned my constant lie of having a boyfriend to get out of advances from the opposite sex into a reality. Now at any mention of a boyfriend, all I saw was him, and it crippled me.

My mouth hung there as I searched for the right answer, but none ever came. I guess that in itself was answer enough.

Disappointment washed over his face and his shoulders slouched. "Right." He peeked up at me. "No worries." Standing, he reached for his glass before pulling out the straw and setting it on the bar napkin. "See ya around, Evangelina." He winked, taking a sip of his drink as he casually strode to the other room.

My breathing felt heavy in my ribcage. That one question had made me so nervous. These are the things I should have thought about before throwing myself back into society.

Idiot.

I took someone's drink order, but I still felt off. The way Drew had looked at me was tough to shake. So hopeful and endearing and . . . humble. Like he knew he'd be shot down and was silently wishing he wouldn't. Such good-looking guys usually wore cocky grins and inflated chests. It was refreshing, but it made me feel shitty. I'd hurt his feelings.

Angie's raspy voice in my ear startled me. "That one was a real looker. You know him?"

I jumped away from the intrusion. "Er . . . kinda . . . not really." I stared in the direction Drew had walked off in.

Angie elbowed me in the ribs. Purple hair spiked from her head, framing her dainty features. "You should go talk to him. He looked like he liked you. Or at least introduce me and hook a bitch up. It'd be a shame to let all that man go to waste." She bit her plump bottom lip, narrowly missing the piercing in the corner as she stared into the airspace he'd just walked through. He was already lost in the crowd somewhere.

"I'm not quite ready to move on just yet, but thanks for the friendly concern." I scowled.

Her features softened. "Oh, honey, I'm sorry. I just assumed since it was your decision to end things, that you were good with it. Not handling it well?"

"I don't really want to talk about it," I muttered. Someone shouted for a Coors Light, and I bent, scooping one from the basin of ice. "Besides, it's my first night back, and Rick's not too happy with me, obviously, since he called you in." I eyed her from the corner of my eye as I slid the wet beer bottle toward the customer.

"Aw, sweetie." Her hand blanketed the top of my arm, her eyes speaking for the pity in her heart. It disgusted me knowing what everyone was probably thinking of me. That I was a tragic case. "He didn't mean anything by it. Honest. He was worried sick about you. He just needs to cover his bases here. You can't blame him, can you?" She nodded at a group of anxious-looking girls, and they began spewing off their drink orders.

No, I couldn't blame him. I didn't even trust myself, so I couldn't expect *him* to hold any faith in me. I just had to prove to him I could be the employee he needed me to be. Then I had to prove to me I could be the student I needed to be. Time to get my goals back in line. No more pity party and no more putting people ahead of myself. It was time to get my life back on track. I was so close, and I'd let it all get torn away.

With a grin and a renewed outlook, I called to my left. "Hey, Rick, am I singing tonight?"

A slow smile spread across his face until it reached ear to ear. "Sure are, darlin'." He winked.

My heart widened a fraction. I could feel it. Feel *something*. It was a start.

Live me.

The empty chair called to me. I stuck my finger in my ear and wiggled it, shaking out the Blake, and carried on.

I BUSIED MYSELF A SHORT while longer, using all my power to keep my eyes away from Blake's empty place at my bar. Around ten thirty, there was a break in the music and a tap on the mic. I looked toward the interruption and was met with Rick's kind gaze.

"Some of you might've noticed we were missing a piece of our family for a while there. Our Eva took a short hiatus, and we missed her terribly." He found my eyes and smiled sincerely. "But she's back now. Aren't you, darlin'?" His smile widened.

I nodded once, returning his smile and blowing him a kiss.

"Well then, it's been long enough. Get your pretty little butt up here and give us a song. I miss that voice." Rick beamed, and the crowd howled.

Despite the rowdiness, I could hear my heart beating in my chest. No matter how many times I did this, I always got nervous. The past few weeks had been spent singing by my lonesome, once the pain in my throat subsided after having my stomach pumped. I'd have to get used to this again. There was something liberating about letting a crowd hear the words in your heart, though, and I could use the release.

Lonesome.

A smile crept across my face. Feeling the words of the song overtake me, I leaned in to tell the band to play Christina Perri's, *The Lonely*. I shook out my hands by my sides and closed my eyes, letting it all sink in as I waited to begin.

A puff of air escaped my parted lips, and I opened my eyes, sliding my fingers up the cool metal of the silver pole in front of me. I didn't focus on anything in particular as the notes on the keyboard started. Instead, I pulled my attention inward to connect with my soul. To the parts of me I'd been ignoring. With a soft voice, I closed my eyes and let out the truth, admitting that I was just a ghost of someone I wanted to be, a shell of a person I used to know.

The inflections in my voice touched each chord as Blake's eyes took over the darkness behind my lids. Wetness pooled at the seam of my lashes.

Can the lonely take the place of you?

My voice cracked, picturing all of my lonely lullabies. Nights spent rocking in the darkness as the lonely came to claim me. My octaves dipped lower, telling how the loneliness was what put me to sleep.

I wrapped my arms around my middle as if that would shield the words pouring out of me and make them any less true. My voice grew stronger as I fisted my sweater, belting how I had to let him go and let the lonely in.

And then it came.

The moment of real truth.

In a light voice, the lyrics portrayed our reality. *Broken pieces of, a barely breathing story.* My voice was wrecked, light, and airy as the tears flowed, sending me into the powerful ending. I took a shuddered breath, all kinds of pieces of broken. Then my eyes opened on the last note of the keyboard, glowing a bright green from moisture, I was sure. I swiped the wetness from my cheeks and bowed my head before excusing myself to break some more in the back room.

The lonely would come to claim my broken pieces tonight for sure.

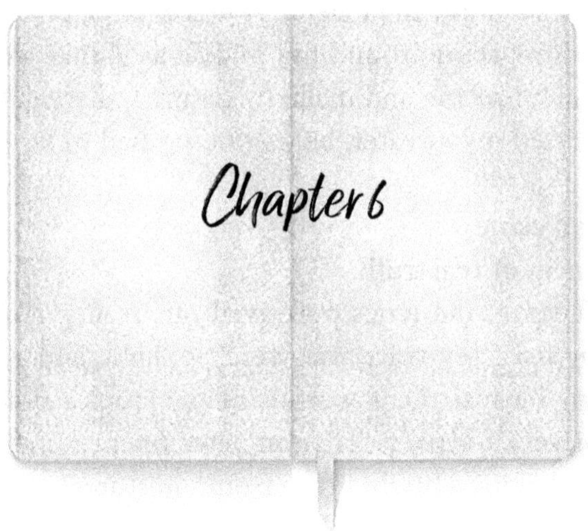

MY NIGHT TERRORS WERE BACK in full force.

I bolted up, covered in sweat, panting. My eyes darted around the room, taking in my isolated surroundings before the searing pain closed in. I glanced down to where my nails were rooted in my forearms and peeled them away, wincing.

Jace had been spending the nights with me so he could wake me when they started, but he'd gone back to sleeping in his apartment. I was pretty sure it was his tough love approach in the hopes I'd get fed up enough to fix myself. All I knew was there wasn't much more I could handle. I'd left the bar last night thinking I could finally start to heal—that I was strong enough to do it on my own. But this—waking up rocking and screaming alone—was a wakeup call. I needed help.

I rolled onto my side and slid my hands under my cheek. No matter how much I had tried to push Blake from my mind, his majestic blues kept popping up, and the vision stuck behind my lids held only disappointment and sadness. His eyes reminded me of my failures and shortcomings. My losses.

Loss.

Abby.

It seemed everything always made my mind drift to her. I'd been avoiding her calls, scared she would hear it in my voice. Know what happened.

"Hey, Eves. Still not answering the phone?" Silence. "Well, I just wanted

to let you know everything is cool with Damon and me. He kept apologizing and begging me to forgive him, and well, I have. He is Damon, after all. It's not like he's going anywhere." More silence. "Anyway, he's taking me on a shopping spree to make up for what a dick he was. Maybe if you answer the phone, I'll share some of my goodies with you." A chuckle that doesn't play its part in trying to seem happy passes her lips. "So, um, call me back. Love you."

I knew this would buy me a few weeks. Whenever she was in her Damon-bliss, she thought all was right with the world. I texted her and told her I had broken up with Blake and that I wanted space to work through my feelings. I'd use the time to get my shit together somehow before she came sniffing around again.

How would I explain it? I knew I needed to tell her. I couldn't let her marry him. But how? I'd agreed to the whole thing from the start. How do you then call rape?

You don't.

But it was. Wasn't it? When you didn't want it? He'd never really known how badly I didn't want it, though. Or had he? God, I didn't fucking know. Everything was turning to gray again. Blended fucking areas that made no sense.

Each time that I contemplated telling my family, my past would float to the forefront of my mind, and the cold sweats that followed would make me think better of it.

I'm going to tell them.

I'm going to tell them.

I'm going to tell them.

I repeat the words over and over as I walk with purpose down the stairs.

Abby's voice floats through the entryway to the kitchen. "Oh my gosh, mom, did you hear?"

I slip into the room just in time to witness my mom barely look up from whipping her mashed potatoes. "Hear what, baby?"

"Cammie called before and said that Maggie isn't coming back to school."

"Oh, that," my mom sighs. "Yes, her mom called me. Such a shame, she had so much going for her."

"What happened?" Damon asks, his voice startling me. He's here. *I jump back and brush against a far wall, trying not to draw attention to myself. Telling them what had happened between Damon and me would have to wait, but now*

I'm stuck here because it will draw attention if I leave too soon.

"You remember Seth who was in our Chem class last year?" Abby asks Damon.

"Yeah, what about him?"

"Well, apparently, he and Maggie were at a party or something and one thing led to another, and they slept with each other. He says it was consensual, but she's saying that he raped her."

My face tightens, flushing in a hot wave as my stomach knots into a ball. I clutch at it, praying no one notices.

"I feel so bad for them," my mom adds. "I mean, I know her mother said she had trouble with her sneaking out and telling lies and whatnot a couple of years ago, but this is much more serious. As much as I don't want her to have gone through that and for it to be true, I do hope she's not trying to tarnish that boy's reputation to save her own skin."

My knees almost give out, and the room begins to swim around me.

"Do you see how she dresses?" Abby exclaims.

Forgetting they aren't talking about me, my eyes drift down to the sweatshirt I'm wearing. I'm relieved briefly, but then I quickly remember the lower cut shirt I wore the day Damon had come into my room, before Abby's voice cuts in again.

"I'm always staring, waiting for a boob to pop out the top of her shirt. I mean, no wonder . . ."

"Now, Abby, that's not fair to say. If what she's saying is true, it's very serious. Her wardrobe doesn't mean anyone has the right to touch her without her consent."

Her consent. I said yes. *Damon's words of being a tease slam into me, and I swear I almost fall from the impact.*

Damon sends me a side-eye. "So many girls want it and then when people find out that they're sleeping around, they switch up the story. It's disgusting if you ask me. They're just liars, and they have no concern for what it will do to the guy's life. Or how bad it makes them look."

I shrink against the wall, my heart sinking into the paint with its loss of hope.

"Well, I for one am more than grateful that my Abby found you. At least I know you're a gentleman and won't hurt my baby girl." My mom's smile practically touches her ears.

"Never." Damon slides an arm around Abby's neck, pulling her in to kiss her cheek. "Your daughter's chastity belt is safe with me."

"Damon!" My mom laughs, flinging a kitchen cloth at him.

"What?" He chuckles, ducking to the side. "Am I lying?" He directs the question at Abby.

"Not lying. This guy is the perfect gentleman. I'm the luckiest girl in the world." She beams.

"Now, I just have to be sure my Eva gets just as lucky." My mom's eyes slide to find mine, but she doesn't focus enough to see the tears begin to cloud my vision before she turns back to dinner.

"Eva, now she's *the one you have to worry about. She's the flirty type. Aren't you, beautiful?" Damon regards me, but the ringing in my ears nearly drowns out his voice.*

My tongue is trapped to the roof of my mouth, prohibiting a response.

"Leave her alone, Damon." Abby swats at him, but she never takes her eyes off him. It's like I'm not even here. Like all they see is him. All they hear.

Where's my voice?

As Damon kisses the top of Abby's head, his eyes find mine once again, a sliver of a smile slithering into her scalp, the happiness bright in his brown irises. Any hope that I have of getting support from my family over what had happened flits out the window. They would believe him. And I would be deemed a slut. An outcast. I'm not sure which would be worse. Holding all of this in and dealing with it in silence, allowing it to rot my insides, or letting the truth out and wearing the scarlet letter brightly for the world to see. To scrutinize. To call me a liar. To say I wanted it. Asked for it.

You did ask for it.

That fact lodges in my throat and I know if I stand here any longer I'll break down in front of them. They go back to their discussions as I flee from the room, covering my ears so I can't hear any more of it, taking the stairs in clumps at a time to get as far away from them and that topic as quickly as possible. My mind is made up. My questions answered.

I slam my back against my bedroom door, shutting myself inside. Shutting all *of it inside. For good.*

With a groan, I sat up and swung my legs off the side of the bed. The engagement party was set for the end of spring, and the wedding wouldn't be for a year after that. That gave me about a year and a half to find a way to break them up. I could do that. I hoped.

All of the physical marks Damon had left were gone now, but I saw each one of them as though they still lined my skin. I rubbed my upper arms as I stood, making my way to the window in my living room. The sun was fully awake, and although I had gotten home from my shift only hours before, so was I. My forehead dropped to the glass, and I peered down at all the tiny things passing by, the seemingly muteness of the busy city below. Then my gaze fell to an empty pot of dirt on the balcony. The one Blake had left, which used to house his forget-me-nots.

Technically, according to him, they were still in there and wouldn't die. They'd regrow in the spring and get a second chance at life.

Second chances.

Could we have a second chance?

I wanted so badly to believe we could, but I knew I wouldn't let myself go there again. If I loved him as much as I knew I did, I needed to let him go. To heal myself of this somehow and let him heal himself—of me. Rid himself of my toxic-ness. But it was so damn hard to live without a piece of yourself. For your heart to beat without its drum.

Live me.

I crushed my forehead against the glass and banged it once, twice, three times, wondering when those words would go away. I still felt him inside me. Knew that I had, in fact, been *living* him all along. Even now, in his absence, a sense of him still lingered in my pores, danced beneath my skin, and traveled through my veins. I wondered for the millionth time if he still felt me inside the same way that I did him. And then I reminded myself how selfish that was of me.

He needed his freedom, and so did I. I needed to be free of this burden. I wished I was able to do that, get it out. Instead, it was festering, killing me from the inside.

I dropped to the couch and tucked my knees under my chin, ready to contemplate how I got here when just a few short weeks ago my life had been the picture of perfection—perfect guy, good grades, seeing my family again, and making close friends.

My phone rang, startling me from my thoughts. I was greeted with Abby's name across the screen. No more blowing her off. It was time to face the music.

I dragged my lower lip between my teeth, closed my eyes, and slid my thumb across the screen to answer the call. "Hello."

"Wow, Eva. Are you really answering right now?" Disbelieving sarcasm dripped heavy from each word. "Should I tell Mom to call off the dogs, or will you be going back into hiding after this?"

"Stop it. It hasn't been that long, and I've been emailing Mom."

"Nice to hear from you, too. I've been good. Thanks for asking." She wasn't even trying to hide the cynicism in her voice. "I thought we were past this. What the hell happened again?"

Your psychotic fucking boyfriend happened. "Please don't start. I've been busy. How've you been? How's everything at home? Mom and Dad?"

A knock sounded, and I glanced at the door, baffled. "Oh, you know, same ole, same ole," she said as I made my way over, confused who it could be since Jace had a habit of just walking in unannounced and I wasn't expecting anyone. I opened it warily. It was so early and no one ever just dropped by. Phone to her ear, Abby was standing there, right in front of me, with her eyebrow raised and her lips puckered in a cocky little grin.

"Gotcha." She smiled.

My mouth fell open. "W-What're you doing here?" I scanned to the left and right to be sure she was alone.

"Hello to you, too." She rolled her eyes. "Such a warm welcome. I'm overwhelmed." She brushed past me and stood in my living room, hanging up her phone. "I knew if I wanted to see you it'd have to be a sneak attack, you little wench. I thought we were cool now, but then you went all clam on me again."

When the initial shock of being caught off-guard subsided, and the ease at seeing she was alone washed over, I took two long strides and grabbed her by her shoulders, pulling her to me in a tight hug. I sucked in the scent that was unique to my sister, roses with a hint of cotton candy. *Abby.* Last time I saw her, she'd looked like a distraught mess, but there was life in her eyes again. She looked content. That made me feel better.

And it worried me at the same time.

I took her fingers in mine, ignoring the rock perched on her left hand. Seeing her now formed a lump in my throat. I always forgot how much I missed my family until I saw them again. "I can't believe you're really here."

"Believe it." She squeezed back. "Now, show me your place, and then you can take me out for breakfast. I'm starving." Her eyes widened as she finally looked around. "Wow."

"I know, right? I scored with this place. I love it." My eyes trailed behind hers.

I gave her the grand tour of my tiny, one bedroom apartment. In Manhattan, even a studio cost a fortune, so although it was small by real-world standards, it was a palace by ours. I was grateful my parents had foot the difference, or there'd be no way I could afford it. That was the price they were willing to pay to have me in a building with a doorman.

She poked around in the living room while I dressed and gathered my thoughts. With the toothbrush hanging from my mouth, I stopped scrubbing my teeth and closed my eyes, collecting myself. This had to be it. It was my chance. We were alone—a rare occasion, and I needed to put a stop to this before she did something crazy and eloped or something.

When I made my way back to her, Abby was staring out my window at the barren flower pot. She turned with her eyebrows screwed together. "What's with the dirt-pot out on the balcony?"

I rushed past her on a breeze, a dismissiveness in my tone that I didn't want her to miss. "I don't want to talk about it." I swiped my jacket from the arm of the couch.

Abby's eyes widened. "Was that a Blake thing?"

I glared at her before stuffing my arms into the sleeves of my jacket.

Abby sobered. "So it's true then? You guys broke up for real?"

"Still don't want to talk about it." I snaked my hands between my hair and my neck, and freed my mane that was trapped in my jacket, then grabbed my keys. "Coming?"

Crossing her arms over her chest, she stuck her tongue in her cheek and popped her hip. Not feeding into her 'you're going to tell me now' look, I spun on my heel. "Well, I'm going for breakfast. You're welcome to join me if you'd like. If not, you can find your way out." Sensing her jaw drop behind me, my lips quirked in a smirk. Served her right for meddling.

"Eva?" Abby rushed behind me. "Talk to me."

"There's nothing to talk about. Now drop it before I drop you." I kept a brisk pace.

"Whoa, this is a sore topic, huh? You're threatening violence and everything. What's gotten into you?"

I stopped short and turned abruptly to face her, forcing her to skid on her heel. "Please stop. Yes, it's true. Blake and I broke up. For good. For real. Now if you don't drop it, I'm really not going anywhere with you."

"Okay, okay. Jeez."

I gladly turned and pushed open the door, exiting the building. Squinting, I searched the street, trying to figure out where we should go eat. Then I remembered a small diner not far away, so I took off in that direction.

"You're not making this very enjoyable, I gotta tell you." Abby struggled by my side.

I slowed my stride, and my shoulders slackened, showing me just how tense I'd been. I turned to face her. "I'm sorry. You just keep hitting all my buttons." She picked at the ends of her hair that draped from the braid over her right shoulder. "Truce?" I held my arms open for a hug.

She stepped in and squeezed, looking at me through eyes that were identical to my own. "Truce." We laced our fingers and finished the short walk.

The bell chimed, and the smell of coffee flooded my senses, telling me how overdue it was in my system. I chose an out of the way booth and slid in so we could have the most private conversation of our lives. A pit solidified in my stomach, but despite that, we ordered our usual plethora of breakfast assortments. We never finished it, but we always ordered one of everything on the breakfast menu so we could have a bite of each.

Oh, Abby. How am I going to tell you that most of your life has been a lie?

The waitress set a steaming mug in front of each of us and, when she retreated, I curled my fingers around the warm porcelain and leaned into the table, staring at my sister who was color coordinating the sugar packets.

"You still do that?"

"Uh, yeah." The octave of her voice rose as though she couldn't believe I was questioning it. "You know I can't sit at a table when the sugar packets are screaming at me to put them in order. It irks me, and then I can't eat. I've tried to ignore it, but I've just accepted it now."

I gave a small, lost laugh as I continued studying her. "So, what've you been up to?"

Her focus on the colored pouches broke. "Mom's been on me to plan the engagement party, so I've been doing that. It would be super helpful to have the aid of my maid of honor, but, you know, she doesn't like to answer the phone." She raised an eyebrow at me, but it wasn't a mean eyebrow. I could tell she was just messing with me still for ignoring her. "Speaking of which, you look like shit."

"Well, gee, thanks." I fluffed the side of my hair sarcastically.

"I'm serious." Her hands dropped to the table, dismissing their task as she trained her eyes on me. "Should I be worried? You're all frail-looking and pale, and your hair could use a fresh cut and the swipe of a highlight. How is Jace standing for this?" She took a sip of coffee.

"He doesn't hold my hand in public anymore." I smiled softly, trying to look unaffected that my disarray was now outwardly showing. "But you shouldn't be worried. I was sick for a while. Winter and all. I'm feeling better now," I lied. I was feeling a million times worse. Unbeknownst to my beloved sister, her crush on Eric was what had gotten me into this situation in the first place. Damon seeing her drooling all over Blake's best friend had set a fire in his ass, and the flames shot right out at me. Needing to change the topic, I cleared my throat and took a sip of coffee. "So, you and Damon then? You've been okay since . . . that day?" *The day he came within inches of brutally raping me.*

She lowered her voice and looked down at the table, picking at the edge. "I don't like to think about that day."

Me either.

"Yes, he's been on his best behavior. Holding my door open and kissing my feet and shit. He feels bad, and I've forgiven him. He was just drunk. He hasn't had a drink since."

"Abby . . ." My words were stilled when the smell of bacon and syrup crawled up my nose as the waitress set a plate beneath it. I sat back momentarily and let her finish trying to find room on the table for all the breakfast we'd ordered. But now any hopes I'd had of eating were long gone, and the smell was only making me nauseous.

Abby didn't waste any time digging in. She was buttering an English muffin with zeal when I dug up something from deep inside, threw caution to the wind, and decided to start this long-dreaded conversation. "Abby . . . What if Damon wasn't just drunk?"

Her knife stopped, and grease hung from her fingertips. She seemed to consider it for a moment, but the deep pucker between her eyes gave away her confusion. "What do you mean?" She grabbed a jelly packet and peeled back the top.

My voice was small, uncertain. "I mean, what if that was the first sign that Damon can't be trusted? That maybe he's not a very good person?"

Abby scoffed. "Oh, please. Do you realize who we're talking about? It's Damon, Eva. The most untrustworthy thing he's ever done is use his dad's company's postage." She chuckled through pounding a ketchup bottle, ensuring it would pour out quickly.

That was a punch to my guts. I fisted the shirt over my belly and pressed on. "What if you're wrong?"

She poured syrup over her pancakes and made a slice. "I'm not wrong. The guy's all bark, no bite." She sunk her teeth into a fluffy bite to accentuate.

Oh, he bites all right.

I leveled my gaze, trying to remain undeterred, though my confidence was waning. "Abby, what if I told you that he's already hurt someone?"

"Yeah, okay." She rolled her eyes and shrugged, still intent on consuming her meal. "I'd say you were crazy."

I swallowed hard. That was a bitter pill to swallow, but if I wanted to get through this, I'd have to force it down. Not knowing what was going to get her attention, I blurted out the first thing that came to mind, despite the knocking in my chest. "What if I said he's hurt me?"

She looked up then, searching my face. "Are you saying that?"

My mouth dried. It was now or never.

I steadied my gaze, unwavering. "What if I was?"

She studied me a moment before wagging her hand at me and

laughing once again. "Good job, Eva. You almost had me." She shoved a piece of melon in her mouth.

I took a deep, calming breath, replenishing my air. "What if I told you he hurt me, Abby?"

She paused. "Truth?"

"Truth."

"Truth." She let out a deep exhale. "Truth is, if you or anyone else told me Damon had hurt them, I'd call you . . . or them . . . a liar." Her eyes held no uncertainty. "That guy wouldn't hurt a fly. We all know that." She waved me off, dismissing the topic. "Now stop messing with me and eat your breakfast."

A liar.

My insides coiled and pieces of me chipped off and flitted away. "I'm not hungry," I murmured.

My eyes glazed over and I felt myself beginning to break. I had been right all along. She'd never believe me. She was so blinded by him and his evil fucking voodoo that any attempt to tell her would be seen as a joke, or worse, a lie. It was exactly what he'd said would happen.

"I don't feel so good." I slid out of the booth and grabbed my belongings.

Abby began to choke on her bite and took a few big gulps of orange juice to try and clear her throat. "Where're you—"

I tossed a twenty dollar bill on the table. "Here. Sorry to cut things short. I'm glad you came to see me. I'll call you soon."

Even hearing her yell my name from behind me, I kept going, not knowing how long I would be able to keep it together. My worst fears had been confirmed.

I'd never be free of this.

Never be able to tell her.

If I wanted to have any type of relationship with my sister, and my family, I had to keep this to myself.

Forever.

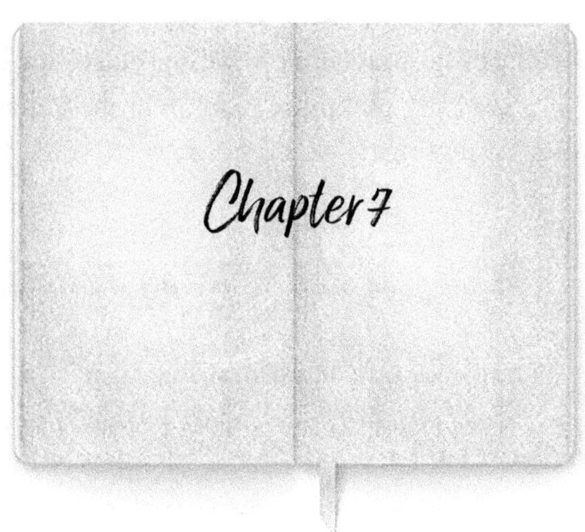

Chapter 7

I DROPPED TO MY KNEES and looked up, pleading for some direction from my friend Bertha. Though Blake had only introduced me to the old willow a few months ago, I felt like she knew so much about me and my past. *So much more than anyone . . .*

The second I was in her presence, I felt comforted—protected and guarded as she continually helped hide my ugly underneath her massive beauty. I rested my back against her trunk.

"What am I gonna do? I knew this would happen, Bertha. She's never going to believe me, and I'm never going to be free of this. Free to be with . . ." It hurt too bad to even have his name on my tongue, so I kept it to myself. Anxiety bubbled inside at her silence. She bared no hint of what my next move should be.

"Talk to me. Help me! Please." I crumbled, sobbing helplessly into my jeans, feeling like a broken soul. Empty. Hollow. *Useless.* I needed him as much as I needed my next breath.

Breath.

Blake.

Breathe.

The more I pictured the serenity behind his eyes, the warmth under his fingers, the solidity of his touch, the more vibrant I felt.

Life.

Live.

Live me.

It already felt like it was coming back. Feeling an overwhelming need to purge, I pulled my phone from my rear pocket and opened up my notes as quick as my fingers would move.

I feel him
Though I know I should forget, he's there—picking at the scabs he left behind

Try as I might, he remains
Slipped under my skin, he circulates through my veins

He asked me once to live for him
Little did he know, he was bound within

Locked inside my being, floating around my soul
His absence a constant reminder of why my heart will never be whole

Why my lungs don't expand quite the same
Why my guts are limp inside and lame

It's an unkind, cruel joke when life rips away a piece of you
Tears away your flesh with empty promises to start anew

For this is a wound that is not meant to heal
There will be no Band-Aid, my scars will not seal

Though I'm no stranger to suffering, this breeds a whole new kind of pain
It's blinding and searing, like a poison rushing through my veins

I'm in him, and he in me
And only when I allow that to happen, can we ever truly be.

I looked toward the horizon through the blurry pools in my eyes, then up to Bertha as a smile appeared on my face for the first time in weeks. Realization spread like wildfire, creating a sizzling warmth I'd forgotten about. I needed him. I couldn't do this without him. Good or bad, right or wrong, I had to find him.

Now.

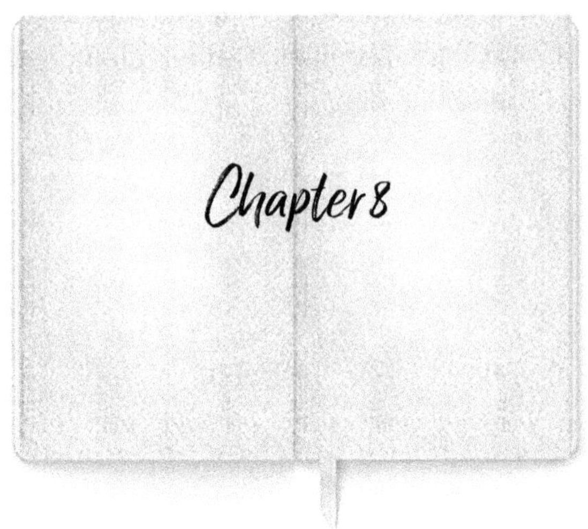

MY BODY ROCKED SIDE TO side as passersby bumped into my shoulders, but I kept my course, undeterred. I had to get to him and tell him how I felt. Apologize. God, I hated myself for the way I'd hurt him. My heart skipped a beat, worried that I may have used up all of my chances. That my three bug-outs had been real and Blake wouldn't forgive me.

I'd pushed him away so many times. So many. How much could one person take? A person with as much love to give as Blake?

My shins burned with the effort of my clipped pace. I ached to stop and stretch them out, alleviate it, but there was no time to waste. I prayed I hadn't already succeeded in extinguishing what he felt for me. Because I needed him. God, I needed him. I couldn't do this on my own. My insides were crumbling.

With a heaving pound in my chest, I rounded the next corner and stopped abruptly as the air sucked out from me in a quick suction.

There he is.

My gaze floated from the leather jacket stretched across his broad back, to the raven hair brushing his collar, up to the camera propped in front of his icy-blue eye. My chest felt full, like my heart had grown a fraction at the mere sight of him. One of my pieces returned.

With a smile, my sights drifted across to the object of his attention—*her.*

A girl who bared a striking resemblance to me was leaning over the rail at the top of the steps leading into his apartment. She was staring off at something, her blonde hair blowing in the wind as he scrutinized her.

I covered my mouth as tears welled—my weak legs giving way, sending me slumping to the ground. *She's gorgeous.* After a moment, she straightened and smiled wide at Blake, who was inspecting the newest found treasure on his viewfinder. I watched his lips spread into an appreciative smile before he motioned for her to come down to him.

She bounced to his side, looping her arm through his, and peaked up on her tippy toes, leaning into his shoulder to look at the image. It brought back so many memories—the way he looked at that screen, the way he looked at her. That hurt worst of all.

Through his smile, Blake said something to her, and she nodded enthusiastically. He grabbed a bag that had been lying by his ankles and slung it over his shoulder. I rushed to get to my feet and out of the way before he turned and saw me.

I pushed up from the ground just as she slid her arm back through his and they both turned. A wave of nausea rocketed through me at the eeriness of seeing him with someone who looked so much like me. It was easy to imagine that was still me by his side.

Unable to peel my gaze from them, I backed up, hitting the brick wall behind me just as his eyes locked on mine. Even from here I could see the paralyzing intensity his gaze held. He dropped his arm, his smile fading as he instinctively took a step in my direction. Gathering myself as quickly as I could, I pushed off the wall and took off around the same corner, running as fast as my weak legs would take me. As fast as my blurred vision would allow.

A car whizzed by, and I stopped short, narrowly escaping running into it. My chest heaved, knowing how dangerous that could have been, after seeing what had happened to my friend Sandra last semester. Our carelessness while crossing the street had landed her in the hospital with numerous injuries, almost dead.

Once in my apartment building, I ran past the doorman, ignoring the wave of his lifted arm. When I got to my floor, I banged on Jace's door repeatedly until he threw it open.

"What the . . ."

"Oh, Jace," I wept, falling into his arms.

"Baby girl? What's the matter?" He squeezed me tight, and I felt the pounding of his heart beating in the same rhythm as my own.

"It's . . . so . . . bad!" I hiccuped.

"What is? Talk to me. You're freaking me out! Did he hurt you again?"

I brought my head back and searched his eyes. "Wha . . . no. No. That's never happening again." I sniffled, wiping my arm along my nose and making my way into his apartment. I plopped down on his sofa.

"I saw Blake. With a girl." My breath hitched through my sobs. "He was taking a picture of her. She looked just like me . . ." My voice trailed off.

"Fuck, Eva." He exhaled, relief filtering through his irritation. "I thought someone died. Don't do that to me." He pulled a few tissues from the box on his coffee table and threw them at me before sitting across from me.

"He's moved on, Jace. For real. We're over." I searched his eyes, panic rising in my chest. "What have I done? I've lost him." Memories of all the times I'd asked him how Blake was, only to get silence in response, flooded back, and I felt my face flush in anger. I narrowed my eyes. "This is why you never answered me? You knew, didn't you?"

He seemed to pull himself back to reality. "No, I didn't know. Why would you think that?"

"I can tell even now you're not telling me something. You've been hiding something ever since . . ." I looked away. I still couldn't think about that day.

"Eva, I wouldn't hide something like that from you." The bluntness in his tone had me believing him despite the way his eyes skirted from mine briefly, giving me the impression he wasn't being completely forthcoming. "Maybe it's a misunderstanding. Where did you see them?"

"Outside his apartment."

"Why were you at his apartment?"

"I was going back to him, Jace. I can't do this without him, and now I have no choice."

Jace straightened his spine. "Well, good then."

"Excuse me?" I narrowed my eyes at him.

"Blake is not your crutch, Eva. He's a man who loved half a girl.

If it's ever going to work out between you two, you need to be strong. Whole. You need to fix yourself. Become that bad ass bitch I remember. And you need to do it on your own. Pussy-up."

His words scared the shit out of me. I didn't want to be alone anymore. I'd spent so much time by myself, screaming in dark rooms, shivering on cold rooftops. I wanted Blake's warmth. His protection. His security.

I lowered my voice. "I don't want to be alone, Jace."

"Then tell your family. They can be there for you." He flung the words at me as though it were common sense.

Another punch to the gut. "I tried. That's the other thing." I gulped. "I met with Abby this morning." Jace stopped fidgeting and honed in on me. Uncomfortable, I lowered my gaze. "We went for breakfast. I asked her what she would do if she ever found out Damon had hurt someone, and you know what she said?" I snickered with heartbroken sarcasm. "She said she wouldn't believe them."

Jace paused briefly, searching me for the truth in my words while he tried to decide whether or not they were valid. Finally, he let out a comforting sigh. "You're not just anyone, Eva. You're her sister. She'd believe you."

I shook my head. "Wrong again. I asked her. I said what if it were me." I looked down at my white-knuckled fingers tied in knots.

"And?"

"Same response."

Jace waved me off and crossed his legs to the other side, hurriedly. "I don't believe that for a second. She couldn't have been taking you seriously."

"I don't have the answer to that, Jace. All I know is that both of my worst fears were confirmed this morning." Fresh tears began to stream down my cheeks.

Jace soothed me for what felt like hours, the tears a never-ending flow. When his shirt was soaked through with my sorrow, I finally peeled my head away. Ironically enough, I needed to be alone. Without a word, I kissed him on the cheek and left.

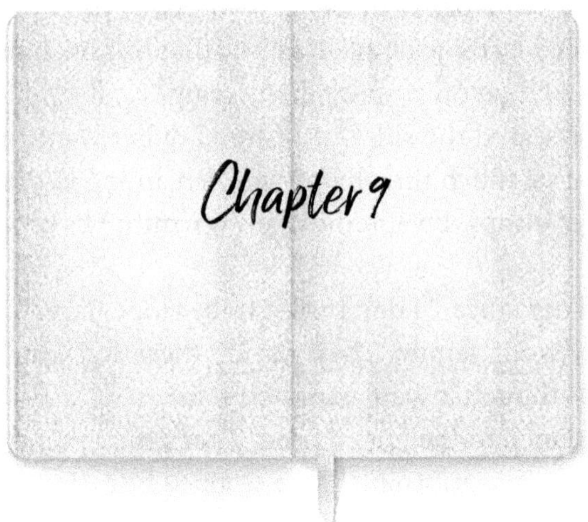

THE SKY GLOWED A BRIGHT shade of orangey-pink as the sun set, but as beautiful as it was, I couldn't enjoy it. So many rises and sets of the sun had been wasted on me, usually seen through a blurred, liquidy vision. I was still in the same spot on the roof I'd crashed in when I had left Jace's place, thankful once again for landing an apartment on the top floor that gave me easy access. Where I could hide. Sing out my sorrows. Music from my iPod flowed into my ears, my brain numb from the heavy words each song spoke. I couldn't feel my fingers, so I knew I'd been up here much longer than I should have been, but I just couldn't seem to make myself move. My heart, a faint, unfeeling organ beneath my ribs, was just as lifeless.

With my eyes closed, my head swayed as the soft words to Sara Bareilles' "Breathe Again" drifted from my solemn lips. Her lyrics brought me to a painful place, reminding me of the life I had left in my rearview mirror the day I was forced to turn my back on all that was important to me.

A tear trickled into my mouth as I sang of wanting to breathe again. Needing to inhale his air—knowing he was mine. I remembered it all. In flashes, everything dashed before me as the heavy words passed my lips.

The first day we met when he'd donned me with the name Angel.

Him in my doorway wearing a black suit, his sparkling blue eyes peeking over a red rose the night of our first date.

The first time we had made love and the fire it stoked within me, feeling us become one.

Nestling beneath Bertha, learning each other.

Bertha.

Lying on the cold dirt, staring at the glimmering gold chain Blake had given me for Christmas dangling from his fist.

It hurts to be here.

The secrets.

Him begging for the truth.

Running away from him.

Running toward him.

Deciding I wanted him back.

Her. Him with her.

What am I gonna do?

My hand instinctively wrapped around my throat, trying to aid the constricting burn of too little oxygen—thin, lifeless air that was all too familiar, mixed with the fire of a watery death as I swallowed my salty emotions.

I'm sorry I pushed you away.

He's the air that I would kill to breathe.

God, I can't fucking breathe.

With a shuddered sigh, I dropped my head to my knees, succumbing to the burden I had been carrying around and the heaviness weighing down my limbs. Tired and numb, everything inside of me was giving up.

Jace slipped next to me on the lounger. "There you are."

I jolted, startled I didn't hear anyone coming. When I realized it was him, my body relaxed into his, and I dropped my head to his shoulder. "Here I am."

"I think we should go out," he stated as blandly as if he were talking about the sunset.

I sniffled. "I'm a fucking mess, Jace. Going out is the last thing I need. Just leave me here. I'm used to this. I'll be fine."

"Yeah, so um, no." He grabbed my hand and tugged.

I winced at the immediate soreness to my muscles that hadn't been stretched in hours. "Jace, come on. Really. I'm not in the mood, okay?"

"I already called the girls." His eyes held no room for negotiation as they zeroed in on me. "They miss you, and they're excited to see you, so you're coming. We'll go to The Backdoor so you don't feel uncomfortable. I'm not asking, honey." His eyebrow raised, daring me to counter.

He dragged me down the stairs and straight into my bedroom before he started rummaging through my closet. I plopped down on the bed and watched him in a somewhat catatonic state.

He turned to face me. "Uck, you look wretched. Go wash yourself, please. We're not going to a rodeo." With the flick of his wrist, he dismissed me to the bathroom.

An hour later, I was deemed "passable" to Jace in my skinny jeans, peach silk top, and wedges. I'd even curled my hair and put on some makeup. It was the most attention I'd given myself in a long time, and it felt good.

I took a deep inhale. "Let's go."

THE MUSIC WAS PUMPING WHEN we swung the door open to The Backdoor. The bar was packed and stocked with three bartenders, and for a moment I was jealous I wasn't one of them. They would make a killing tonight.

I zigzagged through the crowd in an attempt to make my way over to Rick and say hello when I was pulled back by my waist and enveloped in a tight squeeze. "I missed you soooo much!" Jessie squealed in my ear. "Jace said you were coming, but I didn't believe him."

I turned my head, my face brushing against Jessie's wild blonde curls, and spoke over the music. "Nice to see you, too." A genuine smile warmed my lips.

She laced her hands with mine. "Come on. We have a spot already." With her enormous Jessie-smile, she spun around her curls twirling with her. "Hi, Jace." She placed a kiss on his cheek and then tugged my hand toward the bar. Sandra and Jeremy were sitting close to each other, smiling and deep in conversation.

"Look who I found!" Jessie announced.

Sandra spun to face me, her face instantly glowing at the sight of me. "Well, if I didn't see it with my own eyes. Hey there, girl." She hopped off her stool to wrap me in a hug.

"I didn't die, guys." I fisted my hips.

"You'd never know." Jessie hopped onto a stool, lounging over the bar. "Hey, Rick! Thirsty here!"

Rick held up a finger without turning around, counting the stack of money he was depositing. He shoved the drawer shut with his hip and turned, his smile illuminating when he saw me. "Well, it's about damn time you came out. What can I get you, darlin'?"

"Not you, too." I rolled my eyes. "Amaretto on the rocks, please."

"Changing it up, I see. Will do." He turned his attention to Jessie. "Another?"

She tipped her empty glass toward him and pushed it to the other end of the bar. "Give me two if you're going to take forever every time."

"Packed bar here," he retorted, lovingly. "Be patient, Princess."

Jessie blushed at the use of her pet name. Rick was a few years her senior, and for some reason avoided their connection even though it was blatantly obvious the two of them had the hots for each other. I never understood why. There was always something off about it.

"You know, *I* don't have a pet name." I glanced at Jessie from the corner of my eye.

"Put a cork in it. I want to enjoy myself."

"For now." I took a deep inhale and looked around, trying to relax and just focus on having a good time for once.

Rick returned with our drinks, and I wasted no time sucking down half of it before asking him to bring me another. It was the first time I'd drunk since I almost killed myself with alcohol poisoning, and it immediately shot to my head and made a swirl in my belly.

Rick leaned in. "You good?"

"I'm good." When he turned to get my next cocktail, I faced my friends. "Thank you for dragging me out, guys. I needed this."

Jace wrapped his arms around my waist. "Dance with me. I miss you."

We hit the dance floor, and my body took over, remembering its dance partner for life. Jace and I always put on quite a show and tonight was no different. By the time we returned to the bar, my chest was heaving as I reached for my sweaty, watered down drink.

Jace swatted my hand. "Have I not taught you anything?"

I raised my eyebrows at him.

"You never drink anything left unattended. Unless you enjoy roofies." He raised his hand. "Rick! Bring her another one, please." He turned back to scowl at me, but his twisted pout was short-lived. Jace's spine sharpened, and I could practically see the hitch in his chest as he looked past my shoulder. He swallowed hard. "Be right back." Then he disappeared into the crowd.

A few minutes later, I caught sight of him talking to a cute guy who I thought looked slightly familiar. *Is he that twin? Or maybe the football player?* A fresh drink plopped in front of me, and I gave up trying to analyze Jace. He changed men like I changed underwear.

Rick wiped the bar clean with a rag. "So, Eva, you singing?"

"Not tonight. I'm off the clock." I traced wet swirls in the wood with my finger. A familiar laugh swarmed my ears, breaking the monotonous sound of the crowd. The hairs on my arms rose, realizing if he was close, Blake was probably closer. I flipped my hair to the front of my shoulder so I could bury my face in it while turning my head to peek.

Eric snaked his arm around some bountifully-bosomed redhead and rubbed his nose along the edge of her jaw. She giggled and meshed further into him, slapping him playfully on the chest.

I looked around—no Blake. My body relaxed and then tensed once again as Eric's hand drifted to the mound of the redhead's ass, another throaty chuckle rumbling from his throat. My insides churned. Any hopes I had of him being Abby and my savior were flitting away on a wave of this girl's fire engine red locks.

I rolled the drink between my fingers and took a sip, begging for it to live up to its name of liquid courage. Maybe he would tell me who the girl was that Blake was seeing. I needed to know. Needed confirmation that what we'd had was over and that I should move on and set him free.

I probably shouldn't have been intruding on their moment, but I couldn't help myself. Downing the rest of my drink, I turned, determined to get my answer. I nudged his side with my shoulder, and he rocked into his female companion before turning to face me, his eyebrows pulled together in anger.

When he saw it was me, a slow smile spread across his boyishly handsome face, and his mint green eyes came to life. "Well, look what the cat dragged in," he slurred.

I nodded toward the girl. "I see you downgraded. Didn't take long to move on, huh?"

He moved from her and slipped a heavy arm around my shoulder, the alcohol seeping from his mouth to imbed itself in my nostrils. "Seems we all gotta do what we gotta do to move on these days, *Angel.*" He winked.

My stomach shriveled at the use of Blake's pet name. I swallowed hard. *It's true.* "You've seen her before, then?"

"Amanda?" He shrugged. "Couple times. Right, baby?" He turned toward the redhead and blew her a kiss. She merely smiled, then eyed me as she stuck her straw in the corner of her mouth and took a pull. I thought I would be sick, visions of them double dating rotting my insides.

"I gotta go. Thanks, Eric."

At his puzzled expression, I squeezed past him and made my way back to my friends. "Hey, guys, I think I'm gonna head home." I kissed Jessie on the cheek.

"You sure? I feel like you just got here," she whined.

"Yeah, I'm not feeling great. I'll call you tomorrow."

Jace had returned in my absence and ambled to my side. "You sure you're okay? You don't look so hot."

"Perfect. Love." I recited our unique term of endearment and kissed his cheek.

"Love," he replied with a questioning glance.

OUTSIDE, MY LUNGS OPENED UP, inviting in the cool air. I hadn't realized how claustrophobic I'd felt in there. I pulled the edges of my jacket shut and bared down to the cold, the few drinks I'd consumed doing their job of warming me, and began the walk home.

One, two, three . . .

Lost in thought, I counted the cracks in the sidewalk, making sure I didn't step on them. I wasn't sure what I thought would happen if I did. World termination?

I dug around in my bag and pulled out my iPod, needing to distract my brain from the dark thoughts I felt clawing their way toward me.

Ever appropriate, the somber sound of a guitar filled the silence as *What If You* by Joshua Radin began.

His voice, his words tore through me. Maybe the saddest combination I had ever heard slapping me in the face. A song built around love lost, around one last chance to feel. Tears welled in my eyes as goose bumps lined my skin. He would never know what his absence was doing to me, how it was gutting me and shredding any hopes I had of feeling whole, human.

I superimposed Blake and me into the lyrics, picturing myself lying beside him for one final goodbye before I disappeared from his life for good. I wished for one more chance to feel. To be close to him, knowing it was impossible. I pictured the look in his beautifully pained eyes when he would wake the next morning to find me gone.

A set of familiar concrete stairs with gold drizzled throughout taunted me. They weren't my own, but they begged me to use them. My body always had a way of doing what it wanted without me even realizing. I walked absentmindedly into the lobby, waving to the doorman in a dream state, wishing for one more chance. An opportunity to say goodbye the way we should have. The way I needed to.

I opened the zipper in my wallet, extracted a lone key, and dangled it from the red satin ribbon it was anchored from. I watched it twist and twirl, and felt my stomach do the same.

Blake's spare key.

I hadn't given it back. His words when he gave it to me replayed in my head. *Use it anytime. It's just as much yours as I am. You're always welcome.*

I bit down on the edge of my bottom lip, contemplating what I was about to do. Sure he wasn't mine anymore, but he hadn't asked for the key back either. He knew I still had it, so if I were no longer welcomed to use it, he would have changed the locks, right?

I glided the brass between my fingers, flipping it over and back again, uncertain. My chest weighted, the pull to be near him stronger than anything I had ever felt. Then, with a racing heart and trembling fingers, I slipped it into its home. With a turn and a click, the seam of the threshold parted and a wave of Blake rushed out, causing a burst of anticipation to surge from my lungs. I closed my eyes briefly, enveloped in memories and familiarity—letting him invade me as an acquainted comfort wrapped itself around me.

Home.

I closed the door as quietly as I could and stepped inside. Remembrances swarmed me—his leather couch, and the day I'd first said yes. Told him I was his and would never leave him. The first time he had touched me. The day he had called me a unicorn and the adorably confused look on his face when I didn't understand why.

Lies.

I hung my head, ashamed that I hadn't kept my word, and moved toward the kitchen. The table sat bare but for the streak of moonlight. In my mind, it was covered with books, and Blake was wearing a mischievous smile as he gave me a lesson with his unorthodox teaching skills.

I looked up then, squinting through the darkness as I searched for the first photo he had ever taken of me, which had been framed and displayed on the counter, but it was gone. Glancing around, it hit me—there was no sign of me anywhere. Nothing of mine remained. No pictures lining his walls. No flowers.

I tucked my hair behind my ear and pushed through the burn in my throat, making my way toward the back of the apartment. I envisioned yellow caution tape that once blocked the bedroom door in Blake's attempt to keep his hands off me, and despite my melancholy that he had just about erased me from his life, a small smile met my lips at the fond memory.

I pressed my palms to the wood and rested my forehead against it, knowing he lay just on the other side. I wanted so badly to be near him but couldn't shake the feeling that I just didn't belong here anymore.

One last time.

I squared my shoulders, gathering strength before I broke the seal.

In the dim light of the room, I was able to make out a giant mound beneath the covers. Soft breathing floated from below the comforter, and my heart skipped a beat as his aura slipped out and deposited itself under my skin. Whether I could have him or not, this man owned me. I didn't think I would be able to soak up enough of him to last me the rest of my life, but I had to try.

I slipped my shoes off and crept inside, discarding my jacket as I walked farther into the room. When I reached the side of the bed, Blake's face was finally visible. The soft illumination from the moonlight played on his relaxed features, making him look younger, more boyish than I remembered, despite the extra scruff he wore on his face these days.

With a slight part of his lips, I watched the air filter in and out of his mouth in a relaxed rhythm, remembering the smell of his breath, the taste of his tongue. Gently, I moved to my knees and put my face within millimeters of his, closing my eyes and allowing the oxygen to pass between us, recycling from his lungs into mine.

I opened my eyes and sat back on my heels to study him. He was on his side, one bare arm lying over the cover. His face looked so peaceful, completely at ease without a crease or worry line to mar his beautiful features. His soft hair hung loose, framing his eyes, and I recalled how he'd fought to keep those eyes open the night of our first date. That thought brought a smile to my lips and a sadness to my heart. I pushed that away before it could deter me from what I was here to do.

Not wanting to disturb him, I walked around to the other side of the bed and slipped underneath the blankets, trying to get as close as possible without waking him. The coolness of the empty side—my side—sent a harsh reality rocketing through me that it no longer held that title. I suppressed the tightness in my throat and inched my way closer to him, the sheets becoming warmer the nearer I scooted.

Then I was beside him, feeling his heat spiraling beyond his body. I stared at the ceiling, choking back a sob as a million memories flooded me. Happier times which made me long for even the not so happy times, just because they were still *our* times. One by one, visions of the *us* I'd left behind crashed into me—the feel of his skin, the power of his arms and the intensity of his gaze. The feeling of gentle possessiveness he held over me, and the way he'd claimed me as his in a non-threatening, non-dominating way that only *Blake* could do. The way he'd called me *Angel* and really believed that I was when, in fact, it was him who was the angel all along.

A tear trickled from the corner of my eye into my hairline and I thought I'd wake him if I didn't stop, but I couldn't bring myself to. I needed this—had to let him go properly.

The words to *What If You* came to mind and overtook me . . .

It's come to this . . . release me.

Another tear. Swallow.

I'll leave before the dawn.

My breathing hiccuped in my silenced throat as I wiped the back of my hand across my eyes and slid my arms around his bare chest. I did it lightly so not to disturb him, but my fingers were trembling along each brush of his ribs. I ran my toes along his calf and snaked my body around his.

Blake's breathing faltered, and he adjusted himself, pushing back against me, and I heard the distinct sound of him smacking his lips together in his sleep—the most adorable little habit I'd ever encountered in my life—before the movement of his rib cage evened out once again. I held my breath, fearing I would wake him and be caught, but he seemed to have drifted back to wherever he'd been. I exhaled and relaxed into him once again, breathing in the scent of him. His soap and his skin—his Blake.

The song replayed in my head as a flicker of hope stupidly slipped into my psyche. My heart rate sped up as I wondered . . . *what if?* What if I woke him? Would he be happy to see me? Or done and disgusted?

What if you could wish me away . . .

What if I could take back the words . . .

God, I needed him.

I had to tell him. I had to take a shot.

I leaned up on my forearm and stared down at his beautiful profile. The profile of this man whose inside was as beautiful as his outside. I ran my nose along his neck, drawing him into me, hoping a piece of him would permeate me and stay there forever. A line of goose bumps raised there, but again he didn't stir, and I knew I was on borrowed time. I closed my eyes, ready to tell him I was sorry. To take the plunge on a leap of faith.

Making my way around the hard line of his jaw, I opened my eyes, searching to see if he'd felt me when my eyes caught the faint outline of a picture. With no other trace of myself in his apartment, I was curious which memory he'd decided to keep close. Long blonde hair draped over a dainty shoulder, but there was something off. As I squinted, I couldn't make out the surroundings. It wasn't ringing a bell. Reaching over his shoulder, I fingered the photograph lying on his bedside table and pulled it closer to inspect it. My breathing caught, and my heart began to bang around in my chest. Though similar in many ways, this was not me. It was *her*. The girl from earlier.

Amanda.

Smiling a soft, contented smile, she wasn't looking directly into the lens. She was looking past it somewhere. The shots I knew Blake lived for. And it was right beside him in the night. Replacing mine. Where he could study it and fall asleep to it. Dream about it.

With a start, I backed away, clutching my chest and wondering if that was where his mind was as I lie in his bed. With her. In that photograph, reliving a happy moment.

Ice seemed to line the mattress, making me feel like an intruder in a place I no longer belonged. I dropped the photo and slid out from beneath the covers as delicately as possible. As almost an afterthought, I reached into my pocket and extracted my key, placing it in his drawer. Then I slipped on my jacket and shoes and turned to look at Blake one last time in a final goodbye.

But when the sun hits your eyes through your window, there'll be nothing you can do . . .

My throat began to close, and I knew it was only a matter of time before I lost it. I shut the door behind me and ran from the room, not stopping until the cool night air slapped me in the face. I dropped to his stairs, weeping into my knees.

I'm too late.

My legs refused to take me away. I rested my chin on my arms and brushed my fingertips along the concrete, remembering so many walks into and out of this building, up and down these stairs.

Flash.

A memory of him taking a picture of that girl flashed before my eyes. Just as quickly, it was me standing as the object of his attention again.

Flash. Flash.

I winced.

She's skipping down the stairs toward him, looping her arm through his. Then it's me again, snuggling close to his side.

Flash.
Wince.
She's laughing, her blonde hair swiping along his arm.
I crumbled.
I have no one.

I FELT HER.

With her living inside me for so long, it was impossible for my body to not know when she was close—even in my deepest rest. It took everything for me to pretend I was asleep, just to get as much time with her as possible. I erased her from my place for my own sanity, the constant reminders too crippling, but doing the same to my heart wasn't so simple.

God, she felt so fucking good. I couldn't help my skin from reacting. From coming alive with her wrapped around me. A couple of times I thought she'd figured it out, but then she stayed, coiling herself further. When a unicorn approaches you, you don't stir. You stay as still as fucking possible and take in their beauty before they disappear again.

She'd left so abruptly, I didn't understand why. I'd laid there, hoping she was coming back, but she never did. I rolled to a sitting position, dropping my legs from the side of the bed, and switched on the bedside lamp. I scrubbed my palms over my eyes and took a deep inhale, looking around. The smell of her still lingered in the air, on my skin.

Something on the floor caught my eye, and I rubbed it again, squinting. The picture of Marybeth. I picked it up and put it back on my nightstand, wondering briefly if Eva had seen it and if that had sent her running.

Didn't matter. Clearly, it was over.

I couldn't shake the undeniable feeling that she had just said goodbye for the very last time, and part of me was almost relieved. This girl had wrecked me from the inside, broken something I'd thought unbreakable. I'd had a thick skin my whole life because of my father, set my heart in a sheath of armor so it couldn't shatter, and she'd blasted it. Scattered the pieces like they'd never been part of one beating organ in the first place.

I'd given her everything. All my faith. My love. My heart and soul. Hell, I'd given her my fucking veins and insides. She owned me. Lived in me. And now, I was dead. A carcass of a man, lifeless and broken. And I didn't care. My reason was gone, and she'd taken me with her. There was only so much a person could endure, and I'd reached my limit.

I lay back in the bed and buried myself under the covers once again, attempting to block out my Angel, once and for all.

Chapter 11

Be there in fifteen.

JACE'S TEXT RATTLED MY PHONE. I was in no mood for company. After the night I'd had, and the realization that I would never have Blake back again, I was done. The fog clouding my head had never been thicker, and it was suffocating me. I needed a game plan, I knew I did, but I was too feeble to come up with one, and my lack of strength was taking away any care I had to try.

Pound. Pound. Pound.

The harsh knocking shook my door with force.

Is he kidding banging like that?

I twisted the bolts, unlocking them, and tugged at the handle. "What the hell is your—" Sooner than I could get the door fully open, it whacked into me, shoving me backward. Before I could register what was happening, Damon's large body was over the threshold—pure rage rolling off of him, his fists clenched into tight balls at his sides.

I gasped. "Wh—what are you doing here?" I choked out, stumbling back in disbelief.

Am I having a nightmare?

"What's the matter, beautiful? Not happy to see me?" he mocked as he kicked the door shut, a vein streaking the side of his neck in a pointed bulge.

Paralyzed, I couldn't answer, still in shock that he was standing in my living room. He took my lack of a response as an invitation to come in farther, and I instinctively backed up at his advance.

He narrowed his gaze. "What did you say to her?" he demanded, the evil in his eyes unmasked—focused and aggressive.

What is he talking about? Even though Abby had made it seem as though Damon was fine, he had been unraveling last I'd seen him, so I wasn't sure how mentally stable he was. Memories of him pinning me to my mother's cushions slammed me from all angles. I cupped my cheek, remembering the harsh slap he'd laid there. Sure, the visible mark was gone, but the sting still lay deep within my flesh. I shook my head, trying to remain focused, the reminiscent stench of old beer curdling my stomach.

"What did I say to who?" My voice shook with the fear in my gut that he was here to hurt me, my eyes darting around to find any sort of weapon should I need it. "What are you talking about?"

"Don't play dumb. Really, it's ugly on you," he accused, raking a hand through his hair with impatience, the threads of his demeanor beginning to unstitch.

Another step.

My gaze dropped to his advancing legs and then rode back up to his face, which looked as though it were planning all the ways to dismantle me behind those odious eyes. The farther and farther he came into my apartment, the less hope I had that I would get out of this unscathed.

My mind whirled, grasping at straws through the panic. The only thing I could think to do was feign indifference. Make him think he was crazy. "Damon, I have no clue what you're talking about. I've barely talked to anyone in my family in months if you haven't noticed." My voice was shaky despite my words, my eyes prickling with tears of fear. *Where is Jace? Hurry up!*

"She was here," he spat matter-of-factly. "She *told* me she came here. And she came home all fucked up. Said you ran out on her, talking about me hurting people and shit. Is she lying?" I flinched as his voice banged off the walls with a roar as his tolerance depleted.

When he took another step, I recoiled, shrinking into my skin as bile pooled in my mouth.

Fucking Abby.

A cool sweat broke out on the back of my neck.

A lump traveled from the pit of my stomach to the back of my throat. The look in his eye, the feel of him closing in on me, stealing my air . . .

Seconds felt like hours as different responses ran rampant through my head.

Yes, she's lying.

No, she was never here.

I said it, but only as a joke.

Get the fuck out, or I'm going to scream!

And then a whisper.

Don't hurt me.

"You ungrateful bitch." The words slithered from his mouth, the disgust in his tone slinging dirt at me. He wasn't yelling which frightened me more. This was eerier, as though he actually believed I'd disregarded a favor. He was so sick and twisted.

Another step, closing in my world a bit tighter. My lids fluttered in a dazed fog as I became lightheaded. I retreated, but he didn't seem to care as he took one step after another.

Unhurried.

Deliberate.

"You fucking promised," he spoke calmly like he knew what was coming and was just trying to convince himself he was right in his actions. "I told you before we ever did anything that you could never tell because she'd get mad. That she'd never forgive me for not telling her." He dragged air into his flared nostrils.

My apartment was small. There wasn't much more room to go until I would be backed against a wall. Claustrophobia crawled up my throat, its nails a prickling scratchiness. I couldn't find my words as he moved me farther and farther inside, trapping me. Each step trampling on my hope that this would turn out okay.

"I *forced* myself to fuck a prude so I could help you out, and now that you're over it, you want to ruin my life? Act like you didn't ask for it?" He scoffed. "Did you forget you told me you wanted it, sweetheart? *You* needed *me*." He stabbed an accusing finger at me and then back at himself. "You were so desperate to learn, you practically *begged* me for it.

Pathetic." He spat out the word.

I clutched my chest. He was sicker than I thought. *Does he actually believe that? Is that why he never stopped? Did he truly think I wanted it? Liked it?*

Bubbles rolled from the pit of my stomach to the base of my throat, threatening to spill out of my mouth. I forced a narrowed, dry swallow. The whole thing was a mind-fuck that I couldn't wrap my head around.

Shaking at the prospect of what would surely come once he was in grabbing distance, I glanced around at my belongings. My purple hoodie hung from the peg beside the door, and my schoolbag sat on the chair pulled out from the table in the corner, the sun streaming in from the glass door leading to the balcony. My home.

My new home.

This was the one place in my life that wasn't tainted by him. There weren't any hauntings trapped inside these walls. I couldn't allow him to add another one to his collection.

I sucked in a breath, trying to steady my trembling lip while squaring my shoulders. "Get the fuck out." My voice was all-but a whisper, but it was laced with an authority I wasn't sure I possessed. Still, little pieces of me began to float toward my center as a confidence built.

His eyes trained on mine with a cocky assurance that told me he couldn't care less what I had to say. "I'll leave when I'm good and ready. You're gonna get my point. You want to see what *forced* feels like?" He took a giant stride toward me, clasping my wrist in his huge paw as he tugged me to his chest.

I yelped, my heart banging against the confines of him caged up against me—my insides raging in fear. The edge of his lip curled in disgust. "Look at you. You're all skinny and frail now. Even easier to manipulate how I'd like." He flicked my chin to prove his point with a sneer, and I tossed my head to the side, panting in desperate spurts. Lowering his mouth to my ear, he still managed to keep the hatred in his focus on my eyes. "But probably one terrible *fuck*." The last letter clicked from the back of his tongue and nausea rolled through me in waves.

I buckled down, pretending to be strong when inside I was as brittle as a dried out leaf. "Jace is on the way." I shook out. "So, unless you're ready to go *very* public with *our* little secret," I leaned into his ear, mirroring his hateful look through budding tears but not taking my eyes from his, "I suggest you take your hands the *fuck* off me." I accentuated the same word, struggling against the quiver in my lips.

After a long stare-down, my wrist throbbing with a hot, pulsating pain as it lost its blood, Damon threw my arm back at me and retreated, causing me to bow forward in a *whoosh*. He sized me up with each of his backward steps, a sneer amongst his cold, icy glare. I rubbed the ache in my wrist, trying to figure out his next move, not trusting that he was really done with me.

"One of these days, I'm gonna find a way to put that little pussy in his place, too." He cocked his head in thought. "Although he might enjoy it." His smile was sickening, laced with a revolting promise.

Bile rose in my throat, and I knew that if I didn't get him to leave now, I'd be sick right here on the carpet. "He's probably outside right now. Why don't you tell him that yourself?" It was a bold move, but the only thing I could think of to possibly scare him enough to leave.

"Just remember what I said." He bore his gaze into mine, attempting to coax me into believing his words. "You wanted every bit of what we did together. Fuck with my relationship, and I really *will* make you a victim." He tossed the words at me before curling his hands around my doorknob. "Make it right, Eva. Or I *will* be back. I think you know that."

I jumped as the door slammed behind him, rattling the frames on the wall beside it. My chest filled and hollowed in a hurried rhythm as my lungs sucked in whatever air it could find. Although his presence was gone, his aura still lingered, tainting me with his filth as I dragged it inside. Covering my mouth, I ran at full speed to the bathroom, tripping over my feet to reach the bowl before I lost the contents of my stomach. My knees slammed into the tile as my back heaved.

"Eva!" Jace's voice bellowed through my apartment.

I couldn't answer as the next wave caused my back to buck. A second later, Jace was at my side, scooping up my hair into his hands. "Are you okay? I just saw Damon in the hallway. Did he hurt you? What the fuck was he doing here?"

"I'm okay," I breathed. "Just give me a second."

I sat back on my heels as he filled a cup of water and brought it over to me. When everything that Damon had said—everything he could have done—barreled back toward me, the tears began to flow in a never-ending loop. I couldn't voice what was going on inside, how sick he was.

Eventually, my tears seemed to wash away my fears, leaving me with a cold kind of numbness. An awareness filtered in as I sat crumbled into my best friend's arms on the tile floor of the bathroom.

I was done.

So done.

MY TOE DUG INTO THE spout of the bathtub as I twisted and turned it, my eyes stuck in a deranged, mad state. Clutching a wine glass to my chest, I stared at the motion. *Back and forth. Back and forth.* I pictured things I shouldn't, imagined things that rotted my insides.

Ending Damon's life—his blood splattered amongst the tiles.

And then my own, trickling down my wrists.

With a vibrating clank, I set the wine glass on the ledge, my eyes skirting to the razor sitting beside it. My chest filled, sucking in courage. My eyes welled, blurring. My lips parted, trembling. I wrapped my fingers around the edge of the blade, its cool, hard smoothness sending a rocket through my chest.

A fat tear bubbled. I blinked and felt it roll from my saturated lid, freeing itself to mingle into the water below. *Sobs.*

My chest hitched with spasms as I held a shaky hand to the delicate flesh of my upturned palm.

Sobs.

Sobs.

Sobs.

Not again. Don't let him take you again.

I stared at my quivering hand, felt the scratch of the blade as my fingers trembled, heard her voice trying to reach me. *What am I doing?*

With a splash, my hand dropped along with my foot, the water spattering on my face and mingling with the tears that now poured. My distraught body gave way, slumping and shaking beneath the water.

And everywhere that Mary went, Mary went, Mary went . . .

Chapter 13

It's a funny thing what happens when you're stuck between never and nowhere. A faint shutting down of sorts. Time drips on, seeming to soak into the linoleum beneath your feet. Motionless. Meaningless. You stare at nothing, nowhere, wondering where you are and how you got there.

Paint chips. Love morphs and wilts. Crinkles and splits to your existence happen, but you're impervious to it.

You don't remember who you are. Why you are. You just stop. Cease.

The death before the rebirth.

And then you awaken.

I NEEDED HELP.

My heels scraped along the carpet as I paced, waiting impatiently for my name to be called. I needed the poison out before I didn't believe it *myself* anymore. Before I lost the nerve. Something bubbled inside, and I was ready to combust like a boiling pot of tea. I wiped my sweaty palms down the front of my thighs as a middle-aged woman approached on long, sleek legs. A cheerful smile welcomed me from red-painted lips as she stuck out her hand in greeting.

"Nice to meet you, Eva. I'm Doctor Christianson."

I returned her handshake with a feeble slant to my mouth and followed her into the next room. It was cozy, made to look like a worn-in living room. My options were a recliner and a couch. I chose the couch and took the opportunity to peruse my surroundings as she gathered a pad and pen.

"Chilly today, no?" Her smooth voice pulled me away from her bookshelf and the prestigious degrees on the wall.

"Hmm? Oh, yeah. Guess so." I was trying to appear calm, having just met the doctor, but my knee was bobbing up and down, giving me away.

A slow smile spread while she analyzed me from the tops of her eyes. She was a pro about it, discreet, but I was a pro at noticing when people were doing it.

I fidgeted more.

"So, Eva. Tell me why you're here."

"I was raped." The statement toppled from my mouth, and I straightened my spine, unbelievably unsure of why the words picked that moment to do so. I stood and began to pace, shaking out my hands at my sides. "Crap, that felt good. I always beat around the bush, y'know." I took a deep breath and smiled, enjoying the liberation and forgetting I wasn't alone.

A glance out the window showed me a busy city below. People going about their business as though I hadn't just unloaded the heaviest three words I had ever spoken. Movement in the glare of the glass caught my attention, and I turned to find Doctor Christianson analyzing my demeanor, my actions.

She brushed a stray hair from her forehead, except there wasn't a highlighted hair out of place. A tell sign that she was just as taken back at my abruptness as I was. She really should pay better attention to her *own* actions if she didn't want to show her hand. "Well, that was very brave of—"

"I've never said that before," I exhaled, not caring what she had to say as the enormity of what I had just admitted crashed all around me. "Not the actual words." I suddenly felt self-conscious and made my way back to sit on the couch. My hands shook with the weight of my words, and I knotted them into a ball in my lap.

"Well, that's quite an accomplishment then. I'm honored you picked me to share it with first." I could hear the smile in her voice, but I couldn't look at her. I wouldn't say anything more if I did.

"I guess. It won't do any good, but my friend is harassing me to talk to someone. So . . ."

"Sounds like a good friend," the educated woman stated.

"Sorry I blurted that out like that. It's just I've been holding it in for so long. And I'm tired." My voice lowered, and I wasn't sure if I was still speaking to her or myself. "I'm so fucking tired."

"That was a big step. We can backpedal in a moment, but I'm glad you unburdened yourself of that. It had to be pretty heavy carrying it around all this time."

"You have no idea," I huffed, relief swarming me.

Doctor Christianson's smile was adrift, reminiscent, and I wondered briefly if maybe she *did* know. "So, who's this friend of yours?"

"Just Jace, the friend who gave me your card. He's hard to forget. I'm sure you remember the gorgeous, eccentric gay boy."

The doctor cocked her head to the side. "I don't know anyone like that."

"You sure?" I questioned. "He left me your card and badgered me that *you* were the doctor I should call. Like he'd looked into you and knew you'd be perfect for me."

I scrolled through pictures on my phone and brought up one of him and turned it to face her. "Here."

The good doctor smiled. "You're right. I *would* remember him." She chuckled and handed me the phone back, then folded her hands in her lap. "But I don't. I've never met him."

So strange. I shrugged and played it off like it was no big deal, but something about that didn't quite sit right with me. *What's that boy hiding now?* Brushing that thought aside, I started at the beginning. At the safe stuff. My background and my home life, not really touching on the details of my past. We would have to ease back into that.

WHEN MY HOUR WAS UP, I exhaled a liberating breath.

"Not so bad, huh?" Doctor Christianson's smile was warm. Over the past hour, she had dug into me here-and-there, loosening up as she got to know me a bit. I could tell that if she had more time, she could easily be a little bit of a pit bull and even though I was still very fragile, I couldn't help but think that might be exactly what I needed.

"No, not so bad." I returned her friendliness, genuinely surprised at how easy that was. "I needed that more than I realized."

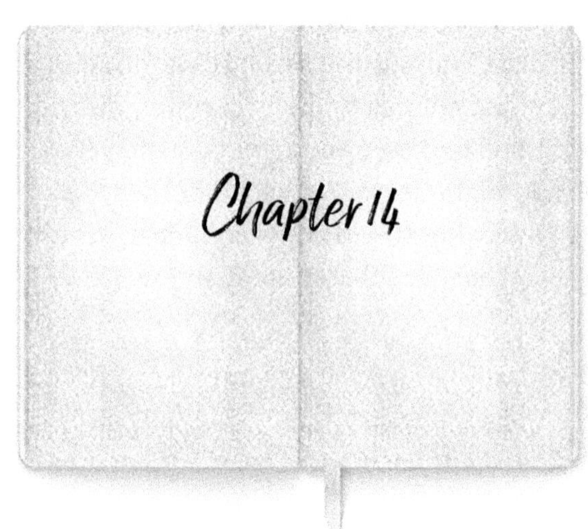

The Basin

A tub of water
fissures down the surface
I hear the noise and know it's coming
crackly splits as the tub forgets its purpose

It's been holding the burden for much too long
fighting the pressure and caging it in
Staying strong against the windy tides
not realizing eventually the liquid burden would win

Millions of drops of water
although nothing by themselves
together form an overbearing force
to which only the strongest dare to delve

A concrete power
strong in every way
Its duty in this world—

keep the rush of the monster at bay

This goes on
day in and day out
Seems so powerful
who would know, who would doubt

Nothing lasts forever
eventually, everything will wither
Even concrete has its breaking point
fighting will always declare a winner

I've been this basin for so long
fighting the turmoil from inside
Not wanting to admit that I was breaking
wanting just to shelter my pride

I've been silent all these years
while my insides slowly splinter
What was once a beautiful flower
has crumpled up and withered

The inner turmoil, just like the water
cannot stay trapped when it wants out
My flesh, as unbending as the concrete
Leaves breaking and cracking its only route

Once I'm broken, what will happen
Can the pieces be re-glued
Not knowing is so scary
Can my being be renewed?

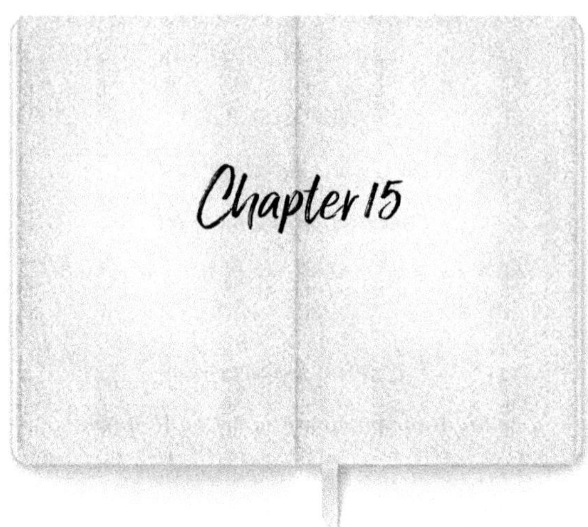

Chapter 15

THE WALLS ARE DRAB. AND *the paint is chipping. That reminds me . . .*

My gaze drifted to my lap where my fingers rested. My manicure hadn't survived the week well and looked much better the last time I had sat on this couch.

"Eva?" Doctor Christianson's inquisitive voice pulled me back to her. I never did answer her question.

"I'm going to school for psychiatry."

Her smile was inviting, probably why she was so successful. "Are you? Well, keep me in mind when you're ready to intern. I'd love to give you a hand." When I didn't answer, she continued. "So, why psychiatry?"

It didn't take me long to spit out my well-rehearsed answer. "I want to establish myself. By myself. I never want to have to depend on anyone."

She crossed her legs in the opposite direction and stuck the cap of the pen between her teeth, but she didn't offer anything, so I continued. "I want to have enough money to be able to pack up and run wherever, whenever, and make it on my own."

"Sounds lonely." She scratched something out on her canary pad.

Ew.

I stilled at her brashness, then my shoulders relaxed as I relented. "Excruciatingly." I let out a puff of air, relieved at her lack of phoniness.

"So, why then? Why plan your life around being alone?"

I quirked a brow. "Jumping right in, huh?"

She shrugged. "I laid back the first session to ease you in. I can coddle you if you'd like. It's your dime."

Bitch.

I liked her. I was starting to get why Jace made sure I came here.

I sighed, silently promising myself to do this right. "The person who rapes—" I stopped short. The present tense of that word implied that it would happen again, and it wouldn't. Ever. I cleared my throat. "The person who *raped* me is very close to my family. Too close, actually. I've never been able to get away from it." I looked her straight in the eye. "Until now."

"College," she stated, enlightenment emerging behind her intuitive eyes.

"Yes. *Away.* And I don't plan on having to be back in that situation any time soon." I crossed my legs to the other side, pleased with my response.

"I can appreciate that. So this . . . family member?" She raised a questioning eyebrow at me, nudging her head forward.

"Practically," I responded.

"This practically family member," she continued, "has repeatedly raped you?"

Hearing the words from someone else was a punch to the insides. Even Jace never said it directly to me. It was so dirty, I instantly felt ashamed and exposed. Tugging the edges of my sweater closed, I crossed my arms over my chest. An internal metal gate came slamming down with a crash, and I flinched.

"Eva?" Doctor Christianson seemed ready to push at that reaction. I wasn't sure I was quite ready to handle that.

"He . . ." Her face didn't budge while I sought out the best words to explain what had been happening to me. She showed no signs of this subject matter intimidating her or making her feel uncomfortable. I suppose I should have felt more comforted by that, but the whole thing was making me feel ready to lose the small lunch I'd forced down.

"I guess you could say that, but he's not entirely to blame."

That earned a raised eyebrow. "Go on."

"The first time, he—I . . ." I trailed off. I always hated this part. I wished more than anything I could go back and slap myself in the head for believing his damn lies.

Doctor Christianson placed her pad on the table beside her. "I'm not here to judge you, Eva. If it helps, think of it as though you're talking to yourself. I'm merely a catalyst. The help you need to sort through your own head and make sense of what's going on. This is all to help you help yourself." Her eyes softened with a smile. "I'll prod where I need when you get stuck, and I'll ask you questions to try and help your process along, but this is going to be you. If you start thinking of it that way, I think it'll be easier to open up. When I leave here, I've got my own laundry list of problems on my mind."

Although I wanted to call her a bitch again over that last statement, she was right, and I appreciated what she was doing. This wouldn't work if I clammed up at the part that mattered most.

"I agreed to it the first time." My words were timid, cautious. "I was young and stupid, and he preyed on that. I was nervous to go to high school as a prude, and he was always around, and my sister—"

"Your sister?" Her eyebrows knitted together with her disruption.

I locked eyes with her. It was now or never. I'd gone this far. "My sister's boyfriend—*fiancé*—is my rapist." That tasted bitter as it left the pit of my stomach to ride my tongue on the way out, but contradictory because it was such a sweet release.

Doctor Christianson sucked in a breath, a lapse in her cool façade as she let that soak. "I see."

I gulped, shame creeping along my skin, threatening to halt my words. But I couldn't let it win. "Way back when, he had me convinced that this was what people did. Learned on one another." I shivered at the memory, the familiar foolish feeling picking at the edges of my brain for entry. "I was so eager to avoid being made fun of that I fell for it." I hung my head, feeling stupid. *Who falls for something so blatantly abnormal?*

Dr. Christianson seemed to melt with enlightenment, as though a door had just opened allowing her to see the light. "I know plenty of people who used someone else to *learn*, so-to-speak. There's nothing wrong with you for believing him."

"You do?" Pure shock engulfed me.

"Sure." She smiled convincingly. "Kind of along the lines of a best friend's pact that if you reach a certain age without getting married, you'll wed each other. It's perfectly normal, Eva. Don't beat yourself up over that."

Well, that was unexpected. I'd never thought of it that way. Now that I had, I couldn't help the encroaching dread of realizing that this was why I had allowed him to do this to me repeatedly all of these years. Why I had kept silent. "I guess you're right, but it was my sister's boyfriend. I had no right going near him." That was the only thing that would rectify that I had suffered all of these years for no reason.

The light now shone brightly in the doctor's eyes, illuminating brilliance, in the hopes of making me understand her full meaning. "Did you go near *him* or did he go near *you*?"

I frowned. "I don't get your point."

"Who approached *whom*?" She accentuated that last word.

I shrugged, not understanding where she was going. "Well, he approached me, of course. I never would have thought to do that."

"So *he* approached a young, naïve minor then? Is that what you're telling me?" She raised her eyebrows. Not a question, but a nudge to get me to see the picture that was beginning to focus.

"Y—Yes," I stuttered.

"And you have guilt because . . ." She let the question linger there.

"Because I betrayed my sister by saying yes." Wasn't that obvious?

"How did he convince you?"

Thinking back sent a nauseous roll through my stomach. "He said he knew I'd never kissed anyone. Told me Abby wouldn't care," I scoffed. "It was only supposed to be a kiss." My voice lost its backbone, and I barely heard that last part.

"And he pushed to take it further?" she prodded, stern in her point.

I pursed my lips and nodded.

Her posture relaxed as though she had just finished pulling an impacted tooth. "That's the most common thing victims of incest hear," she revealed. "That they should experiment with one another. And it sounds like this guy is more like a brother than anything." Her eyes softened, her true compassion for the delicate situation I found myself in making itself known. "You can't blame yourself for this, Eva. Rape is rape. And a rapist will *always* throw guilt at their victim, make them doubt where the fault lies."

This was all too much. I felt as though my entire life was a lie. I looked down at my lap and toyed with my nails, unsure of how to respond to this new information.

"Why haven't you told anyone?" the doctor asked.

"They love him. They'd never believe me." My voice was soft as I continued to process this new information.

"Do you hear what you just said to me?" The sharp tone of her voice brought me back to the present.

The strength of my voice built. "Trust me, you're not the first to point out how illogical that sounds, but it's true."

Doctor Christianson paused, studying me. "I think since you lost faith in yourself, you assume that everyone else did as well."

I sat up straighter. "You don't understand. He's a master manipulator. They all eat out of the palm of his hand—the same hand he has been touching me with for years." I shivered, then in a condescending voice added, "The good 'ol American boy-next-door would *never* be capable of anything like that. Plus, like I said, I agreed the first time. The bastard even made me say it out loud so there'd be no confusion. After that, I almost think he deluded himself into thinking I was a willing participant. But he'd always threaten our little *secret* getting out. *Ours*. Makes me sick." I clutched my stomach.

Doctor Christianson analyzed my words with a nod. "I think step one is remembering your worth and trusting your family enough to let them know what's been happening to you all these years. I'm sure you'll find you suffered far too long when you could have just told them years ago and they would have had your back." She sat forward in her chair, the wisdom of her experience shining in her eyes. "Be kind to yourself, Eva. What you've been through is significant, even if you've been convincing yourself for years that it isn't."

The burn of tears prickled in the corners of my eyes. I plucked a tissue from the table next to me and looked up to the ceiling, dabbing my duct. "I'll try. Thank you." I half-smiled, truly wanting to give it a fair shot. Everything she said made sense, brought with it a clarity that I was never able to see. It was like I had finally gotten the right prescription after being legally blind for so long.

"Good." She relaxed back in her chair again and picked her pad back up, jotting something down. "Step two comes next and kind of goes hand-in-hand. I want you to tell anyone who will listen what happened to you. Build a support system and learn to lean on them. You'll want as much encouragement as you can get, so leave out any negative nellies."

"So leave out everyone then?" I blew out a small, sarcastic laugh, trying to lighten the heavy situation, but the good doctor wasn't amused. I cleared my throat and put on a more serious face. "I have to tell them now. The bastard went and proposed. I can't let her marry him no matter how scared I am of losing them." I wrung the tissue between my nervous fingers.

Dr. Christianson raised a sassy brow, getting comfortable with our exchange. "Well, at least you've got *that* figured out."

"Don't get cute, Doc." I wagged a warning finger. "I like you, and I'm glad I can talk to you, but let's hold the sass for now. I think you've bitch-slapped me enough for one day." I smiled, looking at her from the corner of my eye.

She smirked, the friendly gesture easing my remaining tension. "Very well." Doctor Christianson glanced at the clock beside the door, then rose to her feet, chatting about when I should schedule my next appointment.

I didn't expect it, but disappointment that our hour was up rushed in. I felt as though I could keep going and I didn't want to lose that. I was a fickle bitch these days, and the good doctor might not find me so willing to share next week. I was about to ask her if I could see her again in a few days, co-pay be damned, when a set of familiar eyes stopped me in my tracks as my foot hit the threshold. "You?"

"You." Drew smirked, a small indent forming right outside the edge of his mouth as his eyes danced with insight.

"Well, I guess you found out my dirty little secret." I rocked back on my heels, embarrassed. I didn't like to show weakness.

"As did you," Drew stated the obvious.

I hadn't thought of it that way. Comfort moved into my stomach, replacing the uneasy that had sat there a moment earlier.

He shrugged one shoulder. "To be honest, I'm just glad to know you aren't really made of porcelain." He smiled his friendly smile.

"Ha ha. Very funny." I rolled my eyes.

Doctor Christianson stood in the doorway with her clipboard, checking her watch. "You ready, Drew?"

"Coming, Doc." He bounced up and made his way over. I stepped aside, allowing him into the threshold. Doctor Christianson held the door for him, but he paused in the entrance. His back was terse, unmoving. He turned back to me. "Hey, wanna wait around and grab a coffee or somethin' after this? You can tell me all about your boo-boos, and I'll tell you about mine?" I recognized that hopeful look. He wore it each encounter we had, and I was tired of being the one to squash it.

I bit my lip, contemplating his offer. I never spoke about my problems to anyone, but after unloading all that on the doctor, I didn't feel done, and my next appointment seemed like it was an eternity away. Besides, it might be good to talk to someone who had issues as well and wouldn't judge me. "Sure. There's a coffee shop on the corner. I'll meet you there when you're finished."

A slow brightness dawned on Drew's face, and I thought that look suited him much better. "Sweet. Be there soon." He walked past the doctor, who was wearing the faintest of smiles before she shut the door after him.

Guess that was the right answer.

With a lightness in my step, I fished around in my bag to switch the ringer back on my phone. As I made my way to the elevator, my mind replayed all that I had unburdened myself of in the visit, ping-ponging to what might be coming once I met with Drew as I clicked the button.

> *Damon: Just making sure we're still clear and you haven't forgotten what I said. I could always stop by and remind you if you need me to.*

Chunks rose in my throat as any strength I had grown plummeted to the pit of my stomach. The fucker was careful enough to get his point across without saying anything incriminating. It was bad enough dealing with him in person, but now he was going to start taunting me when he wasn't around, too?

I tossed the phone into my bag and wrapped my arms around my middle, ashamed that I was always so weak the second I was pushed. Something had to give.

Chapter 16

THE BELL CHIMED, AND THE smell of freshly brewed caffeine danced its way toward me. It did its job of pepping me up a bit without even entering my bloodstream. After close to seventy-five laps around the block, second-guessing this meeting with Drew, I made a mental pact with myself not to let Damon's text message get the better of me. And I came.

I tucked a strand of hair behind my ear and looked to the left, searching the tables. Warmth met my cheekbones when my sights landed on Drew's waiting gaze. Both hands were curled around an ivory ceramic mug, the tips of his dirty blond hair falling into his hazel eyes. The hazel eyes that practically danced with a hopeful promise.

The corner of his mouth rose in a half smile, and he nodded to the empty chair across from him. I smiled and bit the edge of my lip, a nervous flutter smacking me in the belly. I clutched at it as the realization hit me that I'd felt that. Felt *something* after being numb for so long. I stood before him, a lightheartedness washing over me at the prospect of some type of *normal* returning to my empty life.

"You came." He wet his lips before a full smile complemented the sparkle in his eyes.

"I did." I removed my coat and draped it over the back of the chair, then pulled it out and took a seat.

A peppy young waitress appeared, her blonde hair pulled back in a haphazard bun. She extracted a notepad from her trim waist and snapped her gum. "What can I get ya, hon?"

"Hazelnut coffee, please."

"Sure thing." She looked at Drew, a pink hue meeting her cheek. "You good, sugar?"

"For now. Thanks." He winked, and her breathing ceased for an instant before she walked away, reminding me of why I'd referred to him as a runway model when we had first met.

He turned his sights back to me. "Now, where were we?" He adjusted himself, leaning farther across the table, locking his focus on mine.

"Right here." I relaxed, grateful for a distraction from my normal heartbreak.

"I didn't think you'd come."

"I wasn't sure I would, either. I contemplated standing you up, but I didn't want to disappoint Doctor Christianson." My tone was clearly playful as I lightened the mood.

His shoulders visibly relaxed, making me realize Drew was good at the game but felt more than he let on. He sat back in his chair, analyzing me. "That all?"

I smiled a purposely sarcastic smile and nodded. "Yes."

What began as a slow crawl spread into the widest smile imaginable, lighting up his face. He dipped his head back in a hearty chuckle. "This is why."

I blew on the coffee the waitress just deposited in front of me. "Why what?"

He didn't answer right away as if trying to find the right, safe words. "Why I'm glad you came."

I smiled and sucked down a sip of coffee. "So, now what? We trade woes? Sing Kumbaya and throw our arms up to the universe, giving her our middle fingers that she's fucked us up the ass of life?"

Drew chuckled. "Well, I was hoping to maybe just get to know each other a little first. I need to be sure I *want* to trust you with my woes." Always wearing a friendly smile, I wasn't sure if he was being sarcastically flirty or if he had really meant that.

I'd normally never open up to anyone, certainly not an almost stranger, but he apparently had his own mess of shit. If he was in therapy, he was used to the whole confidentiality thing, and I could really use somebody to talk to.

"Okay, I can agree with that." I sat back in my chair. "You first."

Drew seemed to roll his thoughts around, before finding his starting point. He scratched the ceramic cup a couple times in thought before beginning. "I'm twenty-two. I started martial arts when I was fourteen, and loved it so much I got a job to pay for extra classes. I became a black belt in a year's time. Now I teach a combination martial arts, self-defense course."

I perked up in my seat, intrigued. "Go on."

Drew paused, seeming to size up his next words, rolling them around, judging what he did and didn't want to say. "I'm a foster home kid." His eyes roamed my features. "Took me a while to find the right family, but once I did, a lot changed for me."

I fidgeted in my seat, uncertain of how to respond to that little tidbit.

"It's all right, Evangelina." He chuckled softly, trying to ease the heavy topic. "I'm a grown up now. You don't need to feel sorry that I didn't spend my childhood dipping silver spoons in caviar."

My cheeks flushed, embarrassed I'd given him the impression he was less-than. "That wasn't what I was thinking. I was just surprised is all. Go on." He opened his mouth, but I waved a hand, shushing him before he could continue. "And call me Eva."

A slow smile crept up his face. "Progress." Then his gaze fell as he focused on the wood grain in the table before inching up to meet mine once again. "Well, I love chocolate and coffee, and girly pop music." His smile mocked himself over that bit of trivia. As almost an afterthought, he threw in a bonus. "And, I've never had a steady girlfriend." He took a sip of his coffee. "Done. Your turn."

I blushed and tucked a strand of hair behind my ear. "Fair enough. I sing and write poetry. I appear to be in shape, but I'm totally out of shape since I don't remember the last time I saw the inside of a gym. I grew up in New Jersey, have one sister, and love chocolate as well. Oh, and my best friend is gay, but you've met him already." I smirked.

"How could I forget?" Drew purposely rolled his eyes and we both laughed, lifting whatever tension remained. We were still strangers essentially, so it was odd that either of us would want to open up to the other. It felt good, though, and I didn't want to stop, so I wasn't about to question it.

Suddenly, Blake's face flashed before my eyes, his dimple proudly displayed as he peeked over a long-stemmed red rose and a pang of guilt knocked into my belly. I closed my eyes briefly, wanting to soak up the memory of him and savor it. Then a new vision appeared, a photograph of him and his new girl, replacing his kind, loving face, and the sourness in my stomach rose and filled my mouth.

I swallowed down my guilt, remembering he wasn't mine anymore. I'd sent him away. Though I wished more than anything that I could take it back, I knew that I couldn't.

When my eyes reopened, they met Drew's watchful gaze. "Penny for your thoughts?"

I chuckled and clutched my cup tighter. "You'd need hundreds." I took a deep breath, needing a distraction. "So, tell me more. Why Doctor Christianson? Or do you have another test for me to see if I'm woe-worthy?" I cocked my head with a playful tilt on my lips.

Drew laughed lightly and leaned across the table once again. "You'll do." He inhaled deeply and blew a burst of coffee-infused air out of his mouth. "In a nutshell, foster care is not the place to be when you're two, three, and four." He paused, sending his hidden meaning straight for me. "Or seven, eight, or nine. Get my drift?"

He pushed back the sleeves of his forearms and rested them on the table, leaning forward. A small silver circle about the size of the head of a cigarette rested in the flesh, and I swallowed hard, hoping that wasn't what I thought it was. Drew followed my line of sight to the scar. "It's okay. It was a long time ago." He gave me a moment to process, and I did so with tears welling in my eyes before he continued. "Eventually, even the smallest boys get bigger." A confident smile replaced his woe-stricken face. "I started karate lessons, began disappearing to the gym, and got a part-time job so I could take self-defense training. I became a well-oiled machine. A bull. I had a ton of rage, and no matter how I tried to cage it, it always simmered just beneath my skin."

He took another sip, looking far away into his past and I knew he was no longer with me at the table. "One night, after a bad day, I went home and let's just say, when I saw the shit-storm brewing, the tables got turned the opposite way. I spent a month in juvie for hospitalizing my 'father,'" he air-quoted, "and then I was placed in a different home with three other *brothers*. We became real tight. Because of my past, I refused to go anywhere without them, thinking I needed to protect them or something." He flicked his head in a nod. "You saw them the day I met you. We're rarely apart."

Thinking back to that day at the pizzeria, I recalled a table full of guys, a light bulb slowly illuminated in my mind.

Drew continued. "My new parents were amazing. I never knew a love like they showed me. Little by little, the hostility faded away, but the scars never did. It's all good, though. Every now and then I need the reminder of how harsh reality can be and how much better off I am now." He puffed up his chest, gaining confidence in his new reality. "I kept training, and I always will. It's good for my head, and I never want to feel weak again. Besides, I get to harness all that and use the experience to help my students. People that can't help themselves. Show them how to find their strength and how to take down the scum in the world. That it's possible."

I gaped at him. He always seemed so happy and carefree. This was the furthest thing from what I'd imagined he would tell me. Although his story was devastating, a swath of jealousy found me that he had found his strength, and for a fleeting moment, I wondered if he could help me find mine. But then I pushed that small bit of hope back into its box.

"So go ahead. Your turn." He winked.

I expelled the largest exhale ever. My legs were numb beneath the table from the prospect of letting it all out right now. Then I remembered Doctor Christianson's words: *you need to set it free. Let go of the evil trapped inside of you. Tell everyone who'll listen until you rid yourself of it. Free yourself, Eva.*

Free myself, my subconscious scoffed.

But he's the wrong person.

I'd always imagined the day I unloaded this. I would be looking into the eyes of the man who'd stolen my heart.

He's not yours anymore.

And there she was with a dose of the harsh truth. My subconscious was never far away when it came to mocking me.

This felt like such a betrayal, but my insides were so saturated with the weight of my misery. I was never able to tell Blake because he was too close to it. He would have done something, pressured me, and I wasn't ready for that. Or worse, he might have even killed him. I had to protect him.

Drew is safe.

He wasn't romantically involved, and he didn't know my family the way Blake did. He was an outsider. And for fuck's sake, I needed the poison out already.

I allowed my eyelids to drift closed while I gathered all my words. Blowing out a full breath of air, I let the first one leave my mouth. "I was fortunate enough to come from a great family. We were always very close, still are for the most part. I was probably part of the family you thought you envied growing up. But all that glitters isn't always what it appears to be." I dragged in another large breath and swallowed hard, finding Drew's eyes for confirmation I should continue.

With kind eyes, he reached across the table and covered my hands with his own, stopping me before I could make the skin around my nail beds bleed. I hadn't even noticed I'd been picking.

I smiled softly and drew them onto my lap. "From as young as I could remember, Damon was around. He was the cliché boy next door, always in our yard and at our dinner table. He was older than me, and once puberty hit, he took a shine to my older sister, Abby. For years I was the tagalong. I wanted so badly for them to see me as mature—not to treat me like a baby." My chuckle at the remembrance was humorless.

"Well, one day . . ." I looked up and buried my gaze into his, trying to drive home my meaning without having to voice the words. "One day he did."

With a sharp gasp, Drew's mouth clamped into a hard line, the bones of his jaw protruding as his eyebrows pulled inward. When tingles prickled my forehead, I realized I had stopped breathing to analyze him, and my chest began a deep rise and fall to gain some lost oxygen. But damn, that had felt good. Not only did I say what had happened, but *who. Fuck it.* I'd lost it all anyway. Lost the one person who mattered most, and my sister and the rest of my family would soon be on his heels, leaving my life as well.

"I was fourteen when he began to *notice* me." My line of sight dipped back to my nail beds. "He still does."

"What do you mean he still does?" At the harsh tone of his voice, my head whipped up to meet the hard line between his eyebrows. "She's still with the bastard?"

"It's a long story, but yes." I exhaled, feeling myself shrink a bit in embarrassment.

"What kind of people are your family for allowing that to happen?" The redness of his skin and flare of his nostrils spoke for his outrage.

"They don't know." My voice was meek, barely registering.

As good as it had felt to finally get it off my chest, I was starting to feel claustrophobic and stupid. I wanted to end the conversation and run.

My back stiffened and all the hair on my body prickled. "You know what? I think this may have been a bit premature. We're perfect strangers really, and all this stuff is personal." I shot to my feet just as Drew did the same, his hand shooting out to cup my shoulder and place pressure downward.

"Sit down, Eva." The forcefulness of his tone took me by surprise, but the command in his eyes gave me pause. It wasn't one of a controlling demand, but one that you would expect to see from an army drill sergeant or a person of power that had every right to tell you what to do because they knew what was best for you. Although under every other circumstance, I would run from this kind of situation, the look in his eyes halted my pursuit. Drew was a helper of the weak, and it radiated off of him. I was sure he was genuinely concerned and looking to help me, not hurt me.

Keeping my eyes on his, I returned to my seat in a slow slump. His shoulders relaxed marginally, but not enough to drop his guard or whatever this protective thing that came over him was. He sat, chomping down on his jaw.

"You can tell me. I'm used to this stuff."

"Maybe that's enough for today." I'd lost the drive I had earlier to share, my voice weakening.

"Don't clam up on me, please." Drew's voice softened. "I want to know. Go on."

I took in a large breath of air. "The first time it happened, I agreed.

He tricked me, I know that now, but my whole life he's had me convinced they'd never believe me because I said yes. That they'd see me as the whore who slept with her sister's boyfriend." I rubbed the tops of my arms and held myself tight. "So I've never said anything."

"And why not tell them now?" His forehead still had tight confused lines crisscrossing it.

"Because I'm still scared they won't believe me." Defeat started to creep inside again. "Or, even if they did, I'm afraid they'd think it was my fault. They love him." The idea of them giving their love to that monster both infuriated and disgusted me to my core.

Drew covered my hand with his own once again. "Eva, I'm sure they love you more."

"But, I *did* agree! I did it, Drew!" I looked around, ashamed and nervous that someone may have overheard. Then I licked my lips and tucked a lock of hair behind my ear.

"You were a kid," he said quietly but emphatically.

I squeezed my eyes shut. "Don't you think logically I know that?" I shook out my head. "Don't ask me to explain how my mind works because I can't."

Drew paused, chomping down on his jaw, while a wild ride swam in his eyes. I could only imagine what he was thinking. Before I could get too self-conscious, he relaxed back in his chair, as though a decision had been made. "So what happened recently? This have anything to do with your breakup or the fact that you're half-skeleton and look like you haven't slept in months?" He motioned to my body with his hands.

"Gee, thanks." I fidgeted and sat up straighter.

"Well?" he asked, not backing down.

"Jeez, you're a tough one. You realize we just met, don't you?"

"Yes. So?" His gaze never faltered.

I sighed. "Well, besides the fact that she's agreed to marry him—"

"You've *got* to be kidding me," Drew interrupted.

"I kid you not." I cleared my throat. "More recently, he's turned it up a notch. Our last encounter was pretty violent, and I basically tried to kill myself after. Put myself in the hospital." I looked away momentarily, gathering my shame. When I looked back to Drew, there was an enlightened understanding in his eyes. Tension whooshed from me, making me feel lighter than I could remember, and I was grateful I had listened to the doctor and unloaded some of this. It was surprisingly easier than I had thought it would be.

"I'm just done with it all. I tried to tell my sister, and she brushed it aside like it'd never be possible."

Drew's face hardened. "I've heard enough. You need to protect yourself."

"Pfft." I rolled my eyes. The thought of me doing anything physical was comical.

"I'm serious." His face hardened. "You need to learn how, and I can help you." He sat back in his seat and crossed his arms over his broad chest.

I hadn't contemplated something like that, but I wasn't sure it was even necessary anymore. Or that I would have the strength.

"I appreciate it, Drew. Really, I do. But I don't plan on going back there until it's absolutely necessary. Right now I have to figure out how to stop Abby from marrying him, and I'm just tired of it all. I'm tired, Drew."

Saying it out loud brought that feeling to the forefront. I was exhausted. Drained. Daily I carried around limbs that felt too heavy, a head that felt too clouded, and a heart that felt too lifeless. And I was exhausted. Of everything.

"You can't just give up on yourself. Let me do this for you," he insisted. "I pray you never have to use any of what I teach you, but if nothing else, we'll get you strong again. Build you."

"Build me?" I asked, uncertain.

"Yep." There was a light in his eyes I'd never noticed before, like glowing embers as he seemed to envision the possibilities. I could tell he lived for this, and that the thought of passing on his knowledge made his pulse quicken.

I mulled it over, tossing it around in my head like a game of *Toss Across*.

Do I? Don't I?

Build me.

Live me.

I swallowed that down and let it settle in the pit of my stomach.

You might as well. You're only rotting away anyway.

Was I strong enough? Did it matter? *Eh, fuck it.* "Okay, I'll try."

A smile crept up his face until the corners of his eyes crinkled in delight. "Don't worry. I'll take care of you. But be sure to bring your A-game. You'll be sore as hell after. Be well-rested and get your head ready. We'll be working on that, too. Your body will never be able to handle what I'm going to put it through without that." A gleeful warning shone in his eyes. "Be at Hard Knock's Gym tomorrow at seven sharp."

I gulped. His words made me nervous, and I wasn't sure I'd be able to handle it, but I had to try. A small tick-tock in my chest, the faintest firefly in my heart, flickering as it awakened.

Try or die. Those were my only two options.

Chapter 17

"COME ON. WORK!"

"I can't anymore!" I grunted through gritted teeth. A bead of sweat dripped between them, coating my tongue with salt. I could barely see out of my eyes, I was so drenched with my struggles.

Drew was above me, my arms were pinned above my head, and if I weren't completely fucking wiped, I probably would have been terrified. He hadn't given me the impression he would ever harm a hair on my head at any point, so my mind didn't go there, but . . .

"Fuck! Let me up!"

Drew kept the smug smile pinned to his face, his own beads of sweat trickling down his forehead. "No, sweets. You're stuck, ripe for that fucker's taking. Now—What. Do. You. Do?" He dug his fingertips into my wrists and bore his weight down further.

"Ahhhh!" I screamed, rage bubbling from my core in volcanic waves, racing through my body like a white-hot light. "Get off of me!" I bucked up with my chest, tossing my torso side-to-side to try and free myself. The air in my lungs was thinning, and I had nothing left to fight with.

Drew lowered his face to mere inches from mine, sweat dotting the cockiness plastered all over it. "Make me."

My chest heaved, unable to withstand his weight much longer, and my eyes widened, fear whipping over me that I was going to pass out before he set me free.

His breath met my ear, hot and struggling. "C'mon, *beautiful*. Get me off of you."

My breaths broke around his words as Drew's face was swallowed by the cloud of a memory.

"C'mon, beautiful. Get me off. Touch it for me." Damon is sitting with a wide part to his legs, palming the hard line beneath his sweatpants. I sit across the bed from him—my bed—in the home where I was supposed to be safe.

I'm never safe anymore. He's always here, and my sister is always sleeping. Tears prickle in their ducts. I can't move, and I pray he can't either.

"Don't look so worried, I'll get you off, too." The promise in his gaze is enough to bring up my lunch.

He licks his lips, and his eyes drift closed as he begins to prime himself. A soft moan follows the breath of air that leaves his mouth and my stomach contents curdle. I can't speak, though. Not even when he gets to his feet and makes his way over to where I'm still rooted to the edge of the bed. My hand instinctively reaches to touch the soft fur of Mary's head, the stuffed lamb my sister had given me to ward off bad thoughts.

Damon stands before me, his eyes following the movement. "Kinky, I like it. That might feel nice."

"Don't touch her," I growl. I'm not sure where that comes from, but the thought of him touching Mary disgusts me even more than the thought of him touching me.

He cocks his head slightly, seeming to mull over my demand, and I draw her behind my back, moving her beneath my pillow.

"Whatever. It's you I want anyway." He grabs my hand and wraps it around the solid bulge in his pants. "Make it feel better, beautiful. Touch it." He guides my hand to stroke him, closing his eyes as he uses me the way he wants.

I close mine, too.

And everywhere that Mary went, that lamb was sure to go.

My eyes flew open with a start, feeling as though they were glowing with fire. Drew's eyes seemed to register the change in mine, and the edge of his lip twitched with satisfaction. In a last-ditch effort, I did the only thing I could think of. I swiped my tongue along the outer portion of my top lip, removing the sweat lined there, and drove my knee upward, incapacitating him.

He rolled to his side, groaning, and I rolled the other way, bent on one knee, and propped myself up with the other in case I had to move quickly while I caught my breath. He was on both knees in a ball, clutching his stomach, his face lost in his chest, and I delighted myself with a ginormous smile. A smile to make up for all of the smiles foregone. *I did it.*

"Good girl." Still heaved over, Drew turned his head to catch my eye, sending me a reaffirming wink. "See you tomorrow. Same time."

I nodded, determination to see this through forming. There was a tingle in my veins that I wasn't used to feeling. A spark that I hadn't realized I was craving. When you're lost in an abyss, it's easy to forget what life feels like. That it's possible to climb back. I had allowed Damon to take me and lock me away all of those years. But now it was my turn.

I was taking me back.

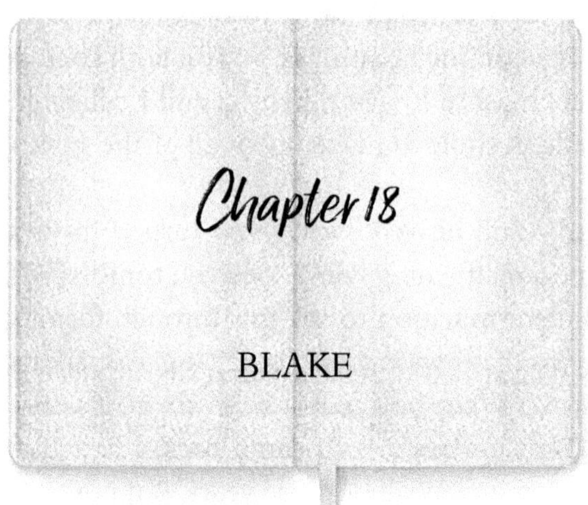

Chapter 18

BLAKE

"GLAD TO SEE YOU'VE COME around, son."

I sat across from my father, the shiny gleam of his cherry wood desk mocking me. The cocky look on his face was enough to make me walk right back out the door I'd *willingly* entered a few minutes ago, but if I was doing this, I had to play along.

When Angel left, she'd stomped me right back into the dirt that my father helped lay at my feet, obliterating the strong pieces of me that I'd built up in the time we were together like a heavy swing of a sledgehammer. And now, as I struggled to gain back even a third of that man, to try and rebuild, it felt as though a strong gust of wind would threaten to take me down.

I pushed past the clenching heartache I felt and pursed my lips, nodding at the overbearing man gleaming at me. "I was wondering if there's a firm you'd like to set up an internship with before I look into them on my own."

Next year I'd be a senior, and I needed to secure a summer internship—it would look good on my resumé. There was nothing stopping me from moving forward with my law career now that I'd lost Angel. Besides, I could use the distraction. The numbing boredom went well with the colorless life I was destined to lead.

The smug bastard staring back at me couldn't have been happier. I had always craved seeing the happiness I saw on his face now. Yearned for it my whole damn life. But today as I looked at him, all I felt was icicles running through my veins, showing me that all he loved about me was a phony imposter. Reminding me of all the honest, unconditional love I had lost.

The ache in my gut was another reminder of all that had changed in my life since I'd met Eva. I never imagined this day would feel so heart-wrenching—the day I'd longed for since I was a child. The day my dad finally looked at me like I was worth something. Except that worth came at the most expensive price—the price of my soul.

"Just don't let 'em steal your soul. I hear you have a good one." Eva's dad's voice rang in my head, tightening the knotting ball in my gut.

Although I'd considered not going to the photography classes Eva had set up for me as a Christmas gift, nervous they'd be too much of a reminder, I had decided to go anyway. They were paid for, and I needed an outlet. It made me feel as though we were still connected somehow. At least I had that. That's where I'd met Marybeth. She was sweet and reminded me a little of Eva. Blonde hair, green eyes, tiny . . .

But something was missing.

As dull as Eva may have felt, she carried around a light she didn't even know she possessed. I'd seen it when she couldn't. And now I missed it. My world seemed so gloomy in its absence. You never feel the dark until your light is gone.

Sound funneled into my ears, a low, monotonous tone turning to actual words, and I realized my father had been talking. I'd zoned out. Seemed I did that quite often these days. I cleared my throat and straightened in my seat, trying to appear as though I cared about whatever he was going on about. Thankfully, this time his words weren't directed at me.

My dad's smile reached the telephone receiver. "Thanks, Chuck. He'll see you first thing Monday morning."

He hung up the phone and grabbed for a pad. The scratch of his ballpoint pen felt like it was grazing my brain. The tear of the page from its adhesive binding cut through the air. Positioning the paper between his index and middle finger, he slid his arm toward me. "You're to meet Chuck at Lawson, Clark & Stein LLP, nine a.m., Monday morning."

My mouth went dry as the desert while I watched the yellow piece of paper sway. I never imagined a four-by-six, college ruled notepad could be so paralyzing. Knowing my fate was sealed once I accepted this offer, I kept my hand rooted, strangling the armchair.

When I didn't move, his eyebrows rose and he inched his arm a bit closer. With no other saving grace, I peeled my fingers away and met his hand, mine shaky as shit as I took the paper from his waiting grasp.

He deflated back into his leather chair. Bobbing back and forth, he entwined his fingers over his belly. "You seem different." He studied me, his shrewd eyes analyzing.

With a firm set to my jaw, I bit down any emotion before it could take hold and give me away. It was my father's job, after all, to weed through the bullshitters. "Determined, that's all."

"Hmph." He examined me further, and I could see the suspicion in his eyes. Never once, though, did he ask if I was sure this was what I wanted to do. And never once did I fool myself into believing that he cared about that.

He stopped bobbing and honed in. "This have anything to do with that girl?"

Prickles danced along my scalp, chasing each other down the back of my neck. A bit of numbness stretched to each of my fingers and toes, and my breathing sat low in my chest at the mere mention of Angel. I was always on high alert where she was concerned, especially when her name graced my father's crude mouth. It had only been a few weeks, but no matter how much time passed, I didn't think I'd ever shake the possessiveness I felt over her. I sat, ready to pounce like a ferocious lion any time she was the topic.

I pulled forward in my chair. "I'm not sure what you're referring to. I'm here making good on your wishes. Surely you're not looking down on that." I dared him, *wanting* him to try me. It might feel good to get stuff off my chest.

He rolled the edges of his fingers around, not letting what he was thinking slide from his eyes as he worked over his thoughts. "It was a smart move disassociating yourself with that one. You may not see it now, but you will one day. Trust your old man."

That's like asking me to trust a tumor. "What's done is done, but I'd rather not talk about it." I rose and looked down at my father.

"I'll be at your friend's office on Monday."

Chapter 19

"TOSS ME THAT ALLEN KEY, would ya?" Sweat lined Drew's brow as he worked to keep his foot on a rowdy piece of metal while simultaneously holding its adjacent part lined up.

"So, an Allen key would be . . ." I bit my lip and searched the scrap scattered along the empty corner of my apartment.

Drew swiped his forearm across his forehead, still holding the bulky piece of steel, and looked at me like I had sprouted ten heads. Working so closely with him the last couple weeks I was getting to know him better, and I could tell there were a million wise-cracks dying to come out of his mouth. Instead, he just used his "I'm talking-to-a-child" voice. "L-shaped object. Inserts on the ends. Please." He stretched out his hand.

I tossed things aside until the tool he'd described appeared. "You know I've never built anything in my life, right? I'm not *really* a dude just because you're trying to turn me into one." I tossed the tool, and he quickly dropped what he was holding to clap it between his hands.

A low growl rumbled from his throat. "You're lucky you're cute."

Ignoring his scowl, I hopped to my feet and brushed off my hands. "Want a drink?"

"Water. Thanks." A few clanks later, I knew he'd gone back to his project of building me a home gym.

A melancholy feeling settled over me as I stared at the set of biceps working vigorously in my living room. Not that I was nervous to have him in my apartment alone with me, but it only reminded me that it was the wrong set of biceps. I was more than grateful for the support Drew had given me, the sacrifices of his time and his income to train me. He was a good friend. But all of my accomplishments, any of my growth was stunted when I couldn't share it with the one person who mattered most. At least once a day I would convince myself that I could go back to Blake, give up the charade and beg him to take me back. But then all of the reasons why I couldn't do that would creep back in. His new girl. And the fact that no matter how much better I was starting to get, I was far from fixed enough. After what I had put him through, I needed to be one thousand percent sure I would never even have an inkling to walk away from him again. To hurt him like that again. No, when I went back to Blake, I had to be ready. In mind, body, *and* heart.

I filled a cup with tap water and then grabbed two bottled waters from the fridge, setting one beside Drew whose tongue was pressed into his top lip with his struggles, before I stepped out to the balcony. Why I continued to water the pot of dirt that sat out here was a mystery, but something in me kept hoping Blake was right and the flowers inside would live to see another day. Or maybe it was just another pathetic attempt at feeling close to him, like a part of him was still here.

I squatted and watched the water absorb into the dirt with my slow pour, my mind reminiscent, the memory as fresh as the day it was etched into my brain.

Forget not . . . you're cared for.

I hung my head, the cup hanging between my bent legs, allowing myself a weak moment while I was alone.

Drew's knock at the glass brought me back to the moment. He didn't look happy as his choppy hand motions and bugged out eyes beckoned me back inside. "You know this is for you, right? You could at least give me a hand." Drew suspended some unidentifiable bungee-thing from the top of the contraption.

"That's debatable. I think you're just trying to make your job easier." I loved messing with him. He was too easy. "What do you want me to do, crybaby?"

Drew let out a weighted huff, losing his patience. "You know, sometimes I question why I bother with you at all."

"Lies." I grabbed the edge of the elastic band. "You want me to hold this?" Before I could secure it tightly enough, the cord slipped from my grasp and whipped Drew on the arm.

"Ouch!" He flung to the side, sending the piece of metal he was about to attach clamoring to the floor. He rubbed at the welt. "You're killin' me," he joked through the pain.

"Sorry . . ." I reached out, wincing as I inspected the red swell on his bicep.

"Helloooo . . ." My front door opened without a knock, and Jace stepped inside, talking without looking over. "Feed me, I'm star—" His tone immediately took on a new sound as he eyed the bulky bicep I was holding. "Well, *hello* there." He sauntered over. "And who has the pleasure of meeting me?" One hand was tucked to his chest while the other reached toward Drew for a shake.

"Jace, I think you have that backward." I rubbed my thumb over Drew's wound and smiled up at him. "You'll live."

"Honey, trust me, I'd know if I was *backward* in that man's presence. And it would certainly be his pleasure." Jace licked his lips.

"Jace!"

Drew laughed and stuck out a hand. "Drew. And we've met. I guess I'm just easy to forget."

"Algebra is easy to forget." He waved a gesturing finger, his eyes salivating. "You, my dear, will be on my mind all night. And recalled on as often as needed, if you get my drift."

Drew's face turned pink. I slapped my palm to my forehead and shook my head. "Welcome to the crazy, Drew. Grab some popcorn and enjoy the show."

"It's Oscar-worthy." Jace used his pinky to swipe along his hairline before blowing Drew a kiss.

Drew chuckled, shaking his head as he bent to pick up the pieces he had dropped. "I remember."

Jace waved his hands. "What's all this man-stuff, and why is it in my bitch's apartment?"

"Hey, I resent that. It's not man-stuff, it's a home gym. Don't be so sexist." I laughed, grabbing the elastic more carefully this time. I liked the fact that Drew was setting this up here. It would serve as a good outlet to get out my frustrations when things were too tough.

A smirk crawled up Jace's face that could only mean one thing was coming. I cringed, waiting. "Honey, I've had a Jim at home, too, but he left in the morning. He didn't set up shop." And there it was.

All of the air rushed out of my nose in a snort. "Oh my god!" I laughed so hard, I doubled over, letting the elastic fly once again.

"Eva!" Drew yelped.

"I'm sorry!" I apologized, still laughing as water filled my eyes. Grabbing the elastic for the third time, I turned my focus to my best friend and pointed a free finger to the floor. "Down, Jace. Heel."

Jace popped to the floor, pulling his legs in enthusiastically to a criss-crossed position. "I bet he looks even better from this angle."

Drew's eyes nearly popped out as he paused in his struggles and gaped at Jace.

Jace licked the line of his upper lip.

"Enough!" I yelled at him. "Can we get this done, please? My arms are killing me."

Drew finally hooked the piece that was laboring him. "This is today's workout. Stop crying. I've done worse to you than this."

Jace made the sign of the cross and propped his hands to the customary praying position. "Dear Lord, please let this man do worse to me. I've been a bad boy. I deserve—"

"Jace!" I launched a screw at him. I couldn't take much more. Drew clapped a hand to his abs and bent back in hysterics. "Don't encourage him." I frowned.

"I'm sorry, but he's fantastic," Drew said around his laughs.

"Please, can we finish?" I exhaled, exhausted. As much as I wanted to seem like all was okay on the outside, holding that face in place was hard after a while and I wasn't in the mood to keep it up much longer.

"Okay, okay." Drew hung a punching bag from the top of the sophisticated piece of equipment, then he opened a long cardboard box and hung a mirror on the wall behind it, before lining up some free weights and workout balls below it. Bulky as it was, it fit right in as though it was meant to be there.

"I'm thinking I might not even need you anymore." I eyed his finished product, impressed and eager to use it.

"You'll always need me to kick your cute little ass." Drew crossed his arms over his broad chest and rocked to the right, nudging my shoulder.

Jace hopped up, jumping. "Oh, Oh, Oh. Kick mine! Kick mine!"

Defeated, I hung my head.

"Let me try." I heard Jace through the blonde waves hanging in my face. I brushed them aside just in time to see Jace grabbing onto the piece of elastic that had tried our patience moments before. "This is like a ginormous sex toy." He tugged and swung, lifting his legs in a chicken flail as he bobbed, laughing.

I chortled into my hands as Drew tried from every angle to grab hold of one of Jace's body parts. "You're gonna break it!" Drew yelled, anxious at the prospect of all his hard work going down the drain.

Jace hopped off and curtsied. "The only thing I'd break is you. Your machine-thingy is safe." He blew another kiss before turning to disappear into the kitchen. "Now feed me already."

Drew followed. "Yeah, I could use a sandwich myself. That was worse than a workout."

My gaze roamed the small corner of my apartment from the home gym to the floor mat, to the weights, before finally landing on my reflection in the full-length mirror. Something was always missing, but a small piece of me felt okay. As heartbroken as I was, parts of me were beginning to feel fulfilled. Like a salve had been spread over a bunch of tiny cuts lining my body, and it knew that in the end there would be healing because of it.

I promise to give this my all. I'll make it work. For me. For Blake.

For us.

A smile found my lips and then fell just as quickly when my phone pinged.

> *Damon: How's Blake? Oh, wait, you're alone now right? Want company?*

Chapter 20

"SO, WHERE THE HELL HAVE you been?" Jace popped his gum across the table from me. I had a quick break, so I'd decided to meet him in the cafeteria. I hadn't seen him in about a week—it was a new record.

"With Drew, fricken killing myself." I scowled, but really, I was beginning to look forward to our training sessions. I could feel my body getting stronger, and it wasn't such a struggle to pull myself out of bed in the morning these days, despite all of the random text messages from Damon. They always managed to knock the wind out of me until I could push away the anxiety and remind myself he was far away. But still, he seemed to be becoming more and more obsessive lately.

"You're like a hottie magnet." Jace fanned himself, bringing me back to the present. "Remind me to thank you for tying your ass to me eternally."

"You're welcome." I smirked at my best friend. "Speaking of—you've been quiet on the boy-toy talk lately. What gives?"

Jace stiffened, his jovial behavior melting from his expression. "Nothing. Just haven't been doing much. I'm in a slump." Jace tipped so far back in his seat, the two front legs lifted from the floor. I followed his line of sight to a jock in a tight-ish pair of jeans meandering tables, books dangling from his side in his upturned hand.

"You don't slump, you slant," I stated in disbelief. I couldn't believe those words were leaving my best friend's mouth. "Exhibit A." I motioned in a grand gesture.

"Huh?" Jace answered without truly acknowledging me.

I cleared my throat with a loud, "Ahem."

He turned his head to me, still perpendicular, and then glanced the expanse of his tilted body before bouncing the legs back forward, laughing wholeheartedly.

"See? Slant." I joined him in a belly laugh.

"God, I needed that." Jace's expression was one of pure relief, and I wondered what my best friend was keeping from me.

"You're welcome." I appraised him another moment. "Wanna talk about it?" I tiptoed around what was sure to be a heavy topic if it had him this troubled. Chewing his lip, he stared at me, unsure. I covered his hand. "Come on, love. It's me."

"There *is* somebody. A real somebody, I think." Jace never lost his sullen expression, and I wondered why, when this was such fantastic news.

"Jace, that's great. I'm so happy for you. Who is he? I want to know every—"

"He's in the closet, Eva," he replied quickly. "A big, fucking metal closet with locks and bolts and chains."

"Oh." I rested against my chair as it all sank in. "Oh, Jace, I'm so sorry." His first chance at something real and it probably wouldn't bear fruit. And even if he did stay with him, he would need to skulk around in quiet as if their love for each other was wrong. I squeezed his hand. "Why didn't you tell me?"

He looked at me matter-of-factly and stated, "Closet," as if that explained it all.

I stroked the back of his hand, trying to soothe his ache and get him to open up. "Come on, Jace, when did secrets ever matter between us?"

"You're right," he sighed. "But this one hurts. I'm scared, love. And I don't scare easy. I don't even like admitting it. I'm trying not to think about it." He shrugged. "But if he leaves . . . If he gives up on this . . ." His voice was replaced by a shudder that I was sure rocked him deeper than I could see. As flamboyant and full of himself as Jace might have appeared, I knew he had always had some deep-rooted acceptance issues.

"You'll be just fine," I assured him. "You're Jace-fucking-Dayco, bitch. You bow to nothing and hold no prisoners. You know this." He looked into my eyes, a film of hope seeming to wash away a fraction of the gloom I saw there.

"Besides," I patted his hand and straightened, brightening my tone, "we're not going to think that way. If you're this serious about him, then I'm sure he loves you, too. He'll see the light, and you'll get your happily ever after." The irony of those words were not lost on me. Regret of what might have been crashed into my chest like a wrecking ball. I swallowed a long, hard gulp and tried to seem unaffected and be strong for my best friend. I was sure everyone was sick of the constant pity-party that was my life.

Always in my head, Jace noticed. It was both a blessing and a curse. "Still stings, huh?"

I joined the tips of my fingers and picked at the skin surrounding my nails, dropping my gaze to their undone state. At one time they had always been manicured. And pink. Blake loved when they were pink.

I sucked in a breath and tossed the thought aside. "I'm sure it always will." I stood. "Come on, walk me to class."

Jace hooked an arm around my waist, and I rested my head on his chest as we walked. "Why don't you go talk to him? There's no sense in being alone, Eva."

"He's moved on, Jace." The words were bitter and disgusting leaving my mouth, like day old coffee.

"I don't think that's true, love." He softened. "I don't think he'll ever be over you."

"I wish that were the case, but I saw it with my own eyes. I have to let him go. I need to give him a fighting chance at a normal life."

He stopped walking and turned to me. "I just don't buy it. I don't care whose eyes saw it. You need to try."

"Doesn't matter. I won't go back to him unless I'm sure I can completely fix myself. Be what he needs. He deserves that. And I know him. He won't settle for less."

"Yeah, but—"

"Topic change." I flicked my wrist in the air, making it obvious this discussion was off the table.

Jace exhaled and snaked his arm around my waist again, moving me along. "So, you and Drew, huh?"

"Yeah, he's been so helpful. I'm really glad I took him up on his offer. He's an outsider but still feels like an insider. I can tell him this stuff without having to worry that anything will come of it. It's been refreshing."

"You sure he's not looking for more than you're giving him?"

I stopped walking.

Except for in the very beginning, before we really knew each other, Drew had never given me the impression he wanted anything more than friendship from me. Once he knew my past, it had been strictly business—training, and a regular friendship off the mats. It's why I was so comfortable being around him. "I don't think so. Drew and I are just friends."

Jace raised a perfectly sculpted brow that I'd been jealous of since middle school. "All I'm saying is you guys have been spending an awful lot of time together. I'd make sure he doesn't see a pot of gold at the end of that rainbow you're shitting."

My forehead tightened with the pull of my eyebrows. I never considered he might still be looking for more than I was willing to give him.

Chapter 21

DOCTOR CHRISTIANSON SAT ACROSS FROM me with her stockinged leg crossed and bobbing, a pricey black pump dangling from her toe. She wore a look of confusion mingled with pleasure, although she was definitely trying to hide it. She studied me, a yellow notepad on her lap, rolling a pen along her bottom lip.

"You're different," she finally stated.

Unsure of whether or not I truly was different, and not yet ready to waste hope, I answered her with a fidget as I changed the direction of the cross of my legs.

She finally allowed a soft smile. "Have you been talking with Drew?"

I nodded and flipped my hair to the opposite side.

Her smile expanded. "That's it?" She re-shoe'ed her foot and placed it on the floor beside the other, sitting up straighter. "Eva, that's fantastic news. This is a big step for you. Have you been able to open up to him? I believe the two of you could benefit from one another. Be a Band-Aid of sorts. Not just him for you, but you for him as well. Perhaps you guys could find solace in each other."

Solace.

The word brought the Sarah McLachlan album to mind. Lots of times I'd used her songs for comfort, but what was his? I immediately felt sorry I hadn't offered him as much of the shoulder he'd lent me. He was always so focused on training that, besides that first day when we'd met for coffee, we barely spoke of our pasts. I was sure that would change once he thought he'd gotten me on the right track.

Right now he just seemed determined to turn me into the female version of the Terminator. Which I probably wouldn't mind since I'd always been jealous of that chick.

"I have." I smiled fondly, thinking of him, grateful for all that he had done for me. "He knows everything. He's been training me. Wants me to get strong. There was no fighting him. He's a stubborn son-of-a-bitch."

Doctor Christianson allowed herself a heavy chuckle. "That he is. But he's also a genuine son-of-a-bitch. He'd give you the shirt off his back. Just be gentle with him, too." The corners of her mouth relaxed, but the smile in her eyes remained. "So . . . did it feel good?"

"It felt . . . wonderful." I exhaled, finally releasing the remaining tension. "Refreshing and liberating. I had a weak moment where I almost didn't go through with it, but he pushed me. Like I said—stubborn." I rolled my eyes before looking back to her and tucking away an errant curl. My voice softened. "But I'm glad that I did. I haven't felt this good in a long time." My mind instinctively started to recall days with Blake when I was happier, but I stopped them quickly. If I was going to be successful in my growth, I had to set those thoughts aside. They would only tunnel me back into the what-might-have-beens, and those were dangerous. They usually resulted in me rocking in a corner.

The good doctor didn't seem to notice. "Well, Eva, I believe you've reached step two." The smile on her face could light up a room. "Don't stop with him, though. I want you to keep going. Talk about it until it doesn't seem shameful. Until you've reached step three." She focused her eyes on me as if to gauge whether or not she thought I could do it by my reaction. "Forgiveness—both for yourself *and* Damon. Let go of what he's bogged you down with. Give it back to him. It's his cross to bear."

When I didn't answer, unsure of my ability to do any of that, she continued. "You will heal, Eva. It's possible. This will always be a part of you like any other scar, but it does *not* define you. The sooner you realize that, the sooner you will heal. And you *will* heal."

The determination in her stare sent a chill through me, and I had an eerie glimpse into my future of a strong woman harboring a scared little girl inside, petting her on the head and recognizing the fact that she would carry her around for the rest of her life, but that's not who she was anymore. And as I watched that vision of a life I prayed I would see, a butterfly—just one stray butterfly—took flight in my belly.

SUNSHINE POURED INTO MY ROOM and, for the first time in months, it felt as though it was seeping into me as well. I'd always been affected by the weather, my day piggybacking the forecast, but lately, every sunrise left me in a gloomy fog. I'd been starting to wonder if I'd ever enjoy another kiss of the sun as it said good morning.

But today? Today, it made me feel alive. Warm.

I stretched my arms as high as they would reach and elongated my toes in the opposite direction, breathing a deep breath of air through my lungs. Although my heart was heavy, I was starting to feel stronger. My muscles were becoming more defined, even the one sitting inside my head. The one I always tried to keep numb. It fizzed and sizzled and made itself known a little more with each passing day. As each piece of my physique was called to play, being pushed beyond its limits in an attempt to strengthen, my brain was being fortified as well. I was building a mental rock. One that couldn't be fucked with. And then . . .

Then I was going to slam it down over that fucker's skull.

Picturing Damon's face sent a wave of adrenaline pumping through my veins. I leaped from the bed, making my way to the home gym Drew had put together. It served as my early morning workout on the days we didn't go jogging together. Good thing for free financing or I would be eating a hefty load of ramen noodles.

This was one of the days I dreaded most. The day I would have to sit in class with Blake and pretend that my heart wasn't pounding out of my chest the whole time. That my head was paying attention to the professor in the front of the room instead of twelve rows back where he sat. He hadn't made any more advances since the *unicorn* note, and I hadn't glanced behind me. Not once.

You have to try.

Shut up, Jace.

Even though he wasn't here, I knew he had heard me.

I WALKED INTO ENGLISH, STEELING myself for the punch to the gut that I got every time I entered this class, but it never came.

For the last couple months, twice a week I would cover my face with my hair and keep my chin tucked to avoid looking to the back of the class where *he* undoubtedly sat. The fifty minutes I was forced to spend in that confining box was pure torture, feeling the heat of him searing me from behind, the soul-crushing guilt that I was hurting him plaguing me. You've never felt *difficult* until you've been put in a room with your soulmate, unable to acknowledge it.

And like every morning, I stopped at the very first desk in the front of the room. But this time I stared down at it. Noticing its confines. Somehow, even in this open room with a bunch of seats and people, it looked so secluded. A mockery of my existence.

Maybe I could blame the sun. Or the little bits of added strength I'd gathered. What came over me at that point, I couldn't say for sure, but—

I looked up.

Finally.

Blue diamonds stared back at me with a cinch between them. I couldn't stand how worried he looked. How pained.

I did that.

I was sick of me, too.

You have to try.

Logic moved aside at that moment. All I could concentrate on was how hard it had been without him by my side. How futile my efforts to grow without the biggest piece of life inside. I didn't think about his new girl. I didn't think about the pain. I thought about him. Only him. About the hands of comfort that I wanted to feel. The hands of comfort that I wanted to offer.

You have to try.

Grabbing my courage by the balls, I moved past that desk, then past the next, working my way to the back of the room. Blake straightened at my approach, his gulp visible. Without a word, I slipped into the seat beside him.

Out of the corner of my eye, I saw his leg bobbing to a hurried rhythm beneath the desk, his hand in a tight ball on top of it. With a calm hand, and confidence that I wasn't exactly sure where it came from, I reached out and covered his fist. His body tensed. I looked over at my hand blanketing his tension, and all I could think about was bringing him some serenity again, easing his anxiety. I stroked my thumb along the outside of his fist, willing him to relax. To feel me. Slowly, the muscles began to lax. I could hear Blake's breaths as I rubbed back and forth, soothing, reassuring.

We were going to be okay. We had to be.

He relented, opening his hand and turning it upside down. I slid mine along his before interlocking our fingers. I closed my eyes briefly, feeling the tracks of my lifelines matching up with his, knowing this was where I was meant to be, even if it hadn't been the most direct road getting here. I needed to fix him, eradicate the grief I'd given him. Share mine with him so we could begin to heal. Together.

No words were spoken, we'd never needed them anyway. I knew the professor was speaking, but hell if I heard a word. All I could concentrate on was the feel of Blake's skin. The warm moisture that was collecting between our palms, the evened-out breathing of our chests. The realization that, without speaking or looking at each other, that one point of contact was enough of a Valium to each of our pained hearts. An agonizing calmness. So close, yet worlds apart.

At the dismissal of class, we didn't move. I simply stared at the clasp of our fingers, unable to bear the thought of losing that one small connection. I imagined he was feeling the same. Knowing one of us needed to make a move, I dragged my thumbnail along his palm, before giving his hand a squeeze and beginning to let go, but he tightened his grip which made me look over at him. Finally. He wasn't looking at me, though. He was still staring down at our hands, grinding down on his teeth, a sort of manic expression on his face.

"What are you doing to me?" His voice was rough with ache.

Those words. All I could feel was the hurt in those words—both to me and to him.

They tunneled me back to the reality I chose to ignore at the start of class. To the fact that there was someone else in his life now and he'd finally moved on from me. To the fact that I had to protect him. From me.

What was I doing to him?

He was right.

If he'd finally found someone else, why would I step in the middle of that instead of allowing him to be happy?

Defeated, and second-guessing everything, I began to pull my hand away, but his grip cinched. I opened my mouth to apologize, to voice my heartache, my selfish need to be near him. But before I could get a word out, Blake was on his feet, and I was watching the hard lines of his back as he walked away from me.

A swift emptiness swooped in, leaving me hollow. After how patient he had always been, I'd never imagined he would really push me away. But everyone's first instinct was self-preservation, I supposed. How many times could you break a person before they became unfixable? Before they gave up?

With a hole in my heart and an ache in my chest, realizing we were really over and he was gone, I exited the building. To my surprise, my gaze immediately landed on Blake's broad, slumped shoulders. Relief and tension rocked me simultaneously. Though light-years from what we were, the fact that he was there—waiting for me snuck a sliver of hope into my crumbling heart.

But then I noticed the torment laced in his posture. He was sitting on the steps with his legs parted wide, an elbow on each, and his head in his hands as though he were experiencing the worst migraine of his life. And maybe he was. Maybe I was just a constant headache to him. A nagging ache.

When I walked to the back of the classroom, it was to offer comfort, to *ease* some of his grief, not to make it worse. And it had backfired. Now, as I stood here, confusion swam inside not knowing what to do. What to say. The last thing I wanted was to cause him more pain, and maybe I should have walked away . . .

But I just couldn't.

Not when he was breaking.

I squatted behind him, my head swimming in a fog of having his aura so close. Unable to stay away, longing to ease his suffering, my trembling fingers reached out. But his back tensed, seeming to sense it. My hand paused, suspended in mid-air. Agony rolled from each of his exhales and I wasn't sure if my touch would bring him comfort or hurt him worse. I was thankful the campus was quiet at the moment and that there wasn't anyone around to witness our wreckage.

His fists knotted around his hair, and then he raked his fingers through the ends and turned, shooting a look over his shoulder at me. I'd never seen that look in his eyes before, and I wasn't sure I'd ever forget it. Anguish laced with something bordering hatred dancing around a broken love. That was the only way I could describe it. That look slapped me across the face without ever touching me, and I abruptly rose to my feet, stumbling back to get away from it. Blake immediately stood as well, his fists in tight balls at his sides.

"Do you love me?" His eyes were wild, searching mine.

Not the words I was expecting.

I opened my mouth to respond but found my tongue immobile. *How could he even question that?* But before I could find the right words, he advanced up one step, his hateful expression slicing me open and I fumbled backward, feeling my heart trip in my chest.

"Can't answer?" He cocked his head to the side, an unhinged sort of madness spiraling in his sapphire orbs. I had never seen him this way, and it stunned me, my brain unable to form an answer to that very simple question. To tell him just how much. All of the ways that I adored him. Missed him. Longed for him. All of the cries that I'd wept for him and the nights I hadn't slept with worry for him.

He took another step, stole another beat of my heart.

"C'mon, Angel. It's a simple question," he scoffed, glitters dancing in his watery eyes. "Do. You. Love. Me?" he rasped.

More than air.

But the words didn't come. Of course I loved him. I loved him with every molecule of my being, but I didn't know if hearing that would make him feel better or worse. And I loved him enough to sacrifice my need for him if it meant he would be better in the long run. My brain was scrambling, trying to figure out the best approach, but he didn't give me a chance.

"What are you doing to me?" His steely exterior began to flake away, his chest noticeably flying around his speeding heart. An unmasked pain etched every inch of his face, making him look older than his years. "You push me away. You shut me out. And yet you keep coming around, leaving your little drippings in my life just to be sure I can't forget you."

Two more steps.

My shoulder blades met the bricks behind me. There was nowhere else for me to go, my body as immobile as my tongue as he closed in.

"Tell me," he demanded, his eyes grazing my features so roughly I could feel them scratch at the flesh of my face, imploring. Begging.

"I—"

The distraught look smeared across his face stopped me. Telling him how much I loved him would just be another selfish act on my part, and I had to put him first from now on. I owed him that much.

His frustration bubbled over his cracking exterior. With a growl, he eliminated the remaining space between us and came at me hard and fast, caging me against the brick wall. My chest heaved, the air I sucked in suffocating me.

"What the fuck are you trying to do to me?" he thundered, pain bleeding from each syllable. He fisted the shirt over his chest, twisting with a pull before banging on it. "I gave you every piece of me. All of it! And you fucking shredded me. I'm not your personal plaything, Evangelina. And now, you can't even say the words?"

His face was so close, his nose practically touching mine as a wave of his scent crashed into me. A soapy, musky, manliness that mingled with his own personal sweetness. I remembered that smell as much as I remembered its taste. It took everything I had not to crumble into him, but it hit me then how badly he was crumbling, too.

"I miss you," I whispered, the words floating out on their own. They brought with them a fear of rejection. But it was liberating to admit, even though they didn't hold the weight of the words he was looking to hear.

"Humph." The sarcastic grumble fell from his mouth. Blake pushed off the wall, allowing a gust of clean air to slap me in the face and I gasped, trying to take it in. He leveled his eyes at me, soaked in disappointment. "You wrecked me, girl."

I could see the calm sweeping into him the way it does after a rush of adrenaline. For a split second, something flickered in his eyes making me wonder if the nostalgia of *us* was hitting him as much as me. Knowing how hard it always was for us to stay away from each other. We stayed locked for a second, or maybe an hour, but then he turned away from me, leaving me pressed against the brick. Alone.

Anxiety began to crawl up my neck, knowing that our moment was over. That he was leaving me and my mind grasped at straws, not knowing what to say. How to make him come back. Sorry that I didn't say more.

I remembered the girl in the photo and all the reasons why this shouldn't happen. I called out just before he got too far, "I hope she makes you happy," and then my heart broke. Because as rancid as those words tasted, I knew that I had meant them.

Blake stopped in his tracks and shoved his hands in his pockets. Without turning around, he replied, "Yeah, well, someone has to."

And then he walked away without another word, taking another beat of my heart with him—a slight thrum that he could slip into the pocket of his heart or throw into the trash. Whatever suited his fancy.

Either way, it no longer belonged to me.

Chapter 23

PFFT.

The sound of my padded fist meeting muscled flesh thumped the air, the whoosh of my breath pushing in and out of my mouth, coiling around it in an intricate rhythm.

"Harder," Drew prompted, dancing around me.

One—Two

I jabbed, my knuckles connecting with his ribs.

"Faster." On the balls of his feet, his movements were light as air. He was like the Fred Astaire of the ring.

One—Two—Three

I increased the frequency with each punch, which used to kill my wrists, but even they seemed to be getting stronger.

"Harder, Sunshine. Make me feel it!" Drew shoved my shoulders, and I stumbled back. He banged his gloves together and came back at me with a determined stalk.

I sized up each of his steps, trying to foresee his next line of action, but he wasn't showing any tells.

Pfft.

He landed a quick jab to my side, and I collapsed inward to protect it.

"You're off your game. Pay attention to every move I make." He shoved my shoulders again, and I stumbled back a few more feet as he advanced, not waiting for me to find my bearings. My encounter with

Blake must have been distracting me. I hadn't been this clouded in the ring since Drew and I began working together. But ever since Blake had walked away from me, he was all I could think about even when I didn't realize I was. I pulled myself back into the now, trying my best to calculate Drew's steps—right, left, right, hitch to the left with a crouch.

Duck—Block

I knew the right fist would be coming that time.

One. Block left.

Two. Slide right.

Breathe.

Uppercut. My fist connected with his jaw, sending his head flying back.

He recovered quickly. "Again."

Masochist.

One—Two. Block. Block.

His flow was gaining speed.

One—Two—Three. Duck, swerve, sidestep.

Punch back.

I hopped from foot to foot, dancing on the balls of my feet as my ponytail swayed behind me. My entire body was slick with moisture as sweat dripped between my shoulder blades and breasts.

Unlike in the beginning, my stamina nearly mirrored Drew's now. He was turning me into a machine.

He flurried his shots. I bobbed and weaved, managing to escape most, coiling in from the few that I'd miscalculated. I'd been trained to keep going, despite the burn, numb to the ache. There was a way of turning off your brain to the pain. Convincing your body it hadn't felt anything when everything inside of you felt as though it were fighting a fire.

I retaliated.

One—Two—Three—Four.

Drew had a hard time blocking, and I lunged, seizing my opportunity. I moved on to my next blow, immediately after landing my last, barely giving him a second to recover. He recoiled, and I advanced, driving him backward, and I saw his eyes spark. He loved it when I came into myself and went into attack mode.

My top lip curled back over my teeth, exposing my grit. *Breathe.*

In quick succession, I landed blow after blow. Drew's gloves were raised high, protecting his face as his elbows stayed tucked tight to his body. He jostled left to right, taking each blow before barreling at me and wrapping his gigantic arms around me, locking my hands at my sides. I squealed and rocked, trying with everything in me to get him to loosen his hold, but his strength was incredible. He squeezed like an anaconda, and I felt my head becoming dizzy with the lack of oxygen. A black and white static crawled into my field of vision from outside points, and I knew it was only a matter of time before I collapsed.

Knowing Drew's first rule was "*there are no rules,*" survival instinct kicked in, and I brought my knee up, connecting with his precious jewels. He expelled a pained sound, but never loosened his grip. The man had the most insane willpower I'd ever seen. We tumbled to the ground, bouncing off the mat in a heap, winded and sweating, gasping and swallowing hard. I lay on my back, Drew still wrapped securely around me, neither one of us able to catch a breath.

Air pulled and pushed through the wide part of his lips as his chest pressed into mine with each exhale. Something in him shifted suddenly. The hard pull of his eyebrows slackened through each of his pants as his eyes concentrated, like he was trying to look into me, showing me so much of his unspoken troubles.

"You okay?" I immediately felt bad for not being the friend that he had been to me.

Drew's face sobered, but he didn't answer.

"Want to talk about it?" Our breaths were settling, slowing.

He rolled off of me. And rested his forearm on his bent knee, talking down toward his leg. "You never *did* give us a chance. Why?"

His question knocked into me, startling my anxiety. I sat up. "Drew—"

He peeked over at me. "Before you go getting all 'we're just friends' it's not like that. We *are* just friends now, and I love you like a sister, that's all. It's just . . ." he sighed and I could tell whatever was troubling him was something he was ashamed of. Something he didn't want to say out loud. "Is there something wrong with me?" The pinch between his eyebrows, the insecurity behind his eyes, broke my heart. How could he ever think that?

"Wrong with you? No. Why would you even say that?"

"I've never had a real girlfriend, Eva. Never had a steady anything and it's not for lack of trying. What am I doing wrong? Am I that tainted? Do I scream psycho-problem-child or something?" He tripped over that last statement and looked away, his cheeks reddening.

"Stop that right now. You are so amazing, do you hear me? Any girl would be more than lucky to have you." I slid my hand onto his arm and tugged, forcing him to look back to me. "Pay attention to me. I'm serious. This is not a speech."

"So what is it then? Why does everyone just brush me off?"

As I grazed my thumb along his forearm trying to soothe him, my finger glided over a rough patch of skin, calling my eyes to the discolored circle that I had noticed when we'd first had coffee. It reminded me that his concerns were even more deep-rooted than he was saying. "Maybe because they're not the *right* someone."

Drew rolled his eyes. "You couldn't come up with something a little less generic?"

He finally relaxed a bit, so I decided to lighten the mood. "Well, maybe they're intimidated by all this." I wagged my finger around the expanse of his body, finally coaxing a smile from him. When I could see the tension leave his shoulders, I continued. "You'll find your happily ever after. Your girl is out there waiting for you somewhere, trust me. There's someone for everyone." I tried to remain positive, but my mind drifted to Blake, and my heart broke open in my chest.

"And you?"

My eyes locked with his as my heart stilled. "I'm a bit of a tougher scenario." I gulped, laying my cards out there. "I found mine. And then I let him go." The corner of my mouth puckered.

"Tell me about it?"

I dragged in some courage. "When Damon attacked me that last time, I couldn't live with myself. I broke in every sense and didn't want to take him along for the ride, so I walked away. But my heart . . ." My breathing skidded to a stop. "My heart will always be his. It's not mine to give away any more," I whispered, lowering my gaze. It was so painful to think of Blake . . . I tried to do it as little as possible. And after the way we had left things the other day, I couldn't stomach the thought.

Drew placed a finger beneath my chin and lifted, forcing me to focus on him. He smirked, the sadness showing through the mask of his smile. "Maybe after all this, there'll be a second chance for you two."

Remember in life there are second chances. Blake's forget me not.

"I . . ." My voice cracked as emotion bubbled up my throat at the prospect of the truth in what I was about to say. "I think it's too late, Drew." The dam finally burst, and I put my head in my hands and wept. Wept for a lost time, for futures that weren't possible, and for the loss of the love of a lifetime. Drew held me, masking his own pain as I crumbled yet again. As much as I knew that I needed to get strong, to be the woman that Blake needed if he ever took me back, to face my nightmares head-on, it didn't help the fact that this was so fucking hard. No matter how strong I became, this was breaking me.

Another chisel to my façade.

Another Band-Aid to one more gaping wound.

Chapter 24

Numbness
Overtakes—bleeds from within
Clouding any form of rational
Making colors bleed into rainbows, melt into grays,
dropping into piles of ash.
Life crumbling—falling to the pits of death
A fiery death that you sit in. Screaming. Weeping.
Breathless.

I PLACED MY TRAY ON the silver rods and slid it to the right, looking at the food behind the glass in the cafeteria. A friendly woman, with a net holding her hair back, smiled wide. "What can I get you, dear?"

Hungrier than usual, my stomach answered for me. I clutched at its boldness and offered a weak smile. "Turkey on whole wheat."

"Coming right up." She did quick work slicing and laying, before handing it over. "I gave you a little extra." She winked.

"Thanks." My appetite was insatiable ever since I'd been working out.

Blake would be so proud. Queasiness rolled through me at the thought of him, but I swallowed it away.

Number seven-million-four-hundred-thousand and ninety-two. That was how many times something had brought my mind to him, and I was sick of it.

I paid the clerk and collected my tray, brushing past a few tables in search of a free one. Ironically, the one I'd occupied on the beautiful sunny day I'd officially met Blake was empty, sunlight pouring in, creating a dusty ray across it. My fingers tightened around the plastic, and I drew the tray into the ache in my belly.

Number seven-million-four-hundred-thousand and ninety-three.

With a loud silence, I lowered the tray and took a seat. Staring out the window, I took it all in. The weather was changing, and the beauty of it was something you could almost feel. Spring always gave me the impression it'd bring with it a happier time. It felt promising, like a chance to rebirth and start anew.

A few months ago, I couldn't wait for these days—to enjoy the outdoors with Blake, lazing beneath Bertha and staring up at her new hair swaying in a gentle breeze. Our fingers entwined while he drew circles on the palm of my hand with his thumb over and over. Picnics and early morning kisses.

A bluebird perched itself on the small windowsill and cocked its head, staring at me. He was so beautiful and so far from home in the big city. I wondered what he was doing here. His eyes studied me, almost seeming to convey concern if that were possible. Sunlight played on his beautiful feathers, and I fumbled, trying to find my phone to take a picture without taking my eyes off his for fear he'd fly away. I didn't want to miss getting a shot at one of those beautiful moments.

Number seven-million-four-hundred-thousand and ninety-four.

My fingers tripped around in my bag as I stayed focused on the tiny animal when the distinct sound of a click rang in my ear. My hand froze, and my body stiffened, the hairs on my arms shooting to attention all at once while bending to the left of me. Toward where I knew, without a doubt, *he* was sitting.

The blood drained from my face, taking my belly with it.

The bird flew away.

"Hi," I whispered without turning to see him. I didn't need confirmation of his presence.

"Hello." The smooth, familiar tone of his voice sent a fissure down my heart.

I closed my eyes, swallowing down a lumpy burn, my eyes turning hot with unwanted tears. I fought past the knot. "He made me think of you. That shot was too beautiful to miss. I'm glad you got it."

"I didn't take a picture of the bird." His clipped tone stilled my heart, and I stiffened.

"Oh."

We sat in silence for a while, comfort seeming to fall over our closeness while at the same time quietly breaking because of the tiny distance that still remained. Though small in proximity, it was as wide as a canyon in reality—and we could feel it. Like a giant, empty bubble between us.

He might as well have been states away, rather than a foot behind me.

I finally broke the silence. "I'm sorry about the other day. I wasn't thinking about how hard all this is on you. It was selfish of me."

"It was," Blake's tone was short, "but I'm sorry for the way I reacted. You reached out, and I pushed you away, and I shouldn't have. I wasn't ready. I can't control what this does to me. That day it was just . . ." His words drifted off before coming back lower, but with clarity laced through them. "That was a bad day." His aura seemed to deflate, and the air around us softened.

A heat traveled up my spine, and I knew he'd settled himself closer. I took a deep inhale, my body desperately searching, to draw a little bit of him inside and get a small fix of the drug it'd been craving. A faint wisp of Blake-infused air met my nostrils, and I pulled it in sharply through parted lips, my tongue dancing on that small taste.

"I miss you." The words tumbled from my mouth before I could catch them. But I did. God help me, I missed him so damn much.

"Not as much as I miss you, Eva."

Eva.

Not Angel.

That name knocked the wind out of me, the ache I heard when he said it practically bringing me to my knees. It didn't sound right leaving his mouth.

When silence ballooned once again, I stated again on a quiet sigh, "I really miss you."

Then he was on me.

Fire met my back as he pressed his chest there, his hands cupping my shoulders as he buried his nose in my hair. "I'm sorry. I can't help it, I'm sorry. You can pretend I didn't touch you after, but I can't just sit here and not feel you." His voice cracked with his confession. "I'm not strong enough. God damn it, Angel, I'm not strong enough."

I felt the weight of him crush against me, and I wrapped my arms around my middle, my fingertips gripping onto his shirt behind me to hold him close as I fell forward with quiet sobs.

"What are you doing to us?" The plea in his voice was gut-wrenching.

The tears falling back down my throat burned so damn bad, too bad to allow a response.

"I know you came to see me that night," he breathed into the wisps of hair falling around my ear. "I felt you there. I could never *not* feel you there." The beats of his heart massaged my back in skipping little thumps. "That's why I freaked out that day in class. I thought you were coming back to me that night and then you disappeared again. Same like you always do," he trailed off.

"I tried. I've been trying so damn hard to stay away, but it's too much sometimes. That night . . . I needed to say goodbye." My voice was so soft, I wasn't sure if I'd spoken at all.

He stilled, and I felt his forehead rest on the back of my neck. "Goodbye?" he repeated, emotion thick in his throat.

"Yes. Properly. I never got to say goodbye properly." I sniffled, angling my head toward him.

"And were you able to?" He continued to speak from behind me, his voice wrought with purpose. "Were you able to say goodbye to me, Angel?" His weight left my back, and a chill slithered into its place.

Never.

I stiffened as my mind instinctively floated to the memory of the photo, the one on his bedside table. *Of Amanda.* I sat upright, forging strength. "I started to, but then I saw her. Next to your bed. And it was too much to handle."

"Eva, it's—"

"It's okay. You don't owe me an explanation. I'm glad someone can bring you joy. That's all I ever wanted for you." I hugged myself, rubbing the tops of my arms. "Coming to you that night was wrong of me. Coming to you in class was, too. I just can't help it sometimes."

His finger met the bone at the top of my spine and began to trail its way down slowly over each of the nubs. "Your body . . . It looks so different. Are you okay?" His voice was soft and distracted as he ignored everything I'd said. "I worry about you."

I curled in marginally, protecting myself, even though my body reeled from his touch—that one point of contact like a lit poker to my skin. And as a moth draws to a flame, I skidded toward it, rather than skirting away. "I don't want you to worry about me."

That was only a partial truth.

I walked away to spare him of having to worry about me, but the truth was, having him here, feeling his concern for me, felt good. Like my favorite cozy blanket that I had just found buried in an old closet, its smell tainted with a settled film, but still there deep within its woven threads. I shook off the feeling of wanting to grab his arms and entwine them back around me, putting his needs before my own, the way it should be. "That's why I walked away in the first place. I want you to be happy. Let her make you happy."

He ignored that, too. "What happened to you?" he coaxed gently, his voice soft and supple like warm chocolate. "That day. What happened to you? Will you tell me now?" He continued his slow progression down each of my vertebrae, and I sat in silence, gnawing at the inside of my cheek.

I'd be lying if I said I didn't want to open up to him and finally clear the air between us. Already just having him so close to me, I was starting to feel a bit less crumbly. The selfish bitch inside scratched at me to be set free. Wanted me to hand him my troubles once again and allow him to fix them. But my love for him knocked that bitch aside.

Because Blake was not the Blake I remembered.

Blake was no longer strong enough to handle both his own burdens and mine as well. Blake was crumbly now, too. He needed someone to shelter *him*. So even if he didn't understand, even if it made me seem heartless or like I didn't want him, we had to stay apart. For now.

I concentrated on the feel of his fingertip roaming my back, the comfort of his support. With each brush, I could sense how badly he wanted to know. And with each swipe, I knew just how badly I wanted him to. I closed my eyes, handing over a piece. "I got hurt again," I whispered.

His finger stopped moving and pressed into me a bit roughly. Although I couldn't see him, the air was so tense that I knew he was chomping down on his jaw, trying to work through what to do with that.

Instead of the response I'd been waiting for, Blake stood and collected our belongings before taking my small hand in his. "Come with me."

I didn't second guess my reaction to concede to his wish. Hand in hand, and with no words spoken between us, I allowed him to lead me straight to the place where we had originally opened up to one another.

Bertha.

She was so enormous. So proud. And, if I wasn't mistaken—happy? Yes, she looked happy. I allowed a small grin and looked up at her, nodding once. She seemed to glance down, welcoming me back.

Blake laid down on the grass and lightly tapped beside him, asking me to join him. I wasn't sure I could do it—lay beside him so close and not touch him, so I compromised. I laid in the opposite direction, my face aligned with his and rested my hands on my stomach, gazing up through Bertha's thick mane. Blake exhaled a deep breath beside me, as though it was the first time he'd breathed in months, and I thought that that was exactly what this felt like.

Breath.

Air.

If I turned my head, I knew I'd meet his blue diamond eyes. I felt them piercing into me, noticed the heat they sent into my pores. My skin was waking up, welcoming the familiar heat of his gaze the way a flower blooms at the start of Spring. Pieces that had been dead for so long were now buzzing and feeling, as though they might live again.

Live me.

Shhhh—I hushed that thought. It was too soon to go there.

Instead, my mind drifted to the box of forget-me-nots that Blake had left on my balcony. I now understood what it would feel like to regrow. To feel the thrum of life inside parts that were once dead.

In life, there are second chances.

I continued to look up through Bertha's branches, unable to face those eyes in this proximity, and I felt his gaze leave my skin as he did the same.

Then the air hardened.

"Who hurt you?" Blake's voice was rigid.

My newfound breaths caught in my throat and I tried to figure out how I'd get around this. How I'd tell him *without* telling him. It was time he knew the truth, but how much could I actually get away with and still protect him?

"It's someone very close to me. Very close to my family."

If the air had been thick between us before, it somehow became even more swollen, almost ceasing to exist, even in this open space. There was no movement beside me. I wanted to reach out and place my hand on Blake's chest and remind him to breathe.

"Who, Angel? Talk to me."

Dirt invaded my fingernails as I dug them into the grass. Damon's seething hatred of me that day flashed before my eyes—his teeth bared, his bloodshot eyes. I inhaled a deep, shuddered breath. "I can't say who. I want to, and I promise I will. Just not yet."

The air slackened, and Blake let out a large exhale, making me aware of how closely he was hanging onto my every word.

"You can trust me." His compassionate tone, soaked in comfort, massaged the delicate situation, but still urged me to have faith in his words. "Don't you know that yet?"

With my life. It was that bastard I didn't trust. He would push the situation into something that would compromise Blake, and I wouldn't have that happen. "Of course. My doubt was never in you. But I need to do this the right way. For *both* of us. Do you trust *me*?"

Blake remained silent, and I wasn't sure if it was because he didn't think I needed the reassurance of a yes or if he didn't want to lie. I didn't want to pressure him one way or the other, so I took away the moment.

"When the time is right, I promise I will tell you. I just . . . not yet, okay?"

The air was stagnant and stiff before it seemed to melt as Blake relented. "What happened then? Can you tell me what happened?" he probed, grasping for whatever glimpse I could give him.

"I went to see Abby that day." I sucked in a deep breath. "I went to see Abby . . . and he was there." I turned my head and finally looked in Blake's direction. "And she wasn't."

Even the hair that fell onto the grass behind his head seemed to stiffen. His air cut off again, and his Adam's apple rode a tense line inside his throat. He turned his head and our eyes finally locked. So much concern rested there, the purple circles under his eyes showcasing nights filled with worry. I wanted to reach out and touch him, wipe his heartbreak away, but my hands were glued to my sides. Instead, I allowed my gaze to touch all the parts my fingers couldn't. His plump lips that were slightly parted, permitting sharp gasps to both enter and retreat as he seemed to be working over my features with the same intensity. His high cheekbones and strong jawline. He was undoubtedly the most magnificent thing I had ever laid eyes on. I'd forgotten how beautiful he was. The bright light of the new spring sun danced along his features, highlighting each incredibly striking piece.

My Blake.

But he was no longer mine.

A sheath of regret blanketed me, and I fought to keep tears tucked into their ducts. I wanted to take it all in, unsure I'd ever get another opportunity like this. We were both so volatile. So back and forth with our emotions.

He turned on his side and tucked his hands underneath his face, meeting me head on. Without thought, I did the same.

"Are you okay now?" He searched me for the truth.

I wasn't sure what *okay* was anymore, but I was better. "Okay as I can be for the moment. I'll never be perfect, but I'm getting there."

A *humph* escaped his lips in a hushed scoff and his eyes locked on mine. "You couldn't be more perfect if you tried."

Wordless, we stayed here, suspended in time where what-ifs and what-might-have-beens danced around us, mingling with unanswered questions and the fears of the what-can-nots. It was both awkward and familiar, uncomfortable yet the most comforting place I'd been in months. My fingers twitched, wanting to touch him. My lips dried, needing to be coated with his. My heart bled in my chest, begging in agony for me to get closer to him as my breaths danced in spurts from my mouth.

Blake brought a pair of shaky fingers to my lips, and they parted, sucking in a gulp of air that tasted like his skin. His eyes told so much—longing I never knew possible was screaming from their depths. My eyelids drifted closed as he outlined the curves of my mouth. He rested the palm of his hand on my cheek and delicately stroked the bone beneath it.

"Angel?"

"Yes?" I answered, breathless. I couldn't open my eyes for fear that this moment would evaporate, that one of us would think better of it and run away.

His breath was hot against my lips, moisture from the warmth skimming the supple skin. "Don't move."

I sucked in one final breath as his mouth covered mine. Light exploded in blinding stars as everything that had ever been right in the world slammed into me with his taste. His love. What I had missed for so long penetrating my senses in a rush of Blake. I nearly crumbled as my chest concaved under the rush of air that left me, the feeling of being *home* barreling into me—overwhelming and glorious and all spiraled into one man, one heart, one soul that was the perfect match for my own. Hot prickles swarmed the corners of my eyes, but I choked down the sentiment and soaked in the Blake.

He kissed me softly at first, as though he was testing whether or not he could go through with it, learning my mouth once again. I didn't move. I couldn't. I merely breathed as much of him into my lungs as I could, savoring his sweetness. Still upside down, his tongue dipped into my mouth with a groan, the pad skimming along the top of mine, and I fell into a dazed, sated, and numb abyss where there was only him and me.

A sense of comfort washed over me, relaxing any tension my body was harboring in his absence.

No pain.

No sorrow.

No regret.

Just love. Undying love.

He continued to kiss me, still slow and unsure, as though he was scared if he was pressing too hard and I would realize what was happening and end it.

But I couldn't.

His hand moved, tangling in my hair, and the breaths that he breathed into me began to quicken. I knew then what was happening to him because it was happening to me as well. The weight being placed on my chest was all-consuming. Even if this didn't end in *us*, I needed to feel as much of it as possible.

Without breaking the connection of our mouths, I lifted and spun myself so I was horizontal with him and could enjoy him properly. One of his hands fisted the hair behind my head while the other stayed at my cheek, and we indulged in each other, licking and sucking and drinking in each other's aura. His hands skimmed down my sides before coming up beneath my arms and tugging, bringing me on top of him. My pieces sunk into his, each crevice fitting like a puzzle as our hearts beat against one another's. They had missed each other. I could tell by the way they aligned, landing in perfect sync to beat the other's drum. It was a rhythm unique to them as they chased each other on high and low waves.

I finally parted our mouths and sat up, scared that I was falling too deep and wouldn't be able to dig myself out again. We both stared at each other, our chests heaving in tandem. I brought my fingers up and touched my lips, swollen with Blake as tears pooled in my eyes.

"Angel . . ." Blake sat up and snaked his hand around the back of my neck. "Stay with me."

Somehow I knew he didn't mean physically. He could probably see what I was feeling. Knowing that this couldn't happen.

"Blake—" My voice cracked.

"She's just a friend."

"What?" My breath trapped in my throat.

"Marybeth. I know you saw her picture that night and she's just a friend. She's my partner in the photography classes you set me up with. She knows all about you, and she means nothing to me."

Marybeth? I thought her name was Amanda. Didn't matter now. I closed my eyes as relief sunk in.

In a voice so small I almost missed it, Blake added, "Don't run."

I opened my eyes and trained them on his sparkling blue irises, the bend between them sending an aching ball into my stomach. "I won't." I shook my head, promising both him and myself. "I'm not. But we can't do this. Not yet. I'm not ready yet." They were words I was so sick of throwing at him, but Jace was right. Blake deserved a whole woman, and I was close—so close, but still not where I needed to be.

Blake seemed to find what he searched for in my eyes because his shoulders relaxed, his features calming. Always patient, the corner of his mouth rose in a half-hearted smile. "Whatever you need." Those words were a horrible reminder of the day that he had walked out of my life and I didn't like the sour they created in the back of my throat.

"I'm sorry." I hung my head. No truer words were ever spoken, but if I wanted to be fair to him, and to me, I had to do this.

"So am I." The defeat in his eyes, the disappointment in his tone spoke more than his words even though he tried to mask it. "I'm sorry that you won't let me fix this for you."

I cupped his face, willing him to see past this denial to my growing strength, to the truth in my heart. "I wish you could, but it's up to me. When I give myself to you again, I want you to have someone that's whole, not be picking through my fragments." I rubbed my thumb along his cheekbone, and his eyes drifted shut.

He took my hand in his and brought the inside of my wrist to his lips. Then my always poetic Blake let the most beautiful words caress the delicate skin. "I wouldn't care if you were particles of dust scattered in grains of sand. I'd still fix you." His eyes trained on mine, stealing my breath. He laced our fingers and rested our hands between our laps with a sigh. "But, for you, I'll wait. Because what just happened reminded me what having air feels like, and I'm not so sure I could go back to suffocating anymore, Angel. I can't bear the thought of it."

I threw my arms around his neck and crushed him tight to me, squeezing. For the yesterdays lost and the tomorrows I wasn't sure we would see, I held him for today and hoped it'd be for eternity.

Damon: How come you're not answering? I've been trying to get you. Because I've *been working on getting* you . . .

LIKE MOST MORNINGS, THERE WAS a soft rapping of knuckles at my door. Since my afternoon with Blake, I had thrown myself into my doctor visits and workouts hardcore, anxious to fix myself, seeing a shard of light at the end of this long, dark tunnel.

When I couldn't work out with Drew, the home gym he had set up was quickly becoming the perfect outlet to get my frustrations out. I would plug music into my ears to try and lull the static that was always in my head, while bashing away at my body, trying to shred my muscles and sweat out my pain. The sun hadn't risen yet, and my muscles already ached to my bones, but it felt good, like an accomplished ache. I opened the door with a smile and kissed Drew on the cheek.

"Mornin', Sunshine," he quipped.

"Morning, Rainbow," I replied as I did most mornings.

He laughed lightly. "Where'd that nickname come from anyway?"

"I don't know, it just came out one day." I placed my hands on my lower back and bent backward. "It suits you, really. You're always bright and hopeful. You're a rare find, and you make me smile when I see you." I pulled the string on his fuchsia hoodie. "And you *are* very colorful all the time." I winked.

Drew laughed, deliberately this time. "Well, regardless, I like it, even if it is a bit feminine. Shows you care." He tapped the edge of my nose. "Come on, show me your muscles." He did this to me every day, sort of like you would do to a child who just ate their spinach.

I held up both arms and flexed. Drew curled a large hand around my bicep and squeezed. "Impressive." He raised his brows. "You must have a good teacher." His boyish grin was contagious, and I couldn't help but smile along with him.

"Eh, he's okay. Although sometimes, when he pins me down, he smells. Someone should teach him the value of a deodorant stick." I pulled my door shut and locked it with a smirk, sensing Drew's discomfort behind me. I turned as he was sniffing his underarm, confusion swiped across his face. I pushed his arm down. "I'm kidding, Rainbow, you smell like roses. God, you're easy." I wasn't sure where the extra playfulness was coming from today, but I could only hope it was a sign that a change was taking shape inside. A good one.

He narrowed his eyes at me. "Just for that, you're getting five extra laps."

"Whatever," I countered, raising my arms above my head in a stretch as I walked past him.

He hurried along beside me, continuing his goad. "And just wait until we spar later. You're working for it today, Sunshine."

Stopping at the bottom of the steps outside my apartment building, I placed my hand on his forearm and pretended to be nervous. "Please take it easy on me. I'm fragile."

Drew studied me a moment before seeing through my rouse. "Yeah, okay. A month ago I might've bought into that fragile crap, but now? Your ass is mine. I want to see action today when we hit those mats."

"Yes, sir!" I sent him a customary salute and began a slow trot toward the park.

Drew kept pace with me as we meandered the early morning city streets, never coming to a full stop as we waited at the crosswalks. Dusk coated the air, rich with the smell of dew, but we weren't alone despite the early hour. You could never truly be alone in New York City. That was until you hit the park. Not many lingered there this time of morning. That's why we had chosen it.

I jogged down the long staircase, Drew at my heels, and turned to face him at the bottom, my feet never stopping all the while. "You ready?"

"Let's do this." Drew clapped his hands together and nodded.

With a smirk, I popped my earbuds in. "Eat my dust, *Rainbow*."

I pushed play on my iPod and then took off to the trails, seeing Drew scurry to catch up out of the corner of my eye. I laughed to myself, thinking what a good guy he was. I was lucky to have found such a genuine friend. He never made me feel like he was doing this for anything other than my benefit. He'd learned how to read me in the short time we'd spent together, which may be part of his trade. He sensed the need to protect himself and knew how to calculate people's actions *before* they actually acted.

With me, he knew when to push and when to back away. Like right now. He could easily outrun me, but he remained a few feet back, giving me the space I needed. He had said he wanted my head strong as well, and something about the solitariness of your endorphins waking up as your stride built always aided the cause.

In the beginning, I tried to push away all of the thoughts that would barrel into me. Stomped down on the memories and the feelings they would bring with them. Even the happy ones left a gaping wound inside because they were memories of a past life that didn't exist anymore. But now, in the face of budding strength, the hurt ached a little less, the pain ebbed a little more. Just like a wound in the process of healing—you know you should take off the Band-Aid, expose it to the air so it could finish curing, but you keep it covered still, trying to shield it as long as possible. That's the stage I was in. I was protecting my aches, but in doing so, I wasn't allowing them to fully heal. It was time to rip the Band-Aid off and deal with the raw state of the wound.

My feet hit the pavement pound for pound as my workout playlist trickled into my ears, handpicked to ensure optimal motivation. My heart beat at a steady, quickened rhythm, each lyric bringing added strength to my stride. For the first time, I allowed myself to truly feel it. Allowed myself to absorb the loss, the solitude.

The ache.

The scratch of a record followed by a strong piano began as Linkin Park's *In the End* started. The words blasted into my ears, a reminder of all the wasted days of my life—how hard I had tried to pull it all together. So close, *I was almost there . . .*

Until that prick had ripped away all that I had worked for once again.

And in the end, here I was. Alone still, trying to pick up the shattered wreckage of my existence for the millionth time.

Fuck him.

I sucked in a sharp breath, keeping my stride steady even though my heart was hurting, making it harder to keep up with the unintentional increase in my step. The weight of everything sat like a boulder inside my chest, saturated with hurt, with pain. All that I'd been keeping bottled up inside for so long felt as if it no longer fit in there. Like trying to keep it contained was breaking me from the inside.

I tried.

Damon's boyish smile flashed in front of my eyes. His old face. The one I had trusted, laid all my faith in. With a sparkle in his eye, he sat down on my bed all those years ago, and I wavered, my feet almost tripping at the recollection, the promise that he was there to make my life *better*. Easier. My nails bit into the palms of my hands to the point of pain, but it only drove me harder, pushed my heels deeper into the ground.

As I remembered my past, his face began to morph, ultimately turning into the Damon I saw when I looked at him now. For as much as I tried to turn off each time he had touched me—to go away somewhere so that I didn't allow it to seep in—it was all there, loitering under my skin like a pesky vermin.

I sucked in the air that was becoming harder to regulate through gritted teeth. *So much time gone.* I remembered all that was stolen from me, and I had to fight to remain focused. I wanted to run to his house and pummel him until he no longer existed for taking it all.

But then the reminder came of how far I had come.

If he could see me now, he wouldn't even recognize what I was becoming. I had trusted that prick with my life. But it was over. It was all over. He'd taken it all and, in the end, none of it fucking mattered. I'd lost it all anyway.

The ending few notes rang in my ears, and I knew what was coming, the playlist engrained in my memory.

Alive.

A slow but determined chord began, followed by Sia's low, pained voice and I let her words of growing up overnight trickle into my stinging veins. The steady beat of the drum banged through my ears into my chest, fueling me. I had spent my life in the same place she talked about, surrounded by stale air and demons in a barren, lifeless land. Days bleeding into nights, shaking with tears soaking my pillow. But I had survived . . .

Barely.

Her voice cracked with emotion, and I felt it cluster in my throat. My eyes pinched shut as I continued to run, knowing that I had continued to breathe all these years that he had tried to squish me into a quiet little box.

I air-punched my fists, breathing in deep clumps of air through flared nostrils as my eyes reopened. The pattern of my footfalls gained speed as I shook my hands out at my sides, focusing on his face, scenes flashing before me like a movie.

His hands pawing at me.

His ugly fucking eyes.

His lies.

I let the fact that I was still breathing fuel me as my pace quickened.

And then it came.

The song blasted at its peak, creating an ache in my eardrum to match that of my heart, the crack of pain doing its job as the beat rocketed into me. I took off like a bullet in a burst, the balls of my feet breaking pavement as my chest opened, drawing in much-needed oxygen. Synapsis sparked and burned, and my eyes were stinging with the effort of holding it all together.

Every word she screamed slapped me in the face, punched me in the guts.

All that I took.

All I had to face.

Anguish.

Pain.

Despair.

Loss.

Fucking empty.

I wanted it back.

I want it back!

Fuck!

I pushed harder, deeper, the tears an uncontrollable veil in my eyes. I swiped the back of my fist across my cheeks as they poured, fighting against the blur they created. I wanted my muscles to burn like fire. I wanted the pain of it to make me feel.

Fucking feel!

I drove harder, taking turns now at speeds that I couldn't keep up with, not bothering to stay on the park's trail. I stumbled onto the grass, dirt flying behind me with the efforts of my feet to gain traction as Sia's broken voice cracked and screamed along a single guitar strum, and her final resolution to the world that she was alive sent me in a broken heap onto my knees.

"FUCK YOU!" I screeched into the early morning air at the top of my lungs, matching her volume.

Drew landed on his knees in front of me, his chest flying up and down, unable to catch itself. His eyes screamed without words, yelling his panic, his worry. He ripped the earbuds from my ears before another word could pass into them, letting the deafening silence slam into them. All that was heard was the sharp breaths desperate to escape from the both of us. The wheezes as our lungs tried with all their might to expand.

He shot to his feet and backed up, holding out his arms with a slight squat. He clapped. "Come at me." He bore his eyes into mine, yelling at me to get off the ground. "Now! Get up and come at me—NOW!"

"Ahhh!" I propelled to my feet, blindness and white light exploding behind my eyes as I crashed into him with the force of a herd of elephants. I came at him with fists, teeth bared, pummeling them down. All I saw were snippets of my past. *Him.* What was gone and the agony that was still there. I wailed and screamed, feeling dizzy. I had no control over what was happening. Drew had completely taken the form of Damon in my mind, and I wanted him dead.

"That's it. That's it! Get it the fuck out of you!" he bellowed in my face.

"I hate you! I hate you for what you did to me! Look at me!" I threw a punch to his ribs, and Drew tried to block it but was unsuccessful. He dragged his arm in to protect himself, and I carried on with my assault.

I kicked and punched and slapped until pieces of me began to give up, the physical exertion moving past the emotional need. My body tilted forward, my limbs weighing down at my sides.

Strong arms wrapped around me before we both came crashing to the ground in a jumbled wreckage. I clutched at Drew's shirt, which was soaked with sweat and tears, and held on so tight my fingers cramped. "I'm so fucking broken!" I wailed.

"You're wrong." He palmed the sides of my face and tilted my head back. "You're so wrong, Eva. You've eradicated him. I don't know what brought that on, but I'm so fucking proud of you." He pulled me into his safe cocoon once again.

Familiar blue eyes that never left smiled in the darkness of my mind, a dimple that always greeted me, confirming it was Blake. The hope of him. Of us. The taste of his lips, and the reminder of all that I lost was what triggered such a monumental moment, I was sure of it. I had him to thank for that breakthrough.

Panting, still trying to steady my breath, I spoke into Drew's moistened hoodie. "Sorry I hurt you." I sniffled.

His chest began to regulate. "You didn't hurt me. I've never felt better."

He put his chin on top of my head and pulled me in close, burying my face in his chest. I was grateful because it covered the rest of the pieces that were crumbling from me.

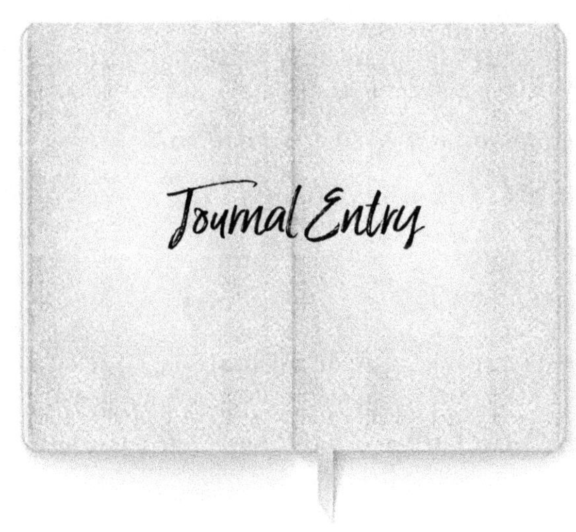

I should have felt better.

I should have felt better, and I didn't.

I should have felt better, and I didn't, and I don't know how to fix it.

What happened yesterday was a huge breakthrough, letting the venom out of my system a relief. But while I was lying in a heap on the ground, all I could think of were the pieces of me that were missing. The piece of me that was missing.

Yes, I needed to rid myself of Damon's poison.

Yes, I needed to recognize that what happened to me wasn't my fault.

Yes, I needed to stand up to him and out him to my family and the world. Let them know there's a deceitful predator amongst them. And, in order to do that, I needed to be strong. To believe in myself as much as I would need them to believe me. To take my word over his.

But . . . without him?
Without the love of my life.
Without so many of my heartbeats.
Without what I want most of all.
Without.
Without.
Without.

Damon: It's almost time to come home. I can't wait to see you.

I plucked that queasy little butterfly out of my belly and flicked it to the floor. *Be careful what you wish for, asshole.*

"YOU HAVE TO WORK OUT your quads more. Chicken legs aren't gonna cut it. I want twenty wall squats an hour, every hour you're home for the next eternity." Drew popped a plum tomato into his mouth and chewed, gripping a fork upside down in his fist. With all the grease in this pizzeria, I don't know how he had the willpower to stick to salad.

"Shut up." My eyebrows pulled in. "I do not have chicken legs. And, if I remember correctly, there was a time you coveted those chicken legs." I stabbed a green olive off his plate and darted it into my mouth.

A smirk slid across Drew's face, remembrance alight in his eyes. "That was never the part I wanted."

I threw a piece of bread at him, and he ducked as he laughed.

"Besides." He waved me off with a twirl of his fork. "That's a horse of a different color. This is coach-talk. I need you more fit."

"Let me enjoy my lunch, you drill sergeant," I quipped.

"Amateur." Drew rolled his eyes and stuck a bite of salad into his mouth.

"Topic change. Can we hit the bag later? Since my breakthrough the other day, I've been dying to kick ass." I began to sway from side to side. "I just wanna punch and bob and weave. I want to see veins in my teeth." Life was beginning to spiral through me ever since I had broken apart while running with Drew. Between that and my time with Blake, I was feeling energized and new, determined to fix myself completely so we could finally be together. And I wanted to harness it every chance I got. Between classes, work, my doctor appointments, and my training sessions, I hadn't gotten to see Blake again, but I felt a small piece of him inside in the spots that were usually empty.

"Easy, killer." Drew laughed.

I chuckled, not remembering when I'd felt this alive. It was like I'd been walking around, covered in sandbags for years, and they'd all just melted off and dropped away. All I could focus on was striking back. And, in the end, I was going to get that fucker if it was the last thing I did.

The chair scraped beside me, and I jutted to the left just as a familiar, heavy arm coated my shoulders. Though I usually loved the feel of that arm, something about it was off as it wrapped me in tension rather than security. I gulped, heat slamming into my cheeks as my line of sight slid from Blake back to Drew. The same tension immediately wrapped around our small table like a rubber band, constricting. Although I knew I hadn't done anything wrong, my body couldn't help its nervous reaction. Drew straightened, his eyes hardening as his hand, which was poised to place food into his mouth, fell to rest on the edge of the table.

I looked at Blake, surprised to see him here, but then I shrunk under the hard set of his jaw and the flare to his nostrils that he was trying to keep contained. In all the catching up we did the other day, we never *did* get around to talking about Drew. I instantly regretted it, not wanting him to get the wrong impression. Drew and I were only friends, and it would have made this situation a lot more comfortable if it wasn't coming as a shock to him.

My line of sight swung back to Drew who dropped his fork and stood, his chest broadening before my eyes. "There're only three people who are allowed to get that close to her. One is me, the other is gay, and you better pray I find out you're the third."

I rose to my feet quickly, as did Blake. Pushing one palm into his chest, I held the other out across the table in Drew's direction, calming the over-protective beast. He had never met Blake, and for all he knew, this could have been Damon, so I didn't blame him, but he didn't need to come on so strong.

"Drew," I warned. "This is *Blake*. Blake, this is Drew, and he's a *friend*." I tried to accentuate the word friend, even though I was sure the vein protruding from Blake's neck wasn't paying attention.

Drew's shoulders relaxed marginally, although the rigidity in them still sat around the edges, tensing his jaw with a tight-lipped smile that didn't reach his eyes. Drew wasn't used to trusting people and it was obvious from the moment he first met someone that he was sizing them up and deciding whether or not he deemed them trustworthy. "Ah, the infamous. Hat's off to you, bro." I couldn't tell if he was being serious or sarcastic.

"Eva, is there a reason why this clown is giving *me* permission to be near you?" Blake scowled at Drew, seeming as though he were standing on a bed of needles.

Their eyes never unlocked, the testosterone-infused air zapping between them like a live wire. They were both so important to me, but I'd never thought this part through. I wanted to talk to Blake privately, break him in softly to the idea that I had become so close to another guy in his absence. Reassure him that Drew could never take his place. My eyes skirted around, discerning if anyone was watching although the guys didn't seem to be fazed by our audience. I was met by the wide eyes of a couple of teenagers at the table next to us whose eyes skirted away from mine as heat swelled in my cheeks.

Drew shook his head with a sarcastic laugh, his eyes downcast. "As much as I'd love to jump all over that statement, I care too much about her to do it." His line of sight locked with Blake's once again. "I'll accept your apology for the name calling when you're ready to offer it." Drew rounded the table and held his arms open for a hug from me. "I'm gonna bounce. I'll see you tonight."

"See ya." I stepped into him, and he wrapped his arms around me, lingering a few seconds longer than comfortable as he, no doubt, stared over my shoulder at Blake thanks to his jab. A pit solidified in my stomach, weighing it down with a hefty twist.

"Find your happy," Drew whispered in my ear. When he finally pulled back, he placed a kiss on my cheek and cupped my face in his hands. "Take care of her," he commanded Blake, still looking at me. I took a step back, and Blake's hands covered my shoulders once again.

"I always do," Blake responded, but Drew was already walking away.

With a deep breath, I turned to face Blake. He was staring in the direction Drew had walked off in with a hard set to his jaw, although the boyish uncertainty swimming in the blue pools of his eyes gave away how nervous this all made him. "Wanna tell me who that was and what that was all about, Angel? Because I'm freaking the fuck out right now and praying there's a good explanation."

I sighed. "He's just a friend, Blake. I was only having lunch."

"Why didn't you mention him?" His eyes finally met mine, and the unspoken accusation I saw there stiffened my spine.

"I didn't get to." *What is this?* I understood that a lot happened between us, but the look on his face—the one telling me that he didn't trust my word, my actions—it cut deep. I searched his eyes, looking for my easy-going mate to return, but he didn't. After our time at Bertha the other day, I thought we were finally at a good starting point, but now I wasn't so sure as Blake looked at me, harsh and unforgiving. I got that he was scared, unsure, upset even, but I had no intention of hiding my friendship with Drew and I hadn't done anything wrong. "What is all this?"

"I don't know, babe." His sarcastic tone overrode the term of endearment. "You tell me. You cut me out of your life for months, and here I am thinking you're having a hard time when you're actually hanging out with some dude. You guys looked quite cozy if you ask me. That doesn't happen overnight."

Whoa. "Blake, it's not like that." I tried to make him see. "He's a *friend*. I'm sorry I didn't get to warn you, but there's nothing going on between us." I covered his forearm with my hand, trying to make him see my side of things.

Blake dropped his arm, and mine fell to my side. I gulped, recouping for a second before crossing my arms in front of my chest, anger beginning to take the place of the sympathy I was feeling. "What's with the caveman attitude? Am I some piece of property now?" Frustration at the feeling of being controlled when I was finally starting to gain my independence angered me. "Why every male in my life thinks he owns me is beyond my comprehension."

His edges softened, but a pained expression twisted his eyes, a defense mechanism kicking in. He held up his palms. "Hey, listen. Trust me, I'm quite aware of the fact that I don't hold a claim over you," he half-growled. "You've made that painfully obvious. But I was just wondering, for as much as you say that you love—" He cleared his throat. "*Loved* me," he corrected, squaring his eyes, "why it is that I needed to promise you my first born to get the time of day out of you, and yet here you are, all giddy with some stranger not long after we've broken up? Kinda cheapens what we had, no?" His voice cracked on that last word, a small fracture in its sound as he fisted his hips, his eyebrows pulled so far into the center they created a ripple as he waited with hollow breath for my response.

I didn't want him under the impression I could be controlled, but my intention wasn't to push him away or make him feel insecure either.

"Don't go there, Blake. Nothing will *ever* cheapen what we have, and you know it." I softened my voice, sympathy creeping back in to cover the bits of anger I was feeling. "Drew and I have never been anything more than friends. He's had a rough life, too, so we've been able to connect. He teaches self-defense, and he's been training me. That's why we've gotten close. But he would never take your place. No one could." I waited, letting that sink in. "I'll talk to him and tell him to lighten up with you, too, but you can't go getting all territorial with me. I don't want to feel controlled anymore."

I didn't know where that had come from, but as the words passed my lips, they tasted good. I'd never realized how free I was beginning to feel and I didn't want to lose that. If Blake was going to be with me, he was going to be with me as an individual. I didn't want to be dependent on anything anymore. Not even him.

Blake's shoulders sagged. "I wasn't trying to control you, Angel. You know me better than that. At least I thought you did." He paused, his face squishing in to mirror pain.

"I know that. But the way you just got all possessive and stuff, I didn't like how it felt. I want to be my own person, stand on my own two feet. You can understand that, can't you?" I implored, needing him to see me as an individual as well as a half to our whole.

Blake rushed a hand through his hair. "Yes. No. I just . . ." His breath left him on a defeated puff as he shook his head. "I feel like I don't even know you anymore. You're so distant, and you've pushed me so far out of your life. It makes me wonder if what we had was just a figment of my imagination." A light dawned in his eyes then, his features smoothing in recognition as the interrogation fled his face. He put his hands in his pockets, and his eyes drifted away to a far off place while a sarcastic little laugh fell from his mouth. I faintly registered him whispering the word "unicorn" before he looked back to me, his voice sturdier. "I always knew that was fitting." His blue eyes met mine, and the coolness I saw there soaked with regret terrified me. A gate was coming down in front of him, I knew it all too well. *Don't lose him.*

"Blake—"

He straightened, strength bulking up his stature as an emotionless expression sat on his face. "Don't. I'll get out of your hair. You're right, it was stupid of me to barge back into your life when I don't belong there anymore." When he went to turn away, I put my hand on his forearm.

"Blake, stop . . ."

He paused and glanced down at my hand, hurt crackling amidst the icy blue of his eyes showing how his air was strangled as his tongue slipped over his teeth behind his lip. His face pinched in pain. "Does he know?" The words floated on a broken whisper.

Another crack to my heart.

His gaze lifted to meet mine, a twinkling of moisture speaking for itself behind the question lying there. "Does he know everything?"

I swallowed hard. I knew I had my reasons for telling Drew the whole story, and I knew my reasons for withholding it from Blake were just as valid. But when faced with the hurt in that one tiny question, I was second-guessing the whole thing, scared of what the prospect of him knowing would do to him. To us. But I didn't want any lies between us. I deflated, my insides already feeling what was coming, the disconnect, the hurt. "Yeah. He does."

"Humph." The weight of his breath left through another sarcastic smile. He shook his head, glancing down.

"Blake . . ." I wanted to coax him into seeing reason but my hand dropped to my side as he began to walk away. *No.*

He stopped, only partially facing me. "Did it ever cross your mind that *I* could've been that for you?" His eyes cut to mine. Betrayal and disappointment were all I could find there. "I could've been whatever you needed me to be. Your help. Your trainer. Your *anything*. You never even considered it, did you? Never had the faith that I would find a way."

I sagged. "You *know* I couldn't do that. It's complicated." Although I wanted him to understand my reasoning, I could understand why he didn't. He didn't know the reasons why we had to stay apart all that time. Why I couldn't share with him the name of the person who had hurt me. He didn't know that it was all for him.

"You're right, it is. And I don't have the head for it anymore." He placed a soft, lingering kiss on my cheek, the warmth of his lips contradicting the chill that ran through me. An overwhelming sense of finality rested there in their wake. He pulled back to look at me one final time. "Thanks, Angel." He swallowed, collecting himself before his eyes slid back to mine. "You just made this a lot easier." He turned his back and left me here, staring into his vacated air.

Chapter 28

BLAKE

SHE JUST LEFT HOOKED ME in the fucking jaw.

I'd been naive enough to believe there was a chance for us. Floating around like a happy idiot, thinking we were on our path to finding our way back to each other after our afternoon at Bertha. Stupid. I was so fucking stupid. *Again.*

When I first saw her sitting there, I couldn't believe my eyes. I was sure it was her, though—laughing, giggling, reaching across the table to touch his arm. All I could register were the surges of white-hot flashes barreling through my veins, the sound of blood pumping ferociously in my ears, the sickening punch to my guts.

Without thinking, I moved past the glass of the storefront and entered the busy midday crowd of the pizzeria, praying it wasn't what it looked like. After everything I had given her, all the time I had waited, could she really do this to me?

All I knew when it came to her was that she was mine—even if she wasn't. And in a move that may have admittedly been a bit dickish, I interrupted their meal with the slip of my arm around her neck. But Angel's shoulders tensed. Her reaction to my touch should never be one of discomfort, and the fact that it was served as a slap in the face.

The look on the fucker's face was enough to make me want to lunge across the table at him. I didn't know who he thought he was talking to, acting like *he* was going to protect her from *me.* She had obviously never told him who I was, which served as a second slap.

When we all wound up on our feet, the look in Angel's eyes was one of part fright, part discomfort. I hadn't wanted to upset her, but what the fuck was this? All this time I'd thought once she healed, we'd be back together. Or even if we weren't, I didn't think she'd run into the next set of open arms.

She rushed to assure me he was just a friend, but the possessive look in this guy's eyes begged to differ. He had something for her, I could feel it.

I bit the inside of my cheek, forcing myself to be courteous enough to let her explain why, when all I wanted to do was tear through that place. When she turned to me, the apprehension on her face scared the piss out of me. And when she crossed her arms over her chest, I realized her concern was for him, not me.

Slap number three.

Then came the full-out punch. She had confided in him. She felt comfortable enough with this *stranger* to tell him what had happened to her when *I* still didn't know the whole truth.

How could she?

I was supposed to be her rock, the place where she was comfortable enough to just be her. And now it seemed like everything I'd thought we had was a fucking lie. A game. And the joke was on me. How many times could I let this girl trash me before I learned my lesson? Took her fucking hint instead of dangling from her measly little string. If I let it keep going, she was going to leave me in a pile of dust.

So I left.

The realization that we were really done slammed into me like a bag of rocks, and I didn't want her to see me break. When I left her standing there, I didn't know where I should go. Every turn always seemed to lead back to her. I'd never felt so lost.

"She loves you, ya know."

That voice stopped me.

Who the fuck was *he* to tell *me* how she was feeling? Had we really grown that far apart? "What are you, some kind of authority?" I couldn't hide the venom in my voice. I had controlled myself once, but this guy should know better than to approach me again.

"Something like that." The assuredness in his tone, talking about *my* girl, made me want to break his jaw.

With clenched fists, I turned to face him. My whole body was rigid and erect, each molecule ready to pounce if needed. As defeated as I felt, prodding me would be like antagonizing a rabid dog. My emotions were so all over the place that I didn't even recognize myself anymore, she had me so ragged. And I didn't know what to expect from myself at the moment. "Watch it, man. I've had just about as much as I can take where she's concerned. I'd tread lightly if I were you."

He studied me, seeming to size me up, sending a bunch of discomfort racing up my spine.

What's this guy's story?

Rolling up from the squat he was holding against the building, he brushed off the front of his thighs before walking toward me. "You can relax, man. I'm not after your girl."

Tiny pebbles began to flake from my stoned exterior, that small feeling of relief nearly bringing me to my knees. I hadn't realized how wound I was, but I knew I was one more encounter closer to an inevitable heart attack.

"So what was that whole show in there?" I jerked my chin toward the pizzeria.

Drew sighed, releasing a big puff of air. "Listen, I'd be lying if I said there wasn't a time I hadn't hoped to be with her, but it's not our fate. She's wrapped up in you." He threw a hand toward me, then paused, letting me soak that in. "And we've become good friends. All I want is for her to be happy. I really mean that." He clapped me on the shoulder and held his other hand out to me.

I stared down at it, unsure of what to do. My mind raced through all of the emotional beatings I'd had to endure at this girl's hand.

His voice lost its edge. "I mean it, dude. Far be it from me to stand in the way of what she wants. I can tell you love her as much as she loves you. I just want to protect her. We're on the same side."

I dragged my line of sight from his hand to his eyes to see if I saw any deceit there, but I didn't. Even if he *did* have feelings for her, I could tell that him wanting what was best for her trumped them. He pushed his hand toward me, and I clasped mine with his. We both cinched tight, squeezing just a pinch more than necessary as silent threats passed between us. I hardened my voice to match the fire in my eyes.

"Don't make me regret this."

I DIDN'T GO AFTER HIM when he left me standing there. I wouldn't know what to say. On the one hand, I was upset that I'd had to defend myself when I hadn't done anything wrong. But on the other hand, I got it. The hurt in his eyes and knowing I had caused it felt like my body was covered with tiny paper cuts and doused with vinegar.

I unlocked the door to my apartment and tossed my keys into the fishbowl by the door. Once I was hidden away inside, I fisted my hips and looked down, trying to gather my thoughts. I'd spent these last few months trying to get my life back—my identity, my strength. I hoped, in the process, I hadn't lost another piece of myself, of my heart. How could I let him walk away while under the impression he'd meant anything less than everything to me? My Blake?

I filled a glass of water and opened the door to the balcony, allowing new air to filter in. It smelled like spring. My gaze dropped to the box of dirt that I'd continued to water in the hopes it would show signs of new life, and something caught my eye as the last drop splashed off the contents. Something green and new.

The sting of me falling to my knees was nothing compared to the squeezing burn in my heart.

Forget not in life there are do-overs.

Second chances.

I covered my face and curled forward, rocking. "Oh, Blake."

What have I done?

I rubbed my finger along the engraving in the front of the box—*To plant a garden is to believe in tomorrow.*

Did I believe? I felt strong. Like I'd been revived physically, mentally. But something was still lacking. My heart. I was doing it all without my heart. How could it ever truly work without that?

It couldn't.

I'd been a fool wasting time, waiting to feel ready when I would never feel one hundred percent without that last ingredient.

Idiot.

Examining the direction of the sun, I tilted the box so it could drink in as much life as possible. Then I laid on my belly like a child and put my chin in my hands, staring at it as though I'd be able to witness it grow. I swiped the back of my hand across my nose, my tears a constant stream, in awe of the symbolism that one flower and I shared.

It was as though it had died with me and it was letting me know it was okay to grow now, to move on and take my second chance at life. Except my sun was gone. My light. There'd be no way for me to grow without it. No way to live.

Live me.

I did.

I do.

I will.

My knees scraped along the concrete as I pulled them in, but I was numb to it. I checked to be sure the flower was placed correctly one more time, and then an enormous tear-filled smile split my face. "Thank you," I spoke in a hushed whisper.

I kissed my pointer finger and pressed it to the box, a new awareness consuming me. It started in my heart and ballooned outward, shooting to my belly and through my limbs, sparking and crackling each cell, sending tingling prickles along my flesh.

It was time to live.

I CAUGHT SIGHT OF HIS eccentric hairdo, coiffed to perfection, bee-boppin' down the pavement. Without thinking, I barreled toward him. "Why didn't you tell me about him?"

Jace turned with a start, his hand flying to his chest before taking inventory of his attacker. "Calm down there, tough stuff. Tell you about who?" he clucked.

I narrowed my eyes. "Don't play the innocent card with me. We both know you're anything but."

Collecting himself, Jace crossed his arms and straightened his spine. "Talk or I'm walking. I have an eyebrow appointment, and Ankie waits for no one."

I was losing my patience with this whole situation. "Jace, for once be serious," I huffed.

He looked down at his watch, tapping his foot.

"You know what, man?" I raised both palms. "I thought we were in this together. Maybe I was as wrong about you as I was about her." Jace and I had formed a powerful alliance after Eva's visit to the hospital, and I didn't think he would keep something as big as a new guy in her life from me. We had been conspiring, and he had kept me informed of each step of her recovery ever since I found her a doctor.

I turned to walk away, but Jace's don't-go-there-honey tone called back to me. "Never doubt me, sugar."

My morbid curiosity stopped me. I turned to face him. "I'm

listening."

He sauntered toward me. "You're speaking of Drew, I assume? The insanely good-looking boy who has his hands all over her sweaty body every day?" He raised a brow.

"Watch it, Jace," I warned. "We've already been down this road once, and I promised you I'd never lay a finger on you again, but I don't like the path you're taking through Jaceland. Just spit it out already. Don't toy with me, dude."

"Fair enough. Just use that beautiful little head of yours to think for a minute." He hesitated, before pointing upward. "I feel I should clarify. I meant *that* head, honey. Even though I'm sure the other is just as beautiful." He licked his lips.

I felt my cheeks get hot. *Did I just blush?* "Get to it," I demanded.

Jace's lip curled in disgust as though he had tasted something bad. "Ugh, I can't stand you these days. You're no fun at all." He waved a dismissing hand. "Besides you—and me, of course, Drew is the best thing that's ever happened to Eva."

That comment made my skin crawl.

"If you love her as much as you say you do, you'll let it be and support it. I didn't tell you because . . ." He zigzagged a well-manicured finger in the vicinity of my body. "All this jazz." He rolled his eyes. "I knew you would try and stop it and she needed it—*needs* it," he corrected. "As much as I adore you, sugar, she's my number one concern. Always will be."

Though I appreciated how faithful a friend he was to her, the stab he delivered almost reached my marrow. I narrowed my eyes. "How could you ever think I don't have her best interests at heart?"

"Because yours is broken." Jace raised a brow while that festered. "Look, it's not that I doubt your love for her, but, again." He zigzagged his finger in the same pattern.

I raked an unsteady hand through my hair. "I'm trying to figure out when *I* became the bad guy in all this."

Jace sighed and looped his arm through mine. "You aren't the bad guy, honey. You're the knight in shining armor. But you're too hurt to see past the armor, and she's still locked in her tower. Wait till she's ready to throw down her hair. She'll come to you."

I wasn't sure why it didn't feel odd to be walking arm-in-arm with Jace. "You just don't get it." I shook my head with a sarcastic chuckle, pulling us to a stop. "I've done *everything* I can, yet there she is with some other guy—telling him everything." I swung out a frustrated hand. "And I'm supposed to just wait until she comes to me?" My fingers banged off my chest with a knock.

Jace nodded, a curt little *bip* as if it was as simple as that, but it wasn't. None of this was simple, and it was time that I stopped pretending. "I know you want me to understand, and maybe I'm an asshole for not, but I think . . ." I sighed, dropping my head with the exhaustion that I felt. "I think I might be done, Jace."

Jace's tone sharpened with his shoulders. "Nonsense. Don't sling crap at me. You'll never be done with her." He tried to pull me forward once again, but my feet were unforgiving as realization set in, my stomach sinking with the letdown of my heart.

"I'm serious." My eyebrows pinched in, the truth of all this bringing the larger picture into focus. Even though I told her at Bertha that I would do anything, give her the time she still needed, I didn't think I could handle any more. "This kills too damn bad. The phrase 'love hurts' never met Angel. She runs through me, and it feels like acid these days. It's debilitating."

Jace smoothed a hand over my bicep, his voice pleading for the girl that he loved. "Don't give up on her. She'll come around. I know she will."

"Come around?" My voice raised, incredulously. "Is that what I'm waiting for?"

"It's not like that," Jace huffed, and I could tell he was struggling to find the words to make this right. But he couldn't. Not anymore.

"Save it, Jace. For once." Fatigue laid heavy in my words, them giving up with me as I stuffed my hand into my jeans pocket, and drifted to walk away.

"She needs him." Authority rang in his tone, his perfunctory statement protective of his friend.

My eyes cut to his, my own defenses kicking in. "And I needed her," I spat, truth swollen in those words. My mouth closed around them quickly, ashamed at the admission, but it was confessed just the same.

I clasped my hands behind my head and pushed out a breath. Love should be more than *coming around*. It should be something that your soul can't live without, depriving yourself of it unquestionable. "Honestly, I'm frustrated as hell, and I might just be ready to finally jump off her hot-and-cold merry-go-round. I tried, I *really* did, but I can't keep track of it anymore. She wants me one minute and then pushes me away the next, and yet she confides in another man? It's a slap in the face, and you fucking know it."

Jace's curt expression didn't look pleased, but he didn't refute.

"This isn't just about him. It's about us. What's it say if she can go to some stranger before me? Not much."

"Pull your shit together. Drew is helping her, that's all, and that's why she had to tell him. She loves you, you know that. She just has to figure out that she loves *her*, too."

I considered his words. I knew she had a lot of self-loathing to work through, but I also knew that if she loved me even an ounce as much as I loved her, she would never be able to put me through the wringer like this. "This isn't love, man. She's destroying me."

I shoved my hands into my pockets and walked away, not sure of anything anymore.

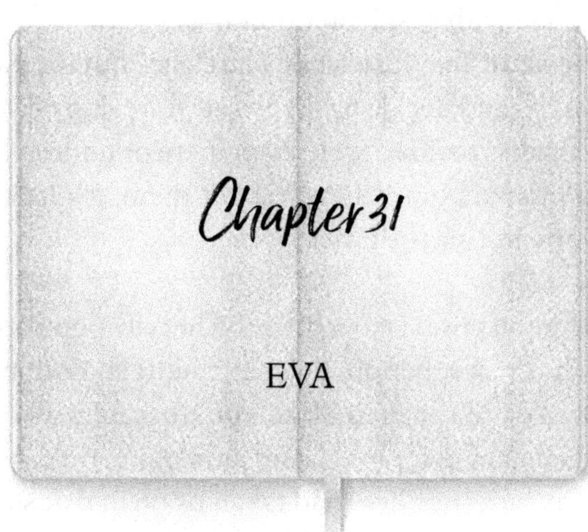

Chapter 31

EVA

Breathe him in on an inhale.
Exhale out the sorrow.
Breathe in change—
Liberation
Air
Healing
Blake
Exhale out me—
Seclusion
Suffocation
Pain
Damon

I NEED TO FIND HIM.

Tell him.

Reassure him.

Make him realize . . .

Make him realize.

I needed to get him back. Help him understand that this was all done for us. Every move I had made since the moment I walked away from him was done with good intentions.

There's a sense of freedom when you figure out the path you're supposed to take in life and decide to act it out. A freeing of your own inner chains that you hadn't realized were even there or noticed how they were constricting your air supply. When you cut them, it's like everything releases at once, and the air rushes in.

That's how I felt.

Moving with purpose, I navigated the heavily populated city blocks, anxious to reach my destination, determined to let nothing and nobody stand in my way. I'd only been to Blake's photography school once before when I'd bought and paid for his classes as his Christmas gift. Hard to believe the different paths our lives had taken us on in that short amount of time. At this moment, I was grateful to be a pack rat that never deleted the email confirmation for the time of his class. If I hurried, I'd make it in time for his dismissal.

The building was in sight, but I was nervous I'd missed him. Moving through Manhattan was never an easy task, and he'd been done with class at least five minutes already.

I wiped the sweat from my brow with the back of my wrist and marched toward the door. I was about to put my foot on the first step when a low, familiar laugh trickled into my ears. It was a sound I'd never forget. The fact that it was mingled with another higher pitched giggle made my belly clench. I sucked in a breath before turning to face him—and the object of his amusement.

Blake was bent on one knee, his camera propped between his hands, looking through the lens—at her. A soft breeze blew an unruly piece of hair across his forehead, drawing my attention there and then lower to the smile on his face. The one he was directing at *her*. Her leg was wrapped around the trunk of a tree, and she was dipped back, playfully, the tips of her blonde hair nearly touching the ground. She looked fun and carefree. Burdenless. It reminded me of the type of girl Blake ought to be with. The kind of relationship he was meant to have.

The overwhelming need to run bubbled up my neck. Paralyzed, I almost succumbed and turned on my heel, but I couldn't. I wouldn't let myself. This time, rather than be intimidated by the fact that Blake deserved something much better than me, *I* wanted to be the girl he deserved. Give him the type of relationship I couldn't before. I had come here to do something, and if it killed me, I was still going to do it. If he pushed me away, at least I'd know I tried.

Giggles must have caught sight of the weird girl eye-balling them because her smile faded and she lowered her leg. When I still didn't move, she nodded in my direction. Blake, never one to miss a moment, snapped one more photo before lowering the camera.

When Blake's eyes met mine, the carefree smile melted from his face, replacing it with a hard-set jaw. His eyes, which had been dancing with enjoyment, now seemed to ice over as he pushed off his knee. She met him at his side, and again I felt the ache of seeing them so comfortable next to one another.

Seeing he wasn't budging, I took a few steps forward. "Sorry to interrupt. I came to talk to you, but I didn't realize you might be . . . preoccupied." My eyes flickered to the girl at his side.

She straightened her spine. "I'll leave you two—"

"No, it's fine," Blake cut her off. The ice in his tone froze me to the bone. "Marybeth, this is Eva. Eva, this is Marybeth. She's just a *friend.*"

Pot meet kettle.

He was proving his point, but I'd never thought he'd hurt me to do it. I deserved it, though, I supposed, knowing he had probably felt the same way seeing me with Drew as I do now. Or worse.

"Nice to meet you." I nodded in her direction.

"Likewise." She fidgeted with her fingers and rubbed her palms together as though she were trying to disperse the sweat that lined them. "So, um, I'm gonna get going."

Blake turned to her. "You sure?"

"Yeah, I've got this killer migraine." She pushed the tips of her dainty fingers into her temples. Dropping her hands, she waved one in a semi-circle in my direction. "Nice to finally meet you, Eva."

"Same to you." Our eyes met briefly, but I dragged my gaze away, tucking my hair behind my ear. It hurt too bad to look at the girl who'd been keeping him company all these weeks we'd been apart.

When I looked up again, Blake was studying me, and the ice I had seen moments before seemed to be thawed by a fire. One that was burning a hole through me. I could see everything he wanted to say whipping through his head, and I was scared of what would fly out first. He clenched and unclenched his fists, his legs parted and rigid. I'd never seen him so uninviting.

"What do you want?"

Talk about to the point.

"I wanted to apologize for how I reacted when you met Drew. I would've told you about him sooner, but I didn't have the chance. We're so weird these days." I pulled my hair over my shoulder and picked at the ends. I was waiting for him to relax a bit, but he never let up. "She's pretty."

He crossed his arms in front of his chest. "Is that all you want?"

"Don't act this way, Blake. I said I was sorry." I stepped forward. "I miss you," I whispered, lowering my gaze.

"What? I didn't hear you."

I looked up, sure that he'd heard me the first time. "I said I miss you."

"So today you miss me? I'm sorry, but I'm not in the mood to play the hot-cold game with you."

His brash tone took me back, but I couldn't let that stop me. I understood the pain I'd caused him, and his reaction was only fair, but it didn't make it hurt any less. Didn't he know how hard all this was for me? No, he didn't. How wrong of me to shut him out, no matter what the reason. All this time, he had just wanted to be a team.

The light inside his eyes was gone now, the spark that made him Blake. That was such a special spark, and I prayed he could get it back. Though the way he looked at me now almost seemed to border hatred, and I wasn't sure he'd ever allow me the chance to make it right.

Forget not . . . Me. Blake's last forget-me-not. *I could never.*

When we had finally gotten together, my heart had felt whole for the first time, as though it'd found its other half. Now, as I looked into barren eyes, I felt it crack in two. How had I allowed us to drift so far apart?

I took another step forward, ignoring the ice in his eyes, determined to make him feel something. "Your flowers started to grow. The dirt pot . . . you were right."

He flexed his jaw, looking as though he wanted to soften up, but wouldn't allow himself to. I was all too familiar with that feeling. It was called being guarded, and up until this point, it was how I'd had always lived my life. I guess Blake had gates now, too.

I broke him.

When he didn't reply, I kept going. "I miss you."

"What do you want, Eva?"

"Eva, huh?" I couldn't mask the hurt in my voice.

Blake sighed, and his head dropped forward as he pinched the bridge of his nose. "Angel, please."

I could tell how hard it was for him to keep up this tough-guy act. It wasn't him. I wanted him to know it was okay to drop his guard. That I wouldn't hurt him anymore. I took another step forward, leaving only a bit of space between us and decided to just let my heart speak for once.

"I miss you so much my skin aches."

He looked up.

"When I imagine a life without you, it feels like I'm suffocating. These past few months have felt like I've been walking around with missing pieces. Nothing makes sense." My voice cracked, displaying my vulnerability. I wasn't sure how to verbalize all of the thoughts running through my mind, and I was certain, from the fact that he still hadn't softened up, that it was coming out all wrong. I didn't know how to make him see.

"I know I hurt you."

Blake's posture and features were so rigid and uninviting, but the lines of exhaustion were evident on his face. "I'm still not hearing what you want, and I'm done trying to interpret your riddles. You can't keep coming around saying you miss me and then running away the first chance you get only to come back around again. Save your charms for someone else."

I recoiled from the harsh lashing. I knew he was testing the devotion in what I was saying—trying to gauge if this was just another swing of the Eva pendulum. But it wasn't. I was at a standstill. Time had stopped, and the only direction it pointed in was Blake.

"Blake . . ."

The tension in his shoulders melted a little, giving away that this, too, was a facade. I was so sick of the games. All I wanted was some real.

If he was softening, even a little, I knew I had a limited amount of time to sneak myself inside. His pain was torturing me. I could feel it barreling around inside of me. It was venomous and foul. He'd been carting it around for months. No wonder he looked so distraught.

Tears welled in my eyes, knowing I'd been the cause of so much misery. "I love you." My voice splintered with emotion. "I love you so much, Blake." I rushed the rest out, not sure if he'd give me the chance to finish, but needing for him to know. "I didn't say it when you asked because I wasn't sure it was what you needed to hear, but I do. I always have and I always will."

"Angel, don't." The plea in his eyes sliced through my center, the hurt in his voice, unmasked. He finally took a step forward. "Don't do this to me again. Please. If you ever loved me, just let me be. Every time you come around with your false fucking hopes, you smash something else inside of me. Are you going to keep swinging until there's nothing left?"

I pushed a palm into my chest. "That's not what I ever wanted to do. Please, you have to believe me. All I've ever wanted to do was protect you. To keep you away from all of my hurt."

Blake scoffed, seeming to sarcastically laugh at some fleeting thought. Then he turned his determined eyes to me and took another step forward. "What do you want?"

"I want this to be all better. I want you to be okay. For the spark that made you *you* to be back." I skirted around the point as much as possible.

With another step, Blake was nearly nose to nose with me, and the feeling of it flooded my bloodstream in a tidal wave. The smell of his soap and his cologne. My eyes drifted to the swell of his bottom lip and my mouth watered, remembering the taste of it. I sucked in a breath as the sensations crashed into me all at once, making it hard to breathe.

"What do you want? Say what you want!" he yelled in my face with such force, the energy in his breath swooped over my skin, taking with it the last of my resolve and breaking what little resistance I had left.

"I want you!" Tension swelled, boiling over as it poured from my lips.

Blake retracted a little, his eyes dancing around from mine to my lips to my stance, as though he were trying to figure out if there was sincerity in my words.

In a tinier voice, I repeated, "I. Want. You."

In a split second, I watched Blake's walls shatter and explode. He wrapped his arm around my waist and pulled me into him as our lips came crashing into one another. Feet suspended from the ground, I cupped his face in my hands and attacked his mouth, dragging as much of him into my system as I could. Panting and pawing, my back suddenly slammed against the tree, his hand coming up to tangle in my hair.

My heart swelled, coming back to life with each of his breaths that I dragged into my lungs. This was my home. My life.

All of my holes began to fill in, my cracks began to mortar. How I'd gone on for so long without him was a mystery to me. At this moment, I'd never felt so alive, so free and so fulfilled.

Blake broke the kiss, his lips swollen and panting. "I can't do this." He released me, setting me on shaky feet as he backed away. Something punched me in the heart and my eyebrows knitted together. The look of mortification on his face was the last thing I had expected to see as he slowly backed away from me.

No.

"Blake?"

"I can't do this, Eva. Not again. It hurts too damn much every time I have to let you go, and I don't trust that you'll stay. Not yet."

A few more steps backward.

No. No. No.

"What are you saying?" I squeaked. "Why did you . . . why did you insist on knowing what I wanted? Why did you kiss me like it was what you wanted, too?" I touched three fingers to my lips, which still tingled with the burn of his passion.

Blake shrugged, a twitch of cockiness at the corner of his lip. "I told you once before, I'll take what I can get." He was acting aloof, but I knew him too well. The slice between his eyebrows betrayed his nonchalant shrug.

I forged ahead, determined to make him see how serious I was this time. "But, you can have *me*! I don't want to be apart anymore. It's torture."

He shook his head, disbelieving as his gaze withdrew. "Until the next time." The more disconnected he became, the more my heart whipped with panic in tandem.

"There won't be a next time," I promised. "You have to trust me. I won't hurt you."

"I've been burned by believing you before, Angel. I just . . . I just need time." An exhausted sigh floated between his lips as his posture wilted. "I thought I could do it. Thought I could wait and bear whatever you dished out, believe there could be an us, but it's just too much. I'm not strong enough to survive another round in the ring with you." His breathing slowed, and he swallowed hard. "I'm sorry."

"This isn't a battle!" my voice squeaked.

He stilled, a look of remorse washing over his face. "You're right." His eyes met mine—washed in solace, bathed in regret. "I surrender." Then they slid closed for a brief soul-crushing second.

I gasped, my legs barely holding me upright as I clutched around my middle with one arm and sobbed into my palm with the other.

No.

Then he handed me my heart, shoved his hands in his pockets, and turned, leaving me here feeling broken open and bleeding.

Chapter 32

EVA

PAIN.

Broken.

Confused.

Alone.

Guilty.

There wasn't a word for what I felt.

What just happened?

So many emotions swirled through the pit of my stomach, taking turns punching me in the gut. I had known Blake was hurting, but I hadn't understood how much until that point. So much had changed since our moment at Bertha. An unspoken wall of distrust stood immovable between us.

I hung my head. I'd never intended to become the enemy. If time was what he wanted, time was what I'd give him. It was the least I could do, but I wouldn't let up. He was going to know that I wasn't going anywhere. If I had to deliver my heart on a silver platter, I'd hand it over to him. As much as this hurt, I wouldn't let it break me.

That fact was an eye-opener.

It proved how much stronger I was now. I was a survivor. But I was also hurting. And so was he. Together we could be each other's salve. I just didn't know how to convince him of that. Funny how the tables had turned. Blake had spent months trying to persuade me of the same thing last semester.

I drifted through the streets on my journey home, feeling lost and uncertain. Without stopping, I kept walking to the back of my apartment in the same dream-state, depositing my bag and jean jacket as I went.

Am I supposed to prove my love or let my love be?

Something called to me, pulling me forward, but I was unsure what it was as I dropped to my bed and put my head in my hands. My hair fell around my shoulders in a blanket while my mind and my subconscious warred. The most ironic part of all of this was that I was finally becoming the woman Blake deserved. I was put together better than I had ever been, which was what I had been holding out for, and now that it was here, he wouldn't have me. My subconscious scoffed at me.

I pushed play on the dock beside my bed, hoping for a sign. Sliding my back down the side of the mattress, I landed on my behind with a thump as Christina Perri's, *Distance* began. Her words were bittersweet as she spoke of a love not returned. Unheard I love you's as she kept her distance. But the distance was kept to protect him.

How did we get here? After all that we had. Because in my quest to get better, I lost sight of what we had. Of our love and our connection that was stronger than anything. Of the Blake and Angel.

Of the Blake and Angel.

I gripped my shirt in a clump over my chest, the weight of it feeling like a heavy blanket as she sang of her trouble breathing. The realization that I may have pushed him away for the last time was too much to bear. I pictured Blake beside me, knowing I'd already given him all of my broken heartbeats, wondering why I waited so long in the first place.

Recalling a day from months ago, when I'd stood in this room a very broken girl, I lowered my head to peer under my bed. There lay the journal Blake had given me, which I'd tossed aside in my desperation to rid myself of any reminders of him.

Sprawled on my belly, I stretched my arm until I could reach the place where it had been discarded. Feeling the supple leather in my hand again brought with it a wave of emotion as I remembered the day he had given it to me, and the love that had radiated from his eyes. That day I was sure we would last forever. I never would have thought that I was days away from losing him.

A tear splattered onto the leather as I swiped my forearm along my cheek and peeled the book open, each memory coming at me like a slap in the face. All of the pictures he had put there, the notes he'd left me on the trails he'd set out for our first date, the page which held my necklace. I fingered my bare neckline and pulled the book to my chest, crumbling at the reminder that I'd broken that gift and tossed it aside, along with him.

How did I let this happen?

My heart broke around that book. The book that was intended to be the *happy* one. The one meant to be kept separate from the original, which held only heartache. I squeezed it to me, allowing it to absorb some of the pain bleeding from me.

Then, frantic, I pulled it away, not wanting it to be tainted by any of my negative energy. I left the room in as much of a dream-state as I'd entered it, my eyes a bit more sore on the way out. I placed the journal on the floor where I could see it, then secured my hair in a ponytail, and jabbed my finger into the play button. My workout playlist came on with a blast through the speakers surrounding my gym nook, and I jumped with a start. Grabbing my chest, I dialed it back a drop. The blood pumping in my veins was the wakeup call I needed to snap me back to reality.

Standing, I stared at myself in the mirror. My shoulders appeared squarer lately, though at the moment they were drooping around the edges. My legs were tighter, defined around my calves and thighs. Arms that used to be slightly boney now wore a bump around the bicep and lines defining muscles twining to my wrists. Physically I was strong, tight, unbreakable.

I stared into the green depths of my eyes as though I could show myself inside. Though heartbroken, a confidence showed through my irises that had once been so hollow, so guarded. That was the biggest difference. There was a sense of freedom that showed there. Along the way, I'd begun to let go of the past, and the weight of it was missing there, the gates that never invited anyone in were almost gone.

I ground my fist into my chest, the callouses on my palms making themselves known on my fingertips. I was still missing one more piece. A solid body, a strong mind . . .

And a broken heart.

The other two could never operate at full capacity without the latter.

I scooped up my free weights and curled up, repeating countless repetitions as I mulled over all of these thoughts. Over and over again, I had begged Blake for more time, and each time he'd given it to me. How could I not give him the same courtesy?

Because you're scared the time has passed and he won't be back.

I threw the dumbbells down and grabbed my gloves, needing to pound on something. The speed bag would bear the brunt of the torture I felt in my heart. My mind kept reeling through the *barra-ta-ta, barra-ta-ta,* of the bag as it jolted from each whack of my fist. My playlist switched to *Fight Song,* by Rachel Platten, the slow piano not really matching the strength in my strides. I punched one final blow with the side of my fist before discarding the gloves and dropping to the mat.

Crunch after crunch, my abs burned each time I would rise up and punch the air.

One—Two.

My fight song.

I was a fighter now.

Crunch. *One—Two—Three—Four.*

Can you hear my voice . . .

My lip curled over my teeth, sweat dropping through them as I pushed harder.

One—Two.

Take back my life . . .

I popped to my feet and threw punches toward the mirror, watching my form as I danced around with myself, shadow boxing.

She sang about not caring if nobody else believed, and it hit me how done I was. I was done caring, too. The truth was the truth, and I needed to be rid of it to feel clean again.

I returned to the floor to do burpees, while the song picked up the pace. Each drop brought me eye-level with Blake's journal. So close my nose was practically touching it.

My fight song.

Hop up. Down.

Take back my life.

Journal.

Forget not . . . you're a strong and incredible person.

Another of his forget me nots. I *was* strong now.

I was a fighter, the burn in my veins reminded me. So why not fight for the thing that mattered most—the war of my heart. A sweat-soaked grin split my face as I lowered to the floor on my last rep. With my weight on my wrists, I leaned forward on my toes and placed a kiss on the top of the journal before bouncing back to my feet.

Game on.

Chapter 33

BLAKE

I AWOKE WITH A START.

Bang. Bang. Bang.

"What the . . ." My gaze fell to the clock on my bedside table. Apparently, I'd slept in because it was already ten a.m., but it was still too early for anyone to be visiting.

I dragged myself from the bed and pushed my palms into my eyes, shuffling down the hall. When I reached the door, the burn of my morning wood stopped me. I looked down to the pajama bottoms hanging off my waist as the obvious arrow beneath it pointed toward the door. "Just a second." I palmed it, trying to get it to tame itself before I scared whoever was on the other side. Figuring half-mast would have to do, given the fact I was commando under those pants, I peeled back the door, hoping whoever it was would keep their sights on the upper portion of my body.

Warm, chocolate eyes peeking out of worn, tanned skin greeted me. They were familiar. I tried to place them as the smell of fresh coffee and bacon entered my system. Still half asleep, I racked my brain, scratching the back of my bed-head, knowing I was missing something.

"Señor." The crinkle in his eyes gave him away, instantly shriveling my semi. How could I forget that face? He'd been so excited to deliver food to Angel the morning of our date. He had spoken broken English, but love was a universal language, and I could tell he was a romantic.

Nausea encroached as I stared at that brown paper bag. For the past couple of days, I had been trying to bring myself to terms that things were done between Angel and me, and I knew whatever was inside that bag was about to fuck that all to shit.

Chapter 34

EVA

"WHAT DID YOU DO?" JACE slid his coffee cup to the center of the table and leaned forward on his forearms.

"Nothing." I shrugged nonchalantly, taking a sip of my drink, but I was sure the smirk I couldn't contain was giving me away.

"Eva . . ." Jace's voice raised slightly as he dragged out the end of my name, clearly knowing I was lying my ass off. "You forget I know that pretty little head just as well as my own. Whatever it is, it's juicy, too. I can taste it." He smacked his lips together and crossed one leg over the other, leaning forward to rest his chin in his palm. "Spill it or I'll—"

"Hey, guys," Jessie's sweet voice cut over Jace's. She seemed oblivious that we were in mid-convo as her mega-watt smile greeted us. She slid into the chair beside Jace, whose face pinched together as though he smelled something rancid.

"Oh, no, honey. What is all that?" He circled his fingers around Jessie's head.

"All what?" She palmed the side of her hair, self-conscious.

"Being it's still early, I'm going to pray for your sake that it's I-was-fucked-all-night-hair." He paused, leaning back to allow his gaze to rove over her. "And well." He winked. "But that's still no excuse for leaving the house like that. And sharing a table with *me,* no less. Get your ass over here and let me work some magic or I'm afraid you'll have to vacate the premises."

I giggled as Jessie hissed through clenched teeth. "Jace. You're embarrassing me."

Jace palmed his chest. "I'm embarrassing you? Honey, if that nest on your head isn't embarrassing you, nothing will. Now, come on, scoot." He swished his hands at her. She rolled her eyes but grabbed the edges of her chair and scooted it toward him.

Jace dug in, ripping and separating and twisting. "I mean, honestly," he said under his breath. Then he turned his attention back to me. "Don't think I've forgotten about you, miss. You're not off the hook. Spill. Apparently, I've got time." He scowled at the back of Jessie's head.

"Ouch!" She winced. "Be careful."

"Take your punishment, bitch. Next time you'll think twice before coming out in public looking like a hot mess." Without switching his focus, Jace stopped just long enough to point at me. "Talk."

I sat back and crossed my legs, studying my nails. "I've just decided to fight, that's all."

Jace waved his hand in a circle. "More specific, darling. You've been fighting for weeks. You already look like She-Ra." He placed his fingers back inside Jessie's curls.

"Not that kind of fight. And excuse me, but She-Ra was hot." I crossed my legs with a smirk.

"I much prefer He-Man. And his *sword*. By the power of Grayskull." Lifting a leg, he accentuated each word with fire-rolling thrusts of his hips.

I snorted. "I forget how quick you are."

"Hey, I resent that. I am *so* not quick."

"Sorry. You come *back* quick. Better?"

"Thank you." Jace's eyebrows rose with an innocent modesty. "But I'm sure there's another pun in there somewhere. I *do* have a rep to protect, ya know. Now stop distracting me. I've had five shots of espresso already. I'm wired as fuck."

"I can tell." Jessie winced again.

"Hush it." He pulled her hair and spoke around her head. "Anyway, I'm on my game, so stop beating around the bush. We all know you don't have one."

Jessie was mid-sip and spit her water out in a spraying-splash.

"Jace!" My eyes nearly popped out of my head.

"The longer you wait, the more I say. I live for this shit. I can go all day. And night." He fingered the corner of his mouth with his ring finger and crossed his legs in the opposite direction. "There. You're done." He spun away from Jessie, who was pulling out a pocket mirror, and turned his full attention to me.

"So this fight . . . Who are we fighting? Is it a pussy—" He cleared his throat. "I mean, a cat-fight? Do I need Vaseline?"

I sobered. "I'm fighting for him, Jace."

A spark flared in Jace's honey-colored eyes. He tried to cover it up, but it was too late. I'd already seen it. "Fighting for who, honey? Drew? That boy's always looking to fi—"

"For Blake. I'm fighting for Blake. I'm gonna do whatever it takes to prove I'm worthy of him."

Sparks danced around in Jace's eyes as he leaned forward. "Come again?"

"I said I'm fighting for Bla—"

"I heard that part," he interrupted. "I want you to repeat the part that came after that."

I repeated the words quietly as their meaning and the fact that I had said them so effortlessly floated together. "I said I'm going to do what it takes to prove to him that I'm worthy of him."

"That." Jace pointed. "That last part. Tell me those last four little words again." He leaned in closer, cupping his ear.

"I'm worthy of him." The strength of my voice grew.

Jace sucked in a sharp breath, but composed himself quickly, his hand still on his ear. "I'm sorry. I think I misheard you. What was that again?" he challenged.

Until that point, I don't think I'd realized that I even felt that way. I was so used to looking at myself with filth that I hadn't noticed the change until it flew out of my mouth.

Do I honestly believe that?

I thought I did. The awareness of that made my scalp prickle. I wasn't sure I would ever be one hundred percent, but I knew I could be what he needed me to be. That I could show him more love and devotion than anyone else in this world.

"It's hitting you, isn't it?"

My thoughts were halted by Jace's voice, and I focused my eyes back on him.

"Uh-huh." Jace relaxed back in his chair and brought his hands together in a slow-clap before raising his palms to the sky. "A-men, praise Jesus, hallelujah. I never thought this day would come."

"Me either," I replied, half to myself and half to him.

"This calls for a celebration." Jace stood, glancing around. "Where's the alcohol when you need it?"

"Jace, it's ten-thirty a.m."

He waved a dismissive hand. "You know my theory about that."

"It's five o'clock somewhere," I mumbled, rolling my eyes.

"Yazzz, sugar. Now let's go." He tugged at my arm.

Jessie clicked her pocket-mirror closed then looked back and forth between us, tucking it into her bag. "You guys are really going drinking right now?"

Jace and I stated in unison.

"Yes."

"No."

He peaked an eyebrow. "Don't challenge me. What's the problem?"

"I can't go anywhere today. I have plans."

Jace flung an eyebrow at me. "What could be more important than the biggest breakthrough of your life?"

I sucked my lower lip between my teeth and looked up at him through lowered lashes, finally realizing with certainty since the moment we met he had always been the most important thing in my life.

"Winning him back."

I STARED BLANKLY AT THE smile pinned to the delivery man's face. It felt like I'd been kicked in the balls as a slow ache crept into my lower abdomen. I didn't know how much more my heart could handle, what I could trust.

"Señor?" The man's eyebrows rose in a question as he nudged the brown paper bag tucked inside a plastic bag toward me.

Knowing damn well I would never *truly* deny anything she was offering, I nodded and took a deep breath, readying my heart for its next jolt.

The man seemed to study my movements as I took the package by the plastic handles and deposited it on the side table before turning to him. He clutched an envelope between both hands, close to his chest. Suddenly his demeanor changed, and he seemed unsure of whether or not he wanted to pass it along to me as he swayed from foot to foot.

I held my hand out to him, knowing that I needed that little piece of her to get me through the day. It was what I'd been surviving on these last few months. The little bits of Angel that I'd collected along the way. "For me?"

"Sí." He smiled before slipping the hard paper into my hand. His eyes found mine, and they told a story about an overlooked wisdom. "She very beautiful, your girl."

A knot took shape in my gut. I swallowed and extracted the envelope from his fingers, then tapped it against the edges of mine and gave a short, sarcastic laugh, looking down. "Yeah, well, she's not mine anymore." Saying those words still felt so foreign even though I was the one to give her the final shove away. I swallowed down the rock in my throat so that I didn't lose my man-card in front of this guy.

"She always yours, Señor." His sincere voice snapped my head up. I sought out his eyes as he sent a shy smile my way. "Read you card." He clapped me on the shoulder and squeezed. "Please don't mind if I say . . . sometimes . . . in life . . . people need a second chance."

I sucked in a breath at the familiarity of those words.

How did he know?

"She very beautiful, your girl." He winked, reiterating his statement as truth before turning to walk down the hall.

I watched him until he disappeared, contemplating his words and steeling myself for what I was about to find. I needed the right frame of mind to stand toe-to-toe with her. No matter how strong I tried to pretend I was, she always managed to bring me to my knees.

I shut the door and laced my fingers behind my head, feeling the envelope rest against it. Blowing out a breath, I stared down at the brown paper bag. It smelled like the most amazing breakfast food, but I had no appetite to offer it. My nerves were jumping out of my skin, my finger twitching, causing it to brush against something soft in contrast to the hard scratch of the envelope. I brought my hands down to examine it. When I flipped it around, what I saw sucked the wind out of me. Taped to the center of the envelope was a tiny blue flower, its star-shaped center giving it away immediately.

A forget-me-not.

It didn't look as pristine as I was sure it did when she'd taped it on, but I'd guess we were both a bit worse-for-wear at this point. Below it was Angel's scrawl—*Read me on the couch.*

My brows furrowed at her instruction, but as usual, I did as she asked. I lowered myself to the cushion and wiped my sweaty palms along my thighs. Did I want to play this game? I still wasn't sure that I did, but my curiosity was piqued, and my heart was racing. Deep down, I knew I'd always be a sucker for her. It was just a matter of coming out alive on the other end.

I opened the flap of the envelope. My fingers stilled when they met a familiar glossy feel, and I readied myself for what I would see. With a shaky hand, I tugged and was greeted by an image of Angel. It was my favorite, the first one I'd ever taken of her the day I'd shown up at her apartment with lunch. The look in her eyes . . . She was so unsure of what she was feeling, but she wore her emotions all over her face and her posture. I'd known she was trying hard to push her feelings aside, but when she'd forgotten that bogus guard and looked at me like that—with flushed cheeks and a heavy chest—she told a story without ever speaking. Of a princess locked in a tower. An angel fallen from heaven that was so lost trying to find her way home. I had tried to be that for her, and still, I had failed.

I stared at the stilled eyes staring back at me. She wasn't even here in the flesh and yet I couldn't look away. It was as though she was trying to speak to me. Trying to will me to do something. To feel something.

I dragged my fingertips along the image, trying to remember the feel of her skin, the scent of her hair.

Behind her sat a single flower. It had been the point of focus for the first picture I'd shown her how to take. A small smile met my lips as I recalled how flustered she'd become when I'd slipped myself behind her, wrapped my arms around her, and breathed her in. Her scent was a mixture of sweet drizzled with fire. It was unmistakable, and its effect on me was lethal. I'd do anything to get my fix, including, apparently, breaking myself.

Unable to look at that image any longer, I tossed it aside and poked around in the envelope, but my fingers came up empty. My eyebrows drew in as I pulled the edges apart and peered inside its barren opening. Confused, I looked back at her picture for an answer and was met with more of her penmanship. Her note was on the backside of the photo.

To my BFF

I cupped my hand over my mouth and laughed slightly into it, grateful I was alone as I fought the burn behind my eyes.

Good morning. Today is going to be all about you. About us. It seems the roles have reversed somehow, and you've taken to running, but I'm going to attempt to slow you down a bit. A long time ago you told me that if I ever forgot, if I tried to run, you'd make me remember. Well, it's time now for you to remember. At the front of this envelope was a forget-me-not. It's our second chance flower from the pot of dirt that sat vigil outside my door since you gave me them last fall. You were right, they got a new chance at life. But Blake knows best, right? ;)

I laughed once again, in awe that she was making this type of effort. The girl that I'd chased for months. From the second I saw her, I knew I'd do anything for her. Wait forever if I had to. Somewhere along the line, I had forgotten that part.

If you listened to me, you're sitting where we officially began all those months ago. When I came to you so scared, but so sure that I wanted to be with you forever. I'm sorry I got lost along the way, but I feel as strongly today as I did that day that we are meant to be together. If you'll come find me.

Remember to always remember.

Remember to forget me not.

Love forever and always,

Angel

I dropped my head into my hands and drew in a hefty breath. There was a pound in my chest that wasn't there before. It banged my blood into and out of my veins, forcing a bit of life through limp limbs at the prospect of there being hope for us.

Second chances. Hope.

I had asked her to live me like I lived her, but I think we both died a little that day, along with those words. Flowers were one thing, and I talked a good game trying to convince her we could have the same scenario, but I wasn't convinced we could resuscitate what we'd had. How could I trust that she would stay still this time?

With a heavy heart, I raised my head, and my gaze immediately fell to the brown paper bag. I moved the package to the table in front of me and split the seam.

The first container I pulled out was eggs. Taped to the top was a packet of salt. That memory brought a smile to my lips as I remembered the first time I'd heard her laugh outright the day I'd tossed it on her desk. Seeing the packet there brought my thoughts to what had prompted me to toss it at her in the first place—those pretty pink nails that I was trying to salvage because she was chewing the hell out of them. A tightness began between my legs, and my dick twitched against my thigh, reminding me that I still had one.

"Easy there, professor," I spoke aloud, adjusting myself.

I placed the container on the table and reached into the bag, removing the next item. A short-stack of pancakes. I'd called her that on more than one occasion because of her tiny frame. I was beginning to see a pattern. And damn her to hell, I was beginning to like it. A grin played on my lips, a thrum ticking in my heart.

Next, I extracted a slice of angel food cake. A label was placed on top of the container. In smaller words, it said, "I know it's not Tuesday, but . . ."

EAT ME.

Pussy. I swear I'd turned part-pussy because I couldn't deny that punch gave me fucking butterflies. My dick purposefully slapped me that time.

Was she fucking kidding me? The least she could have done was give me a fighting chance, the cunning little minx.

God, I fucking loved her.

She knew just how to get to me. Put a burn in my veins, a fire in my heart, a dilation in my pupils. This tingled all the way to my scalp, and I wasn't about to walk away from the feeling of it any time soon.

The next item I pulled out of the bag was a peach. It was supple in my hands, ripened to perfection, and my mouth watered. She tasted just like a fucking peach. Below it, resting at the bottom of the bag, was a small manila envelope. Beneath the hard, orangy-yellow paper were three mounds. Like an anxious kid, I couldn't wait to see what was inside. Pulling back the metal tongs, I released the flap and let the contents drop into my palm.

The first item was unmistakable. It was a small canister of lavender scented bubble bath. The other two had me perplexed. They were vials containing about an ounce of white liquid in each. I peeked inside the envelope and, sure enough, there was another letter.

Can you feel that? It's me taking shape in your pores, in your veins. Feels good, doesn't it? Like your body is remembering life? You always demanded that I tell you what I wanted and that's what I'm going to do. I want you to keep feeling . . .

All the way down.

A hard gulp rode my throat.

If you're wondering what the white juice is, you've tasted it before. Though I might have added an extra ingredient with my finger this time ;)

Fuck me.

Crack it open and put a small amount on your tongue and see if you can remember. Go ahead. I'll wait.

My cock stiffened like a rock, forcing me to widen the part of my legs. I opened the vial and its sweet scent dispersed into the air. It smelled familiar. I dipped my middle finger into the liquid and braced myself as I slid it into my mouth. My eyes closed, recalling her words, knowing drops of her were undoubtedly mixed into the sweet concoction on my tongue. The familiarity of this taste sent a wave tingling along my skin. I shuddered, allowing myself this moment. Unable to stop myself, I emptied the entire contents down my throat, its fiery sweetness reminding me of the taste of my devilish Angel.

She's going to fucking kill me.

With that tingly burn added to my veins, I picked up her note and continued.

So can you guess? That's right. That's Angel's Tit on your tongue (and some extra Angel juice). I was sure you'd never forget the taste of that special shot I hand-picked for you. Now, here's what I want you to do. Bring this pair of tits, the peach, and the bubble bath to the tub with you. It's the same scent you bathed me in the night we got together. Remember, baby? I want you wet, I want you hard, I want you eating and drinking me, and I want you playing with yourself, imagining the day I played with you in that very same tub.

Holy shit. My hands were visibly shaking as I tried to make it through the rest of the words on the page.

When you're done, and you're nice and relaxed, come back here and eat your breakfast. There's another note taped to the bottom of the bag. Now go. I'm waiting for you in the bath. Make me feel it.

Hugs & Kisses,

Angel

Holy mother of God, I think I might have come in my pants. My dick was so fucking hard, I didn't know if I'd make it to the bathroom. Somewhere, I knew I shouldn't be doing this, but I was swimming in a fog of Angel-infused lust so thick I was near-drowning in it. There was no way I could go another second without a release. I grabbed all of the items she mentioned and jetted to the back of the apartment.

I turned on the faucet and twisted off the cap of the bubble bath, taking a pull of its scent before tilting the bottle into the stream and watching the tub fill up with rainbow-tinted circles.

I hooked my thumbs into the waist of my pajama pants and tugged down, wincing when they got stuck on my stiff cock in the way. When I tugged harder, it bobbed free, eager and anxious. The smell of lavender coated the misty air filling the room, taking me back to the day we'd shared this very spot together.

After laying the peach and the vial containing the shot on the edge of the tub, I lowered myself into the steamy, soapy water and shut the tap, letting my body adjust to the temperature. I'd been trying to block her from my mind for so long that, now that all of these reminders surrounded me, I had to retell my body what she felt like. Convince it that it was okay to let her in, even if only just for now.

I closed my eyes, and a vision of her in this very tub took shape clear as day. Her back pressed against my front as my dick played against the crevice of her ass, the head licking the base of her spine. The look of the creamy, ivory skin at the back of her neck, daring me to lick a sample of the droplets of sweat mingled with bathwater.

My head dropped back against the tile, and my eyes pinched shut as

I sought out the base of my cock that was now swollen and throbbing. Parting my legs further, as though she still rested there, I fisted my shaft and tugged up slowly as her giggles seemed to echo through the air before slipping into a moan as I brushed the pad of my thumb along her nipples.

She was alive in this room now, and every action I made seemed to coincide with what I imagined I was doing to her. And what she was doing to me.

I pressed the pad of my thumb into the slit along the head of my cock, spreading my own pre-cum over it, mimicking what I envisioned doing to her hardened nipples. A hiss escaped my lips as I palmed my swollen head and then closed my hand around it again to descend back down.

Although I was harried inside, I took my time, wanting the feeling of having her here with me to last as long as possible in case I never got to feel it again.

With one hand on my cock, I used the other to seek out the drink she had given me. The name of it alone was enough to make me blow. I used my thumb to twist the cap off before bringing the vial to my nose and taking that in, mingled with the lavender fumes from the tub. My eyes rolled behind my head, and I licked my lips.

Picturing the liquid poured onto her ample chest, dripping between the peaks of her breasts, almost did me in. I drizzled the liquid onto the back of my hand and licked it off, envisioning my tongue lapping it up from between her perfect tits.

I reached for myself once again, grunting, my movements becoming a bit more desperate. Keeping my release at bay was proving to be a task. Before I finished prematurely, I took the soft-as-fuck peach and sunk my teeth into it with a throaty groan, letting the juice roll onto my tongue and down my throat, wishing with all I had that I was sucking up her juices instead. I strangled my cock, squeezing as I rolled my fist up and down, pumping up then sliding my palm over the head.

More of the juice rained down my throat, and I swallowed hard, my nostrils flaring. I ripped off a bite and tossed the rest onto the bathroom floor before reaching down with my spare hand and cupping my balls. I hissed again, grunting and unable to slow my course as visions of Angel engulfed me—the smell of her all over me, her eyes begging me to let her inside, her hands sliding over my skin, her mouth tasting the head of my dick and sucking the whole thing to the back of her throat.

Fuck.

Sudsy water splashed over the edges of the tub as I massaged my balls with one hand and pumped my engorged cock with the other, wishing it was being squeezed by her sweet-as-sin pussy instead. Black and white specs broke out behind my lids, and my eyes squeezed shut as I exploded.

My pace slowed as I brought myself down, taming the wild banging in my chest. When the high disintegrated around me, falling like the scattering of a blown out firework, I raked my hands through my hair and cupped the back of my neck, staring down at my lonely dick poking out from the water.

The fact that she wasn't really here brought with it shame and disappointment. I was mad that I'd let her persuade me so easily. But I knew, if given the choice, that I'd happily relive the moment again and again just to share it with her.

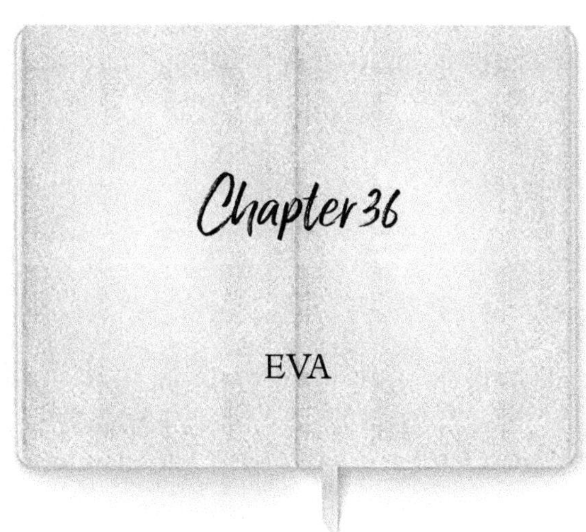

IT WAS HARD TO GO about my day in normal fashion. If Blake was playing along, that meant he was playing with *himself* as we speak, and picturing it was doing unruly things to me. Knowing how delicious he looked wet and hard in that tub turned my insides molten. Add the fact that he was stroking himself with pleasure, thinking about me, and I was done for. Despite that, my insides were in turmoil.

What if he didn't play along? What if he did, but still decided he couldn't be with me anymore? What if what I'd done was irreversible, and he was finished with me?

I chewed at my thumbnail, lost in a fog as I waited impatiently. Finally, the girl I'd been watching for the last half hour stood, the scrape of her chair echoing through the near-empty space. I gathered my belongings and rushed over to the spot she'd just vacated. Waiting for her had set me back, so when memories began to flood at the close proximity of this special space, I pushed them aside quickly before I could get lost.

I placed an envelope on the table and tee-pee'ed a piece of paper behind it. Gripping the back of the seat, I stared down, hoping this would work. Finally, I kissed my fingers and pressed them to the envelope before hurrying away.

AFTER SHOWERING OFF THE REMAINS of my bath, I stood in front of the foggy mirror with a towel wrapped around my waist and palmed the edge of the porcelain. The tips of my hair dripped water down my face and onto the floor as I stood with my head hanging, trying to figure out where to go from here.

Like any addict, the easy thing to do would be to run to her and get my fix, toss her ass in the air, and take her in all of the ways I had just imagined until the heat from my dick thawed the ice in my heart. The problem was she was so much more than a quick fuck. If I ever tasted her skin again, felt her wetness explode around me as she sucked me into her core, I'd be done for. She'd own me once again, and I wasn't sure if I could trust her not to do this to me anymore.

I swiped my hand across the wet mirror and stared at my pained expression in the streak. I never remembered seeing bags under my eyes like this, or such deep lines across my forehead. I took a deep breath and stared into my own eyes. *You're in control.* She couldn't hurt me unless I allowed it to happen. The prospect of happiness—of her—sent a wave of hope barreling through me before I could stop it.

I stepped into a pair of jeans before making my way back to the living room. I'd tried to avoid that bag long enough, figuring the answer of what to do would come to me. And maybe, in a way, it had. Either way, I needed to see the rest.

I dragged a hand through my damp hair before squeezing the back of my neck as I stared down at it. Using my thumb, I cracked one, two, three knuckles, trying to build courage. When the itch got too tough to bear, I dropped to the couch and stared at the bottom of the bag. Sure enough, another envelope lay right where she'd said.

When I tilted it to extract the letter, something brushed past my fingers, tinkling onto the coffee table. I moved the envelope aside and picked up two puzzle pieces. They were only parts of a larger picture, and there was no way of telling what the image was supposed to be. On the backside were a few words, but without the other pieces, they were meaningless. That comparison told a story in itself and had never been truer. She culminated all of my missing pieces, and without her, everything in my world had been incomplete—made no sense.

Oh, Angel. What are you up to?

I placed the pieces aside and withdrew a picture of her sitting in the library with a huge smile, pointing to a paper that she'd gotten an "A" on, while I kissed her cheek. The picture was haphazard since it was a selfie, but it was adorable. I remembered that day. She had promised to *thank me later* for my efforts tutoring her. My cheeks warmed thinking of all the *tutoring* we'd done.

I flipped the photo around and revealed more of her writing.

Good to see you're playing with me.

I didn't miss that hidden meaning.

I'm hoping you're nice and relaxed now.

Relaxed? I was wound like a top.

They say the way to a man's heart is through his stomach, but she was taking a different route. I glanced at the table of *Angel* food and chuckled. Well, she was taking both.

I'm trying to figure out how to prove to you that I'm all yours forever. There are a million ways I can say it, but how can I show you? I could give you . . . me. All of me. All of my pieces. You're holding two of them, so be gentle with me. I want you to own every piece of me, Blake. Forever. Do you remember when we took this picture? Where we were?

My smile betrayed the ache in my heart. How could I forget?

After you eat me . . . I mean, your breakfast, go there. Oh, and one of your white T-shirts is tucked between the paper bag and the plastic bag. I've slept in it almost every night since you gave it to me. Put that on so you can smell me all day.

Love you,

Angel

I separated the bags and, sure enough, wrapped in a Ziploc was one of my white T-shirts. As soon as I opened it, the smell of her invaded me. Not just her perfume or her hair product, her skin was embedded in the threads, sweat and sleep and soap and breath and one hundred percent Angel.

I brought my fist, knotted with the shirt, to my face, and sucked in, giving my veins what they'd been missing for months. The fix they had craved. All at once, sensations flooded me, just about knocking me over as I remembered. When I'd given this to her, and the kiss I'd placed to the tip of her nose after I draped it over her delicate shoulders. And the way her ass looked in her satin panties, barely poking out of the bottom when she swayed her hips. The smell of her lust after I'd fucked her wearing only this, pulling the V in the neck aside to suck on her perfect tits as I pumped in and out of her. How she'd looked rumpled up into my sheets, her one leg hooked along the outside of it and only this shirt covering her top half.

My gaze fell to the red stain at the base of the shirt, and I grunted, recalling the game we'd played with the strawberries that one day. I licked my lips, the taste of her musky scent mingled with their sweetness prominent in my salivating mouth.

I hope I survive this.

I slipped the shirt over my head, feeling her coat me from all angles, then I stood and closed the button of my jeans before slipping on my shoes, grabbing my keys, and running out the door.

Fuck the food.

THANK GOD FOR GOOGLE DOCS. My handsome photographer had uploaded all of our photos since the day we'd met into a shared drive, which had given me plenty of ammo for this little hunt. I prayed this would work.

Laying on my back, I took a quick moment to absorb my surroundings. I stared up through Bertha's thick mane, a soft breeze parting the strands, gazing at the blue sky overhead and remembered all of the times Blake and I had spent doing the same thing. A sense of comfort surrounded me as I wrapped my arms around myself and recalled memories of our past. When my mind inadvertently went to one of our very last encounters, nausea threatened to dominate the good feelings. One of the worst memories of my life was made in this very spot. I'd contemplated leaving this stop out so that it wasn't part of what Blake was remembering, but really, how could I? Good or bad, we were what we were. If we were going to be together, we couldn't ignore all of the bad that we'd been through. We needed to embrace it, hand our heartaches to one another and watch as the other person made it dissolve into their pores. We needed to make all of our troubles our own, share them and survive with them so that neither of us ran. Help each other see through the dark to bring us into the light, solidified as one.

All this time, I'd been running to try to protect him. I'd kept him separate from me, thinking that was what he needed. But every day that I distanced myself from him, I didn't allow a piece of us to grow as beautifully as it could have. The same way the plants he loved so much needed water to see another day, we needed each other to thrive. To survive.

We grew in this spot. Shared so many happy times, secrets, kisses. He needed to come here and feel it. The good . . . and the bad.

Our energy lived in this grass and in Bertha's bark. Laying here, our story whisked around me on the warm breeze tickling my skin. I got to my knees and rested my forehead on her trunk, framing my face with my palms.

"Help us, girl. With any luck, he'll be here soon. Help him see." I scraped my pointer finger along her rough bark, pausing, allowing myself to *hear* her comfort.

The air seemed to still, no movement from a leaf or ripple in the water. As fierce as nature could be, this moment was the epitome of tranquil. The calm before the storm, perhaps, but I knew without a doubt that she was telling me it would all be okay. And at that moment, I chose to believe her.

THE SMELL OF BOOKS HIT me immediately. Old and new pages mixed with thread and leather bindings. It was eerily still, making me self-conscious to move around. Every effort seemed to echo throughout the familiar library, the first study session Angel and I had shared imprinted on its walls.

I stood amongst the tables, my eyes zeroing in on her intended destination for me. In the far back corner, I could already make out something sitting on top of it, even though it was unoccupied. Approaching, the word 'RESERVED' was prominently displayed, a manila envelope that said 'Blake' sitting below it, and a forget-me-not taped to the right edge.

My heart flipped in my chest, making a jerk out of me. When I'd left my apartment, I'd felt so sure I could do this, but the ugly monster of doubt was back. I was trying to be strong, to keep my self-worth intact. But after a lifetime of trying to prove my worth to the one person I would have given anything to impress, only to be shot down time after time, it was getting harder and harder to convince myself that it was there.

Angel had made me forget all of the letdowns caused by my father, believed in all that was me, no matter what that meant. She'd looked at me like I could move heaven and earth, rearrange the stars in the sky to build her whatever picture she wanted to see. And for all that I was, I fucking tried.

After clearing the solid lump in my throat, I pulled back the chair and winced at the loud scraping sound that reverberated through the space. I needed to fit that broken person back into his box and try to be open-minded if there was going to be any hope of this working.

Pulling back the metal prongs, the envelope revealed a bunch of papers clipped together, another picture being the very first thing in the binding. I tilted the envelope on its side, allowing the clipped pages to partially slide out, forcing two more puzzle pieces to slip free and bounce off the table. I picked one up, flipping it between my nervous fingers as I stared at the image of Eva and me lazing beneath Bertha. All four chambers of my heart pulled into the center, creating a slicing burn as it sped up. I pushed my fist into it and rolled it over the pain.

She'd fallen asleep that day, finally comfortable enough to be around me with her guard down. We'd only known each other a few weeks, and I couldn't outwardly call her mine yet, although my heart had given her that stamp already. We had been in class together, and the wonky weather had brought on somewhat of an Indian summer. Knowing the cold weather was coming, all I could think about was enjoying the sunshine with her. So at the dismissal of class, I'd laced my fingers with hers and asked her to play hooky with me the rest of the day.

I would never forget how she'd stared down at our hands intimately intertwined, or the look on her face as she'd dragged her bottom lip between her teeth and bit down on the corner, contemplating my request. It had felt like there were tiny birds trapped in my chest as anticipation ballooned between us. In a bold move, I dragged the tip of my thumb up the center of her palm.

Her eyes flicked up to mine as she released the clasp of her lips to allow a small, sexy-as-sin grin. Then she'd rocked up on her toes with a small bounce in her step. "Okay." And another piece of her snuck inside my erratic heart, slowing it down as it swelled heavier.

I pounded a few taps on my chest as I stared at her golden locks dispersed between the blades of grass that decorated Bertha's feet. I was used to seeing worry etched on her face, even when she had thought she was portraying herself to be *happy*. But as she'd lain there, succumbing to the warmth of the sun and the fresh breeze floating on the wisps of Bertha's long leaves she looked angelic, childlike. It reminded me that, even though she gave off the appearance of an older sophistication, in reality, she was only just coming out of the age of adolescence.

I had laid beside her as carefully as I could, trying not to disturb her, and tried to angle the camera appropriately before closing my eyes and taking the shot. She'd stirred, but instead of pulling away she'd melted herself into the crook of my arm and neck and stayed that way, wrapping around me for the rest of the afternoon.

I flipped over the photograph.

Blake-

In your hand is a list of words that describe what I've been through on my journey to you, to where we are today. I used your study tactic as a guide, though my meanings are the real deal. (I left the dirty talk in the tub.)

I hope this helps you understand me a little better. I know you think you know me more than anyone, and maybe in a way you do, but I'm giving you a front row seat to an inside viewing. So get out of the VIP section. You don't belong there anymore. I'm pretty sure you never did. Go to the spot in this picture for your next clue.

Yours (I hope),

Angel

I placed the photo aside with the puzzle pieces and picked up the page in front of me. The fact that she was making an effort to allow me into the place where she kept her secrets and insecurities counted for more than she knew.

In my hand were college-ruled pages with words listed in the left margin. There was a fold down the right half of the papers, hiding the meanings. When Angel had been having a hard time remembering her vocabulary words, I had done this for her so she could study easily when I wasn't there to test her. Though, my meanings had been a bit . . . unorthodox.

My gaze fell to the first word on the page, and it swooped into my chest, taking my breath as my forehead immediately dropped to it.

Innocence.

Silent cries rocked my shoulders, and I allowed it, releasing all that had been pent up for so long. I'd always believed myself to be a strong man, but even I had a breaking point. The heaviness of that one word was enough to take me down.

My mind immediately went to a blonde-haired, green-eyed little Angel as I imagined a wolf circling her, licking his chops. My stomach rolled, and I dry heaved. I had never allowed myself thoughts about the reality of what she'd been through. Sure, I wasn't stupid, and logically I'd known, but that image . . .

I shuddered. Sucking in a ragged breath, I pressed my thumb and forefinger to my tear ducts, squinting and pulling myself upright, then I opened the flap in the page.

Innocence—(n.)

-the state, quality, or virtue of being innocent, especially, freedom from sin, moral wrong, or guilt through lack of knowledge of evil.

-used euphemistically to refer to a person's virginity.

I moved to the next word.

Manipulation—(v.)

-control or influence (a person or situation) cleverly, unfairly, or unscrupulously.

My heart crumpled.

Abuse—(v.)

-treat (a person or an animal) with cruelty or violence, especially regularly or repeatedly.

(n.)

-the improper use of something.

The list was endless.

Fear

Shame

Isolation

Then I came here and met you.

Freedom (n.)

-the power or right to act, speak, or think as one wants without hindrance or restraint.

-the state of not being imprisoned or enslaved.

Acceptance

Happiness

Love

Nightmare

Weak

Worthless

Rebuild

Strength

Healing

Courage

Forgiveness

Devotion

Unity

Commitment

Worthy
Live

Live (v.)

~ make one's home in a particular place or with a particular person.

Home . . .

This was killing me.

Each word was listed with its meaning, each another clue of the path her life had taken. To see it written out in black and white was such an eye-opener.

The end of this list remains to be written, but when I look into a future with you, this is what I see. I want you to be my happily ever after. My rainbow and unicorns. My white knight. Be what you want, just be mine so I can live. Because when I'm with you, I don't have to remind myself to breathe.

I sucked in a hefty breath. She had taken the words out of my mouth.

Chapter 40

EVA

MY BREADCRUMBS STOPPED HERE. WISPS of hair whipped into my face on a soft breeze as I stared into the horizon. Though it now shined bright with the day, a visual of the most beautiful sunrise I'd ever seen graced my memory, bringing an airiness to my chest as I recalled it.

Rooftops had become an anchor in my life, simultaneously representing both seclusion and freedom. Air and suffocation. Much like myself, they were the perfect oxymoron. Most of the memories of the sunrises I'd witnessed up there were torturous, comprised of me singing through my pain.

All but one.

I looked out at the same landscape from my memory, a soft smile tugging at the corner of my mouth in silent prayer that, in a short while, I wouldn't be alone anymore.

For good.

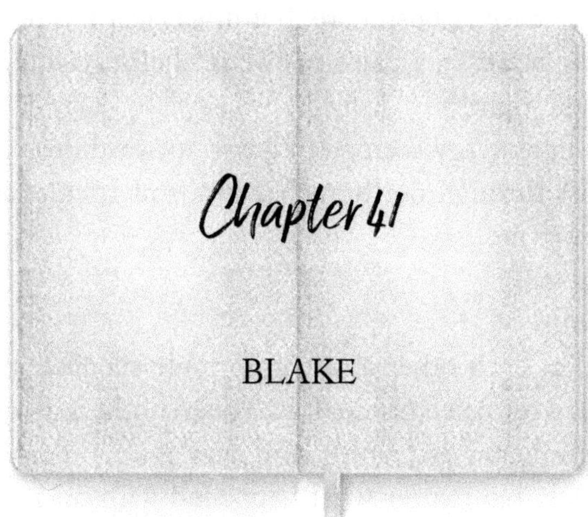

I APPROACHED BERTHA SLOWLY. SHE seemed to bristle when she saw me, most likely feeding off my energy. This whole encounter had me pretty uptight, not knowing what the end of the line would mean for us.

Though I had come here with Angel that one day, I hadn't visited Bertha regularly in a while. It was too painful. I had tried once, but all I kept picturing was Eva crumpled under the tree, broken and weeping, and I couldn't bear it.

I didn't know what had made me bring her here that other day. Hope that things would turn around, maybe? That we would both find comfort? Whatever my reason, it had worked momentarily. But our wounds were so deep, the cuts spreading venom like a bacteria. A part of me did pray we would find the antidote. That we would be able to somehow bury all the hurt and pain.

From the corner of my periphery, I spotted a large envelope at Bertha's feet, but I chose to ignore it for now. First, I needed to make amends with another special lady.

I stood beneath her and shoved my hands in my pockets, rocking back on my heels. A gust of wind blew one of her long branches in from the side to swish across my face. I chuckled and cocked my head to the side, staring up at her. I deserved that.

"Hi, Bertha."

No response.

"I'm sorry I haven't been here, but it was just too painful. I lost my heart here and, in a way, a piece of me died along with it. You know I love you, though, right?"

Just then, her energy seemed to burst outward in a ring, the breeze seeming to pass through her branches in a soft trickle, and a sense of calm washed over me.

I was forgiven.

"Thank you."

We stared at each other in a comfortable silence, and I finally felt peace. Like I had returned home. It had been bothering me that I hadn't been able to be here. As painful as it was, I was thankful Angel had brought me back. No matter what happened with us, I'd have to thank her for that.

I nodded toward the envelope. "That for me?" I bit down on my jaw with a tick in her silence. "Right." Then I bent to one knee. I paused and squinted up at Bertha with a playful smirk, trying to lighten the mood. "Hold me?"

I picked up the envelope, which had another forget-me-not taped to the corner, and moved to sit with my back against Bertha. There was some kind of hard object in this one, which piqued my curiosity. I shook it, trying to decipher what was waiting for me like a kid who'd found his present the night before Christmas.

Unable to wait any longer, I tore it open and let the contents fall into my palm. As before, I held two puzzle pieces. The front had another indecipherable picture and the back, a few words. Confusion found me at the last item though—an iPod.

When I'd found out about Angel's night terrors, I'd given her an iPod, downloaded with a bunch of songs to help her think of me, hoping it would make her feel better when I wasn't there to do it. I wondered briefly if this was the same one.

I closed my fist around the mechanism and reached inside the envelope to find my note. The picture I'd taken of us watching the sunrise from the roof of the hotel of our first date was clipped to the top. I'd forgotten how beautiful she'd looked that day with the soft light of the breaking of dawn playing on her flushed, recently sexed features. I'd been so nervous, I hadn't slept a wink, scared I would wake up to find she'd changed her mind. When I couldn't find one trace of doubt on her face, my heart had swelled even more, knowing she really was mine. That she'd finally given herself to me.

I rubbed my thumb along that image of the beginning of us, remembering how I'd felt, the completeness. I had been certain we'd never be apart again. My soul had felt fulfilled. I'd finally found my purpose. Found my girl. The one I'd take care of forever.

Her longest note yet was attached.

Blake—

As this adventure winds down, I hope I've done for you what you would've done for me had I "forgotten" us. Words can't express how sorry I am that I let you down. When I should have let you in and leaned on you for support, I allowed my own doubts and insecurities to get the better of me, and I made the biggest mistake of my life. I locked you out. At least, I tried to. But I soon found out it wasn't possible. Because you live inside of me. With every beat of my heart and pump of blood through my veins, I live and breathe you. This is not an easy admission. Where I was used to isolating myself from everyone, imagine my surprise to find you were rooted so deep inside of me that I could no longer survive on my own. But I wasn't ready to be who I needed to be yet both for you and for me. I needed to be stronger. To know beyond a shadow of a doubt that I would never, ever hurt you again. I've spent the last few months working myself over both inside and out, and I can finally say I'm ready.

I'm strong, and my mind is clear. And I want you, Blake. For good. So I'm asking—no, I'm begging—for you to be with me.

Be my forever.

You asked me once to live you, not realizing that I already was—so much that I couldn't live without you. None of my pieces make sense without you, and I'm asking you to put me back together. Make me whole. I know how hard it'll be for you to trust me with your heart again, but I promise I'm in this to stay. I'm waiting for you where we took this picture, thinking we were starting our forever. If you'll have me, come and get me so we can get our second chance.

All my love,

Angel

P.S. This is the iPod you gave me. I've loaded it with songs letting you know how I feel about you. The ones you originally downloaded are at the end of it to remind you of how you feel about me.

Sucking in a breath, I rested my head against Bertha and looked up at her. "What do I do?" I banged my head once, twice, three times. "Give. Me. A. Sign." I banged one last time before my head came to rest on her trunk. A gust of wind rustled her leaves before a long strand fell like a beautifully decorated rope, landing beside the puzzle pieces Angel had left me.

I looked up to Bertha just as another long lock fell, this one landing softly on the iPod.

"Show off," I mumbled.

Chapter 42

EVA

Rick: Hey, darlin. Can you cover for Jasmine tonight? She bailed on me.

I STARED AT THE TEXT message, then typed a quick response, hoping I was right.

Me: Hi. Sorry, I have plans tonight. Any other time, I would for sure.

Rick: Crap. OK. Thanks anyway.

I closed the message box and laid the phone beside me. A small piece of the hope I'd had a few hours ago flaked into thin air.

What if he doesn't come?

I drew in a breath and checked my watch for the umpteenth time, trying to contain the surge of panic that shot through my belly each time. I'd arrived early to set up our room downstairs and grab a seat on the same lounger Blake and I had watched the sunrise from the morning after our first date. Except for the occasional person coming up to peer out from the hotel's roof before heading back down, I'd spent the last hour or so alone.

Each time the elevator dinged with a new guest, my heart would fly in my chest, wondering if a tall, raven-haired, blue-eyed man would step off, then sink to find it wasn't him. The yo-yo effect was maddening.

What if it's really over?

No. I brushed those thoughts aside. I wouldn't allow those in . . .

Yet.

Chapter 43

BLAKE

WITH A HUFF, I PICKED up the iPod and inserted the earbuds, a soft melody trickling into my ears. I'd never heard this song before, but I recognized Christina Perri's voice immediately. She was one of Angel's favorites. I closed my eyes and rested my head on Bertha, listening to her message. I knew that whatever song she'd chosen meant a lot to her.

The Words.

I imagined it was Angel singing to me in her sweet melody. Telling me how the rest of the world had disappeared for her and all she could see was me. The thought sent an ache to my heart. I curled into myself and resolved to stay strong through this.

I knew how loud it was inside her head because mine was noisy now, too. I'd tried to build up a wall around my heart to stop it from shattering, but the fucking thing was useless. She wanted me to let go of it. Let go of my reservations and my doubts, but I was scared shitless. How do I open myself up to possibly being mangled again? That's what she was asking me to do—fall backward with trust. Saying if I did that it wouldn't hurt anymore. Except it always held the possibility of it hurting worse than before. The truth was what always hurt us. Her truth that she kept so guarded. How could it not hurt us now?

I pinched the bridge of my nose, my throat a knotted ball of fire, my heart engulfed in flames as it struggled with the enormity of this. I'd walked my own personal hell on this journey as well, and it burned. But I was addicted to its heat, every moment of it another tattoo to my being.

Still your mind . . .

She was asking me to choose her.

The song got quiet, her voice telling me she knew how scary it would be for me to let go and trust her. A tear leaked from the edge of my eye. I was grateful to be alone right now. I needed to release the pent-up *bad* if I wanted to make room for the good. If I wanted to go home.

Ironically enough, she'd been home all along, in the center of my heart. That's why it ached so fucking bad. God help me, I was scared. I was so god damned scared of what this would do to me if I just let go.

A strong wind rustled Bertha's leaves, freeing another strand. It flitted to the ground, landing to my left, in the very spot I'd found Angel crumpled in a ball in the dusk the morning she said goodbye.

A chill crept down my spine at the memory. I rose and walked the couple of feet before squatting down. I skimmed my hand through the blades, drawing in the heartache she'd deposited there.

The last of my pieces is in the spot where I broke apart in the first place.

The words from her letter repeated in my mind as I searched the area. Sure enough, I spotted something white poking out. I gathered it and made my way back to the tree.

I pushed my hand into my pocket and extracted the other six pieces Angel had sent me. Sliding down Bertha's trunk, I stared at my palm, wondering if I wanted to see the image all put together. I could see sections of white and blue and . . . blonde.

I placed the top right corner on the flat dirt at the base of Bertha and sought out my courage. Gone was the fearless lover who had fought tooth-and-nail for the girl who'd stolen his heart. In his place was someone I didn't like. Even if it went no further, I needed to do this one last thing for her. Hell, even now, I'd do anything she asked of me, no matter how much I second-guessed it.

Sifting through the pile, I found the ones that belonged at the right edges of the puzzle. I laid them down before searching for the missing one in between. Putting it together gave nothing away. I was only able to make out clouds on top of rolling blue waves.

A beach?

Curious, my eyebrows drew tighter as I worked my way left. The top was more clouds, the bottom more waves, but in the center was something that resembled an angel wing. Three pieces remained. Knowing they'd provide the full picture sent a wave of anxiety through me. The words from her letter whispered to me again . . .

I'm asking you to put me back together. Make me whole.

The bottom left corner went next. It was the lower portion of her body. Her legs were bare, her posture relaxed. I moved to the top, not ready to see it in its entirety. Below more soft clouds was the top of her blonde head, but that's all I could see. The final piece, I knew, would hold the full picture in that one tiny jagged little square. I rubbed my thumb along it, not bothering to peer down at what was on it. Finding the smooth edge, I joined it with the others and brought her final piece home.

My heart pounded at the image staring back at me. It was breathtaking. Unlike the others, this wasn't a picture I'd taken. She clearly had gone through the effort of having it taken—for me.

Set on a beach, she was off-center along the left side, her focus down and away from whoever was capturing it, as though she didn't want them to see inside herself. As much as I could see the pain she carried in the curve of her shoulders, she looked calm. At peace. As though she'd made amends with her demons and had finally learned how to co-exist with the truth inside herself.

A pair of wings fanned out from her back, topping off the angelic photo of her. Dressed all in white, the image was pristine. It gave a sense of her starting anew, coming into her new skin with acceptance. The way she looked away, almost into herself, told me that it was her burden to hold—but she was releasing it into the universe, perhaps into the soft waves crashing around her, as though she was ready to be set free.

The symbolism of this one gesture was enough to knock me to my knees. She was handing herself over to me—giving me her pieces and telling me only I could put her back together, make her whole. It was humbling and eye-opening. For as much as we had been through, I couldn't let her down. But I still needed to think long and hard about whether or not I was up for the challenge of her. If I had the strength left in me to do what she was asking of me or if what we had was irreparable. I didn't want to be her letdown, and I didn't want her to be my downfall.

Remembering all of the random words I'd seen on the opposite side of the puzzle, I scooped my fingers beneath it and flipped it over, careful not to disconnect them. When I set them back down, I braced myself for more of Angel's beautifully crafted words.

Breathe You

Live through air
Float through time
All seems wasted
When I can't call you mine

You asked me to live you

As if there was ever another choice
Trying to deny what we shared, I lost you
Severing a limb, leaving me without a voice

How do you live when you're missing your heart?
How do you function when you've been torn apart?

Drifting . . .

Drift
Search
Fall
Stumble in circles
Until your back hits a wall

My lungs constrict
In a dark, confined space
Knowing that without you
All I am is just a waste

Waste of time
Waste of skin
Crumbling
Dying from within

You're my ailment and my elixir
A wound that only you can suture

I've tried and failed and tried again
To piece together a heart that cannot mend

Pieces of me broken
Lost
Scattered around
Searching for the match, which cannot be found

To live you is to breathe you
To move you through my being
Piece me back to life again
You're the glue to my undoing.

THE SUN WAS SETTING. IRONICALLY enough, I was watching it off the same lounger I'd watched its rise all those months ago except this time I was alone. Still.

He isn't coming.

I inhaled a broken breath. A tear rolled down my cheek, dispersing onto my lips as I said goodbye one final time. The hotel room we'd stayed in on our original date was decorated in memories, but I couldn't bear to see it again, knowing it wouldn't get used. That it was over.

I'd rubbed that keycard over and over in the last couple of hours, so much that it had left an indent on my thumb. I couldn't look at it anymore. I shoved it beneath my legs and unlocked the screen to my phone.

Me: Hey, Rick. Change of plans. I'm free tonight. Still need me?

A moment later, my phone pinged back.

Rick: Hell yes. See you soon.

I tossed my phone into my bag and dragged in my knees before pushing my forehead into them. I rolled my head back and forth. It was just me now. I had to be okay with that. And I would be. I'd grown in the last few months. Though a big portion of me would always be missing, I'd mended enough of my pieces to function.

I just had to learn how to breathe.

Chapter 45

RICK HADN'T BEEN KIDDING. THE bar was packed. I hadn't said two words all night after I'd deposited my bag next to Angie's and then slipped between her and Rick. Drink after drink, I had filled the orders being yelled at me, my body moving around based on memory, unaided by my brain.

Fill glass with ice.

Pour liquid into cup.

Slide across bar.

Exchange money.

Repeat.

Everything feels worthless.

Physically, I could do the tasks at hand, but for what purpose? When nothing in life seemed to matter anymore?

You've got to snap out of this.

It seemed every time I was falling to a low point, my subconscious would come back around. Logically, I knew she was right, but convincing your heart to beat without life behind it seemed so pointless. The decision was made. I would move on and live the path of my altered destiny, but that didn't mean I liked it.

Push lime onto glass.

My favorite cover band was here tonight, the one that always made it a point to play my favorites, but even those weren't doing their job in pepping me up.

Rick brushed past me, leaning in push-up style to take an order from a blonde who seemed to be losing her patience. I had noticed her standing there a while, but I didn't have it in me to move any faster. She blushed and tucked a hair behind her ear with a soft smile as she recited her order.

"You got it." He winked, pushing off the bar, and I had to all-but reach into my eyes to stop them from rolling as she licked her lips and watched him longingly as he moved away to fill her drink.

Rick flanked my left shoulder. "You good, darlin'? You seem a bit off."

Scoop ice into glass. "Yeah, yeah, fine. Sorry, I'll step it up."

"No worries. I always love having you here, but if you're not okay . . ."

A tap knocked off the mic before a quiet organ began. I didn't look up, but I recognized the song as *Fix You* by Cold Play.

"I'm okay. I'm just try—" I squinted, wincing through rays of light that began poking at me. My face, my hands, the bar surrounding me. My eyes jutted to my fingers, then bounced between the flickers spiraling to the melody just as a familiar, horribly beautiful voice cracked out the beginning lyrics.

My head snapped up. Twinkles danced amongst the rays shooting at me from each band member, making it hard to focus, but I honed in, searching, seeking.

Blake.

Hands wrapped around the mic, his eyes reached out to me, delivering his message. Telling me of his—of *our*—struggles, massacring the tune. And . . . it never sounded better.

The sight of him buckled my senses, paralyzing me. After not knowing if I'd broken our relationship beyond repair, then accepting that he wasn't coming back to me and resolving to move on, I didn't know what to think. Scared he would evaporate, my focus never left him as my fingers tightened around the bottle that I'd been about to pour.

"Rick—"

"Go. I got this."

Rick took the liquor from my shaky hand, and I moved as swiftly as my near-numb legs would allow, mindlessly nudging people aside as

I made my way toward Blake. As I approached, all lines of worry on his gorgeous face became clearer. I knew I was the cause of most of them. I hated myself for it, but I vowed, if given the chance, that I'd spend the rest of my days trying to smooth them away.

His eyes followed me through the crowd until I stood before him. My breathing was labored, quieted by the heaviness of his words telling me his light would guide me home. Always the light in my darkness, he shined brighter than anything I'd ever seen, even at his dullest.

Wounded, his posture wasn't as erect or confident as I had remembered, but there was an unmistakable sparkle in his eyes that was unique to him. I hadn't seen it in a while, but it was there, flickering amidst the lyrics. He seemed to be trying to imbed his words, pouring out his heart in promise to allow me back home—to take my hand and show me the way.

As I watched his mouth intently, I noticed he'd shaven at some point. It brought a small smile to my lips, thinking that was step one in the return of *him*.

And I will try to fix you . . .

I'd done as much of the fixing of myself as I could on my own. I needed him for the rest, or I would never be whole again. His cracking voice continued, bleeding out words that cut so deeply, to the root of us. Him telling me he couldn't let our love go—what I'm worth. That was possibly the hardest struggle of all for us.

I couldn't take my eyes off of him as he went into the next chorus, his hands sliding up the mic stand, his gaze drilling into me, seeming to gauge my reaction to what he was saying.

Although his message was clear, I was nervous to find out if what he seemed to be saying was real. I couldn't take another letdown.

I'd drifted even closer, the sliver of metal holding the microphone the only barrier between us. As the song took off in a guitar riff, no words were sung or spoken. None were necessary. None were sufficient to match the pounding in my heart, rapid with hope, the whispering of faith that we were going to be okay. A mirrored image of the same emotions lay deep in his icy-blue eyes. It was both frightening and exhilarating. But before I let myself go free-falling to the other side of hopefulness, I needed to be certain that this was for real.

Blake reached out and brushed his thumb along my cheek, wiping away a tear I hadn't felt. His timid, yet solid palm lingered on my jaw, and I savored his touch, living in the warmth of his skin for a moment. When his heat withdrew, I opened my eyes to witness him kiss the moisture from his thumb. And I knew—he had meant it.

I vowed to do my best to never shed another tear born from heartache as he went into the next verse, reminding me of tears we had both shed from losing an irreplaceable love like we had. The world opened up then, and I almost wasn't strong enough to remain upright as the boulder of burden rolled off my shoulders, freeing me.

A nudge to my back lurched me forward, obliterating the slice of space remaining between us, bringing each of our chests flush against the mic stand. Knowing my heart's pair was beating on the other side of the cool metal sped mine into overdrive as Blake's solemn baritone quaked through the last chorus about his light guiding me back home. The feel of him against me set my soul on fire, lighting a spark that could no longer be contained.

Without another thought, I shoved the stand aside and grabbed onto Blake's shoulders for leverage. I clambered up his torso, wrapped my legs around his hips the way I knew he loved, and swallowed the words 'fix you' as they left his mouth. He stumbled back, fastening one arm around my waist, while his other hand cupped the back of my head.

Blake.

I was home.

A sob choked my throat, but I couldn't take my lips off his. Not even when the taste of my tears saturated the seam. Scared of losing him again, I draped my forearms along the back of his head and held onto his hair, trapping him to me. His arms constricted around my waist as his heart pounded its beats into mine, giving me back some of the ones he'd stolen. Energy buzzed through my veins, a thrum pulsating along each nerve. I couldn't shake the nervous butterflies that this might not be permanent, but right now I just needed to drink him in. I slid my tongue along his and relished the growl it elicited, rumbling into my mouth.

Blake lowered me to the floor. Hesitant to lose the feeling of him, I kept my fingers imbedded in his hair until he stood, forcing my hands to fall to my sides as we stared at each other.

Rick was at our side with a gleaming smile, placing a hand on either of us. "Go in the back, guys. I'm good for a bit."

I only looked away from Blake long enough to thank Rick with my eyes, my words trapped somewhere in my dry throat. He responded with a wink before I headed off to the back room—anxious, hopeful.

Scared shitless.

With the flick of the light, I stepped aside, allowing Blake to enter before I followed. The click of the door was all I heard over my shallow breathing. I stood in front of him, not allowing myself to fully believe what I was reading into his words, afraid to death that he was about to say his final goodbye rather than his forever hello.

"I'm sorry it took me so long to come back to you. I was just so scared," he admitted, still not moving toward me.

A tear rolled from its saturated duct, and my lips parted to allow me to breathe better. *Please let this be happening.*

Blake dipped his chin and viewed me with compassionate, worried eyes. "I've been trying to figure out how to fix myself, but then I realized the only way to fix me is to fix you—to fix us." Blake snagged my pinky finger with his pointer and lightly swung it like a kid would do. "I'll fix you if you'll fix me." The small divot beside his pucker, the sparkle in his hesitant, yet playful eyes, warmed my core.

Faith rose in my chest, even though I was trying to tamp it down. "Is this real?" My voice splintered, unable to withstand the pressure from the burn in my throat.

"As real as a heart attack." Blake smirked at the use of the first song I'd ever sung to him before solemnness washed over his features. "I can't live without you, Angel." He paused, lost somewhere in his thoughts. "Trust me I tried, but I'm like a walking fucking corpse. I'd rather die loving you for even one more day than walk around in this purgatory. You're my life. My living. If we're together, we can fix all that's broken. I know we can."

He stepped forward, a small glimmer of hopefulness sparking in his apprehensive eyes. "Hold me. Here." He rested his palm over my heart, and its beats fluttered beneath it in rapid thumps, aching, longing to be near him once again. To be whole again. He had asked me to give that part of myself to him once before. I had failed him then, but I would never let him down again.

"I never let go of you. I've held you there all along. Even when it stung." My voice lowered to a whisper. "It's what kept my pieces together." Another tear dripped from the corner of my eye, the salt invading my mouth. I was sick of its taste, sick of crying all the time. Of hurting, constantly fucking aching.

We stood a foot apart, connected only by the spot where his hand sat on my chest. The heaviness it created there was a reminder of the weight he held in my heart. The fragments of it so broken, I thought it unfixable.

An uncertainty still lay in Blake's eyes. "You destroyed me, Angel. I have pieces now, too." He looked away with a swallow. His shoulders losing their gumption.

My legs nearly gave way from the new crack that sent down my heart, but I needed my strength. We weren't surviving separately, and I couldn't deny either of us this anymore. I covered his hand with my own, needing to wipe away any remaining reservation. "Then fit yours into mine."

His eyes snapped up to meet my gaze, a new hope swirling in the water that glistened there. I could see the merry-go-round spinning inside his head, the constant loop I'd kept him on taking him on a wild journey. It made my heart skip a beat, and his fingers twitched above it as he collected that one, too.

I exhaled, feeling the weight I'd been carrying all this time begin to flake from my being and sprinkle to the floor like tiny broken pebbles, solidifying my confidence. "It's time to stop running. I just want to stop running." Without breaking eye contact, I stepped out of my shoes, and Blake's hand finally left my chest as he looked down to see them laying at his feet in a silent promise. A promise to be still. To be there. Forever. "Be still with me?"

Blake's jaw hardened around its clench, his eyes raw and begging for honesty. "Angel, if you have any doubt, you need to put those back on and walk away from me right now. I won't survive another one of these." His eyebrows were drawn so tightly together, I hated the doubt I saw there. Doubt in me. Doubt in us. Our love was supposed to be so solid, and I'd reduced it to pieces. All kinds of pieces of broken. But I didn't want to be broken anymore.

"I'm done running, Blake." I bore my gaze into his so there'd be no misinterpretation, then I gave Blake the words he'd given me so many times. "Be with me."

His breathing stilled in his chest and his eyes went wide. He took one step closer. "Say it again."

A brighter light emerged in his eyes, hope peeking its head through his darkness. I took a tiny step forward as well. "Be with me."

He matched one more tiny step. "This is your last chance to back out of this. If you really mean it, say it one more time." He cocked a brow, a tinge of playfulness returning to his gorgeous features. "So you don't forget."

His study tactic.

Anticipation wound around us in a tight binding, my heart thrumming in more of a flutter than beats, stealing all of my air with it in swirls and spirals. My final step brought us chest-to-chest, obliterating any space that remained, the contact forcing my eyelids to drift closed for the faintest of moments while I regulated myself. Blake's chest swelled against mine as he took in a large breath, and the feeling of him pressed against me—of him coming home, took over my body in a tidal wave. My eyes reopened with a reinforced determination, needing him to know how solid we'd be once we were put back together.

"Be. With. M—"

The final word barely made it out of my mouth as his body gave way, the tension it had been harboring seeming to be set loose on a wave. His hands were on me, tangling in my hair as his lips crashed into mine. He attacked my mouth, lifting me from the floor and slamming my back against the wall. I wrapped one leg around his waist, leaving the other dangling down the front of him.

Breaking from my lips, Blake rained kisses to my jaw, my neck, nibbling along my collarbone and trying to talk at the same time. "Your words, your pictures, I could never deny you." He returned his attention to my mouth as he sucked my lower lip between his, running his tongue along it and moaning, his hand roamed to my ass as he palmed it, then dragged it outward to grab hold of my thigh and wrap that leg around him as well.

"You didn't come," I panted into his mouth. My eyes closed in a euphoric bliss as he sucked at my neck once more. "I waited all day, and you never came. I thought we were done."

I dropped my forehead to the top of his head as his hand covered my breast, kneading greedily at their swollen fullness. With his teeth partially bared, he stared at my chest as he spoke. "I needed time to process. I'm always telling you to slow down, woman."

"Mmmmm," I moaned, fisting his hair as he pulled my shirt and bra down in one motion and drew my pebbled nipple into his mouth. "Blake—"

"I need you." Blake's voice cracked with desperation. "I need inside of you, and I won't do it like this. I need to take my time with you. Make you mine again." His eyes were desperate as his erection made itself known between my legs.

"We still have the room . . ." *Crap.* I deflated. "I left the key card on the roof. I was so upset, I didn't think you were coming—"

"This key card?" Blake held the piece of plastic between his fingers, a gorgeously devilish smirk upon his full lips.

I stared at it in disbelief. "You went there?"

"I went there." He smiled and returned the card to his back pocket.

"I could kiss you!" I threw my arms around his neck and squeezed.

"Oh, Angel. You're gonna do a lot more than kiss me." Blake licked a line up the side of my neck, causing a stream of bumps to prickle there. "Come on." He pulled us away from the wall and made his way to the door with me still wrapped around him.

"You're not going to let me down?"

Blake stopped with his hand on the doorknob and swallowed visibly while finding my eyes. "I'll never let you down again."

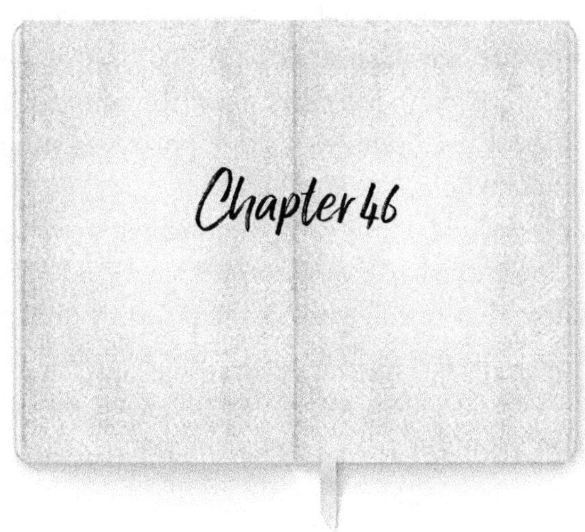

Chapter 46

AS SOON AS RICK HAD excused me for the rest of the night, Blake and I had run out of the bar so fast I wasn't even sure we'd said goodbye.

Soft lighting and the smell of flowers brought a smile to my face and the way Blake's hand tightened around mine puffed up my heart a little more. I hoped he liked what I had done with the hotel room.

Battery operated candles trailed from the door all the way into the room and were scattered around on various furniture. Rose petals were drizzled on top of the bed, mimicking what Blake had done on our first date. Only this time forget-me-nots were mingled amongst them, creating a meadow effect. Dozens of photos of us were placed around the room, and on the bedside table lay two journals. One new—and one old.

"I can't believe you did all this," Blake spoke from behind me. His hands rested on my hips, the tops of my thighs flush with the side of the mattress as we stared at it.

"I didn't know what else to do to prove to you that I wouldn't run anymore. To remind you . . ." My voice lowered as it trailed off, uncertain of how to finish that thought.

"You can't forget what it feels like to live, Angel." I turned to face his heavy words. "You were always here." He took my hand and placed it over his heart. Each pump touched my senses as I collected a few of his beats as well. "When it broke, it destroyed me."

"I'm sorry I put you through that. I broke my promise to you once.

I won't break it again. I hope you believe me." The fact that I had lost his faith stung worse than anything.

"I believe you." Though the shadows of the pain that I'd caused him still lay in the lines of his forehead, his eyes portrayed strength. Faith. "If I didn't, I wouldn't be here."

Those words opened up my lungs, letting in a fresh wave of new air. Even after his song at the bar, I was worried we wouldn't be able to overcome all the hurt. That once we tried, the poison would be too deep in our veins to work past. But I see now that was foolish. This was us. Two as one until the day we take our last breath of life and stop living one another. I'd make sure of it.

I tapped two fingers over his heart. "Mine?"

He rested his palm on my heart. "Yours. It could never *not* be yours."

He stepped forward, the backs of our hands coming together as the fronts still felt the other's heartbeats. We stared at each other, reacquainting with the other's features. He brought his hands up to cradle my jaw, his fingers splayed over my cheeks as he studied me, feeling me, learning me again. Brushing my hair from my face, he moved in to place a tender kiss on my lips before pulling back to look at me once more.

His fingers roamed the sides of my neck, back up to my face through my hair as though he were coveting each inch, each piece. With a soft smile, he leaned in to brush his nose along mine. We locked eyes, both of us silently reassuring the other of our devotion, relishing in the feel of coming back together.

His thumbs slid over my parted lips before he licked the seam, inviting himself in for a taste. A burn crept through my middle as he invaded my being—touch, smell, and everything Blake coating me from the outside in.

It was so hard to restrain from taking my fill of him, but I wanted to take my time exploring him, and I could tell by his lingering caresses, he felt the same way. Sex was one thing, and it was powerful when it was with someone you truly loved, but two souls coming together was something else entirely. It was heart-pounding and genuine and needed to be done delicately.

Blake's fingers mingled into the spaghetti strap at the top of my shoulder, and he kissed it away, dropping the elastic down my side before repeating the same action on the other shoulder, causing the material to pool at my waist. "I missed your skin."

He grazed his hands along my collarbone and up to my neck again. Grabbing each side, he used his thumbs to dip my head back, opening my neck to him. I panted, closing my eyes as he licked a line from the divot in my collarbone, up to my chin, and then stuck his tongue in my mouth in one motion. I gasped into his mouth, taken aback by the demand in his lips, the needy softness. He was taking me slowly, but with a possessive touch claiming stake to my being. The feeling of it made my insides shudder with the thought of belonging to him again.

"I missed your everything," I purred when he finally freed my lips.

He dropped his forehead to mine, his eyes closed, his lips glistening with our combined moisture. "My unicorn." The last part came out as a hushed whisper.

"Not anymore."

Blake's eyes opened, confusion swiped along the hard lines on his forehead. In a soft voice, I clarified, "Unicorns disappear. You thinking of me that way was never a good thing. I don't want to be that girl anymore. I want to be the stays-around girl. Not the runaway. Statue of Liberty. Call me that." I smiled, only half joking.

Blake laughed. "Does your torch only light for me?"

The flutter in my heart sobered me. "Until my last breath."

Blake's smile faded as his mouth descended to mine once again. Cradling my face, he paused a hair away from my lips and spoke against them. "You take my breath away." He found my eyes and sank his gaze into them.

"You give me mine back."

A soft groan left his throat as he massaged his mouth with mine, stealing my thoughts. Lip locked, Blake gently urged me backward. His weight covered me as my back sunk into the mattress, a few petals fluttering around us. He took his time, his tongue dipping in for little tastes of my mouth as his hand skidded softly down the side of my face, his fingers combing my hair, feeling my neck. Tucking my fingers beneath the cotton of his shirt, I groaned at the feel of the tight skin of his back. I dug in, dragging my fingers up the muscles that lined the dip of his spine until I reached his shoulders. I cupped my hands around them, bringing him closer to me, but it wasn't enough. I needed his heat.

Bringing my hands back to the hem of his shirt, I yanked at it. "I need to feel your skin on mine."

Blake sat up and drew his shirt over his head before tossing it to the side, and then he was on me again, the warmth of his body melting into mine. On instinct, I arched my back, pushing my chest into him as I brought my arms around him once again and curled a leg over his hip.

"Yes."

He felt like heaven in the sun on a warm day. The kind you close your eyes at with a smile and tilt your head toward, trying to soak it up so you can carry around the happiness it gives you for a little while.

And he was all mine.

A hiss escaped my lips as he moved the thin lace covering my breast aside and licked the pebbled nipple into his mouth. I moaned and pushed up, wanting him to suck, but Blake had other plans. Two of his fingers worked my other nipple to a peak while he swirled his tongue around my breast, swiping under the heavy flesh at the bottom. I moaned, tingling from holding back as he moved to my other breast and repeated his attention there. I ground myself into him, burning with a need only he could fulfill.

"Bla—"

His tongue was in my mouth again, his weight leaving my chest as he pushed his erection between my legs with a soft grunt. My hands roamed the curves of his biceps, feeling them tense with the effort of suspending himself above me. They glided back up and to the front of his body, down the hard peaks of his pecs, down each ripple of his chiseled abs, before finding the waistband of his jeans. I popped the button and lowered the zipper, then turned my wrist and slid my hand inside, eager to unwrap my prize when I was happily greeted by his hard length—commando. I smiled against his mouth.

"Easy access?"

"I couldn't be bothered with unnecessary things. I just wanted to get to you." He moved his hips, forcing his cock to slide in and out of the circle of my fingers.

I stared down the hard landscape of his body, the crests and valleys of each defined muscle protruding from his smooth olive skin, down to the head of his cock poking out from the denim. A glisten sat on top of it, and I licked my lips, eager for its taste.

"I want you so bad," I moaned, tilting my head back as Blake suckled at my neck.

"You have me. Until my last breath, you have me." Blake pulled back and rested a forearm next to my head. He brushed the hair from my forehead with his middle finger before resting his palm on the side of my face, seeking out my eyes. "I won't lose you again."

"You never really lost me. I just lost myself," I confirmed, resting my hands on his lower back. "When I'd sit in a quiet room, I could hear you inside of me. It was always so loud. I couldn't take it."

Blake answered me with a soft kiss. "I'll spend the rest of my life making sure you're okay. From now on run *to* me. Not *from* me." His gaze seemed to imbed his next words into my soul with more meaning than just words alone. Reassuring everything I was with everything he was. "I love you, Angel. So much that the words seem insufficient. You make me everything and reduce me to nothing all at the same time."

A tear leaked from the corner of my eye. Hearing him reconfirm his love for me, laying in the same bed we had first made love—now sharing the moment we promised forever—brought everything full circle. We were coming together, newly reinforced in an unbreakable bond. Something in me was sure of it. As it had once before in a horrible situation, my life with Blake passed before my eyes. I saw a future filled with laughter and love, blue-eyed babies, and blonde-haired girls. I knew he would keep me safe—do anything to help me breathe in a life that always seemed to be stealing my air.

I lifted up on my elbows and clasped his lower lip between mine, sliding my tongue along the sweet taste resting there. I breathed him in through my nose, tasted him on my tongue, mingled my fingers into his hair as he moaned, sending his voice into my lungs, ensuring that all the air filtering through me would be infused with him.

"I love you so much, it's almost too much to take. I feel so swollen inside, like I could explode if I squish one more piece of you into me."

A devilish smirk slid across Blake's moistened lips. "Well, I hope you have room for one more piece because I need inside of you."

His openmouthed kisses began at the hollow of my throat and

trailed deliciously down the center of my chest. I leaned into him as he continued past the soft skin of my torso, stopping only to dip his tongue into my belly button before swiping the pad from one hip bone to the other. I bucked when he passed an extra sensitive spot, pebbles breaking out along my skin as I fisted the bedspread. Together, his strong hands pulled off what remained of my shirt, my pants, my panties—licking, sucking, nipping, but purposely missing the one place I longed for him.

After discarding both of our clothes, he spoke between kisses up the length of my leg as he stared at me. "Your body looks different, more defined. I didn't think you could get any sexier, but clearly, I was wrong."

I gasped as he bit into the flesh of my upper thigh. "I'm glad you like it." I swallowed, my words wispy as I was held together by a mere thread.

Blake deliberately dragged his nose over my clit as he went for the other thigh. "You still smell the same, though. And your taste . . ." He sucked the skin inside my leg and then came to my center, lightly biting my full lips from the side.

"Ahhhh," I moaned, raising from the mattress with a pant. "You're killing me. God, just do something, please," I begged. The build-up inside was too much.

Starting at my opening, Blake flattened his tongue and dragged it up the inside of my folds, staring at me. My head dropped back with a hiss as he continued up, over my pubic bone, back up my torso, and settled himself between my legs. He held himself above me with one arm while he pushed a finger into my core. "Tell me you're mine, Angel. I need to hear it one more time." He primed me, stoking the fire building within.

"I'm yours. I was always yours." I placed my hands on his face, not wanting to take this final step with any uncertainty lingering in his head. "I just want to be one with you again. I nee—"

My words were halted when the head of his dick replaced his finger. It probed at me, seeming to request acceptance. I widened my legs as he pushed in slowly. With his eyes pinched shut and his lips open, I felt every centimeter of him add to the one before. I could tell he was savoring the feel of me sliding around him. I closed my eyes, too, so I could focus on the sensation of it. The feel of slowly filling up with Blake. When the heat from his pelvis met the top of my pubic bone, Blake paused, dragging a heavy breath into his lungs. The fullness of my heart matched the fullness of him inside of me, and the weight of it at the same time was too much to keep me anchored. As if a dam broke, tears began to spill down my cheeks while my chest hiccuped with tiny sobs.

Blake took my face in his hands. "Angel? Are you okay? Did I hurt you?" He began to pull out, but I grabbed his ass and pushed him tighter inside of me.

"No, of course not. It's just the feel of it. It's too much."

Blake smoothed his thumbs along my cheeks, mingling them with my tears. He kissed the tip of my nose, quieting my sobs, before kissing each of my eyelids.

I steadied my breath and covered his hands that still rested on my cheeks. "I can't believe how close I came to losing you—to never feeling this again." It felt like no matter how deep inside he reached, he would never be close enough.

Blake answered with the soft rocking of his hips as his lips sought out the delicate skin at the base of my ear. "Close your eyes, baby. Feel this with me." Blake's air entered through his flared out nostrils and exited through the part in his lips.

I closed my eyes, trying to put myself in the same realm as him as he slowly moved in and out of my core. Any remaining doubt that Blake and I would be okay blasted into particles and floated away on a puff of his building breath.

His forehead dropped to mine, and he kissed me. "Can you feel that?" Blake shuddered.

"You're all I can feel in every fiber of my being. I feel like you crawled inside of me."

"Keep me there." Inch by inch, push then pull, Blake dragged his cock seductively in and out, each slide opening up a little more of my wetness. The slicker I became, the more urgent his movements became.

Curling my arms around his back, I wrapped my legs around him and sucked him into me, my pussy drawing him in as my body held onto him as though I would fall into an abyss if it let go. I urged him on with my heels, eager to feel him come apart inside of me.

"More," I moaned. "Give me more. Faster, baby," I panted against his earlobe.

When Blake's eyes opened to find mine, they glowed a startling blue. His fingers sent tingles over my scalp as he dragged them into the hair at the back of my head. Blake pulled my hair, tilting my head back at the perfect angle to nip and suck.

"There won't be anything fast about this. You're gonna come slow around my cock so I can feel every drop of you."

I gasped as the head of his dick met me deep inside. The weight of his pubic bone sat heavy on my clit, awakening a need that couldn't be tamped down. I gyrated against it, mewing as my head swirled with lust. A fire seemed to break out along my skin as I moaned, digging my heels into the hardness of his ass. Blake pulled out slowly and then pushed inside of me again until he filled me to the hilt. Over and over, he repeated the motion, waves of pleasure rippling around me, keeping me breathless and filling me with life. With him.

My insides cinched together in a tight ball, and I knew I was close. Instinctively, I used my legs to try to urge him faster, feigning to release, but he kept his pace.

"You're right there. I can feel it."

Sharp jabs of breath broke from my throat, and all I could respond with was an exhausted moan.

"Come for me, baby. Let me feel you." Blake's words hit the over-sensitized skin next to my ear as his hips gently swiveled, bringing with it the first tidal wave of pleasure.

Small bucks quaked in trembling waves, seeming to go on forever as his own release pulsated inside of me. Blake took my lips in his then, sucking in my air as we finished. Every inch of me was numb and buzzing as I kissed him lazily, drunk in euphoric bliss.

Blake rolled off of me, bringing me into the crook of his arm. "Sleep, baby. That was only the beginning. We're not going anywhere for a long time."

I drifted off into a blissful slumber, wrapped in a cocoon of Blake, never feeling more at peace.

AN AWARENESS OF A FAMILIAR hard kind of softness trickled through my subconscious. I curled into it as a musky, lust-laced aroma blanketed me. My head rose and fell on an even, relaxed breath, sending the corners of my mouth into an upturn.

Blake.

I kept my eyes closed so my other senses would be heightened as I absorbed the moment. The baby hairs lining my forehead tickled as his soft breath blew them on each of his exhales. Heat from his bare skin created a moisture beneath my cheek, but I wouldn't dare wipe it away. If anything, I hoped my pores would drink it in and store it for times of his absence. Dragging my toes along his skin, I curled my thigh over his hip and burrowed deeper into his side, circling my arm around his waist. Even in his relaxed slumber, our attraction couldn't be denied as he hardened to life beneath my leg.

Blake's arm tightened around me, and his lips landed on the top of my head. "Morning, Sunshine." Drew's nickname for me on Blake's lips sent a wave of awareness through me. I had wanted to ignore real life a while longer—and I would—but it was a reminder of what today would bring and what needed to happen.

Absolution.

After today, there would be no more secrets. No more half-truths or wondering. I was coming clean. Emptying out my soul of the black gunk that laid like sludge.

I pulled up on my elbow and placed a peck on the tip of his nose. "Morning, baby. Sleep nice?"

"Like a dream." Blake stretched, his words hanging lazily on his smiling lips. "I don't think I've slept that great since . . . well, since ever."

I bent my arm over his chest and rested my chin there. "I know. Even before, as relaxed as we thought we were, it wasn't quite like that, was it?"

Blake looked down at me, his thumb tracing long strokes up and down my spine. "Uh-uh. I feel like my world just came together or something."

"That's because it has." I smiled, staring into the little glitters sparkling in his hazy morning eyes.

Blake squeezed my ass cheeks, pulling upward. "Get up here, woman."

I swung my leg over his hip and landed with a plunk on his steely erection. "Good morning, indeed."

"No. Good morning in *you*."

Blake cupped his hand around the back of my neck and urged me down to him, his smile melting into a kiss as his eyelids drifted closed. His dick twitched between my legs, inviting my hips to start rocking cowgirl style, making sure to keep him right in the center of my wet lips. My pussy licked at him, soaking him as our tongues danced a frantic waltz together. He reached between our legs and thumbed my clit before taking himself in his hand.

"All aboard."

I never thought I could miss a divot so much, but as his dimple plunged into the smooth curve of his cheek, I was reminded how much I adored it. "Take us for a ride."

I TRAILED MY FINGER AROUND Blake's chest, unable to avoid the elephant in the room that was sitting a couple feet away, perched on the nightstand. We had already *made up* several times and now lay in comfortable silence. I pushed a kiss into Blake's cheek and rolled off of the bed, gathering my underwear before dropping his v-neck over my head.

"Stealing my shirt back again?"

I pulled the neckline to my nose and sniffed. "It smells like both of us now." I smiled.

"So do these sheets. And my hands." He covered his nose and mouth with his palm and dragged in a lock of air, his eyes fluttering closed dramatically. "Oh, god." He opened his eyes and looked down at the teepee'd sheet standing at attention between his thighs. He poked and pushed at it with the same palm. "See what you do to me?" He looked at me. "Down, boy." He pushed once more, wincing.

I laughed and came back to sit next to him on the bed, pulling my ankles into a criss-cross one at a time. "Always so eager. But, really, we should talk." I picked at my fingernails, anticipation sitting like a boulder in my gut.

He grimaced. "Already? Can't we just enjoy this?"

"For this, I think you'll make an exception." I reached behind me, twisting to pull my old journal onto my lap. Just as broken as me, it was a bit worse-for-wear with its fraying edges and peeling creases, but it was mine. It was me. At least, it had been for a long time.

Blake's eyes dropped to the worn leather with a hard gulp riding his throat. He'd seen this book many times, even held it in his hands once before. He placed a hand on my thigh. "Angel, you don't have to do this. I'm here. Nothing else matters anymore."

"You're wrong." I blinked back tears, knowing how heavily this moment was going to weigh on us. "All of it matters. I should've opened up to you from the beginning, and I'm sorry I didn't. We lost so much time because of it." I hung my head, causing a few blonde ringlets to cover the wounds I was sure my face was showing. "While we were apart, I started seeing a therapist."

Blake's hand left my thigh. When I looked up, I was met by his strained expression. "Yeah, about that." He scrubbed the back of his neck, angling his head. "If we're coming clean, I guess I should tell you. I kind of set that up."

"You?" I squeaked. "But I don't understand. Jace gave me the card. He said he—*Jace*, that bitch." My hands balled into fists as all the clues began to float together one-by-one. The card, the secretive way he was acting when I asked how Blake was. "I *knew* he was up to something. I'm losing my touch."

He winced. "Yeah, I asked him not to tell you. I didn't want you to not go because *I* was the one sending you there. I researched the best psychiatrist for abuse and gave him her card."

I gulped, my eyes softening from the shock to absorb just how much this man loved me. The lengths that he had gone through even after I had pushed him away so forcefully. "So that's why he was so insistent I see *her*."

He sighed. "Yeah, we've kind of been working together. Well, after that one incident, anyway." His cheeks tinged a colorful pink. It was completely adorable how bashful he became when he had to confess something.

"What's this you speak of?" My eyebrows raised and I sat up straight. "I know of no incident."

He winced again. "I kind of hit him once. But it was only once," he rushed to reassure me.

"Wait. You hit Jace? My Jace?" I palmed my chest, disbelief raising my tone each time his name passed my lips. "Jace, Jace?"

Blake looked into his lap and fiddled with his fingers. "I'm not proud of it."

"Forget that." My eyes widened. "He let you? Like, you're still alive? And your member is still intact?" I blew out a puff of air. "Damn, he must like you more than I thought."

"I was going through a rough time, okay?" Blake looked as though he were confessing to his mother about eating the last cookie in the middle of the night, eyes wide with guilt, canary feathers hanging from his lips. "He knew that. He's not stupid. It was all out of love for you anyway, and I think that kid might love you just as much as me." He lowered his voice. "He really is a good guy, you know? He put up with some kind of torture from me." Blake's head snapped up, apprehension bursting from his eyes as they narrowed. "But don't you *dare* tell him I said that."

I laughed. "Your secret's safe with me." My stomach tightened, knowing the next part would be a sore topic for him, but it couldn't be avoided. I cleared my throat. "That's where I connected with Drew." I peeked at Blake, trying to gauge his reaction.

He stiffened. "So, you're telling me it's my fault then? That I sent you straight to the next suitor?" He crossed his arms over his chest.

I chuckled at Blake's choice of words. I knew he was using it to lighten a topic which still made him uncomfortable whether he wanted it to or not. "Don't be silly. He's only ever been a friend." At Blake's disbelieving scowl, I covered his hand with my own. "I mean it. And he's amazing. I'd love to tell you what he's done for me. I think you'll really like him." I pushed my gaze into his. "And I think you'll be really thankful."

Blake's shoulders melted, becoming more relaxed. He brought one hand to the side of my face and stroked my cheek with his thumb. "If I have him to thank for bringing you back to me, then you're right. I'm more thankful than he'll ever know."

"I'm sure he'd like to hear that." I smiled, feeling anxiety lift from my shoulders. I exhaled. "I feel better already. It bothered me so much that you were hurt by the thought of me being close to him." I took his face in my hands, needing there to be absolutely no doubt of my feelings. "No one can ever take your place, Blake. Ever. So please, don't doubt that you're the only one for me."

Blake answered me with a soft kiss. "Noted. I'd like to meet him one day. Officially. So I can shake his hand and thank him for helping my girl." A small smile tilted his gorgeous lips.

"I'd like that, too." I returned his smile, feeling that one pebble drop from all the weight of our bucket.

My journal sat like fifty tons in my lap, bringing me to the most important part of this. I sat up straighter, forcing a little extra distance between us. Running my palm over the top of it, I stared down as I gathered my newfound courage. Blake sat up taller as well, elongating his back against the headboard. When I raised my gaze to his, I found his eyes fixated on the book as he clenched and unclenched his jaw in a nervous pattern. Behind those indecisive eyes was a barrage of different things tumbling through his head, as though he were trying to pick through them all and find the right set of words. But the words needed to come from me this time.

"Some days are harder than others." I gulped.

That sent his sapphire eyes my way. I smiled to reassure him he could relax. I wouldn't break this time. "When Drew came across me, I was a wreck of a person. Lonely, not eating, confused . . . hurt. I resorted back to the same girl you'll find in these pages. Maybe even worse."

Still seeming unsure, Blake glanced at the book again.

"I want you to have this."

With a hard swallow, Blake's glimmering eyes snapped up to meet my determined stare. "Angel—"

"I want you to have this, Blake. I could sit here and tell you my story, but sometimes the words—they get trapped. This way you can get it straight from *inside* of me. I don't want there to be any more secrets."

A mist encroached my eyes as I transferred the book to his lap. I knew this was a game changer. He would find all of his answers in that book. The why, the when, the how . . .

And the who.

I was ready for it. I'd prepared myself for months. But I wasn't sure he was.

Blake's face crumpled as he lay his hand on my knee. "You don't have to do this, baby, and the fact that you're willing to speaks volumes, trust me. But . . . that's private." Fear shone in his eyes, and I wasn't sure if it was him trying to prove his respect for me or that he was scared of the story these pages told.

"Nothing is private anymore. Not with you. I'm ready to be an open book." A faint smile tinged my lips as I fingered the edge of my journal. "So, here's my book. I'm about done filling those pages anyhow."

Blake's words, when he had given me my *new* journal for Christmas, rang in my ears. When he'd told me he didn't want to mingle our new happy memories with the heartache of my past. I was glad to be rid of the poison held in this book and start fresh in Blake's journal once again.

Blake held the book in both hands, staring down at it with a hard set to his jaw. His unforgiving posture and lack of enthusiasm were not what I'd been expecting.

"What?" Worry wobbled my voice. I didn't like how he looked.

"Huh?" I broke him of his reverie, and he glanced up at me. "Nothing. I just . . ." Blake trailed off, seeming unsure of how to continue.

"What is it?" I pressed, nerves crawling inside at what he was thinking.

"It's just . . . Well, we only just got back together. It means the world to me that you're trusting me with this, really it does, so I don't want you to think I'm ungrateful or undeserving, but before we jump into the bad,

I kind of want to focus on the good for a little bit. On the *us*. Fixing us." He hesitated, searching my body language. I could tell by the worry plastered on his forehead he was scared that admitting that was fucked up of him, but truthfully, I was glad he said it.

I relaxed on an exhale. "Thank you."

Blake's eyebrows pulled in the center. "Thank me? For what?"

"Doing that. I want you to know everything, and if you choose to open that book, you will. But, I was worried about what doing that would stir up, as well. And whether or not we were ready for it just yet."

Blake's entire body deflated. "Oh, thank God." He put the journal on the sheets beside him and tucked me into his side. "I just don't want our focus to be on all that bad stuff just yet. Let's do *us* first. Unless . . ." Blake leaned back to inspect my face. "Unless you need to get it off your chest. Do you need to talk about it? Because then I'm here for you. I'm here for whatever you need."

"No, it's nothing like that," I reassured him. "I've let it out a bunch. I've already begun to heal. I just needed my last piece." I kissed him on the nose and let him know that was him.

"Okay, good. Because I also don't know how I'll react once I know who did this to you. I think I'll need to be mentally prepared for that." His slanted mouth caused his dimple to poke through his cheek.

I just nodded, hoping he didn't notice the lapse in my breath or the color draining from my face. My pulse, damn it to hell, was betraying my healing and growth as it beat in double time at the idea of him knowing who it was. And what he would do once he did.

"Oh, hey," Blake's smile spread as a thought came to him, "I guess this means we're going to Damon and Abby's engagement party together now. I got the invitation last week."

And then—it stopped.

Chapter 48

"HOLD THAT PLANK, EVA. NO slacking now that you're back with your man." Drew circled me, hands clasped behind his back, a smirk on his face. I got the feeling he was pushing me extra hard today. And I was fine with that.

A coat of moisture lined my body, exhaustion making itself known in my muscles, but I had this. Drew could sit on my back and I'd still hold my position. My brain and body were fine-tuned and on the same page for the first time since Damon walked into my bedroom all those years ago.

With my teeth bared, my lips slid into a smile. "I can do this all day. What else you got?"

Drew's legs stopped in front of me. I craned my head and looked up. Still with his arms behind his back, his legs set in a wide part, he peered down at me as though he were sizing up how much he thought I could handle. Then, his eyebrows hardened. "Go get your gloves."

I grinned and pulled my legs in. Hopping to my feet, I bounced and rolled my neck back and forth. "I was hoping you'd say that."

GLOVED, I BOUNCED FROM FOOT to foot, never taking my eyes from Drew, who was doing the same thing in a more leisurely fashion. I'd never seen him so relaxed. It almost gave me the impression he was done going so hard on me. That maybe he thought I'd reached my peak and it was time to take it easy.

I moved in. *I'll liven him up.*

Protecting my face, my ponytail swooshed over my back as I tried to goad him into picking up the pace. He merely stared, still creeping around me. I swung hard and fast at Drew's jaw. He jutted his head back, dodging my punch before quickly returning one to my ribs. I buckled in from the sting of it, cradling my side as I looked up at him. He still bounced in a relaxed rhythm, and it sent a rush of fire sizzling into my veins. I straightened and came at him again, covering my face, trying to decide which body part to attack first, when he landed an uppercut to my jaw, spiraling me back to the floor. I shook my head, dispersing the ringing, and glared at him before rising back to my feet.

"What, are you mad at me or something?" I seethed, coming a bit closer to him than I should have but over-eager to hurt him back.

Whack!

The air whooshed as my back smacked onto the mat, my ankle throbbing where he'd kicked out my legs. "The fuck, Drew!"

He landed on top of me in a rush, squatting over my hips and pinning down my arms. My chest heaved, my heart pounding harder than ever as my eyes searched his face for any sign of my friend, for any clue that he wasn't about to hurt me. He used his teeth to tear his gloves from his hand and covered my neck with a light squeeze, still pinning both of my arms with his other large paw.

"See this spot right here?" he spoke through his teeth, placing pressure with his thumb. A fuzz filtered into my head, making me woozy, my heart unsure of whether it wanted to speed up or lay down. "I've got you right where I want you." His finger probed deeper, sending a spider web effect crackling through my periphery and my mouth opened as my head tilted back, though no sound emerged. "Never get cocky!" he yelled in my face, releasing me to sit back on his heels.

I gasped, sucking in air as I knocked him from my lap and sent distance between us. Coughing, my thoughts raged as I tried to gain composure and air. I had never seen him so intent on hurting me. The look in his eyes ran my blood cold.

He continued to study me, the instructor in him poking through his fury. "There's a difference between cocky and confident, Eva. Confidence will give you the bounce you need to keep your head in the game. Cockiness will give *him* the upper hand to take you down." He stabbed his finger at me, deadly threats beaming from his eyes as he vibrated. "Get it straight and don't fuck it up." He threw a towel at me and turned his back.

I patted the back of my neck, anger simmering into humbleness, feeling as though it were melting away the tension hardening my muscles, deflating me. "I thought I *was* being confident. I was proud of where I was at, that's all." My voice was small, abashed, and quivering.

"And *that* is what made *that*," he pointed to the mat, "where you're at. You're dealing with someone who already knows all your weaknesses, Eva. The day you forget that is the day we'll be peeling you back up off the floor." His eyes trained on me with a passionate knowledge, unwavering and unapologetic.

I propped an arm on one bent knee, contemplating Drew's words. The thought of Damon ever gaining control of me again sent a raging shudder through me. In my mind, I would never allow it. It wasn't a possibility. So I'd relaxed a bit about it. I had forgotten what little choice in the matter I'd had the day he tried to take me forcefully. I gulped and gave a hard nod. No matter how conditioned Drew made me, I had to remember the physical strengths of a determined man.

The bell above the door chimed, indicating someone's presence. Drew grabbed a towel from the floor and slung it over his shoulder without looking up. "We're closed."

A throat cleared. "I'm here to see her."

Drew turned, pushing a thumb into his opposite palm as he addressed our visitor, his eyebrows set in a stern line. The tension between his eyes settled, but his jaw clenched as he dropped his hands. "Well, well, well. I do believe you're the reason we're still here."

I twisted to find Blake hovering in the doorway. Pushing to my feet, I brushed the backs of my pants off. "You came."

Blake's cool gaze that was focused on Drew glided back to me and softened like a child seeing his parents returning to pick them up from school. I scooted over to him. He smiled down at me. "I told you I would. I was happy you wanted to give me a glimpse of what you've been doing all this time." He wrapped his arms around me and dropped a kiss on my nose.

"I'm sweaty." I squirmed.

"You're sparkling." His lips tapped mine in a quick peck before he tucked me under his arm and looked to Drew. I could practically see the hackles raised on the back of Drew's neck like a cat.

Blake tensed beside me. Both guys seemed to be sizing each other up, unsure of what reaction they were going to get from the other. I stepped out of Blake's arms and laced my fingers with his, urging him forward, but speaking to Drew. "I invited Blake to see how you torture me." I smiled, trying to lighten the mood.

Drew's eyes cut to mine, though his words were meant to *cut into* Blake. "Did you tell him you got your ass kicked because your head is in the clouds now?" His gaze bounced back to Blake. "She's a bit too lacksey-daisy for my taste ever since you guys got back together."

I looked up at Blake. "He's being dramatic." Then I looked at Drew, narrowing my eyes with a silent threat. "Message received. Now get the stick out of your ass and come play nice with my boyfriend once and for all, or we're gonna roll around on that mat for real." My look warned him I was only partially joking. I needed them to be friends. They were both too important to me.

Drew could have reacted a number of different ways, but I was pleased when a grin appeared on his face. "There's the Eva I want to see." He made his way over and stuck his hand in Blake's direction. "Told you she loves you."

A smile crept across Blake's face, becoming wider and wider by the second. The tension in his grip on my hand relaxed before he clapped his free hand with Drew's in a firm handshake. "Thanks, man. For taking care of my girl when I couldn't. I was bitter about it at first until Jace reminded me ever so Jace-ly that it was what she needed." Blake looked down at me, though his words were still for Drew. "Thanks for bringing her back to me."

"She's a good girl." His voice was soft as it drifted to a pause. Then it hardened as he brought his line of sight back to Blake. "Treat her right, or I'll have to use you as a test subject." Drew outwardly smirked, but I caught the serious glint in his eyes.

"No worries there." Blake tucked a few hairs behind my ear. "I'll guard this girl till the day I die."

Drew nodded, and in that quiet couple of seconds, a blanket of comfortability seemed to drape over the three of us as the unspoken tension ebbed away and something normal appeared. Blake acknowledging the strength in our relationship status and the friendship between Drew and me. Drew solidifying his role in my life—protector and friend—and stepping back to allow me and Blake our happiness.

"I think we're done for today." I brushed a piece of lint from Blake's shirt.

"That's too bad." Blake frowned, genuinely disappointed. "I wanted to witness you in action."

Drew's smile turned cunning. "Oh, I think we have time for one more throw down. What do you say, Sunshine? You game?"

His cocky-ass grin spoke to my inner lioness. No way was he backing me down.

"I'm always ready to shut your smartass mouth up. Game on, Rainbow." I clapped my hands together and hopped from foot-to-foot, cracking my neck.

"Easy there, whippersnapper." Drew threw up his hands with a short laugh. "Don't scare your boyfriend."

Blake laughed with the lightheartedness that I had missed so much finally shining in his eyes. "Before I forget." He glanced at Drew. "I'm having a thing at my Hamptons house next week. You should come."

Drew nodded. "Sure thing."

And all was right in my world as I landed the first punch to Drew's gut.

Oof!

Chapter 49

"HEY, MAMA-JAMA." JESSIE PLANTED A kiss on my cheek, then plopped into the chair across from me in the cafeteria, plucking a fry from my plate on her descent.

"Hey, girl. Here take 'em. I'm done." I slid my tray toward her.

"Nah, I shouldn't. I started this crazy diet. They looked too good, though." Jessie stared at the fries like a woman stuck on a deserted island.

"Why are you dieting exactly?" I frowned at my perfectly petite friend.

"There are too many rolls in this oven." She pointed to her flat mid-section. "I'm never gonna get a man with all this."

I chuckled. "You're never going to get a man because you're hung up on *one* man in particular." I raised a knowing brow at her.

She scowled. "Well, I'll never get *that* man with these rolls then."

"Stop it, ass." I waved her off, hating when she put herself down. "You're perfect and gorgeous, and you know it."

"But—"

"Zzz—" I made a zipper noise and motioned with my hand for her to shut her mouth.

"Whatever." She shoved a fry into her mouth and closed her eyes, savoring its salty goodness. "God, I love fries." She spoke around her next bite. "Speaking of Rick, I think I'm giving up on him. That's why all of the dieting and stuff. I don't want to be alone anymore." Her eyes were sad.

I shook my head. "I wish I could help you with that one. I don't know what his story is. I can't figure him out." I twisted the cap off my water and took a sip. "I mean, it's obvious he has feelings for you. Everyone can see it, so I just don't get it."

She sighed as she eyed another fry. "I've exhausted myself trying to figure it out. I may just throw myself onto him until he surrenders." She laughed lightly, but unlike her normal Jessie cackle, there wasn't much humor behind it.

"Maybe that's what he needs." I winked.

She waved her hand around. "I don't want to talk about him. Let me enjoy my fries." She popped another into her mouth and closed her eyes along with her lips with a moan.

"'Kay. You coming to the bar tonight?"

She paused and looked up. "Well, I guess I shouldn't if I want to move on, right?"

I shrugged, feeling sorry she had to go through this. I knew how it felt to not be able to be with the one you loved, and it sucked. As I was thinking that, strong fingers slid around the back of my neck, sending a warming tingle over my skin. The touch was so familiar, I didn't have to turn to see who it was. I merely pressed further into it, tilting my head against it. Blake dropped a kiss below my ear and scooted me up a bit so he could slip behind me on the same seat, cloaking me with his manly, musky scent.

"Hey, Jessie." The way his words tickled the little hairs lining my neck, I knew he didn't look at her as he addressed her.

A warm rush raged across my skin at the feel of it combined with his open palms dragging along the tops of my thighs, before coming up to settle right below what would be considered indecent. I turned my face to his, and he eyed my lips. "Hey, Angel." The warmth in his tone heated my core, delivering a rush of blood to my cheeks.

"Hi, Blake." Only a sliver of air rested between our parted lips as we took each other in.

It had been a little over a week since the hotel, and Blake and I were settling back into *us*, taking every advantage we could to be as close as possible to make up for lost time. In our previous relationship together, I had always been somewhat guarded, but after months of therapy and training, and living with a loss that put me in a place so low I thought I would never dig out from it, I was fortified now. Strong. I was in control of every aspect of myself, and I would never lose sight of that again. I made a vow to enjoy every bit of this man at all times, and that's exactly what I was doing.

Both of our eyes remained open as he closed the remaining distance and took my lips in his. The taste of him was enough to roll my eyes back into my head, but the sparkles dancing in the blue pools of his kept me entranced. His fingers bit into the tops of my thighs, and I knew it was taking a lot of control on his part to restrain himself. Knowing the effect I had on him always got me going, I scooted back a little more in my chair, pushing my ass against his growing erection. His eyes widened and then slid closed as he skimmed a hand over my torso and up to my jaw, holding my head in a tilted incline to lick into my mouth. I moaned onto his tongue, drawing it in for a suck before the harsh clearing of a throat called to us from the other side of the table. In a dazed fog, our lips parted, my eyes lazily opening to find Jessie, stunned.

"You guys . . . for real?"

"Sorry about that." I used my ring finger to dab the corner of my mouth and then glanced to my right, heat still soaked into my cheeks. "He's just so delicious."

"Uck, I can't. I'm outta here." Jessie pushed to her feet and picked up her pile of books.

"Hang on," Blake called to her on a chuckle.

She turned, jokingly covering her eyes, and splitting her fingers to look between. "Yeah?"

Blake shook his head and hung his fingers with mine. "My Hamptons house is free for Memorial Day. We're headed there for the weekend next Saturday. I wanted to invite you to come along. There's a bunch of bedrooms, so there's more than enough room."

"Thanks!" Her hand dropped, and her smile returned. "Sounds like fun." She waved and scooted off.

I turned to partially face Blake, and he growled. "We may never get to see anyone while we're there, though. I don't plan to release you from my chambers much." He nipped the edge of my nose.

That brought something to mind. "Speaking of chambers, what's going on with your dad?"

"Now?" His eyes widened in disbelief. "You want to talk about *him* now?" He lowered his voice. "When my dick is hard, and I was about to tell you about the stock I purchased in whipped cream?" He looked down to his lap. "And there it goes," he sighed. "I'm sorry, professor. She didn't mean it."

"I'll make it up to you later," I spoke to his lap.

"Well, in that case." Blake snaked his arms around my waist and squeezed, dropping his chin to my shoulder.

"But you still have to answer the question." I pushed back on his chest.

"Aaaand, he's gone again." He twirled his hand toward his member and relaxed back.

I twisted in my seat. "Is there something you don't want to tell me?" I grew serious, studying him.

Blake huffed. "You know I've been trying to avoid negative areas where we're concerned right now. I mean, I haven't even read your journal yet. I'm just trying to stay in our little happyland bubble a while longer. Is that too much to ask?"

"That's all fine and good, but real life is still happening." I slid my hand over his knee wanting to communicate, for him to know I was here for him. "What's going on?"

Blake deflated behind me. "While we were apart, I decided to go through with my father's plans for my career. I was miserable anyway, so I figured it made no difference at that point."

I slumped inward. Each time I remembered how I'd hurt him, it was like a new punch to the gut.

"Anyway," he continued hesitantly, "if I couldn't be happy, I figured maybe it'd feel good to at least make him happy. So I asked him to set me up with an internship with a firm of his choice over the summer." Blake sent me a sidelong glance.

Visions of us lazing at the beach and underneath Bertha every day evaporated before my eyes. Before we had broken up, I'd been so close to convincing him to give up law. I was sure of it. Now I wasn't sure it would ever be a possibility, and I wouldn't even have this last summer before his senior year to convince him anymore.

"Can you cancel it?" Hope rose in my voice that I could give him a way out. "Say you changed your mind?"

"Cancel? Are you for real? If I want to throw everything out the window and forget I have a father, sure." Sarcasm dripped from Blake's tone, the nonchalance in his features confirming he didn't mean to do any of that.

"Blake," his name rested on a sigh, "why would you do that? You were so close to changing your life. I gave you those photography classes, hoping your love for it would overpower your need to appease him. That you'd want to be happy." The light that he had whenever we were together dimmed with the grim topic, proving my point.

"I didn't think I'd ever be happy again. You don't understand the place I was in. You were—are," he focused deeper into my eyes, "the most important thing to me. With you gone, I would've never been happy anyway. Those classes were all right, but I couldn't enjoy them when I couldn't share them with you."

Sadness crowded my skin. He was wrong. I *did* understand the place he'd been in because I had dwelled there, too. It was a low, dark, and horrible grave. I got it. "But that part of your life is over." I spun in my chair and hooked my legs at the knee over his thick thigh so I could better focus on his eyes which were melancholy and far away at the moment.

"I'm here now." I tried to return some of his hope. "Just tell your dad you've changed your mind and want to take one last summer to enjoy yourself before you have to work for the rest of your life." I smiled brightly, willing it to be contagious, but Blake's shoulders sagged, swiping away my hopes.

"I can't do that, Angel. He set it up for me. It's with a friend of his. It would be too much of an embarrassment. I'm sorry." With his eyes downcast, he looked away.

I wished he had more of a backbone when it came to that man, but we had only been back together for a week. Hopefully, with time, he'd grow stronger. Maybe by summer I could change his mind.

"We'll see." I let my own hope shimmer, certain that I could persuade him before the time came.

"Don't do that." The warning in his tone was clear as a bell, although I chose to ignore it.

"What?" I feigned innocence.

"That." He waggled a finger in my face. "All that. Your brain is moving so fast I can smell it burning."

I laughed fully. "Who are you, Jace? I can't have all of us in my head."

"Just calm yourself. I'll get this over with during the summer, grab the experience I'll need to look good on my resume, and we'll still have more than enough time to enjoy ourselves." He circled my waist with his arms and squeezed.

"Uh-huh," I agreed in my own noticeably sarcastic tone, tilting my neck toward him to invite a kiss.

A ROSY HUE ON A high cheekbone stared back in my reflection. My eyes appeared less sunken in and sullen, the lines of despair that had made themselves known every day now a faded memory. My clothes didn't hang loose anymore. Rather, they were a bit tight from the increase in muscle, and my air seemed to flow freely instead of feeling like I was being strangled all the time.

Blake joined me in the mirror as he snaked his arms around my stomach, pressing himself against my back. I watched as he lowered his head to my ear. "You're so gorgeous." He bit the lobe, and I rocked into him from the heated tickle it gave me. "You sure you have to go to work? Because looking at you in those tight-ass jeans is giving me a raging hard-on." He pressed his erection into my behind as proof.

"Don't tempt me." I dropped the back of my head to his muscled shoulder and closed my eyes.

"So you *can* be tempted then?" His hands rode the curvy lines of my torso before coming up to cup both breasts as he nibbled the soft skin of my neck. "I like when your hair's back."

I sucked in a breath as he suckled the prickling skin. Blake moaned, his hands working the heavy weight of my breasts as his deft fingers brought my nipples to attention. "God, I missed your taste. I don't think I'll ever get enough."

His hands left my breasts and skimmed up to my shoulders, sending a chill through me. He removed the hair tie I'd just spent ten minutes toying with, freeing my hair to cascade down briefly before he scooped it back up into his large palms. With skill and precision, he used his grip on my hair to maneuver my head back and forth as he dropped open-mouthed kisses to the sides of my neck, the bridge of my jaw.

My breathing sat shallow in my chest as I closed my eyes and went limp in his hands, allowing him to control me however he liked and absorbing each sensation. The hard tips of his fingers dragged in and out of the hair at my nape, then down again to clasp it in one bunch to tilt my head to the other side. His tongue started at my ear and then followed the path of my jaw before he lay my head on his shoulder, tilting it at an angle so he could push his tongue into my panting mouth. I spun to face him, slamming his back against the far wall and tangling my own hands in his hair.

"There's my mountain lion." His teeth tugged the flesh of my bottom lip.

"You've got ten minutes," I panted.

Blake's smile lay on my lips. "I only need five. The other five will be a bonus—" He paused to lift me off the floor as I wrapped my legs around his waist and was brought to his gorgeous baby-blue eye level. "For you." His dimple greeted me, and I couldn't help but realize how much I'd missed seeing it as I was whisked off to la-la-land.

"VODKA TONIC!"

"You got it," I called back across the shiny lacquer finish. Blake's "screwdriver" had me feeling more energized than I had been in months. A noticeable pep in my step had my newly smoothed ponytail swishing against my shoulder blades. Rick looked pleased as he maneuvered the bar with me. He seemed at ease for the first time in weeks, finally letting his guard back down with me.

I leaned into the sink, scooping ice into a glass as I glanced to my right, feeling the scrutiny of Blake's electric gaze. A smirk slid across his baby-smooth face which glistened with the glow of a clean shave. He poked a straw between his full lips as my cheeks flushed. Yep, all was finally right in my world.

All but the not-so-tiny matter of Abby, but that would come in its own time. For now, I was going to enjoy my newfound sense of normalcy and strength.

Blake's long pointer finger extended, then crooked as he beckoned me over. I pushed a lime onto the top of the glass I had just filled and slid it across the bar before making my way to him. The heat in his gaze practically ate me alive on my approach.

"I'm thirsty." His eyes dipped to my lips long enough to speed my heart before returning to my own.

"What're you in the mood for?"

He licked his lips. "If you only knew."

Fuck me. Again.

I leaned my elbow on the bar. "Oh, I think I kind of know." My own line of sight dropped to his mouth as heat pooled between my thighs. *Damn this wooden slab between us.* I was all but ready to quit my job just so I could jump over its glossy finish and hump him like a dog in heat. But I smoothed down the front of my shirt and draped my ponytail over my shoulder, feeling like a mess even though I knew it was just my fraying insides playing tricks on me. Knowing I was about to unravel, I decided to speed up the process before I got myself in trouble.

"What can I do for you?"

Blake's eyes widened briefly, a spark zapping them to life as they sparkled above his dimple. He leaned into the bar to meet me. "Maybe you could help me decide." He fingered my hair, twisting it around his finger as he spoke. "I'm not sure if I'd like sex on my face, creamy pussy, or . . ." He leaned in closer so that his lips nearly met mine. "A Suck. Bang. Blow." He blew a puff of air onto my lips before his tongue flicked out to lick them. Then he relaxed back in his chair. "Or perhaps a Royal *Fuck* might better suit my needs."

My air stopped.

Pleased with himself, his throat vibrated with his chuckle. "What do you say, Angel? Any of those sound good to you?"

After months of wishing I could hear some sexy drink melt from his snarky mouth—the fright of thinking I may never get the opportunity again still fresh in my newly-closed wounds, my eyes stung with the prickling of unshed tears. Every now and then the enormity of his absence from my life made itself known, and each time it brought with it a wave of emotions.

Always able to read me, Blake leaned closer once again, helping me block out my surroundings. "I was just playing with you, baby. I didn't mean to make you upset. How 'bout you just make me a rum and Coke?"

His thumb grazed the top of my hand, which was strangling the bar rail. I looked down at the gesture and then back to his eyes, a smile creeping onto my face. No way was I letting him stop his sexy orders. "Don't you dare." I stared him down and waited for the spark to return to his eyes, before returning its light with a smirk. "I just figured you might better enjoy a tall glass of tight snatch."

Blake's Adam's apple rode his throat before coming to rest right above the sexy dip in his collarbone. "Tight snatch sounds perfect. Well played."

Something caught my eye, and I flicked my sights to Blake's left where a stranger was sitting with wide eyes and a wider 'O' on his panting lips. I cringed. "Sorry, we were broken up for a while. I kinda missed him." I winked at Blake, who seemed to have grown three inches as he sat proudly as a peacock on his stool.

"No worries." The man gulped. "I'll take one of those, too."

I laughed out loud, then covered my mouth, hoping I didn't offend him. "Coming right up." I blew Blake a kiss, then turned on my heel to make *two* dirty cocktails.

"Yo, yo, yo!" Jace danced up behind Blake, stabbing his fingers in the air to the beat. Jessie was on his heels, smiling as she played with a tendril of her hair, bopping her head as though she cared about the familiar tune while her eyes scanned behind the bar. Even in the dimmer lighting, I could see the pink swarming her cheeks as Rick raised a hand to her as he poured with the other, finishing off his salute with a wink. Sandra was close behind, and she dropped her handbag on the bar in front of the stool dirty-drink-man had just vacated.

"Well now, the party can start." I plopped bar napkins in front of them. "I was starting to think you guys had changed your minds."

"Blame this one." Sandra thumbed to Jace. "God forbid a highlighted hair is out of place." She rolled her eyes.

"Shrew," he called back.

"Diva," she countered.

"Thank you." Jace pushed a palm into his chest, batting his long eyelashes like he had just won an award. Sandra blew him a kiss. "I prefer Beyonce, though." Jace curled his hand in and threw his head to the side, swiping invisible hair from his shoulder.

"You *are* a queen." I smirked.

"She gets me." Jace pointed to me, flicking his head.

"What're you drinking, Ms. Carter?"

"Kettle, *splash* of seven, and a lime. Make sure it's a splash. I don't want a lot of that soda crap. It's just to take away some of the bite. I got my own." He puckered his full lips.

Blake turned to Jace, offering his straw. "You sure you don't want a tight snatch?" His expression was so straight-faced, it served as its own humor.

Jace's face twisted in disgust. "Not unless it's Madonna's, honey, and that one better come with a side of her tight-assed male dancers to keep my interest."

"More for me." Blake made sure his tongue was visible as he returned his eyes to mine and pushed the straw between his lips.

Jace's eyes were glued to the gesture. "On second thought, I'd take it with a side of you, too." He moved in closer to Blake, practically breathing onto his neck as Blake's back stiffened.

"Hands to yourself, vulture," I warned. "Go play with someone else's meat."

"Greedy." Jace scowled. "You got the Grade-A shit. All the rest of these clowns are like that eighty percent crap they try and sell you in the supermarket. Barf." He stuck a finger in his mouth as Blake puffed up his chest once again, his smile practically touching his ears.

"What do you look so happy about? Want me to agree to it?" I winged an eyebrow at him.

Blake shrunk down, his hand disappearing behind himself to cover his ass no doubt. "No thanks. He scares me."

I snorted as Rick came behind me, covering my shoulders for leverage as he leaned across the bar to give Jessie a peck on one of her red cheeks. "I'd love to stay and chat with you guys, but we're slammed, and I need this chick, sorry." He tugged my shoulders.

"Coming," I called back as he made his way to the opposite end of the bar again to join Jasmine. "That's my cue, guys." I filled their orders quick before spending the next few hours fulfilling my duties.

At some point, Jeremy, Sandra's boyfriend, had wandered in and slipped his arms around her waist, rocking to the side as he reached over to give Blake a pound. He wasn't around much, but her whole face lit up every time he was. I could tell he sincerely made her happy. I guessed a near-death experience aided in assuring you made the most of your life. She had changed so much after that incident, making sure each of her days counted.

When the band was on break, the jukebox took over in their absence. I'd noticed Rick over there a few minutes ago, so I knew some much-loved throwbacks were about to come on. As soon as the newest Miley Cyrus ended, a familiar voice singing about stepping back from a ledge came through the speakers, my keen music-ear instantly recognizing it as *Jumper* by Third Eye Blind.

Jace bopped to the beat, finger in the air, reciting each word. "Dance with me!"

I turned to Rick with a questioning glance.

"Go ahead. I was about to teach Jessie how to mix drinks anyway."

I turned my gaze to her and raised a brow as a bashful smile emerged into a full-bloomed gleam. She hopped off her stool, and we met at the opening, trading hopeful glances. Jace didn't give me much time with her, though, as he yanked my arm, my legs hitching out from behind me in the process. He spun me to sing directly in my face as we stated to each other the truth in the lyrics. He had to talk me down from many ledges. Always with each other's backs and with understanding.

Blake joined us in our happy-bop, completing my heart and bringing everything full circle. I was ready to put my past away and face my demons head-on. The engagement party was fast approaching, and I resolved then and there that it would never have its day.

Drunk, Jace even sang the guitar notes as he air-strummed and I laughed, rocking side-to-side in Blake's arms and loving having the smell of him surround me. Trying to gauge how much time I had, I turned and sought out Rick's approval, but he was noticeably distracted, pouring the bottle with his arms poking out beneath Jessie's. They were both wearing a similar flustered expression and looked like they weren't focused on the bottle they were pouring, though neither could see the other's face. It wasn't lost on me, though.

The lead singer of the Blind Rascals called my name through the mic. "Yo, Eva!" I turned as he motioned me to him. He covered the mouthpiece as the rest of the guys were setting up. "You ready?"

"Sure." I smiled. I'd already chosen a song hours ago, excited to finally sing to my man again. I winked at Blake and lifted onto my tippy toes to give him a peck on the cheek. "Stay close. This one's for you." Blake swatted me on the ass, sending me behind the mic.

I chose more of an upbeat feel to get my point across to him tonight, and I grinned when Rachel Platten's *Stand By You* began. I reached my empty hands out to Blake with a smile as I sang, then turned and wiggled the top half of my back while I stared over my shoulder, telling him to take my wings. At the gesture, Blake tipped his head back with a deep laugh.

I knew I'd walk through any hell with him. He had already helped me deal with so much of what I'd been through, and I needed him to know I would do the same for him. My growth would never have been complete without him. What held him back in life was much different from my pain, but I would be here for whatever he needed to help him soar.

When the song was over, he laced his fingers with mine, a new glitter in his eyes. "We don't have to find heaven. You *are* heaven. You're heaven on earth." He bent to kiss me, the slightest sigh leaving his lips as he spoke. "My angel."

"I will be," I promised. "One day I'm gonna save you the way you saved me."

"You already have." He smiled, light shimmering in his eyes as he stared back at me from the cocoon he held me in, safe and tight in his arms. "I died and came back to life."

"Well then, now it's time to live." I looked deeper into his eyes, hoping he would pick up on all that I meant, when a slap on his shoulder rocked us to the side.

"Sup, bro." Eric held a hand out to Blake, the other still resting on Blake's bicep.

Blake released me to slap Eric's hand, and I stepped back with a small smile, disappointed that our moment was lost. Eric gave me a peck on the cheek, his mint-green eyes alight with life.

"You guys are back together, I see. I'm happy for ya." He dropped his arm around my shoulder and tugged me to him. "Even though I *still* think I'm the better choice."

When I had first met Eric at the frat party at the start of school, a similar situation had made me close to sick, the need to run from it nearly crippling me. Now, I laughed without an ounce of worry. It was just another awesome reminder of how far I'd come.

"There is no other choice." I smiled at Blake.

"Don't be jealous," Blake said to Eric. Taking my hand once again, he deposited me into the bend of his arm where I belonged.

"I'm not jealous. I'm gonna get the other sister anyway." Eric winked, his eyes glistening with promise.

Oh, if only that were true.

"What about your redheaded friend?" I scowled. "I thought you downgraded."

"Who, Amanda?" Eric looked surprised that I remembered. But how could I forget the floozy he looked so keen to wrap himself around? *Amanda.* Suddenly it all made sense. I blanched at my misunderstanding even through the relief of finding out that last little crumb.

"She's nothing." He shrugged. "Did you expect me to be alone? A guy's got to keep up appearances."

I shrugged, not giving away my misinterpretation. "Guess not."

"So when're you gonna get in her ear and hook a guy up anyway?"

"Trust me, nothing would make me happier." I couldn't keep the distaste from my voice.

Blake stepped to the side so he could see me better. "Why do you hate him so much? Haven't you all been best friends since you were little or something?"

I hated how my heart hiccuped in my chest. It both shocked and satisfied me that he hadn't figured it out yet, but I supposed it was for the best. With everything else, I didn't need Blake's prison sentence on my conscience as well. My only answer was to kiss Blake's lips, quieting his questioning mind.

"She hates him because she loves me. And because he's an ass-face,"

Eric yelled over the beginning of the band's next song, disrupting mine and Blake's bliss.

Our lips parted, and we each backed up a step as something caught my attention. A good-looking guy with light brown hair and playful eyes danced toward Blake, placing a finger over his lips while making eye contact with me. With a small leap, he covered Blake's eyes and tugged back. Blake's hands immediately came up to paw at the intruder's fingers, and my eyebrows knitted together. I was worried this might not be a wanted encounter until I heard Eric's hearty, bellowing laugh from behind me.

Blake was able to pry the guy's fingers loose, then he tossed his head behind him, looking as though he was about to rip off the head of whoever it was. But then a smile began to creep across his face, breaking into a full-blown gleam. He immediately grabbed the guy by both shoulders and pulled him in for a hug. "Bray! Is it really you? It's been forever, man." He clapped him on the back before releasing him. "What're you doing here?"

"Eric called me. At least someone keeps in touch, douche!" He shoved Blake's shoulder, and I wondered for the millionth time who he was.

"And I assume this is the girl I told you would be coming to turn your life upside down?" He focused friendly eyes on me.

Blake rubbed the back of his neck, tilting his head as though something had just hit him. "Yeah, I guess you were right about that one." Blake turned a shy smile to me, sweeping his arms out in introduction. "Brayden, this is Angel—I mean, Eva. Eva, remember a while back I told you about a friend that I had for-like-ever that was practically married since he was five?"

"Hey, I was eight." Brayden rolled his embarrassment off his shoulders.

Blake laughed. "Well, this is him."

Thinking back, I did faintly remember a long-lost friend Blake spoke fondly of. "Nice to finally meet you." I stuck out my hand, and he quickly accepted it.

"My pleasure. Thanks for making an honest man out of this guy."

My cheeks warmed. He obviously hadn't been filled in on the train wreck that was our past relationship. Thankfully we would be moving forward from this point on, so hopefully, his view of me wouldn't be tainted.

He turned his focus back to Brayden. "So what's up? Where's Casey?"

I was pretty sure I remembered that being the name of his so-called *wife*. As far as I knew, they weren't actually married yet, and Blake was just being a typical ball-busting guy. My heart was happy to see him so lighthearted, though. I vowed to keep Brayden around.

Brayden's eyes lost a drop of their smile. "She's been busy. Finally finishing up with school and shit."

"Cool." Blake hadn't noticed the tiny missing spark. "Maybe this means you'll be around more?"

"Maybe . . ." Brayden's thoughts were cut short as Jace pushed himself into the center of their man-circle.

"Well, well, well. What's all this?" Jace motioned to Blake, Eric, and Brayden. "This is way too much hot in one spot. We may have to call in the fire department." He fanned himself, then placed a thoughtful finger to his lips. "Scratch that. That'd just mean more hot men."

Brayden's posture became erect, his smile losing its muster as it began to sag in the corners. I was so used to people accepting Jace that seeing it caught me off guard. I hoped Jace didn't notice. He talked a good game, but those types of things always did their job of chipping away a small piece of his ego.

"What's up, sweets? You a phobe or somethin'? I've got special tools for people like you if you are." Jace placed his hands on his hips, narrowing his gaze.

He noticed.

I held my breath and swung my eyes to Brayden's reaction. Thankfully, he caught himself. "No, no. Sorry, no disrespect. You just reminded me of someone, that's all."

Jace's eyes licked with fire as his finger wagged. "Trust me, sugar. There ain't no carbon copy of all this." Jace motioned to his body from head to toe. "But, dirty looks like *those* are the reasons why I'm here solo tonight. You should watch them. The mouth ain't the only thing that talks, honey." He quirked a brow.

I placed my hand on Jace's forearm, leveling him. "He didn't mean it, Jace. Down, boy."

A small piece of tension left him, but most of it remained.

"Whatever's going on with you has nothing to do with him. Come on, love. Make nice," I pressed further.

The rest of his aggression left, and he stuck out his hand toward Brayden who had lost all playfulness. He accepted Jace's offer. "Sorry, man. I got a lot going on."

"Me, too, I guess." Jace smiled from the corner of his mouth, apologetic for probably the first time in his life.

"Come on. Shots on me!" Brayden called out.

"Don't tempt me, sugar," Jace replied, licking his lips.

The smile on Brayden's face told me he had meant what he said and didn't have a problem with Jace at all. But the encounter also told me that my best friend was hurting more than he had let on.

HE POPPED THE QUESTION.

She said yes.

Please join us in celebrating . . .

A week.

There was one week left before the engagement party. I'd been so focused on Blake and me that I hadn't begun to figure out how I would stop this party from happening. After this trip to the Hamptons, I would have to figure it out, but I was going to enjoy a few more blissfully unaware days before I allowed the shit to hit the fan. One more weekend and then I'd make Blake read the journal. *Then . . .*

Then I'd turn my sister's world on end and possibly lose her for good.

The engagement of Abby and Damon.

I clenched my teeth and aimed my blow dryer at the card, reveling in the enjoyment of watching it skid from my counter and spiral to the floor. After I finished my hair, I walked into my bedroom in a red satin bra and matching underwear. Blake was asleep on my bed, his bare back rising and falling lazily, the mound of his ass tucked tightly beneath the towel that was still cinched around his waist. The curves of his spine sparkled with water droplets—the slow, even breaths entering and exiting his mouth on each puff of air, making them look as though they were dancing. I watched one drop topple from the hard peak of his muscle, down the side of his rib, and disappear into the mattress.

I couldn't help myself. I crawled onto the bed on all fours, stopping to hover directly above him, taking in his beauty. The smooth color of his tanned skin, the deep dip down the entire middle of his muscled back. I was even in love with the way he bent his leg to the side any time he slept on his stomach. We had a long drive ahead of us, so I should have let him sleep . . . but I had droplets to taste.

My tongue scooped up the one directly above the towel on the left side. Drop by drop, I tasted Blake's skin, swooping my tongue up along each muscle lining his back, over his shoulder blade, before sucking behind his neck. Little pebbles broke out, mingling with the drops, and I smiled as I made my way down the right side of his back, around his ribs, and right back to where I started, at the base of the towel. I dropped open-mouthed kisses along the perimeter—into the dip of his spine, around the side of his hip—when he finally trundled to his back, sending me between the V of his legs.

He smiled down at me. "Now there's a wake-up."

I smiled back, feeling drunk from his taste, my mind on one thing as he hardened under the soft bends of the towel. I dragged my nails up his thighs, earning a moan from him, the back of his head becoming lost in the pillows. Inch by inch, my hand disappeared under the cotton, Blake's breaths seeming to deepen with each slide that brought me closer.

The hair turned fine, smooth to the touch on his upper thighs, letting me know I was getting warmer. Blake's heavy breaths told me he was heating up as well. I licked my way along his lower abs, right above the tuck of the towel. My fingers roamed the tops of his legs, the curve of his hip, loving the quivers rippling over his stomach with each pass of a sensitive spot.

A hard twitch beneath the towel brought my attention to it. My fingers sought out the source, moving closer to the center. Blake's moaning swallow let me know that's where he needed me. I had the same reaction when I brushed the edges of the cotton aside, allowing it to drape along the outside of his legs, showcasing the hard throbbing flesh between it. I wrapped my greedy fist around it as a strangled groan found its way to Blake's throat. The air hissed through his teeth as I stroked him, soft, gentle strides up and down, palming his head, back down to the base. The moisture that I'd collected on my palm quickly replaced itself at the head of his cock as his arousal heightened. My tongue darted to it, drawing more of his taste inside, his hips bucking at the contact. His fingers found their way to my hair, coming into the soft strands framing my face as his eyes sought out mine in a silent plea for what he wanted.

I allowed him to guide me, show me what he needed as I took him in my mouth. And I loved the strained, pleasure-filled look on his face, knowing I was the one putting it there. He closed his eyes, dropping his head back as he worked me over himself. His pecs bulged with the strain of reaching down to me, his abs tight and bunched while his cock grew even harder in my mouth.

Up and down.

In and out.

His fingers combed through my hair, caressed my face, and stroked the back of my head before locking at my nape. The urgency in his movements heightened, quickening. I rode his motions, letting him use me to bring himself down the other side. I loved that I was what sent the bucking waves of pleasure rocking through his quaking body.

A grin teased my mouth as I ran my tongue along the length of him, and he melted back into the mattress, releasing me. I lulled his dick from the high, kissing and lapping until I knew he was done, sated, and relaxed. Crawling up the length of him, I placed kisses along his happy trail, over his belly button, and the hard lines of his torso, to the valley of his chest before melting into his embrace. He used his thumb to stroke my back, my arms, a soft smile playing on his lips while his eyes remained closed.

"I love you, Blake Turner, if I didn't already tell you today."

"I love you, Evangelina Angel Ricci, if I didn't tell you this hour."

"I'm pretty sure you messed up my hair that I just spent almost an hour on," I teased.

"No way." His breath tickled my ear. "The I-just-swallowed-my-boyfriend's-dick look is *so* much nicer on you. I did you a favor."

I swatted at him. "Watch your mouth."

A devilish grin broke out across Blake's lips. "No, *you* watch my mouth." He flipped me onto my back and began trailing kisses from my collarbone, down my center, headed toward my heaven. And I watched every last drop of those perfectly plump lips to my heated skin until his face disappeared between my legs.

"WHAT SHOULD I WEAR?" I stood in front of my closet in only a bra and thong, swishing hangers back and forth.

"Nothing. It'll make my job much easier later."

I turned to find Blake with one arm propped under his head, still in his towel, staring at me.

I laughed, turning back to my chore. "Now that would make a good headline. Girl arrested for indecent exposure along the expressway."

The bed creaked behind me, followed by some rustling noises, and I assumed Blake was finally up to getting dressed. "Whatever it is, just be sure it matches gold." His breath in my ear startled me, and I jumped, banging off his chest.

"You're never going to stop doing that, are you?" I palmed my heart and turned to face him. "Now, what are y—"

I choked on my words at the sight of my chain dangling from Blake's long pointer finger. The chain Blake had given me for Christmas that I'd torn off my neck in haste the day I nearly killed myself. The chain that culminated all of the memories of our relationship. The chain that I had left for scrap as though it had meant nothing to me when, in fact, it meant the world. The chain with the hanging charms from scattered points that he had put so much thought into.

That chain.

Water filled my vision, blurring its beauty. "You fixed it," I whispered.

"I fixed it," Blake stated, tenderness melting on his tongue.

I threw my arms around his neck and squeezed. My tears rocking me against him. "Thank you."

Blake kissed the top of my head and backed up slightly to clasp the chain around my neck as I swiped at my eyes, sniffling. "There we go." He made one final adjustment to its placement. "You take that off again and you're punished."

I laughed through my tears, fingering my neckline, grateful to feel its return. "Never again."

He placed his hand over my heart, the tips of his fingers resting on the necklace. “Mine.”

I covered his hand. “Yours.”

Chapter 52

"WOW." I STEPPED OUT OF Blake's car onto the circle drive.

"Yeah. Perks of being the son of a Supreme Court Judge." Blake half sneered, half smiled, coming around to my side.

"Might as well get use out of them if you're doing what he wants anyway." I gave him my famous side-eye.

"Don't think I won't kick your ass this weekend, miss." Blake tapped the edge of my nose as if that were a threat.

"Oooh." I shivered sarcastically, shutting the door.

The property was massive. Long white columns twined up the front, leading up to a full wrap-around balcony.

That's a much better balcony than mine.

We left the car next to the fountain in the center of the drive, and Blake cupped his hand around the back of my neck, leading us up to the porch. Before he could get his key in the door, it flew open, and his sister Victoria leaped into his arms.

"You're here!"

The strength knocked Blake back a few feet with a stumble, my body jolting from the force. "You're early." He smiled, setting her on her feet.

"Uh, yeah, I am. I couldn't wait to get out of there." She rolled her eyes.

Blake's mom was a sweetheart, like his sister, but his dad was a monster. I knew that's who she was so anxious to get away from since she still lived at home. With long legs that seemed to stretch to the sky, Victoria threw herself at me next, nearly taking me out with the extra six or so inches she had on me. When she was done squeezing, she whispered in my ear, "I missed you, sis. I knew you'd be back."

I choked up at her words. I hadn't seen her since Blake and I had broken up, and I didn't realize how much I had missed her spunky personality. "Small hiccup. It'll never happen again," I reassured her.

She laced arms with me. "Come on, let me show you around."

"Lead the way." I smiled, taking a peek back at Blake.

His face was twisted in a scowl as he slung our bags over his shoulder. The thump of our heavy baggage landed in the foyer as Victoria chattered on about the artwork on the walls. She was so engulfed, she didn't notice me scale back to whisper toward Blake, "What's wrong?"

"She's early." He frowned.

"Aaand . . . ?" Blake was crazy about his sister. I never imagined he wouldn't be happy to see her.

He bent, the edges of his hair brushing against my ear as his warm breath coated it. "And I wanted to fuck you on every square inch of this house before anyone got here. Starting with that table right there, next to the expensive fucking vase." He squeezed my hip.

My throat went dry, my swallow scratchy as I stole a glance behind me to the piece of furniture that sat as the focus of the foyer, proudly displaying an overpriced floral arrangement. When I looked back to Blake, his eyes were intense as Victoria's words bled into the background.

"Then I wanted you in the pool." Blake kissed the left side of my neck. "Then on top of the bar." He kissed the right. "Then on my face as you fisted the wrought iron rails lining the tennis court." He licked the sensitive swatch of skin right below my ear, sending a rippling wave down to my girl parts.

I stopped breathing.

When his gaze met mine again, he smirked.

"*Hello* . . . are you even listening?" Victoria's voice finally had volume, slicing through the intense moment.

I cleared my throat and tried to speak coherently. "Yeah. Sure. Listening." Fanning a hand to my face, I turned to meet her. "Is it hot in here? I think it's hot in here." It would be indecent to fan where I really needed it.

"Hot?" She tilted her head. "The air is set to like sixty."

"Well, I think it's hot. Blake, are you hot?" I looked at him.

Another dimpled smirk. "You know *I'm* hot."

I fanned faster, turning back to Victoria, whose corner of her lip was raised as though she had seen a bug. "Eww."

"You were early," Blake growled.

"You know I'm your sister, right? I don't want to hear this stuff."

"But—"

Blake tried to explain, but Victoria cut him off by sticking her fingers in her ears like a five-year-old. "La-la-la-la-laaaa. I can't hear you!"

Blake laughed, backing off, and Victoria unplugged. "How would you feel if I was talking about some guy like that?"

"Yeah, all right." His chest inflated. "You're not dating till you're like thirty-five."

Victoria rolled her eyes. "Keep telling yourself that, dear brother."

She patted his bicep and he noticeably tensed. "Uh-huh," Victoria gloated. "See how that feels?" She swayed her curvy hips as she left the room, calling back over her shoulder. "Make sure you pick the room farthest from mine!"

"Well, there went any hopes of a hard-on." Blake shiver-cringed.

I looped my arm through his, a grin tilting my lips. "I'm sure you'll be just fine. Come on, Romeo, show me around."

THE GROUNDS SEEMED TO GO on forever, the number of rooms and wings endless. There was even a mini movie theatre and game room downstairs. I guess this was the type of life Mr. Turner wished for Blake to have. As glamorous as it seemed, I didn't think Blake *needed* it. I mean, sure, who wouldn't love to have it, but at what cost? What was the price of one's soul?

Blake wrapped his arms around me from behind, his chin pressing into my shoulder. "So, what do you think?"

"It's beautiful."

Blake twisted us so he could focus on my face, his eyebrows pulling in the center. "What's wrong?"

How did this boy always know when there was something on my mind?

Tell him, don't tell him?

I didn't really want to ruin our weekend.

"Nothing." I leaned my neck to his lips, signaling he should press a kiss there. He obliged, skipping a tingle down my spine.

"Liar."

"I always tell the truth, even when I lie." I curled my lip with my best Scarface impersonation.

"Okay there, gangsta." Blake spun me to face him and then draped his forearms over my shoulders. "What is it?"

The corner of my mouth puckered and I shrugged. "It's just a bit much, no? Is this what you want to have one day?" I couldn't keep the disappointment from my voice.

"If I get to be with you, I wouldn't mind living in a shoe box." He kissed the tip of my nose and rested his forehead against mine.

"Is that true?" I peeked up at him.

"Of course that's true." He became serious, taken back. "Why would you doubt that?"

Hope ballooned in my chest as I rushed out hopefully, "Then cancel your internship. Spend the summer with me. We can spend the rest of our lives in a cardboard box, singing and writing and taking pictures of it."

I could tell my eyes were alight with life as Blake's began to dim. "Angel, please don't do this. Can't we enjoy our one weekend away?"

"Well, yeah." I lowered my voice. "I just thought, if you really meant it, that I'd be worth giving all this up for." I took a step back. I didn't mean to sling a guilt trip on him. I knew how he felt about me, it was just . . . I loved him. More than life. And I'd push as hard as I had to if it meant he would be happy in the end.

Blake looked at me with all the love in the world. "You're worth giving up air for, and you know it." At my silence, Blake exhaled a deep breath, pinching the bridge of his nose. Finally, he stepped toward me. "I'll make you a deal." I stared up at him as he combed a piece of my hair behind my ear.

"Let me do this just for this summer. Get a feel for the real life of it. And if I really truly hate it, I'll stop."

I took inventory of his reactions to see if he was really telling the truth. "You mean it?"

"I mean it." Blake's gaze was unwavering, truth shining through his eyes as he stared down at me, hopeful.

I threw my arms around his neck and squeezed. "Thank you." I peppered his smooth cheek with kisses. "Thank you, thank you, thank you!"

He chuckled. "You're all I'll ever need, baby. Don't you ever forget that."

As I pulled back, I fingered my necklace, which reminded me of the day Blake had originally given it to me inside the new journal. Which in turn sent my thoughts to the old one he had yet to read. I dreaded that day and hoped that, once he did, he would still mean those words.

"Ditto." I kissed Blake long, deep, and slow, resolving to love him every minute of every day that he would have me. I wouldn't let fear be my ruler anymore. I would always be okay, no matter what.

"Hey . . ." He slapped my ass lightly before resting both palms on it. "Ever play tennis?"

"No, but I'm intrigued." My lips curled. "Does it involve you sweating while we're playing it?"

"It does." Blake smirked. "Wear your bathing suit underneath whatever you put on. We're going there next." The glint in his eye sparkled with whatever was up his sleeve.

THE WROUGHT IRON FENCE.

I swallowed hard. Blake's smirk spoke volumes as my eyes sought him out.

"So th-that's the, um . . ." My eyes went back to the fence.

"The fence that you're going to white-knuckle if you lose? Yep, that's the one." He swatted my ass with the racket, sending me to a skip.

I rubbed it, mumbling. "Hardly seems like a punishment." My eyes brightened. "I forfeit. Can I just lose now?"

Blake tipped his head back with a hearty chuckle, and I loved the way the sun danced across his features.

How did I get so lucky?

"Trust me, Angel, we're both winning." He stepped closer. "I'm still gonna kick your cute little ass, though."

I had no clue what the rules were, and I had no idea if Blake was even keeping the proper score. All I knew was I was having a blast. Tennis was a lot more fun than I expected and probably the ultimate workout. I would have to let Drew in on the secret. I swatted the ball with the backhanded swing I had perfected over the last hour.

"I think I have tennis elbow," I called across the net.

"Tennis el—*Oof*." The ball bounced off Blake's gut, and he folded forward, holding his middle.

"Sorry." My hand reached out.

"Nope. Nope. My fault," Blake coughed. "I hardly think you can get tennis elbow in one afternoon." He half-laughed, half-winced.

"I'm telling you, it hurts in here." I stepped to the net, pulling my arm around to try and inspect it as Blake met me on the other side.

"Let me see." He took my arm in his hands. "Where? Right here?" His fingers moved gingerly over my sensitive skin as he probed, testing.

"Yes." I flinched.

Keeping his blue eyes on mine, he raised my elbow to his lips and placed an open-mouthed kiss on the tender spot. "Better?"

My breathing caught as I watched the motion, witnessing the small shimmer of *kiss* he'd left behind. "Not yet." I shivered.

Blake brought his smiling lips back to my injury and began to suck-kiss it. "How 'bout now?"

"It seems to be traveling. It's radiating up my arm." My eyes never left him.

"Well, we can't have that now, can we?" He kissed up my arm, creating a tingling heat throughout my limbs. My head dropped back with a gasp when his greedy lips met my collarbone. "Here?" He licked.

"Everywhere," I panted. "It hurts everywhere."

Blake's smile widened as he licked a trail to my ear, his words grazing the lobe. "I win." With no other notice, he scooped me up and lifted my tiny frame over the netting that was separating us. I instinctively wrapped my legs around him, whimpering into his mouth as his tongue found mine. He tasted like mint and sweat and lust as he carried me, palming the spandex covering my bottom under the almost non-existent tennis skirt I had borrowed from Victoria.

The fence knocked the wind out of me as my back slammed against it, the push of Blake's pelvis into me forcing a whimpered moan from my lips. Blake bit that moan as he clasped my bottom lip between his teeth, eliciting a second whimper. "I want you." He fingered the thin material covering my pussy.

Do that again. "It's the middle of the day . . . Victoria . . ."

"Is shopping." With no effort, Blake had the silky strap aside as he pushed a finger inside of me. I gasped, but he swallowed that up, too. "Grab the fence," he ordered into my mouth.

I hastily untangled my fingers from the back of his head and reached behind me to wrap my fingers around the iron. Blake's grin was deliberate as his eyes raked over my trussed up body, his fingers making quick work of his pants. His gaze fell to my panting chest and then his face disappeared between it as he inhaled a deep breath of me, biting down on the heaving flesh as he slid himself inside of me. My head dropped back between the bars as he allowed my body to adjust around him, my full weight sitting on top of his erection. Without words, his eyes asked if I was ready, and without thought, my pussy clenched in response.

There's the dimple I love.

Blake's hips began to rock, his tongue mingling with mine once again. His breaths matched his pace as both quickened.

Thrusting.

Panting.

Pawing.

Loving.

I cried out, the back of my head riding between the bars, my arms burning as they held on while he nipped and sucked my jaw, my neck, my collarbone. He palmed my chest, driving into me. I squeaked and cried and moaned as he grabbed the back of my head, forcing my air to pant into his lungs once again as he dragged in each of my harried whimpers.

"I love you," he spoke into my mouth, and my grip tightened on the bars as I exploded around him.

"I love you more." I let go and wrapped my arms around him as he lowered us to the ground, each of us finishing in a slow, magical rhythm. I melted into his embrace, neither one of us willing to move.

This man was my lifeline, and I would let him carry me to the edge of the earth or the top of the sky. Wherever it was, I knew I'd be grounded. And after years of falling into the pits of nowhere, it felt good to finally feel solid enough to land.

"Hold on." Blake's smile was mischievous as he tightened his hold around my bottom and got to his feet, taking off in a small sprint.

"Where are we going?" I hugged myself to his chest to stop from jostling too much.

"Round two." Blake's smile widened further before he slanted to the side and free-fell with me in his arms, my half-screech muted by the rush of water over my head. When we resurfaced, we were both laughing and trying to catch our breaths.

Finding his footing, Blake stood in the pool, my legs still wound tightly around his waist as his hands found the sides of my face. I wondered what he was thinking as he drew in each of my features, his gaze drifting about. I stared at his eyes, glistening a glittering blue as the sun and the reflection of the water danced amongst them, and I thought I'd never seen anything more magnificent.

"I love—"

"Marry me, Angel." Blake's words swallowed mine, making them insignificant.

I couldn't answer, though, because they stole my breath.

"I know we're crazy, young. It doesn't have to be today or tomorrow. I don't know when, and I didn't even plan to ask, but I know it's what I want." His breaths evened out as calm washed over him. You would imagine the opposite happening with such a declaration, but the release of it seemed to provide him with solace more than anything.

When my tongue stayed silent, and my stare remained stunned, he continued. "Nothing functions right unless you're by my side. When you're gone, I wonder when you'll be back and when you're here, I wonder how I can get you closer." He brushed the pads of his thumbs along my cheekbones, still cradling my face. "Marry me. One day—every day. Make me the happiest man alive. You make me whole. You're my air and my sun. My—"

"Yes," I answered without thought. "A million times, yes." My words were soft despite the banging in my chest. I'd never been more certain of anything in my life, though, and I harbored no fear about tying myself to him for eternity. I'd do it today if he really wanted to.

Blake's head dipped lower, a question in his mesmerizing eyes. "Yes? You'll be my wife?"

"Yes. I'll be your everything. Your wife, your best friend, your air, your heart. You're already all of those things for me. My soul already married you the day it met you."

Blake took my lips in his. I felt his smile suck me up before he started peppering kisses on my face. "I love you, Angel. I'll make you the happiest woman in the world. I'll love you forever and ever and take care of you." He continued to sprinkle promises around my face, but his words began to melt into one another as what he was saying really began to settle in.

I would never be alone again.

I would never have to be afraid. No matter what, I'd have him by my side. But, before I could allow him to fully solidify that promise, we needed no secrets between us.

"Blake—" I spoke between his kisses.

"Yeah." He still roamed my neck and jaw.

"You need to read the journal."

Suddenly, they stopped.

THE HEAT OF BLAKE'S KISSES still lingered on my chilled, wet skin. Blinking, he stared at me. Though behind his wordless lips that still lingered in a small pucker, I saw the faintest hint of fright.

I covered the hands that still cradled my face with my own and smiled reassuringly. "You have every nook and cranny of me. You own each piece, forever and always, but I need you to know exactly what has made up each and every one of those pieces."

Blake's breathing faltered, and his shoulders lost their sharpness.

"It doesn't have to be today, and it doesn't have to be tomorrow, but I know it's what I want." I fed him back his same words. The fact that I meant them was a true eye-opener.

"I'm ready," he admitted. "I just wasn't expecting that. I only wanted to have some *us* time, before the weight of that book sat on top of us. But it's time to put it all behind so we can throw it away and build our life free of it." Blake placed a soft kiss on my lips. "I will love every piece of you until I take my last breath, Angel, and I'll never stop taking care of you."

"Thank you." I rested my forehead against his, and we both closed our eyes. You seemed to draw more of the person under your skin when your eyes were closed to other distractions. "Thank you for the unconditional love you give me. For loving my scars and my ugly."

Our eyes met, but our foreheads remained touching. "There's no ugly in you. Only beauty." He skimmed his fingers down my arm. "I'm going to spend every day for the rest of my life making sure you're fine. I promise."

My lips silenced his as my heart ballooned to near-exploding. There was nothing else I needed, and I wasn't nervous for him to read the one piece of my insides that I had always held so guarded. Blake was my home. I had no doubts that, no matter how he reacted to the truth once he knew, he would never leave me. We would be okay.

A contented fulfillment immersed me.

So this is what it's like.

I was finally whole—without doubt and without regret. I was ready to fully own my past, no matter what that meant, and march toward my future knowing I was a strong and recovered individual, as well as half of an iron-clad couple. Nothing could come between Blake and me, I was sure of it, and knowing that seemed to build a new set of walls around me. But rather than keeping people out, they were put there to hold the two of us in. Together we would build our own fortress, our own unbreakable city where nothing else mattered but him and me. I wasn't sure when the shift had taken place, but the world seemed to tilt on its axis and slip us both into a different realm.

We each slid a palm over the other's heart, absorbing the rhythm beneath them.

My beat met his bang, his bounce answering my thump as we created silent music together, mingled only with the soft lapping of the water around us. Our heart rates sped up simultaneously, each of us sharing the same thoughts of how overwhelming the sensation of this was. The suffocating feeling of being so swollen with love, so filled with the other person that you thought you would explode somehow if you didn't find some form of relief from it, but at the same time, wanting to squish even more of them inside of you.

"I feel it, too," Blake said, his eyes gentle as his lips parted as though breathing were a task. His finger tapped my chest each time a beat took flight.

When his lips met mine, they seemed like they were trying to tell me something. Soft and gentle, he dipped in and out of my mouth, placing light kisses with plump caresses, letting me know we had all the time in the world to enjoy each other now. He tasted like chlorine and sunshine and that sweetness only he had. With each light brush, I fell into him further. At this point, I'd fallen so deeply into him that I didn't care if I never found my way out.

Fall into me.

Words that he had spoken so many months ago.

The rest of the world disappeared in a blanket of watery, tender kisses and silent beating promises of finally being able to breathe with breath that didn't hurt.

WHERE DID THAT COME FROM?

I had never planned to ask Angel to marry me, but no words had ever felt more right leaving my mouth. I didn't care how young we were or how short a time we'd been together. None of that mattered. The thought of spending another day without her could buckle my knees. I needed for her to know that wasn't an option anymore. She was my everything all rolled up into a tiny little green-eyed goddess package. I wanted to swallow her fears and comfort her hurts. I wanted to share in each of her joys and kiss away all of her tears. Build her up when she felt like tearing herself down. There was nothing that could separate us anymore, and the confidence I held in that fact made me feel like I could stand as tall as the highest building.

I was going to be *her* everything. Be the man who would make her proud. Nurture her. Protect her.

My heart knocked on my chest. It was time to find out what she had been dealing with. I couldn't be scared of it anymore. It wouldn't ruin us, it would free us. Break the final chains that kept that small piece of us apart. Whatever it was, I would figure out how to fix it for her once and for all. One final weekend of bliss and then we would tackle the demons head-on.

Her journal felt like butter underneath my fingertips. Though, when you caught the edges just right, there were parts that were so worn they could cut you if you hit them at the right angle. I picked my nail over a slice in the far right corner, thinking about what this book held inside. Just holding it rocketed a piece of heartache through me. The weight of her sorrows tucked inside it was unmistakable. I knew she had given it to me to read at my leisure, but I wouldn't look inside without her next to me. It felt like a violation.

We'll read this together when everyone leaves tomorrow.

Chapter 55

"KNOCK, KNOCK!" JESSIE'S VOICE ECHOED through the foyer.

"In the kitchen!" I called back.

"Is Blake serious with this house?" Jessie squealed. "He never said he was royalty."

"He's not royalty." I laughed, rolling my eyes. "This is what you get when you sell your soul to the devil."

Her eyes continued to roam. "Well, he can have mine, too, because this is gorgeous."

"Thank you, thank you." Blake walked in, his body tilted in an incline carrying a case of beer. The bottles clanked with his strides, knocking off his thick thighs as his biceps stretched the material of his black T-shirt. He set it down next to the fridge. "Angel would rather live in a cabin of sweet music and heartfelt photographs, though. We'll be dirt poor and rich in love." With a crooked grin, he bent to line the bottles on the bottom shelf.

A playful grin met my face as well. "Sounds perfect." I swatted his round ass, the sound of glass ricocheting off one another ringing out.

Blake steadied them quickly, jumped up, and grabbed his behind. "You're assaulting me again?" The effect was just as cute as the first time I had done it.

I stifled a giggle, pointing. "I own that ass now. Consider it never safe."

Blake scowled, tucking a couple of bottles to his chest, and turned to unload them, blinking like an innocent fawn, peeking back over his shoulder to be sure I wasn't too close.

"Idiot." I laughed before turning back to Jessie. "Did you drive up alone?"

"Nah, Sandra and Jeremy are bringing all the stuff in." Her face puckered. "They're so sweet to each other they make my teeth ache."

"Don't be bitter." Sandra's voice came from the doorway.

"Oh, there's Miss Sugarcane herself," Jessie mocked.

"You love me." Sandra batted her eyelashes before tucking her auburn curls behind her ear. "Fancy quarters." She smiled at Blake, who was bending to kiss her cheek.

"Thanks." Blake reached behind her to slap Jeremy's hand. "Hey, bro. Glad you guys could make it."

"Course," Jeremy replied. "Thanks for inviting us." Jeremy was on the shorter side and clean cut for an artist. And Sandra loved him madly.

Blake went back to his task. "Go pick your rooms, guys. Consider everything here yours and make yourselves at home."

Victoria danced into the room. Always full of life, she beamed at their guests, sticking out her hand to each of them. "Hey, guys. I'm Tori. Don't let them convince you to call me Victoria." She hopped onto the kitchen island and snagged a peach before taking a big bite. Peaches, grapes, and oranges. I didn't think I'd ever seen a fruit bowl in someone's house that didn't contain apples. But, ever since the incident in the cafeteria when the apple had freaked me out, Blake never had another one around, which made me realize it was most likely on purpose that his bowl lacked their presence.

Will we always revolve our lives around my past?

Either way, I loved him more for the effort.

Jessie bounced over to Tori, her matched spunkiness making me realize they were the perfect pair. I didn't know why it hadn't occurred to me sooner to introduce them. "Hi! I'm Jessie. You can call me Jessie." Her smile practically reached her ears.

"How cute you are with your curly hair. I wish my hair was curly. It just lays there." Victoria fingered her own gorgeous strands.

"You're kidding me, right?" The corner of Jessie's lip turned up like she was disgusted. "You have, like, silk-head. I'd die for your hair. Here's what I can do with this. This . . ." She pointed to the current style of her hair, which was just fluffy curls. "Or a frazzled ponytail. That's it, sista."

"Well, I love it." Victoria took another healthy bite.

"Jace not coming?" I looked at the crew.

Sandra began to answer. "Nope, he said he had pl—"

"Don't you bitches be talkin' about me." The front door banged off the wall, revealing Jace in rose-gold Michael Kors aviator sunglasses. His hair was slicked back, and a bag hung from his crooked elbow. On the other elbow, he was wearing . . . Drew?

"This stud offered to ride me—I mean, give me a ride," he corrected with a grin, "although that still sounds fun." Jace smirked at his own joke, while Drew looked mortified and out of his element around my eccentric accomplice.

"Do you know how long of a car ride it is from Manhattan to the Hamptons? Anyone?" Drew polled us. Judging by his disheveled hair and the stoned look in his eyes, he had clearly been Jace-ized.

Poor guy.

"Don't play like you didn't love every second of it, honey." Jace rolled his eyes as they made their way further into the kitchen.

"I'll never be the same," Drew mumbled more to himself. He shivered, and I laughed, imagining what he'd had to endure in that car. Jace made his rounds, double-kissing cheeks while popping his leg back in the air. And Victoria . . .

Victoria slid slowly down the edge of the counter, her eyes fixated on Drew as though a god had entered the room.

Drew addressed Blake first, reaching a fist out to give him a pound. "Thanks for the invite, man. Nice place."

"Anytime." Blake returned the gesture with a warm smile.

Drew rolled his neck around, cracking it, walking toward me. "Hello."

"Hey." I rose to my toes and kissed his cheek. "You okay?"

"Not yet." He chuckled, glancing around before his eyes snagged to my right where Victoria was now standing, her stare trained on his hazel eyes. She rocked to her left into my arm, nudging me to introduce them. Drew's jaw tightened, his muscles bulging as his grip cinched his bag.

I looked back and forth between them.

"Um, Drew, this is Victoria."

"Tori." Victoria's hand stretched forward.

Drew's gaze fell to it before he slipped his palm into hers. "Drew."

I saw it—the hitch in Victoria's breathing, the lapse in rhythm as her cheeks reddened before her eyes skirted away from his. She pulled her hand away and scraped it along her thighs.

Within moments, Blake was at our sides, his shoulders sharp and straight. He looked back and forth between them as Victoria took a few steps back.

"*Victoria*," Blake annunciated, "is my kid sister."

Drew's shoulders rounded out as if he were a kid who had just gotten all his candy stolen. "She's charming," he croaked out.

Victoria put her hand on Blake's shoulder, and I caught him wince as she squeezed. "Thanks for clearing that up, *brother*. You can be on your way now."

"Don't get cute, Tori," Blake warned.

"Didn't you say you wanted to enjoy your girlfriend? Go. Enjoy." She swatted her hands at Blake, shooing him along.

"Oh, boy," I muttered. I saw the look in her eye, and if I wasn't mistaken, my handsome personal trainer was returning it in ten-fold.

The door opened, and the direction of attention shifted once again as Eric stood before us, beaming. "*Now*, the party can start."

Blake smiled, seeming relieved as though back-up had arrived. "What's up?" He slapped Eric's hand and pulled him in for the customary bro hug.

"Not a thang, not a thang. Been looking forward to this for weeks. I need to unload."

"I thought Brayden was riding with you." Blake looked toward the door.

"He backed out. Said something came up with Casey and he would catch up with you another time." Eric looked around. "Beer?"

"In the fridge," Blake responded, thumbing behind himself. "Help yourself."

"You know I will." Eric stopped to give me a kiss hello before pulling back the refrigerator door.

"You guys trying to kill me?" Jace fanned himself. "All this hot in one room—it's like sitting on the freaking sun. Anyone else coming? Brad Pitt? Kostas?"

"You love you some Kostas Martakis, don't you?" I laughed.

"I do. I really do," Jace replied, wetting his lips.

"You don't even know what he's saying," I said. Kostas Martakis was a Greek singer who, as far as I knew, barely spoke English.

"I don't need to, honey. Those hips move in a universal language." Jace mimicked a hip roll. When he realized all eyes were on him, including Blake, Drew, and Eric's, he smirked. "Uh-huh. It's confusing, isn't it?" He waggled his eyebrows, and all the guys turned to start talking to one another to hide the blush to their cheeks.

"Eric needs no introductions," I stated before turning to Victoria. "Tori, why don't you show Drew to a room." I looked at my other friends. "I'll bring you guys up. Try not to get lost. This place is huge."

"Tori, don't give him my room!" Eric called after us, popping a cube of cheese into his mouth. Tori tucked her hair behind her ear and motioned to Drew that he should follow her. I was in shock. I didn't think I had ever seen either one of them with nothing to say.

"Well, isn't this an odd turn of events?" Jace spoke close to my ear as we walked up the stairs. Sandra, Jeremy, and Jessie were close at our heels.

"I'll say. Blake looks like he's about to have an aneurism." I laughed lightly but was equally concerned.

Drew and Victoria came from two opposite worlds, and her dad was not the most accepting person. Judging by the look in Blake's eye, it didn't seem he would be too quick to welcome a romance between those two, either. I loved them both, and I didn't want to see either one's feelings hurt.

When we got to the top step, I looked to the left. Victoria had her back against one of the bedroom doors, her hand behind her on the knob, and a seductive smile on her face. Drew was directly in front of her, his broad chest not touching her but close enough to be considered indecent if it weren't invited. The muscles on his arms were near-popping, most likely from restraint. She was saying something that I couldn't hear before she freed the door and walked backward into the room.

They're adults, I reminded myself. And they were each the loneliest two adults I knew. I hoped they would catch a break and be able to have some fun with one another without too much of a hard time.

I'll have to keep Blake nice and distracted.

"REMIND ME AGAIN WHY I invited muscle man?" Blake looked toward the steps as Victoria descended, Drew close on her heels. When she got to the bottom, she spun and tucked her hair behind her ear. "I don't like this," he added.

I scooped my arm through the bend in Blake's and tugged him to me, trying to turn his point of focus. "Leave her alone. The girl never dates, and you know he's a good guy. He'd never hurt her."

"He's not for her." The ice in Blake's tone was foreign, but his words were enough to narrow my gaze.

I dropped his arm and turned to face him fully, fisting my hips. "You sounded an awful lot like someone *else* I know just now. What's the matter? Drew doesn't meet your high socialite standards, *Mr. Turner*?"

That was enough to snap Blake's focus back to me. "What are you talking about?"

I lowered my voice and stepped in, poking Blake in the chest. "You know exactly what I'm talking about. I didn't pin you for a stuck-up snob, Blake."

He exhaled. "That's not what I'm talking about, and quit going against me for other guys. What is that?" He narrowed his eyes at me, hurt reflecting in them as he lowered his voice with the question.

"Explain yourself then."

Blake sighed. "He's too hard for her. Victoria's soft. He's had a rough life, Angel." He couldn't hide the concern in his eyes.

I softened a bit, knowing how protective he was of her, but I wouldn't let him believe he was right in his thinking. "Which is why he deserves a chance at some soft." I placed my hand on his forearm, wanting that to sink in before adding, "Leave them be, Blake. Let them *both* have some fun. They deserve to let loose and have a little happy of their own."

Blake scowled in their direction once more before succumbing to my request like he always did. As Drew helped smooth the hair behind Victoria's other ear, Blake swallowed then noticeably forced himself to turn to me. "Come on, make me not think about what's probably about to happen."

I laced my fingers with his and smirked, thinking of all of the possibilities this house had to offer. "My pleasure."

SHOT, SHOT, SHOT-SHOT-SHOT, SHOT, SHOT, shot-shot-shot, shot, shot, shot-shot-shot, shot—everybody!

And repeat.

Wasted.

We were all wasted, and the music was pumping through the deejay's speakers. The sound was banging off the walls so loudly, I was thankful Mr. Turner had built his own compound, and we didn't have to worry about the neighbors calling the cops.

Jace jumped up and down in front of me, punching his fist in the air to the beat, sweat dotting his forehead as he balanced a sloshing cup in his other hand. He tossed what remained down his throat and leaned into my ear. "I'm gonna bounce for a while."

"You're not driving like that," I yelled back, still bopping.

"Nah, I got a ride outside. I'll be back before the sun wakes up. But if I'm not, don't come find me. It means I had a better night than I thought." He smirked. "Love."

"Love," I called back before planting a kiss on his cheek. Then he was gone just as fast.

Everywhere I looked was wall-to-wall bodies. Gyrating bodies, half-clothed bodies, tilted bodies, laughing bodies—all signs of a good time. I wondered if Blake even knew all of these people, and I hoped there was a cleaning crew on hand that would show up in the morning.

Speaking of Blake, him and his sparkling eyes were dancing his way through the crowd toward me. Even from far away, I couldn't mistake the hint of playfulness that shimmered there in the flickering lights, and my stomach bunched in anticipation of him reaching me. In a slow sway, which probably didn't match the beat of the music, my eyes dragged over this man who continued to be the most beautiful thing I had ever laid eyes on. Tonight, he was wearing an ice-blue V-neck, which only helped to accentuate his matching eyes and showcase that dip beneath his neck that I loved to lick. Eyes intent on mine, he stalked toward me, slightly matching the rhythm, the rest of him determined to get to me. His approach heightened my breaths until a wave of his scent rushed my system as his front blanketed mine in a flush coating. Stumbling back a drop, I gasped, sucking in Blake-infused air, a woodsy scent peppered with his own sweet, sweat-laced aroma.

One of his legs landed between my thighs, his left hand combing through the hair at my nape, steadying me while anchoring me to him. Some kind of spicy liquor was present, a warm, moist coating lining his warm skin as I squeezed the round mounds of his shoulders. His smile was crooked in the corner as he tilted his head and bent so his mouth was level with my quickened breaths. Then, without taking his eyes from mine, he pushed his tongue between my lips, tangling mine in a seductive dance. Already buzzing, I groaned from the overwhelming sensation, tasting the liquor resting on his tongue before his lips parted with mine. In a euphoric daze, I lingered as Blake poured a sweet-tasting shot down my throat. His fingers grazed the path of my swallow, heat spiraling through my core as he chased it inside with his tongue—drinking what remained and grinding his erection into me in a fluid motion to the beat of Ariana Grande's, *Into You*.

"You're fucking delicious," he spoke into my ear, cupping both sides of my face, still rocking into me with his dirty little dance.

"Blake," I replied, my head dipping back from his thumbs as he tasted my jaw, my neck, my collarbone, making sweet, seductive circles with his hips. Closing my eyes, I let the warmth of his lips mingle with the tingles, letting myself feel every piece of him enjoy each piece of me. I combed my fingertips into his hairline and rested my forehead against his, my breath catching as he pushed his hardness further between my legs.

Fuck.

I'd lost count of the number of ways I'd had him already since we'd gotten here, but right now all I could think about was hiking up my skirt and fucking him right here on the makeshift dance floor. "What're you doing to me?" I panted, hardly able to think.

"Nothing." He kissed the right side of my neck just below my ear. "Everything." He dropped a kiss on the other side before bending and scooping me up behind the knees and whisking me toward the stairs. My arm draped across his broad upper back, feeling the bulge of his muscles gliding across it with his strides as he weaved through people. But I didn't care who was watching as my man's lips tangled with mine again.

Blake kicked his bedroom door shut, muffling the sound of the music, and didn't stop walking until he was lowering us onto his bed. His weight followed my body, resting on top of it as he scattered kisses along any exposed skin he could find.

I mewled a soft moan, arching my back toward him as one leg wrapped around his waist, anchoring his hardness against the throbbing between my legs. My fingertips explored his body, roaming the peaks and valleys until they reached the waistband of his jeans. I yanked, getting my point across that I wasn't willing to wait to feel his skin on mine.

Blake complied, lifting from me just long enough to cross his arms at his waist and pull his shirt over his head, the strain in every defined muscle layering his body, moving in a fluid dance beneath his tanned skin. Before he could descend back on top of me, I pushed a hand onto one of his pecs and sat up to sample him, swiping my tongue into that divot I loved, then sucking an earlobe, feeling his abs bunch along the edge of his jeans as I lightly brushed my fingertips along it, and then those muscles pulled in tight to make room as my hand delved below the denim to find what I wanted.

"Fuck," Blake spoke into my mouth before his teeth clamped down and tugged on my bottom lip. I rushed to free the button of his jeans before lowering his zipper and shoving his pants down his legs.

"Lift your arms," Blake demanded, fisting the hem of my little blue dress and dragging it up my legs. When it reached my hips, Blake's hands repositioned so that they rode my body the rest of the way, passing the delicate curves of my waist before his thumbs brushed over the hardened peaks of my nipples. I gasped when he lingered there, putting pressure on the tightened buds before lowering his face to mere centimeters of it.

"Well, look at you. No bra," he stated, his breath tickling the sensitive flesh.

"No bra," I replied, scooping my fingers into the hair at the back of his head to try to urge him to me.

Blake didn't move, merely raising his line of sight to my eyes, making sure to keep his lips as close as possible to my chest without actually touching it. "Don't rush me, Angel. I want to enjoy you." His tongue flicked across my nipple before he blew a puff of cool air over my panting chest.

Blake tossed my dress aside and then settled two of his fingers along the wet strip of material between my legs, leaving his thumb resting on my pelvic bone.

Another flick of his tongue forced my head to fall back. "Fuck," I hissed.

Blake's fingers teased the material, rubbing back and forth, purposefully swiping it aside a couple of times to meet the smooth skin beneath it. He sucked one of my nipples into his mouth, coiling heated ripples from each point of contact before one of his fingers found its way inside my core. He dipped in and out a few times, sucking a bit harder as he did, and then his fingers left me to circle around my other nipple. With a sparkle in his eyes, he moved to that one to lick the arousal he'd just deposited there.

A graveled strain coated his voice as he ordered, "Lie back."

With a heaviness in my belly and a hitch in my breathing, I did as he asked, anticipation for what he was about to do with me racing my heart.

Stripping me of my panties in a slow calculating motion, his palms ran over my thighs, my calves, before he tossed them aside. He reached over to the nightstand and collected another shot, and my eyes fell to the amber-colored liquid.

"Open," he instructed.

Parting my lips, I waited to taste the sweet concoction. His gaze fell to the round circle of my mouth, and a heated look swarmed his irises, hooding his eyes. As though he couldn't help himself, he slid his tongue inside—long, deep spirals around mine before dragging it back out with a kiss. Sitting back on his heels, he dipped his head back and drained the shot into his own mouth instead. With fire in his eyes, he lowered his face, tilting his head to the side before dropping his lips to mine, depositing the liquid into my mouth in a slow trickle.

Sweet.

Hot.

Soft.

Blake.

I barely suppressed a moan as I sucked down all that he gave me and then even more greedily on his tongue once it was gone.

Euphoric.

I was drenched with lust and liquor and Blake's intoxicatingness as he reached next to him a second time, swiping the can of whipped cream that I hadn't noticed before.

With a tilt to his glistening lips, he rolled the chilled can back and forth along my chest, sending my nipples to a peak. I wriggled beneath it, the cool of the metal a stark contrast to the heat emanating from me.

"You didn't think I forgot this, did you?" His smile spoke to his satisfaction with himself.

Fluffy white foam erupted over my chest, the round mounds prickling further. With bright eyes, as though he were about to consume the best meal of his life, Blake swiped his tongue through the valley between my breasts, cleaning away the cream. My breath left me in a thick swoosh at the feel of the warm pad of his tongue to my flesh, which was hot yet cold at the same time. He blew on the newly damp skin, causing a wave to ripple through me.

He cleaned every inch of me before the shake of the can rang out again. Another cool line began at the hollow of my throat, but this time his tongue landed on it almost immediately, chasing it as he sprayed the column. Moaning, I opened my mouth just as the soft tip met my bottom lip. Sweet cream exploded into my mouth, filling it before his tongue dipped in—tasting me and rubbing my breasts, which were swollen with need, grinding his cock into my pelvis, feeling as though it was about to start a fire.

"So. Fucking. Delicious," he kissed the words, using his tongue to be sure all traces of his dessert were removed.

"I need you. Please, I need you." I was near-tears with desire for this man.

Blake's grin was infectious, his eyes never leaving mine as his hand moved lower. "I'm not full yet."

A cool sensation met my hot pussy, forcing a struggled groan from my lips as the back of my head pushed into the pillow. "Oh my god," I moaned as the pad of his tongue landed on my clit, a finger pushing into me at the same time.

Blake spoke against the smooth lips of my sex, brushing his mouth side to side. "I always knew you were sweet." He sucked the side of one clean. "But this is sweet enough for a toothache." He bit down, and my body jolted in response. Then he circled his tongue around my clit before taking the opposite lip into his mouth, still fingering cream into me. After placing a bite there as well, he kissed a line down my center, making me buck and whine, before finding my opening. He replaced his finger with his tongue, dipping in to taste both the cream he put there and my desire.

"So fucking good."

My body quaked with a soft release, unable to contain the pressure anymore. Blake lapped at it greedily, savoring each drop with moans of his own. When the small tremors subsided, and he knew none of me would be wasted, he flattened his palms to the backs of my thighs and pushed up with his body, bringing my legs with him as he nestled his cock between my folds. My ankles rested on his shoulders, and I stared down at the swollen head, anxious, waiting. He took himself in his hand and caressed my center, swirling, rubbing. With one final stroke, he was positioned at my entrance.

I reached between us to grab his ass and force him inside. My body arched up to meet his as he fell on top of me, my knees now pushing into my shoulders as he began to rock. He was so deep this way, I could feel him stroke every inch of my channel, hitting each spot that yearned for him. He moved as though he were mapping out each piece of me.

"You feel amazing this way," he breathed into my ear.

I agreed with a moan. No words were adequate to the way this felt—when two souls connected to form one being, knowing when they were separated they were broken fragments of nothing but together made up a beautiful masterpiece beating in tandem and thriving off one another. Even though it locked you into one person, essentially binding you, it was somehow freeing. Like you were finally alive enough to be free to live, where before you were too bogged down with the weight of feeling incomplete to even breathe.

"I feel it, too," he answered my thoughts.

I forced my eyes open, finding his. He stopped moving, leaving himself deep inside of me, and combed my hair from my face, freeing my legs to fall to my sides. He reiterated. "You don't have to say anything. I feel it, too." He pressed his lips to my forehead, then my nose, and finally my own before dropping his forehead to mine and rocking his hips once again.

"Now, stop thinking." He twined his fingers into my hair, sending a chill through my over sensitive body, and kissed me softly, slowly. My eyelids slid closed to focus on feeling him once again just as his eyebrows pinched together and he returned his forehead to rest on mine. "Feel me, baby. Just feel me love you."

With each soft thrust, my body took him into a new crevice, locking him there for as long as I would have breath to breathe. Though he moved slowly, Blake hardened inside me, and I knew he was close. Wanting to experience every pulse of his release, I wrapped my legs around him and used my stomach muscles to tilt my hips, the effort heightening the build-up brewing. On a gentle incline, my arousal skated—

Gliding . . .

Climbing . . .

Reaching . . .

Peaking . . .

Panting . . .

Caressing . . .

Kissing . . .

Breathing into each other as we reached the top together.

I drew his bottom lip into my mouth and held on, my eyes pinched shut as the need to feel him overtook all of my ability to do anything but experience this release with him.

In a sweaty heap, we crumbled into each other—one body, one soul, our hearts finding the rhythm that only the two together could make. They beat in a quick song, each call of his heart eventually slowing mine until the thumps matched our decreasing breaths and relaxation sunk in.

Music still rang out from downstairs, the sounds of a good time bleeding through the seam of the door, but the only thing filtering through my being was the comfort and calm that I felt knowing that, above all else, I was blanketed with love and protection. I felt untouchable by harm, like all of my fears were absorbed into Blake and dissipated from my system as I lay, lulled by the slow circles of his thumb on my upper back.

He kissed me once, then settled his palm over my now steady heart. "Mine."

I smiled, loving that he felt the need to keep reassuring us of this. "Yours."

His lips curved up in the corners as they began their descent toward mine once again but quickly jutted away to face the rapid pounding of a fist on the door.

"Eva! They said you're in there. You in there?"

Bang.

Bang.

Bang.

I knew that voice.

In a prickling draw, the blood drained from my face, the presence of Abby's voice meaning only one thing. "Come out, come out, wherever you are! I'm drunk. Stop screwing around and give me a kiss!"

The voice from my nightmares directly followed hers. "Yeah, beautiful. Come out and give us *both* a kiss."

Damon.

Chapter 57

MY COCOON BURST.

The warmth and security that surrounded me splintered as my eyes sought out Blake's. A smirk tugged the corner of his lips, and I knew he was misinterpreting my terror for shock.

Knock.

Knock.

Knock.

"He-llo! *Sister* outside." Abby's voice had a playful ring to it that only alcohol could cause.

"You knew they were coming?" I sat up, pulling the sheet around me.

Blake twirled a long lock hanging loose down my back. "Yep, Damon called me and asked if I was having my yearly party and said he was bringing Abby for the first time. I thought it would be a nice treat for you to see your sister." He beamed with pride, looking satisfied that he had done something good for his girlfriend.

Oh, Blake. Read the damn journal already!

"Awesome." My sarcastic voice tapered off as I sought out where my clothes were discarded, scared those two would find their way in before I could put them on. I sprang up, plucking my underwear and dress from where they lay as Blake did the same at a much slower pace. Hopping my foot into one side, I called out, "Coming!" But the music was so loud, I wasn't sure she could even hear me.

Any alcohol I'd consumed earlier dissipated with each bang at the door. Staring at the knob, I smoothed my hands down my dress one last time before doing the same to my hair. With one final drag of air into my lungs, I closed my eyes and pulled any stray bits that had flaked off of the steely exterior I had built back into myself. I needed to remember who I was *now* and say goodbye to the scared little girl of my past. I couldn't let being faced with the monster, who'd held me captive in my own silence for all these years, stumble me back to anything other than the strong girl I had spent the last few months building. I was different now.

And it was time *he* knew.

But, I had to be careful. Almost everyone I cared about was in this house right now. Two of them knew who my abuser was, and one was a few pages away from finding out. I needed to play my cards right if I was getting past this weekend. With a renewed confidence, I threw back the door.

Abby, mid-make-out session, fell backward into me, the fall unsealing her lips from Damon's, whose brown eyes immediately landed on mine. Giggling, Abby spun to wrap her arms around my neck, and I cringed, knowing those same arms were just circled around *him*.

"Evaaaaaaa!"

Damon's lip, pink from my sister's lipstick, curled up in the corner. "Hope we didn't interrupt." He dragged his cunning gaze from mine to behind me.

Blake pushed up against my back, reaching over my shoulder to give Damon a pound as Abby pet the side of my face. "I missed you so much, you little stinky-head." The strong aroma of alcohol floated off her breath.

My nose scrunched at the smell. "How many drinks have you had, Abs?" The half-mast of her glistening eyes and waver in her step told me it was probably more than a few.

"Aww, sissy-poo is worried." Damon tapped the edge of my nose. The burst of his cologne rotted the contents of my stomach, sending a ball into my throat. "Don't worry about her, beautiful. She's in good hands." He wiggled all of his fingers at me as though he were about to tickle me, and I cringed at the thought of him making contact.

My back bumped into Blake who was still so close, and he wrapped his arms around me, reminding me of his security. I straightened my posture, not wanting to give away that small lapse of strength, but I didn't miss the tic in Damon's jaw as his eyes drifted to Blake's arms. He quickly pulled Abby into his own, and the inebriated fool sunk into his neck with another giggle.

"Where are you staying tonight?" I asked Abby, even though I was certain she'd go along with whatever the douchebag said. The last thing I wanted was to be under the same roof as him, but it was late and I didn't want either one of them driving back to Damon's place in their current state. Judging by the looks of them, I wasn't even sure how they had made it here.

Before they could answer, Blake chimed in, reading my mind. "There's plenty of space, so grab a room. I don't want you guys driving."

With an evil glint in his eye, Damon answered while looking at me rather than Blake. "Yeah, that's probably best." I shivered at the coolness that floated from his eyes, straight into my pores—the hidden meaning he meant for his words to deliver to me and only me. Damon straightened, loosening his hold on Abby to look first left, then right.

"Any one of these cool?"

His movement forced Abby to stand on her own. Unbalanced, she swayed, palming the wall with another short giggle. Her line of sight followed Damon's, sweeping both ways. As her eyes swung left, a look of fright washed over her porcelain features, a hiccup swallowing her air in a large gasp. Eyes wide, I watched the blood drain from her face in one fast swoop, her smile slumping at the corners. I followed her gaze to find Eric standing at the end of the hall, leering at her. A beer hung lazily from his pointer finger, but his stance was sharp. Although I'm sure a million emotions were running through him, he didn't give anything away. He just didn't move, almost like he was testing out whether or not she would run into his arms. Damon was, of course, her fiancé, so she couldn't do that, but I noticed the pulse in her throat and the small step she retreated from Damon.

Damon's smile sagged as Eric began a slow prowl toward us, his hand flinging up to flip the beer bottle toward his mouth, his eyes insistent on staying glued to my sister. She was usually more careful. I knew if she hadn't been such a drunken mess that she would have anticipated

Blake's best friend being here. Though they had only shared one kiss, and it was a secret only a few of us knew about, it was enough to start a fire that didn't seem to be easily put out.

And Damon felt it.

I knew he did. I only prayed he didn't act on the sudden hatred I saw ticking through his veins. Like a frayed electrical cord, I watched him zap back and forth, twitching, barely containing the lashing I was sure he wanted to dish out. According to Abby, Damon hadn't drunk in months. To Abby that was just a day, but to me it was the day he nearly brutally raped me. Witnessing Eric and Abby together was what had set him off and, as I looked at the deranged swirl beginning to swarm his irises, I saw that same Damon take root. I hoped he would handle the liquor he'd already consumed better than he had that day, and that no one had to feel the wrath of the true Damon.

His fist clenched, and his gaze swung to Abby. On instinct, I stepped between them just as Eric approached.

"Fancy meeting you here." Eric's lip curled as his line of sight finally released Abby and dragged to Damon. In a slow incline, Eric dragged his fist up for a 'pound', his voice low and devious, matching the motion. "Sup, bro."

Damon hesitated, a malicious gleam in his eye as his fist collided with Eric's. "Sup."

They each stared. No smile. No jest.

Just tension.

What was Blake thinking inviting them all here together where the alcohol was pouring from every corner?

I could honestly say the only thing he'd been thinking about was me, and his deep swallow told me he now realized what a mistake that'd been. Blake put a hand on my shoulder. "Babe, go help Abby pick a room. We're gonna go get a drink, aren't we, fellas?"

The apples of Abby's cheeks were so red, I could practically feel the heat coming off of them. Luckily for her, they were still flushed from all of the drinking she had done, so there was a chance Damon hadn't noticed. But, given the fact that they had spent almost their whole lives together, he knew her just as well as I did, and the hard set to his jaw told me he probably had.

His lip tipped in a devious smirk as something surely came to him, before his hand drifted back and swung in hard, making contact with her ass and jolting her back to reality with a squeaked gasp. She jumped as he squeezed. "Yeah, *babe*. Pick us a good room. I don't want *anyone* to hear what I'm gonna do to you later."

I wrapped my arm around my middle, nearly throwing up in my mouth. I knew that statement could have been taken in one of two ways, even though no one else seemed to. Abby didn't say a word. Didn't stand up for herself or tell him to go to hell.

Nothing.

I wonder if she's as broken as I was.

The thought rolled a second wave of nausea through me. Again, I yearned to tell her all that Damon had done to me, to free her of her own set of chains. But, once again, now was not the time. I couldn't out him and embarrass her like that in front of everyone we knew. Besides, she was too drunk to process it the right way. When I told her, it would have to be done delicately, especially after the lack of reaction I'd seen with the crass way he had just treated her. My sister was going to need kid gloves with this.

A lump built in my throat, its burn too painful to swallow, and I had to look away. I laced my fingers with hers. "Come on, Abs. I have the perfect room." When she didn't move, I lightly tugged, squeezing her hand gently as an urge for her to follow me.

Water built in her sad green eyes. "Yeah. Sure." She tucked her hair behind her ear and dipped her head low, following me.

I secretly wanted to kick Eric in the shins for starting anything. He knew exactly what he was doing, setting her up like that. But in his defense, the situation bothered him just as much, and he was only making a play for the girl he wanted as bad as Blake had wanted me. A heaviness weighted my heart, instantly understanding the pain of wanting something you couldn't have. He didn't know the situation he was putting her in or how dangerous Damon could be.

When I came across the first empty room, I quickly ushered her inside and shut the door behind me. Before it was even closed, she crumpled to the carpet, sobbing into her hands. On instinct, I dropped beside her, holding her close with shushing tones while rubbing circles along her back.

"I did it again!" she wailed.

I shushed some more as fresh tears heaved her back. Riding her waves, I tried to tell her it would all be okay, even though a nagging pit sat low in my stomach, telling me I was probably wrong. But everything happened for a reason. I believed in that. There had to have been a purpose for what I had gone through—for the situation we were faced with now. And I had to hold faith that, once the fog I had been drifting through lifted from the murky air, we would all be able to enjoy the rainbows in its wake.

Abby collapsed forward, her forehead buried between her thighs, muffling her voice. "He won't believe me after this one."

Trying to gather my words, I continued to rub her back. When I didn't answer right away, she dragged her head to the side with a sniffle. Mascara tracked her cheeks and streaked her pants. "I convinced him last time that what he saw between Eric and me was all in his head, but he'll know for sure now."

I recited the words running through my head. "Everything happens for a reason, Abby."

She stiffened under my palm. "What are you trying to say, Eva?"

My heart was surprisingly calm as I answered. "I'm saying maybe fate keeps putting you in this situation for a reason." I tried to get her to see the light without having to delve into the truth of the situation. Knowing my sister, she wouldn't make it that easy.

She sat upright. "So my fiancé can hate me and lose all trust in me?"

I repressed a snort and fought hard not to roll my eyes at the trust statement.

Trust.

What a funny five letter word that people put so much faith in. At the end of the day, for most, that's all it was—those five measly, meaningless letters.

She should only know.

I gulped. "Abby . . ." I exhaled, my brain whirling in the blur of a tornado as to where to begin. I took her hands in mine. "Maybe Damon isn't to be trusted, either. Maybe . . ." My eyes roamed the room as though something in it would lend me the right words to use. "Maybe you're meant to explore other avenues because Damon's not for you."

"Not for me? He's only ever been for me! I was just a kid. Remember that?" Her eyes were wild, desperate for answers, daring me to give her the wrong one. I knew my sister was teetering on the brink of a meltdown.

Trying to calm her, I rubbed my thumb along the back of her hand. "When you truly love someone, when it's the *right* someone, they're supposed to be your beginning and your end. Your world should stop and start with them." I explored her eyes, imploring her to listen. "Maybe Damon was your beginning . . ."

She dropped her head, her face beginning to crumble in the center as though she were about to start crying again. I lifted her chin with my finger, intent on getting my point across. "But maybe he's not your end."

"Why do you keep saying this to me?" her voice rasped. "You're supposed to be my support system. My maid of honor. *My best friend.* And all you do is run away from me and spew hatred at my fiancé." She shot to her feet, wiping down her cheeks, muttering, "I'm so fucking stupid."

I hopped up, chasing after her toward the door before she could leave. I reached out for her hand, and the second our skin made contact, she spun to face me like a rabid animal. "I should've never come here. Stupid me, I keep looking for my *sister*—" The tone of voice she used when saying that word was so hypocritical, it was its own slap in the face. "—when all you are now is a stranger."

That stab to the chest made my legs retreat a step. I pushed a palm into my heart, squishing away the hurt they brought. Behind her words, I could see a scared little girl. My big sister. The girl that I idolized and had looked up to my whole life. Who had taught me how to put on lipstick and stuff my bra before my boobs grew. Who had played with my hair and shouldered the blame with my parents every time I'd been about to get in trouble. "Don't say that." My voice was a mere whisper as it floated through the air.

"Why not?" She squared her shoulders. "It's true."

I thought then, about telling her. I thought about finding the right words. The words she would believe over everyone else's. Over *his.* Then . . .

I looked into her frightened, glistening eyes and the red vines slicing through them.

She's too drunk.

Instead, I reached for my bag of tricks—the façade that I had spent the last few months demolishing. The cure-all. I pieced it together and pasted it firmly in place with a deep breath. What used to feel like a second skin felt foreign to me now, like an unfamiliar coat that didn't quite fit right. "It isn't true, Abby." I used my most soothing tone as I stepped toward her, calm washing over my eyes. "I know it seems that way, and I promise I'll fix it. After this weekend, we'll get together, just me and you, okay?" When a pinch of tension rolled off her shoulders, I took one more step. "Right now let's focus on you. On fixing this mess. Deal?"

"I don't know how," she whispered, not really looking at me but somewhere far away. My heart broke for how lost she seemed.

"I'll help you." I scooped her hand into my own, and her gaze fell to the gesture before rising to meet mine. With a sturdier voice, I reiterated, "I'll help you."

Abby's arms were around my neck so fast, the force knocked me backward before I could find my footing. She squeezed hard, the smell of alcohol curling through the cotton candy scent she always wore, reminding me to tread lightly with her.

"Eva?" She spoke into my hair.

"Yeah, Abs?"

"You feel different." She pulled back and moved her palm over my stomach. "Are those cubes?" she squeaked.

I giggled at the look of shock in her big eyes. "Maybe a little. You haven't seen me in a while. I'll introduce you to my trainer. He's here."

Shit. After I said that, I immediately regretted the words. Introducing her to Drew wouldn't be a good thing. It would most likely mean simultaneously introducing him to Damon, which could never happen. Ever.

"Get out! You're, like, all muscle-ly and stuff." She wrapped an arm around my bicep.

"Lil' bit." I smiled proudly. "It makes me feel good."

"I'm glad." Abby smiled back at me, her eyes reminiscent of something her mouth didn't betray. The both of us remained quiet for a bit, happy for the rare gift of being alone in each other's presence.

"Now," I broke the ice. "What're we gonna do with you? You're a hot mess." I laughed, smoothing back Abby's long brown hair.

"Fix it," she stated simply.

"Here's the plan. Let's freshen you up, then you're going to go downstairs and make nice with your *fiancé*." I paused, trying to remain strong through the idea of still calling him that. "Surely after a kajillion years, you know how to do that, yes?" I raised a brow.

"I think I can handle it." She seemed to be brightening.

"Good. I'll keep Eric distracted while you do that—and possibly knee him in the balls for this. After that, you can excuse yourself to bed to nurse the coming hangover you're going to have tomorrow so you can avoid being trapped in a Damon and Eric sandwich again. Cool?"

Abby licked her lips and opened her mouth, no doubt to bite on that sandwich statement, when I held up a hand in front of her face. "Too soon for jokes, miss. Shutty."

She clamped her mouth shut.

"Now come on. We've got some serious work to do," I sighed. "Where's Jace when you need him?"

THE HEAVY BASS BLED THROUGH the seam of the bathroom door, sounds of loud voices and laughter sprinkled throughout the mixture. It seemed the rest of the party was unaware of the shit storm brewing.

Damon in the house with all of the people intent on protecting me.

Angered by the cut to his ego after seeing his fiancée affected by another man.

Watching me—the person who he thought he owned a possessive hold over—outwardly with her boyfriend . . .

All of it was a recipe for the perfect storm.

Drew worried me most of all. I needed to find him and warn him, plead with him to stand back and let me handle it. A final swipe of a Q-tip under Abby's eye had her looking much better. "There." I smiled.

She poked her fingers into her hair, looking at herself in the mirror. "Thanks, Eves."

"No problem." I sucked in a lock of air, dragging it into my lungs to suppress the nerves I felt about leaving the room. "Come on. Let's go make things better." I tucked Abby's arm into my own.

Music pounded through the door as the seam split, my heart scurrying in my chest. Descending the stairs, I squinted my eyes and scanned the crowd from a bird's eye view for any sign of the guys.

There.

Blake.

Eric.

Damon.

Blake was wearing a big smile, which I knew was a forced effort to make light of an uncomfortable situation and try to get the other two to play nice. Thankfully, Eric and Damon didn't look heated anymore. Both just existed beside one another as Blake poured shots from a metal canister.

I drew in a fortifying breath, my arm instinctively tightening around Abby's to aid in calming my raging nerves and convince myself that maybe this would all turn out okay. Remembering that Drew was still out there somewhere, my eyes raked the crowd in swift sweeps, trying to hide the desperation I felt at finding him. Blake lifted an arm above the crowd, calling out to someone with a smile and waving them over.

My eyes dragged to the focus of his attention. To the sandy-blond hair and broad, muscled shoulders making his way through the crowd, his hand trailing behind him, locked with Victoria's. To the only other person in the house who knew what had happened to me and *who* had done it.

Drew.

I should have moved quicker, but my feet stopped, shock numbing their ability to do what they were designed for.

Abby tugged at my arm as my sudden loss of movement knocked her off kilter. "Eva?"

My mouth dried, not allowing a response. Each squeeze past a new person in the crowd brought Drew one step closer to being face-to-face with the one person he would love to extinguish. One step closer to outing my secret to an entire house of people in a harsh manner and from foreign lips.

One step closer to Blake.

Fresh air bombarded my lungs as they gasped me back to reality and the stair I was rooted to.

"Earth to Eva. Come on!" Abby pulled again.

I snapped my eyes back to hers. "Hang on tight. When I get you to Damon, you know what to do." And I took off down the remaining steps. I would need him as distracted as possible.

Once I hit the floor, I dissolved into the crowd. Tiny in comparison to everybody else, I kept my entire body as erect as possible, craning my neck to see as far over the people as I could. Tightening my hold on Abby, I shouldered my way, bodies parting with laughs and smiles, not realizing the turmoil whipping through me.

In glimpses through swaying figures, I witnessed the next few moments like a series of clicks on a childhood View-Master, each image spinning on the tick of the reel.

Blake's dimple.

His jovial, glistening eyes.

Drew's returned smile.

The gap between them diminishing.

Then disappearing.

The movement of Blake's full lips.

The gesture of his hand in Damon's direction.

The smile melting from Drew's face.

Blood draining from the rosy apples of his cheeks, revealing a new shade of pale.

The gulp of his Adam's apple pushing new blood to the surface, a vibrant red overtaking his cheekbones as his eyebrows pulled down.

His shoulders squared as he turned his focus back to Blake, his lip pulling back over his teeth as though a profanity were about to slip past them when—

Slam!

My chest hit Drew's, sending him stumbling back on his feet and simultaneously spilling what remained of his drink between the two of us.

Drew's eyes flashed something I couldn't quite pinpoint. Taken abruptly from his moment of rage, he seemed uncertain of whether he should shove me and swing or pull me close and run. I implored him without words, silently pleading for him to read the panic I meant for only him to see, while trying to portray to the outside world the clumsy stumble of a drunken girl. As if trying to catch myself, I fell forward toward his shoulder, fisting his shirt and pushing my knuckles into his chest while moving quickly to his ear with a whisper.

"Please."

His chest bunched to a rock beneath my balled hands and I searched his eyes once more, begging. His jaw set, nostrils flared, but the look in his eyes contradicted all of it. Right there, I saw something he'd never shown me before—pity.

I sucked the disappointment of that inside, knowing I didn't have a lot of time and continued with my act. "I'm so sorry! I must've tripped on all these big feet."

Blake rushed to my side, scooping up my arm. "You all right?"

"Yeah, I'm good. Clumsy." I smiled and rose to my tiptoes to place a kiss on his cheek. Blake's posture melted and his smile slowly reappeared.

I looked down to the wet stain sliced down the front of my dress that matched the one dripped down the center of Drew's shirt and saw my only out from this ticking time-bomb. "Look what I did." I moved from Blake's hold toward Drew. "Here, let's go clean you off." Looping my arm with his, I urged him to follow me, stopping only to reassure Blake with a smile. "Be right back."

Drew nearly tripped over his feet looking behind him as I dragged him off, then I stuffed him into the closest bathroom. When the lock was securely fastened, I turned and pressed my back against it, sucking in a sigh and closing my eyes.

What the hell am I going to do?

Little flakes of tension began to peel away, having survived two close encounters already, and my body sagged forward, crumbling from the pressure. My palms pushed into my knees as I collected myself, replaying all that had happened on a quickly spinning loop.

"Please tell me your *boyfriend* did not just introduce me to your fucking *rapist*." Drew's voice spliced through the images, causing them to fizzle out before me. I stood up sharply, having momentarily forgotten I wasn't alone.

His red Solo cup landed with a *clank* into the sink, the remnants of liquid splattering on the mirror as he approached. With nowhere else to go, I squished my back to the door as he closed the distance—fists balled so tight the whites of his knuckles bled into the red surrounding them. His body jolted and vibrated as though the raging fire building within him was clawing its way out, looking for any available opening to combust through.

One hand landed with a smack against the door to the right side of my head, and I flinched to the left only to have his other hand fist the knob on that side. "Move out of my god damned way, Eva." The hazel eyes that I'd grown to adore, that were always so intense but always in a good way, were now orbs of danger. I didn't know where my friend had gone, but in these eyes, I could picture the anger-filled teenager on a mission to destroy anyone who had ever hurt him or someone he loved.

My mind raced with how I could possibly control him and step him back long enough for him to listen to me. Then I paused. *I know this boy.*

On instinct, I did the only thing I knew how to do when it came to him. The only thing I knew he would respond to. With a screeching roar through clenched teeth, I fisted his shirt and pushed harder than I'd ever pushed anything, bearing into him to shove him backward. He came to a stumbling skid about five feet from where I stood, my own fists balled, anger bubbling up my neck in crackling whipping fireworks.

"Listen to me!"

Movement ceased, the air becoming stagnant but for the sharp sounds of our breaths wheezing in and out of our heaving chests. I stepped forward.

"I need your word."

Drew's eyebrows pulled in, relaxing the hard edge to his jaw as he tried to find my meaning. I softened my approach a little, but not all the way. I wouldn't let my guard down on the pit bull I was locked in the cage with.

"Your word, Drew. You can't do or say anything."

"You're out of your fucking mind." Drew took two elongated steps, attempting to barrel past me. I slammed my palm into his chest and threw him back once more, his stumble only bringing him back a couple of feet this time. "You won't get one more of those, Eva. I think you know that."

"Just *listen* to me!"

Drew stepped in, cutting me off once again. "How could he? What kind of guy allows the girl he loves *rapist* into his house? Drinking with him like it's no big deal. Just another day." He cackled a sarcastic laugh. "And *you* . . . I thought you had a stronger backbone—"

"He doesn't know." I cut him off.

Drew narrowed his eyes at me. *"Excuse me?"*

I lowered my voice and dropped my hands. "It's not Blake's fault.

He still doesn't know." My shoulders lost the sharpness that held them erect. "Neither does Abby. That's why you can't do anything. They can't find out this way."

"You've got to be shitting me. What's the matter with you, Eva?" The desperation in his tone was unmasked. "I thought since you guys were back together that you were going to get rid of all the secrets and open up to him already."

"I tried. But we were focusing on us." I shrugged, seeing now how ignorant that had been. This was always part of us. "Anyway, I've already planned to talk to them both this week. It's all going to be over. So please, *please*, just cool it for now. Okay?" I begged.

Drew let out a puff of air with so much force the hair that lay over my left shoulder blew to the side. He fisted his hips and looked down at our feet. "I can't believe you're asking *me* of all people to do this."

"Please, you have to. For me. This is *my* story to tell." I stared at him, though he didn't return my gaze.

Drew emptied what remained in his lungs, weakening further. Then he dragged his line of sight to my eyes. "I'm not happy about this, but I'll do it . . . for you. I'm gonna be watching, though. That fucker steps out of line once, and I swear to God, Eva, he won't live to talk about it."

I placed a hand on his arm, relieved. "Thank you." I exhaled. "Don't worry, I got this. I had a good coach." I sent him a sarcastic smirk to belie my nerves.

Drew closed the small gap, his nose so close to mine I could smell the mint on his breath. He grabbed my shoulders. "Remember it all, Eva. Remember all that I taught you. Every word I fucking said, and every time I made your back hit those mats. Remember it and harness it. *Do not* let this motherfucker own you. Not anymore. This is *your* life. *Your* house. *Your* rules. You got it?"

"Got it." I stared back, confident that I was telling the truth, the ferocity in his words building the strength in my core.

"Good. Now . . ." He stepped back and flicked his chin to the air. "Hit me."

"Get out of here." I nudged his shoulder, bringing some playfulness back to us and feeling as though I could breathe a little again. My shove met an unmovable force, not one iota of budge in Drew's stance.

I gulped as my gaze rose to the tic in his jaw, causing the smile that felt so good to slide from my face. "He's not going to do anything. Besides Abby and all these people are here. So, come on before someone comes looking for us."

I tried to grab his hand, but as my fingertips brushed along the outside of his, he slapped it away. "Hit. Me." In a move I'd seen him do more than a hundred times, Drew squatted slightly and held out his arms. "Now."

"I can't do this right now. Let's go!" I yanked at his wrist, panic he would draw attention to us bubbling in my chest.

"I'm not budging." The air was motionless, his stare constant and glaring as my pulse began to knock at scattering points in my body.

Then something else starting knocking.

Knock.

Knock.

Knock.

"Angel, you in there?" Blake's concerned voice slipped through the cracks, floating on the beats of the music behind him.

"Drew, please, he's going to hear us," I whispered harshly, my eyebrows pulled so tightly in fright that I didn't know how he wasn't giving in. On shaking legs I approached him, reaching out to grab one of his hands again. A stab of pain whipped through me as he slapped my hand away for the second time.

Motherf—

"Drew!" I pleaded.

"Hit me!"

"Eva? You in there, baby?" Concern was rising in Blake's tone.

Bang.

Bang.

Bang.

"Come on!" I was frantic now, blood whooshing through my veins on violent pumps of my heart, stealing my breath on each pound at the door.

"Hit me!" Drew yelled in my face.

Suddenly, all I saw was spatters of red, and I didn't care who was at the fucking door. In quick jabs, I punched my fists.

Right—Left—Right—Left.

Only to have Drew block each one with an open-handed slap.

"More. GO!" he yelled, and I flurried faster.

Right—Left—Right—Left—Right—Left—Right.

My breaths raged against my rib cage, my teeth aching as they ground against their opposites, the pain in my knuckles burning. I flurried faster, flailing, wanting so bad to land a shot to his over-enthused, stubborn face.

"Angel!" Blake called through the door, but I wasn't finished yet.

"Coming," I called back with as calm of a voice as I could fake, trying to bide us a few more moments before Blake decided to bust down the damn door.

Drew grabbed both of my wrists and spun me around, locking my arms crossed in front of me while we both fought for a breath. I felt his air meet my ear in quick jabs, then his nose grazed along the rim. "I've got you now, *beautiful*. Now, what the *fuck* are you going to do about it?"

My world stood still as that word slithered along my skin, and I was paralyzed for the small moment that he had always warned me about. The moment you were most vulnerable. Where someone who knew you most would find the opportunity to attack. I saw the instant. Felt it curl around me in a threatening bubble.

Then . . . I demolished it.

"Fuck you!" I screamed through the pounding on the door, feeling each bang surge the blood in my veins. I locked Drew's arms and bent forward quickly, causing his body to tumble over my own and freeing my hands in the process. Drew's legs whisked over the countertop, crashing him down. He hopped back up, and I stepped back, using the opportunity of freedom to gain back an advantage. A smirk broke out on his face as he caught his breath.

"Eva, open the goddamn door!" Blake shouted.

"Good girl. Now you can go out there." I regained use of my air while Drew added, "I'm not going to be far. He does one thing I don't like, and I'll be on him faster than you'll know what to do. I was just making sure you were still on your game." Drew reached behind himself without looking, freeing the lock.

Blake barged over the threshold like a rabid dog, his cheeks red, eyes wild. His hair fell disheveled, brushing along the corners of his eyes. "What the fuck is going on in here?" He looked back and forth between Drew and me.

I collected myself quickly. "Nothing, this jackass just thought now would be a great time for a sparring session." I walked past Drew, biffing him on the head for effect. "Clean your own damn shirt." Drew smirked, not lending a clue as to how serious our encounter was.

Blake's breathing evened, the alarm in his eyes melting to comfort as he accepted the lack of threat between Drew and me. He laced his fingers with mine. "What's with you two with that? Give it a rest already."

"Hey." I stopped just outside the door, something dangerous sparking to life with that rush of adrenaline. Leaning up on my toes, I fell forward, loving the dominating feel of Blake's back bouncing off the wall behind him. I grabbed his face with both hands and forced his lips to mine, letting my tongue invade his mouth, dragging more of *him* into my system.

His strength.

His support.

His love.

That was all I needed. I dropped my forehead to his, focusing only on the matched rhythm of our breathing, loving the shock in his wide blue eyes. A smile crept across my face as my armor locked into place.

"Dance with me."

I FELT AN INTERNAL SHIFT.

Like the prickling of a new fire, the tiny sparks crackling along the dried out earth, looking for each other amongst the wild so they could join and expand into a full-blown flame. Those baby moments where something is born. I wasn't sure what it was yet, but it felt good. It was like a jolt of life trickling in. The feel of Blake's warm palm against mine, our fingers interlocked, the security in his grasp, only added their own set of new sparks, drifting from the tracks of his lifelines directly into mine.

He led me through the house, the music becoming louder, thicker, more intense with every step—his smile widening with each movement forward. When we rounded the corner, the crowd of people was still dense, though slightly less than before. It had to be well past midnight by now, but the party showed no signs of stopping.

Jessie, Sandra, and Jeremy were dancing in the center of the room, drinks in hand. As soon as we reached them, Jessie threw her arms around my neck. "Where have you been?" she slurred. "This is the best. Party. Eveeeer!"

I laughed, jostling from her clumsiness while peeking into her cup. "Whatcha drinking there?"

"Cream soda," she stated blandly, contradicting the sparkle in her eye.

"What kind of *cream soda*?" I pushed.

Jessie shrugged, poking the straw between her teeth. "An adult kind."

"Ingredients?" I added.

"Ginger ale." She sucked.

I watched the beige liquid travel up the clear center until it was in her mouth. "And . . ."

"There might be a Remy in there." She winked. "Or a Jack. Or a Jameson. I forgot his name." She giggled.

"Just don't get sick, okay?" I chuckled at her cuteness. "I've got my hands full tonight."

"Aye-Aye, Captain." Jessie saluted. "Hey, *that's* his name. I remember!" She giggled again and sucked in another sip.

I scanned the crowd. "Have you seen Eric around? Abby?"

"Eric split a while ago looking *pissed*." She widened her eyes and made a grand gesture with her hands, exaggerating her story. "He popped the tab of a fresh beer and left, and I haven't seen him since." She craned her neck, searching the room. "I thought I saw Abby not that long ago. She's . . . yeah, there she is." She nudged her chin toward the far edge of the room. Damon had his back to the wall, sucking down a drink in one hand while the other rested at the base of Abby's spine, bordering her ass as she swayed against him.

"Dance with us!" Sandra exclaimed, her hand still laced behind Jeremy's neck as she leaned over to grab my arm. I looked at Abby and Damon once again just as she placed a kiss on the side of his neck. I turned with a cringe, not wanting to witness any more of their make-up session.

I started to slow bop with my head, easing into it as Blake leaned into my ear. "Be right back. I'm gonna grab us some drinks."

Jessie scooped up one of my hands, commencing the familiar 'girl-dance'—arms locked and raised above our heads, bodies swaying, hands rocking side to side. Both of us wore similar euphoric smiles as I allowed the music in. It always electrified and calmed me, even the deepest of beats, parading happy endorphins through me and spicing up any bland that I had with its immediate high. A beast inside stirred, awakening—a fierceness dancing on each beat—and I closed my eyes, absorbing the rhythm.

Smiling so wide my cheeks ached, I swayed, not caring about

anything but enjoying this. Letting all my worries of Damon, Abby, *anything* melt into the next verse, smashing it away with each rock of my hips.

A school bell rang, then a clapping beat took over the sound system, and I immediately recognized Zara Larrson's *Ain't My Fault*. I jumped up and down. "I love this song!"

And when Zara's cute little giggle rang out, excitement rushed through me. In a bopping, rocking swagger, my hips started moving, my shoulders ticking in time to the beat.

Familiar fingertips ran the length of my back, a firm abdomen riding a path until it was pressed flush against me. Blake's cologne coiled around me as his hand traveled the column of my throat, his heated touch taking my jaw to tip my head back to his shoulder. He rocked with me, a prickling heat set loose throughout my body at the possessive yet adoring way he always held me. His thumb landed on my parted lips, resting his taste there, then dragged down to hook my chin, opening my mouth before trickling a warm liquid into it.

I sucked it down, loving the tingles it added, feeling its zing of playfulness. His heat engulfed me, his thin, warm shirt pressed against my partially bare back, exciting me. I whirled around, wanting to enjoy this moment like two regular young people in love. Wanting him to know he was it for me and how fucking hot he was. My hands landed on his pecs, the hardness beneath them fueling me as my eyes found his. The intensity they held was stronger than I'd ever seen and I knew he was feeling it, too. The finality of the bullshit. The pull of *us* and the 'fuck-the-world' attitude that was crawling up me so fast I could barely contain it.

Though our bodies kept their calculated movement, our eyes were locked on one another's. We moved in tandem—fun, playful, seductive. Bodies crouched, I sang in his face, and he sang back in mine, his dimple in full bloom—up and down, back and forth, together.

When the chorus began, I sang straight at him, telling him how irresistible he was, that I couldn't be responsible for what I did to him. With the clap of the beat of the chorus, I began jumping up and down. Arms in the air, I had fun with it until I came down off the beat. He slid his leg between mine, bucking his hips. He read me, rocking with me, dancing across each exciting note.

The show kept on, people gathering to watch, but we were immune to the stares and screams around us. My hands roamed his body, riding his dips and sways. Singing to him about how good he looked, I flicked his collar, my touch dragging over his broad shoulders, his dimple broadening in response. Blake shivered as my hands roamed lower, grazing every bump of his abdomen before hooking into the top of his jeans and yanking his pelvis toward me so that his body was flush with mine. I danced my fingers back up until the smooth skin of his face was beneath them. I combed them through his hair, then moved them to clasp his hands within my own just as the next chorus began.

In a bold move, I directed his hands along the curves of my body, bordering indecent as I hung my head back and swayed my hips. I dragged his hands along every bend in my body, past the round mounds of my breasts to the hourglass of my torso. Blake's eyes followed his hands, wide and hungry, fueling me further until I laid them to rest on my ass while she sang about them going where my eyes couldn't see. His head dropped to the crook of my neck, his teeth digging in to place a love bite there, and I wrapped my arms around his head, swaying as one body.

When I opened my eyes, they locked on Damon's disturbed stare. Abby still swayed in front of him, playfully trying to dance, but he was looking past her, over her head, straight at me. Instead of the fright that usually came, though, I merely laughed mockingly and mouthed in time to the music, shrugging my shoulder. "It ain't my fault." And a heated blaze seemed to shoot from his flared nostrils. Not far from where he stood, I excited at the smirk on Drew's face as he watched me. I sent him a wink, hoping to keep him calm and reassured I would be okay.

As the song drew out in slower time, I lost myself in Blake again, in the moment, in the sway, the rhythm, the love, the strength. A knowing glitter danced in Blake's eyes, and he intentionally scrunched up his nose, a movement he had mastered that was so incredibly hot, I had told him as much on our first date. Excitement rushed through my veins not having seen it in such a long time, knowing without a doubt that we were back. Before I knew it, I was off my feet, and Blake had me in the air, his hands under my arms as he held me suspended above him. I looked down into the most adoring, most loving set of eyes I'd ever seen, and I had never felt so cherished, so truly loved as he circled, holding me. In a quicker spin, my legs swung out, and I threw my head back with a laugh, love swirling through me as he lowered me back to the floor.

As if he couldn't wait any longer to taste me, his tongue pushed between my lips, the vibrations of me singing into his mouth as we picked the pace back up. We ended the song playfully—breaking apart to brush our shoulders, bopping circling each other. I ignored the heat searing into the side of my head from across the room. I knew what I just did. It was all done on purpose.

Blake grabbed me tightly around my waist, pulling me in to kiss me deeply, claiming me, loving how open and free we were with each other now. I returned his kiss, letting the rest of the world melt away. This was how I would live my life now. Free from fear. Free to love and be loved. Free of *him*.

When Blake rested his head back in the crook of my neck to suckle the warm skin there, I allowed my eyes to drift to Damon in a final farewell. A final send off.

Though my mouth didn't move, my eyes spoke volumes.

Fuck. You.

4:37

I squinted at the bright red numbers on the bedside clock, trying to focus, but my eyes felt like they were stuck together with glue. Apparently, I hadn't been sleeping long, but I must have fallen down hard. Lying on my stomach, I mashed my fingertips into my forehead and sighed. Tomorrow—*today* would be rough. Already it seemed there was a trail of gunk behind my sinuses, and my mouth felt like an entire sack of cotton balls had been stuffed inside.

I rolled onto my side and was met by Blake's warm skin. No matter what the temperature was, he always radiated heat like a small ray of sun. Even through his slow, even breaths, he instinctively reached out, cupping my waist to pull me closer. Wearing only a pair of underwear, I hooked a bare leg over his waist and settled comfortably into his embrace, feeling his warmth coat my nipples. With the soft light of the moon a cloak over our mingled bodies, I almost fell back into a peaceful slumber in the timed rhythm of his breaths. I dozed off a few more minutes, but I couldn't ignore the nagging dehydration that was parching me senseless.

I tried to slip away, but Blake tightened his hold with an adorable grunt, letting me know that he wasn't as *asleep* as I had thought. I huffed a light laugh and traced the outline of his strong jaw. "I need a drink before I die. I forgot to leave one on the nightstand. Be right back." I inched up and kissed the edge of his nose, relishing in the slow smile that crept across his face, though he never fully opened his eyes.

How'd I get so lucky?

I wondered this over and over, but I didn't think I would ever find the answer. I tried as best as I could to recall the end of the night as I slipped Blake's T-shirt over my head. Knowing the house was still full, I opted against leaving the room in just a shirt and underwear and slipped my legs into a pair of his sweatpants as well. He was so much taller than me that the extra fabric bunched beneath my feet and only the tips of my toes peeked out from them. I smiled as I looked down, wiggling my little pink piggies and thinking Blake would love the sight of this. It was a comforting and protective feeling, as though I were actually wearing *him*.

I closed the door behind me with a soft click. The house was much quieter now. Eerily silent knowing how many people still remained. I guessed I wasn't the only one who had crashed hard.

Reaching the top step, my palm fell to the banister and then I tensed. Hackles raised along the back of my neck as my mind immediately went to Abby. I glanced behind my shoulder to the closed door, staring at it a few seconds. Tracing my steps back in that direction, I bunched the pants into my hands as I approached on my tiptoes. Hearing no sound still, I moved closer and pressed my ear against it, listening closely when a loud snore ripped through the room. I rolled my head until my forehead rested against the wood, a long, slow sigh leaving my lips. *Good.*

Feeling more relaxed knowing they were sleeping everything off, I quietly stepped the rest of the way to the kitchen.

What a wreck.

Remnants of the previous night lay strewn about the foyer in a scattered mess. Somehow, a buzz from the music which pumped so loudly still lingered in the air from the deejay equipment which sat abandoned now. Stepping over discarded cans and red cups, I decided not to allow myself the anxiety of looking around. Blake did this every year, so I trusted he had a way of easily righting it again.

The bare skin of my feet met the cool tile, sending a chill up my body. I rubbed away the little bumps traveling up the tops of my arms and then covered my mouth with the back of my hand as a yawn escaped. Through the large picture windows lining the kitchen, the sky was turning a husky shade of off-black, signaling that the sun would be waking up soon.

I opened the refrigerator, searching for a bottle of water, but all I could find was beer and some cheese cubes. *Guess we'll be shopping today, too.*

The dry in my throat was unbearable. With another yawn, I moved to the cabinet, searching for a glass. I filled it with water from the tap and sucked down half of it in hearty gulps. Once the urge was sated, I slowed down and rested my hip against the counter to finish the rest.

The kitchen overlooked the back of the house. Hidden in the darkness were rolling green fields mingling with courts for sports and the pool. The sun began to poke her head through the grayed darkness, an orange hue sneaking into the skyline. A smile spread across my face. I had missed so many of these lately, and that only meant one thing.

I was happy.

Rays of light bled into the dark, illuminating the grounds little by little. My smile grew in a returned *good morning* to my old friend as she greeted me over a very different landscape than I was used to. My smile widened as I caught myself dazzling in a daydream, where Blake was mine forever, and we were raising a family and living out our dream as husband and wife, leaving the rest of the world and our heavy pasts behind us. My life was about to change. I could just feel it.

But then I felt something else.

Something hard poking me in the backside while a firm grip tightened at my hip. The remainder of the sunrise whirled like a kaleidoscope as I spun, praying I'd be looking into a pair of baby blues when I knew, without a doubt, that I wouldn't be. My body was all too familiar with the ice that ran through my veins at this touch. The stench of what I would ultimately see was the second thing to hit me. I'd never seen hatred with such a distinct look as I did when my wide eyes found the dirt brown color of his.

Though my chest was heaving, he barely moved a muscle—his calm, a stark contrast to the banging beneath my ribs. This was normal for him, like air. He the quiet predator, and me the shaking prey. A twitch of a smirk hit his lips, and I instinctively retreated a step, but it only pressed my back against the counter behind me. With a racing heart, I tried not to panic. Instead, I was gathering my bearings, taking inventory of my surroundings.

The room was cast in contradiction, the bright light of the sun just coming awake, meeting the shadows of the setting moon. I allowed myself an internal laugh at the irony of how it so closely mirrored my existence. How fitting a setting it was. I had danced amongst the shadows my whole life, maneuvering through the gray areas just to get by. It was home to me, comfortable. I had lived in this space, owned it for so long. It was time to make it mine.

I crossed my arms over my chest. "What the fuck do you think you're doing, Damon?" I used the quietest voice I could spit out at him.

He remained still, the only movement was his arm as he took a swig of beer. After he swallowed, his tongue came up to cover his top teeth. He sucked back the liquid with a distasteful click, eyeing me like I was poison. The pause and lack of response so unlike him, it skidded a chill down my spine.

Something's off.

Instinctively, I tried to step back once again, but the back of my heel hit the cabinet. Though the beats of my heart seemed to be racing each other for freedom, I huffed, trying to seem bored by his game as I rolled my eyes and pushed off the counter to shoulder past him. I needed space. This spot that he had closed me into feeling as though it were constricting, creeping into me from the outside in. My shoulder banged into his chest, trying to shove him aside, but bounced back off of it as though it was cement rather than flesh. "Get. Out. Of. My. Way." I tried to appear calm, in control.

Strong.

Even though I wanted out of this situation, I couldn't let him see my panic. I wasn't his defenseless *lamb* anymore. I was a lion. A warrior.

He took a step closer and the lip of the counter bit into my back. I gripped it on either side to steady myself. *Blake and Abby are both resting peacefully upstairs.* I pulled all my inner strength into my center as my eyes dragged to the beer bottle dangling from Damon's fingers.

"Binging again, I see? We both know how well that went over last time." I gulped back the memory, knowing that *I* had been the one who'd bared the worst part of that episode.

He took a long pull from the bottle, then smacked his lips together. "Yep. Couldn't resist." He leaned in. "Your pussy feels so much better on the inside when I got a buzz going."

The water I had just consumed bubbled up my throat, but I couldn't give away the shake in my belly. I steadied my voice, not biting into that comment. Knowing I would be dead before he was ever able to touch me again fueled my strength.

I straightened my shoulders, needing some height since he towered mere inches from me. "You need to go to bed."

"Nope." His eyes glistened with the effects of the alcohol.

"Well, I'm going to bed." I tried more forcefully to shoulder past him, but his firm grip wrapped around my arm, his fingertips indenting my flesh.

"Nope," he snarled, so sure of himself. The smell of liquor, stale and new rested on the breath that landed on my lips. My stomach rolled, but I didn't recoil as I stared into the most evil set of eyes I'd ever seen. Dark and daring and partially hooded as if completely turned on by violating me. But they also swam with malice, equally as turned on by the thought of causing me pain.

Get away from him. He's not right.

"Let go of me." I yanked my arm back, but that only made him clench harder to keep his hold. My heart raced faster. The sound of blood banged in my ears as his lips moved closer still, only a whisper away from mine. Right before they made contact, his face swept to the side of my head. His hot breath covered my ear as he breathed the most terrifying word once again. The only word he needed tonight. The word that held all the promise in the world of what he intended to do.

"Nope."

As strong as I was trying to be, I couldn't help the shake that rolled over me. "We aren't alone right now, you sick fuck. Do you realize what you're doing? Everyone will know."

Then . . . the game changed.

All hope I'd had of leaving this situation vanished like a puff of a cloud.

His face emerged back into view as slowly as the rising sun, which now almost completely warmed the kitchen, making it even easier to see the complete state of undone he was in. His clothes hung disheveled, his hair a tattered mess, but his face . . .

His face was so certain, so sure, so unconcerned with my words as a devilish grin emerged.

"We've *never* been alone, beautiful. That's the beauty of it. I've always taken you right . . . under . . . their . . . noses." He tapped my nose at each of those words and my body jolted in response. That earned a deeper smile. "Made you squirm in silence."

"You don't care if Abby knows anymore?" I was desperate, grasping at straws and wanting to protect her.

Then the real hammer came. The truth of how sick this whole situation actually was.

His eyes trained on his finger as it traced the V of Blake's T-shirt, which rested protectively over my heart and my skin ached to concave beneath it. "Abby sleeps like a rock. Always has." His eyes flicked back to mine. "Those little blue pills I slip her every now and then work like a charm." Then he bore his stare into mine so I wouldn't misconstrue what he was saying. "Always have."

I gasped, my breaths halting in a ball beneath my rib cage as my mouth immediately dried. The fuzz in my head from a dawning hangover was making it hard to grasp what he was really telling me.

At my shock, Damon continued. "What? You thought I would ever just leave it to chance that she'd wake up and catch us? Give me a little more credit, beautiful."

"I can't . . . I can't believe you would do that to her." My voice was so low, so soft, so . . . insignificant. Like I had always been.

Damon shrugged. "Wasn't enough to hurt her and it wasn't all the time. Everyone does it. She's fine."

Reality whirled back into me in a blur as his finger dipped lower, between the crevice of my breasts. I slapped it away and tugged back on the other hand that was still holding me so tight. "Get your fucking hands off me," I grit out.

He didn't seem to hear that. Just studied my face as though it were no longer familiar to him. "You think you're cute, don't you? Flaunting, teasing, testing my limits. Dancing all sexy on your boyfriend while you're eye-fucking me. Daring me to come and take you out of his arms."

I gasped. *Is he that delusional?* He was sicker than I'd thought. I half-laughed as I stepped to push past him once again. "You need help. You should seek some out."

He whipped me back against the counter once more, his eyes pinning me to the granite. "Don't play coy with me. Your body may have been dancing with him, but you were looking at *me*. You don't have to beg, beautiful. I'm right here." His hand came down and cupped my sex.

I gasped into his palm as it shot up to cover my mouth. Once I was silenced, his hand began its descent, his fingers plucking at my bottom lip before it trailed past my jaw, skimming over my throat. His nail clipped my collarbone, pricking me just enough to snap my mind back to what was about to happen.

Again.

No.

Suddenly, calm washed away my fear, peace at the fact that this wouldn't happen. I would stop him or die trying. He could fuck a corpse, but he wouldn't take me alive. Not again.

As my body composed, absorbing my new fate, Damon released his grip on my arm, bringing both hands to the flat of my chest to finish his descent down. Still in a haze, Blake's blue, loved-crazed eyes filled my mind, his smile warm and reassuring, his dimple so fucking cute and amazing. Warmth coated me, and I took his love with me, borrowed his strength as a cool hand slipped beneath the cotton of my shirt and squeezed my bare breast.

At the intrusion, Blake's face exploded into a million bright stars, revealing the crazy person standing behind it. I sucked in a breath, Damon's eyes opening wider as that action puffed out the breast he was holding. His greedy thumbs began to circle my nipples, his mouth hanging open as though he ached to taste one. His eyes flicked back to my lips, his face inching toward me to take my mouth. My lip curled back over my teeth, and I took my palm, mushing his face and throwing him back.

Finally.

Damon stumbled, trying to find his bearings, and I took the

opportunity to move away from the counter he had locked me into and gain back a little more advantage.

"Remember it all, Eva. Remember all that I taught you. Every word I fucking said and every time I made your back hit those mats. Remember it and harness it and come out of the gates fucking swinging. Do not let this motherfucker own you. Not anymore. This is your life. Your house. Your rules." The words Drew spoke only hours earlier rushed through me.

Crouching my knees a bit, I sat into them and flicked the sweatpants at my thighs to hike up the extra fabric beneath my feet and give myself more traction. The cool tile sent a wave of energy through me, like a jolt of adrenaline, and I widened my arms. Turning my palms up, I raised a mocking eyebrow, a half-smile crooked in the corner of my mouth as I trained my eyes at my violator. My enemy. "Come at me," I recited Drew's words.

Damon cocked his head, studying me. Then a smile slid across his amused face. He laughed. "You're not serious."

I adjusted my legs, not letting my guard down, then sunk deeper into my squat. "Oh, I'm serious. Come at me. Unless . . ." I quirked a brow. "Unless you're scared." I made a pouty face. "What's the matter? You afraid I'm about to fuck *you* for once?" He stepped closer, and I swallowed deep, knowing this was it.

"Watch your fucking mouth."

"Nope," I spit his word back at him. "I've watched it long enough. It's time for *you* to watch my mouth now."

"Oh, I'm watching all right." Evil dripped from his twisted features his lip pulled back over his teeth, and he took a step toward me. "And I'm gonna shut it for you."

Quicker than I could register, he was on me then, but my body instinctively took over, slapping his hand away as it made to reach for my neck. I smiled once again. "Gonna have to try harder than that, asshole. I've been waiting years for this day, and if you don't care who finds out, then neither. The fuck. Do I." I curled my fingers into his shirt and threw him back.

Damon almost fell, landing in a crouch, one hand slamming to the floor to steady himself. When his eyes rose to mine, a chill washed over my entire body, and I knew it was over. He was coming at me with full force. My breathing loaded as the anticipation heightened.

"You little slut. How many times do I have to tell you they'll never believe you?" He stood and brushed off his hands. "See all this?" He motioned to me. "*You* attacked *me*." He grew more confident as he began to walk toward me. "Everyone saw your little display earlier." Another step. "How you were looking at me, licking your lips and begging for me to touch you. To *fuck* you, as you call it." Damon licked his lips and trailed his eyes down my body, still closing in on me. "Now you wanna cry victim?" He raised a brow, his smile widening. "Doesn't work that way, sweetheart. The world is on to whores like you."

My confidence dipped for a mere second, though my stance never did.

Was he right? Would no one trust my word?

He must have picked up on the hesitation because he took the small opportunity to lunge at me, coming full force for my torso like a barreling football player. My body slapped my mind to the forefront, screaming at it to look alive and do what it was trained for.

Survive.

The flat of my foot met his gut, and all the air whooshed from him in one large *oof*, taking him back a couple of steps. But I didn't stop. Something in me clicked off. Rationale replaced with rage as *I* advanced on *him*.

He straightened quick, attempting to slap my cheek, but I easily smacked that hand away. He tried the other cheek, and I did the same with the other hand, still coming up on him. "Come on, hot stuff. Hit me," I goaded, wanting the excuse to hurt him.

But something happened as Damon realized his position was being challenged. A familiar veil fell over his face, replacing whatever normalcy remained and displaying the true evil underneath.

There he is.

The devil himself stood toe-to-toe with me then. Staring at me on the other side of the island. One finger at a time, his fist curled in, and I knew he'd decided a mere slap wouldn't do. He charged at me. In a flurry of fists, he attacked. But I had been expecting this. Trained to dodge them, no matter what.

One-two

One-two-three

One-two-three-four

I danced. And his breathing became heavy. Maybe too heavy to carry any weight if he was actually able to make contact.

But he couldn't.

I was too good for that.

The air moved through my lungs fluidly. Entering and exiting my mouth in small, quiet wisps as he circled and threw, missing one after another. I couldn't help myself then. I decided to excite in a small victory and take my shot, landing an open-handed slap to the side of his face like the little bitch he actually was.

Damon seethed. His teeth bared, he came at me again, and I covered his other cheek with a full-on punch. His head bucked back, and I moved in, landing another square on his nose, and I delighted at the small red trickle that ran down.

But then he tasted it. Tasted the copper running between his teeth. He swiped at it and stared down at the color swatch on the top of his hand. The anger on his face stopped me cold, making all this too real. "You'll pay for that."

He was too fast.

The moment it took to stun me was all it took for him to be on me, for him to have the advantage. His large fingers wrapped firmly around my neck, blocking off all air and bringing a darkness into my eyes from all outside points. I covered his hands with my own—clawing, pulling, begging with wide eyes for him to loosen his grip, but he didn't. Something completely consumed him, fueling him to follow through with the final betrayal I'd fallen victim to at his hands. At this very moment, he seemed intent on stripping away that final piece of me. My air. My life.

Darkness closed in in graying spider webs, my tongue poking through my lips as a dull numbness prickled the skin on my face. Beneath my skull boomed a pressure I didn't think it could withstand.

The last thing I saw before my eyes lazily slid closed was that swipe of red between Damon's two top teeth and the way his mouth curled around it. The last sound was the beats of my own heart rocking into my ears in slowing thumps. I was swimming. Levitating. Drifting off into a darkness filled with electric blue eyes, spiraling into a tunnel. A low voice whispered from somewhere in the darkness.

You're dealing with someone who already knows all your weaknesses, Eva. The day you forget that is the day we'll be peeling you back up off the floor.

The vision of Drew screamed at me then, hazel eyes blazing with fire. *Go!*

I pulled everything in. Though I couldn't breathe and my arms felt like lead, my eyes shot open, my knee coming up to connect with Damon's junk with as much force as I could find. I choked, coughing as he stumbled back, dragging in whatever oxygen I could while he straightened and came at me again.

"You thought I fucked you against your will all these years? Well, you're about to really get fucked now. Hold on tight, beautiful. Your world's about to end—"

"What the fuck! Eva?" The boom of Blake's voice came from the entryway, and my eyes immediately shot to his, quickly begging him to put the pieces together and understand what was happening as I strained to catch a breath that was barely even there.

Crack!

The world melted away, blurring my vision in a swirl as I rolled over the side of my feet in a free fall. Searing pain met my skull for the second time as the other side of my head hit the granite countertop, a spiral of lights and darks falling with me as the back of my head screamed out in pain once more, hitting the marble tile beneath me. And then . . .

Nothing.

BLAKE

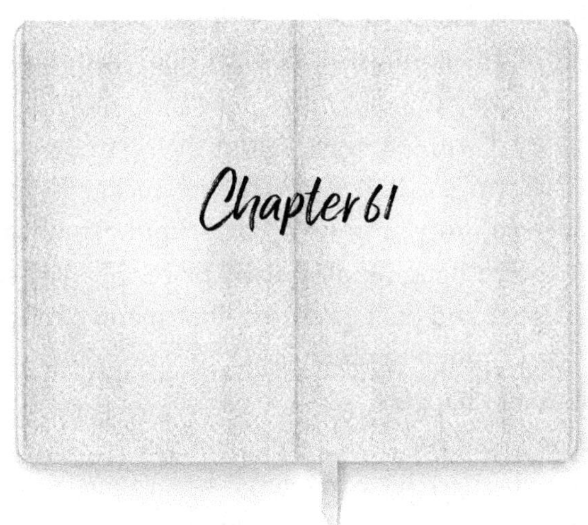

Chapter 61

"YOU THOUGHT I FUCKED YOU *against your will all these years? Well, you're about to really get fucked now."*

Damon's words froze me in time.

Him.

It was him.

How could I not have known?

Angel's eyes locked with mine, desperate and pleading. They were so wide. Begging for me to understand? For my forgiveness? I wasn't sure. I didn't have long to think about it because, quicker than the answer could come, Damon grabbed a stray bottle left over from last night. My lips parted to shout her name once more—to warn her, but the crash of glass slamming into the side of her head was what rang out instead, cracking me in two. The green eyes that I loved so much dulled instantaneously, rolling back to reveal white as she slumped over. I reached out, but it was too late. Her head bounced off the counter like a rubber ball, and I nearly chucked right there before she disappeared behind the kitchen island. With heavy breaths, my eyes shot to Damon, my mind in overdrive and completely unhinged. He advanced toward her with sick, glossed-over eyes, so focused he wasn't even paying attention to me.

But he was going to.

I moved into the kitchen, calculating my moves, knowing first and foremost I had to protect her. And that meant getting him far the fuck away from her. I needed to keep my cool somehow even though my vision was being clouded by a sea of red. Rage pulsated from my fist that was closed so tight, my knuckles ached. I would make sure I was the last thing he saw on his way to hell.

"You," I seethed with enough venom that Damon finally looked to me. "Don't you fuckin' touch her. You motherfucker. I should've known. You've always been a slimy scumbag. Child rapist actually makes sense."

His clothes were hanging all out of place, his hair sticking out in every direction. That and his red-tipped nose made him look disheveled and unhinged, determined to end her life.

But that couldn't happen.

Not if I ended his first.

Damon straightened, his convoluted brain twisting a warped smile on his face. He raised his brows. "I don't know what you're talking about. Your little slut came on to *me*. She's wanted me forever. Begged for it all her life."

Stride after stride, I moved in. Eyes on his throat, I could practically see the tic of the pulse I intended to extinguish. "How could you?" My voice cracked around the quiver in my lip, giving away my vulnerability at the thought of her pain. Vibrations shook me from my gut, making it almost hard to move forward. "She was a child. How could you do that to her?" A rock settled low in my stomach, then bubbled, growing, traveling to my throat as the truth settled deep in my bones. I thought I would be sick from the thought of his hands on her. From the look in his eyes right now as he recalled the times that they were. Lust laying on his disgusting fucking stare.

"I'm gonna kill you with my bare hands, you sick delusional fuck." That last word grading from the back of my throat was all it took to put me close enough to lunge at him. I twisted his collar in one fist and pounded the other one into his dirty fucking mouth. A split ripped his bottom lip into two halves, and the look of blood sitting between it thrilled the fuck out of me. I cocked my fist back a second time but stopped in mid-air as he began to . . . laugh? The fucker was fucking laughing.

Damon's own hands knotted into my shirt, and he tugged me to him, his face so close his eyes were able to see directly into mine. I shivered, witnessing all the years of her suffering in those eyes. In that one stare. Her innocence lying there, discarded, wrecked, and abused.

The alcohol on his breath clouded my vision, but his cold voice tunneled me back to reality. "What's the matter, Blake?" His sarcastic eyes dragging to mine before a smirk split the cut on his lip wider, though he didn't seem to notice. "You mad because I knew what that pussy tasted like first?" He scrubbed the back of his hand across his mouth, then glanced at the blood that lay there. He inhaled a quick breath before spitting a spatter of what remained on to my face.

Thinking ceased.

Logic floated away.

Something else settled in. Something animalistic.

A roar erupted from my throat as I pushed forward, slamming his body against the counter. His back bent backward from the force, his head smacking against the cabinets.

A burst of air pushed through my nostrils as they flared to capacity. The grit of my teeth seeming to crumble them in my mouth. I cocked my fist back into a trembling ball and crashed it down, an explosion erupting in my vision as I heard the bones of his cheek crunch beneath it.

Motherfucker needs to die.

His head snapped back but took the hit, probably still numb from the alcohol. And that was good. I wanted him to take every hit I dished out. Because as long as he did, the more I could deliver.

I landed a kidney shot next, crumbling him to the side. That one he felt. It labored him enough for me to land another to his ribs. A crack splintered the air, and I knew I'd broken at least one. I dug my fists into his polo shirt and spun, swinging his body before tossing him. He slid the length of the island, an explosion of fruit, cups, and liquid flying out in his wake. A groan floated up from the floor as I rounded the corner of the granite. His legs came into view first, curled into him as he wrapped his arms around himself.

Good. He feels me.

I knelt beside him, clutching his shirt to yank him up to me. "Do you know what you did to her?" My spit fell on his forehead as I screamed in his face. "Do you!" My voice was so loud, my ears rang around the words. I bounced my hands down, knocking the back of his head off the tiles.

Blood filled the skin surrounding his left eye, turning it purple as it began to swell shut. The glassy look swimming around his irises let me know I was doing more damage than he was letting on. The cocky smile never left his face, though. Through every grunt and every groan, the stubborn son-of-a-bitch tried to make it seem as though I wasn't hurting him, but that was about to change.

Eva's angelic face flashed before my eyes, her lighthearted laugh fucking with my sense of reality.

I shook my head, and Damon appeared, goading my insides to end him.

Flash.

I'm with Eva again. She jumps on me with a squeal, wrapping her legs around me as I spin.

Flash.

She's younger, sitting on her bed and listening to music. Singing with her eyes closed and a smile on her face, her head bopping in time with the music. Unsuspecting. Innocent. The bed beside her dips down, the smile on her face fading as realization sinks in that she isn't alone, a look of terror replacing the happiness she had moments before.

Flash.

Him. With that same cocky-as-fuck smirk he was giving me right now, lurking beside her. Reaching for her.

"Aaaahhh," I cried out through my ground out teeth, my body quaking with a fury and rage I had never experienced before. That I didn't know how to contain. Somewhere in the black hole behind my eyes, I knew I couldn't let myself crack so deeply, get lost so far in it, but it couldn't be helped.

Another blast of my fist met his teeth, and then I wrapped my fingers around his neck and squeezed, pulling him toward me to look into his eyes. To make sure he knew exactly what was in store for him.

"Get ready." My lips trembled, adrenaline rocking me. "This is gonna make up for five years of her pain." A smile slowly moved across my face as his cocky grin finally slid away.

One breath.

Two.

Crack!

My knuckles exploded with agony as they connected with his temple, sending his skull back against the tile. Anchoring my legs over the sides of his body, I squeezed his throat unmercifully. The whites of his eyes emerged, rolling back as his lungs depleted of oxygen. I wanted to take his air the way he had taken hers. To take *her* air *back* from his lungs.

More grit in my mouth, my nostrils pushed so wide they ached, yearning urging me to deplete him of the one thing he needed to stay alive. This asshole wasn't worthy of a drop of relief.

"Fuuuck!" I screamed as his tongue fell through his teeth, blood vessels crackling along his cheeks in tight little clumps.

I faintly registered screams around me, but I was too distracted watching the fireworks show in the whites of his eyes. Popping and spreading of red streaking the ivory color. His head fell back, and I dropped him in a heap. Then stood and stared down at his worthless, twitching body. With a heaving chest, I brought my foot up, staring one last time at the cause of my girl's destruction, and stomped down with my heel right between his legs. I was determined to leave his dick unusable if he was spared any remaining days.

Strong arms wrapped around me, pulling me aside. I spit at Damon before I was dragged away. "He's not moving, man. You have to stop." I recognized the voice as Drew's, but I couldn't stop the vibrations rocking me. My chest ached with the effort to breathe, my jaw throbbing from being clenched so tight.

"It was him." The words were far away, shaky. "It was him!" I lunged once more, wanting to make sure he never woke up from this, but Drew's hold was solid.

"I know, man. I know." Drew's voice was low, apologetic.

"Oh my god, is he dead?" Abby shrieked. "What did you do?" Her horrified eyes found mine as she slipped on a patch of blood beside her *fiancé*.

My head spun like the exorcist. "What did *I* do?" I pulled toward her but Drew yanked me back. "Did you know? Did you know he was doing that to her!" I yelled, hurt parading off of me in rolling waves.

"What're you even talking about?" she screeched back, before switching her focus to Damon. "Damon? Oh, god! He's not fucking answering!" Eric knelt beside her, taking inventory of Damon's injuries as he tried to shush Abby.

"How could *you* let him do that to her!" I raged, arms shackled behind my back by Drew.

"Calm down, man. She doesn't know." Drew's voice was as tepid as possible." You gotta calm down, or they're gonna cart you outta here, and then you won't be able to help her."

Help her. Angel. Oh my God, where is she?

The frenzy started to simmer into sheer panic, like an icy frost racing into my center.

Angel.

"Angel?" I glanced to my right and saw her toes peeking out from behind the island in the same place they'd been when she first landed. "Angel!" I shrugged out of Drew's hold and slammed to my knees beside her, rolling her over in my arms. Her head dropped back over my forearm, the whites of her eyes peeking through the small slits beneath her lashes. Her cheeks were white, ashen, her lips blue.

My voice was barely recognizable as it tore from my throat. "Somebody call nine-one-one!"

TIME SUCKED FROM ME LIKE a vacuum in a quick whoosh. From the moment I held her limp body on, everything whipped in a mindless cyclone. Simultaneously, I could hear everything around me and also nothing but the faint wisps of air struggling to come out of her mouth. "Breathe, baby. Breathe. She's fucking turning blue!" I yelled, frantic as I spread her body back down against the tiles, the blue-gray tinging her skin telling me how critical she was.

"What!" The cry that tore from Abby's throat was punishing, but I needed her quiet so I could focus.

I placed my ear to Eva's chest, simultaneously pressing two fingers to her throat. Her pulse was weak, but she was there, my little fighter. My body rocked as Abby dropped down beside me, knocking into me in her haste. But, just as quickly as she was on me, she was being dragged away with a yelp, her legs flailing.

"Come on. Give him space. Let him help her," Eric soothed her.

"Eva!" Abby's cry choked amidst her tears. "What happened to her? Eva, get up!"

"Let me in. I'm trained for this," Drew demanded. When my eyes met his, there was nothing but confidence in his stare.

I held her body tight, wanting her to feel me with her, not wanting to let her go. I had made her a promise to never let her down, and I intended to keep it. Had I not needed to back-off Damon, I'd have been to her side sooner . . .

"I got her. I'll fucking breathe for her as long as I have to." My body shook so violently I thought I'd be sick as my quivering mouth met hers. Instead of the warm, supple lips that normally greeted me, I was met with a dry, lifeless response. I squeezed my eyes shut, not allowing myself to dwell on that so I could take care of her properly. Pinching her nose shut, I began to blow into her mouth, rescue breathing for her.

In between counts and small breaks, compressions and breaths, I rested my forehead on hers, begging so low no one else could hear me, but praying somewhere inside her motionless body she could. "Come on, breathe my air, baby. Breathe me." I puffed into her mouth once more, my lips feeling dry to the point of cracking from the repetition. I dropped my forehead to hers again as unrecognizable sobs ricocheted all around me from people that loved her. People counting on *me* to make her okay.

"You're doing good, man," Drew coached. "You need a break?"

"Never." I cupped my hands over her heart, working through another set. "Come on!" I yelled, frustration clawing at my throat that she wouldn't open her eyes and see me. Gag, any-fucking-thing! "Angel." My voice cracked, a tear leaking between the seams of our joined lips as I covered hers once again. A swelling burn coiled in the pit of my stomach at the thought that she might not make it out of this. That I might not be able to save her.

"Fuuuuck!" I sobbed, defeat slipping in despite my attempts to keep it away. "Fuck," I whispered, cradling her face and licking my dry lips, tasting the salt that lay there. Sirens blared in the distance.

A small relief began to bloom until I heard Drew's voice beside me. "You gotta get outta here. You don't know if he's gonna make it."

I stopped the CPR just long enough to follow his line of sight to the floor where Damon lay with Abby hovering over his chest. "I'm not leaving her."

Abby's head snapped in my direction. "For all we know, *you* did this to her. You're not going anywhere near her after this."

Heat rode my spine in crackling sparks, bubbling over my neck in a hot wave, and I fought to remain rooted on my knees and not lunge at her. I jabbed my finger in her direction. "You have no fucking clue what you're even saying. *He* did this to her!" I bellowed.

At her wide-eyed response, Eric spoke for her, his own face reddening. "Hey, don't talk to her like that. She's innocent in all of this."

I was barely hanging on to my frayed endings. "Well, she needs to put her *sister* first for a change. You want to talk about who's innocent in all this?" I bore my gaze into Abby's. She was lucky Drew stopped me before I could finish that motherfucker.

Drew stepped forward. "Look, I didn't see anything." He looked around. "I'm sure no one else did, either."

Slow nods began to bob around the room. Eric spoke next. "Nah, man. I didn't see a thing."

All eyes turned to Abby.

"You guys can't be serious!" she screeched.

Eric put a hand on her arm just as Jace burst over the threshold, knocking him to the side as he ran past.

"None of us understands anything right now," Eric spoke as calm as possible. "But something brought this on, and we're not going to have any answers without all the players."

"What did he do to her?" Jace interrupted, slamming to his knees beside me. "I didn't know he was fucking here!" he yelled again, agony crackling through each syllable as he gathered her in his arms. "Baby girl? Wake up!"

"Jace?" Abby's voice held no weight, but her tear-soaked eyes spoke of her uncertainty, glistening under puckered, heartbroken eyebrows.

Jace's gaze locked on Abby, his whole face crumpling as he pulled Eva into his chest. His eyes held the key to all our unanswered questions—heavy, regretful, all-knowing, and finally, remorseful.

A gasped, "Oh my God," floated from Abby's lips before it was muffled by her palm. Her eyes watered further, one stray tear falling over her lower lid as she looked to Damon. Then the rocking began. "Oh my God. Oh my God," she half-wailed, half-swore as the bubble of shock worked its way around her. Eric was quick to wrap an arm around her, concern etched on his face as he soothed her with gentle hushes.

"Help her," Jace begged, lowering Eva back to the floor so I could continue breathing for her just as the clicks and clanks of paramedic equipment rang out from the front door. "Where is everyone?" a deep baritone called out.

"Kitchen," a bunch of voices replied at once.

"Everyone back, please. What do we have here?" A young, built man, who looked to be in his early thirties, dropped a bag beside Eva.

"We're not sure. They got into a fight. This is how we found them," Drew spoke first. His back was straight as a tack, his face stoic and unreadable as he looked at the paramedic square in the face.

The man looked around the room, and when no one offered anything more, he looked at Drew from a disbelieving side-eye and lowered beside Eva. "What do you have over there?" he called over to his partner, a woman with her brown hair twisted in a bun, who looked like she could kick my ass if she wanted.

"Unconscious male. He's breathing on his own, but not well," she replied, setting up the tools she would need to aid him.

"Bag him and let's get them out of here," he said as he bent beside me. "Sir, you'll have to give us room."

With a tight nod and a hard swallow, I spoke against the kiss I placed to Eva's hairline. "Come back to me, Angel." I kissed her once more and backed away.

Moving to a squat just a foot away, I rested my elbows on each knee for leverage, and pushed my hands to my lips, watching the paramedics assess her. I'd never felt as helpless as I did right then. Having to stand back and watch someone work to save my reason for living, not knowing if she would come out of this all right.

"Oh, god." I dropped my head, rocking on the balls of my feet as the notion that she might not ricocheted through me. As I stood here watching her strain for her next breath, I prayed that I had done enough. Given her enough of my air to save her.

I was defenseless. Powerless. Suffocation clawed at me, seeming to close my throat as the world stopped. I raked a hand through my hair, sending all my prayers up to God. *Please, don't do this to her.*

Small cries caught my attention, and I looked up to find Jessie in the corner with her hand covering her mouth. Beside her, Jeremy rubbed circles on a bawling Sandra's back. Less than a year ago it had been her in this very situation, and I was sure that this hit a little too close to home for her.

Another set of paramedics rushed to their aid as oxygen was

supplied to both Eva and Damon. Gurneys were propped up, machines turned on, things beeping and flashing. The whole thing happened in a matter of minutes, but it felt like hours as they moved about my kitchen.

Once Eva was secured on the bed, they began to roll it toward the door.

"I'm going with her," I said, rushing to their side. Though I could feel the weight of everyone in the house following us through the foyer, I didn't dare remove my eyes from her for one second.

When we reached the door, Drew called out, "I'll wait here for the cops." But the paramedics didn't stop moving, and neither did I. My focus was trained on the guy's hand and every squeeze of the bubble that was taking my place and blowing oxygen into her.

The gurney lifted into the ambulance and, just as the door was about to close, Abby slipped inside. "I'm coming with you."

Chapter 63

BEEP.

Beep.

Beep.

DRIP.

Drip.

Drip.

Chapter 65

"WE NEED A MEDIC IN here!"

"Nooooo!"

Fuck, no! Let her be okay.

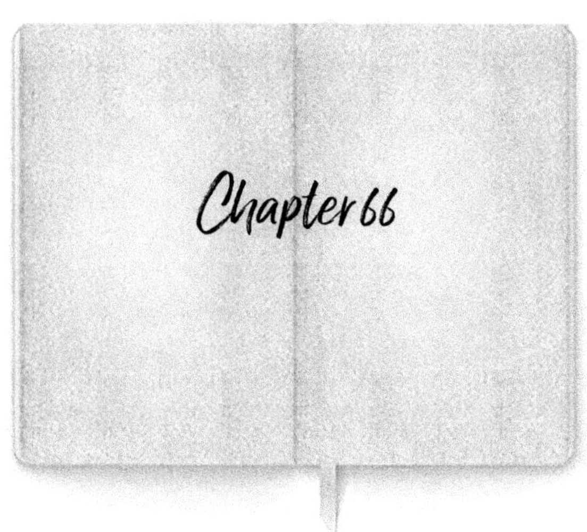

COMMOTION.

Chaos.

Another minute.

Then two.

Then ten . . .

"SHE'S STABLE. YOU CAN SEE her now."

Air.

I STARED DOWN AT THE shiny blue tile, focusing on a chip in the corner of one and watching it blur before I blinked it back into focus. The last couple hours had easily taken ten years from my life.

She has to be okay. She just has to.

The doctors had worked on her so long, so hard. They had told Abby and me that the knock she had taken to her head had likely caused a brain injury, which was what was hindering her breathing. They stabilized her before their white coats were whisking her away for further testing and CT scans to see the extent of the damage.

My poor Angel.

I laced my fingers behind my head and crouched forward on the blue cushioned sofa in the hospital waiting room, buried in my thoughts. In my nightmares.

I swore to all that was holy that if the fucker had caused any permanent damage to my girl, I would finish what I had started back at the house and end him.

Eva's parents were away for the holiday weekend as well, so they hadn't arrived yet, but they were on their way, her mom texting and calling every few minutes for updates. Little did she know she was about to get the shock of her life.

Thankfully, Abby had disappeared again, not wanting to be around me until she knew the whole story, and that was fine. I didn't know how I was going to deal with the barrage of questions that was sure to come.

I didn't have any of their fucking answers, and the one person who did was lying motionless on a slab.

That vision rocked me senseless, and my body jolted up to drag in a gulp of air, trying to calm my rickety nerves. How the hell was I supposed to do this? Without her? Without the whole story?

Then the answer rammed into me so hard, I don't know how I didn't think of it before. Awareness prickled the back of my head, my eyes widening just as Jace crossed the threshold with two cups of coffee. He looked worn, somewhere else as he set the cup beside me on a table without ever really noticing me. Or the new life in my eyes. Or the tic in my veins as I dragged my gaze to meet his.

Bringing his hand up to sip, he lingered with the cup hanging off his lip as he stared, finally noticing what was probably a crazy look on my face. "What's with you?"

A firm swallow rode my throat as my eyes, which felt like they were completely unhinged, locked on his. "I need a favor."

Chapter 69

BEEP.

Drip.

I was surrounded by it. The cool temperature did nothing to brighten up the drab walls of Eva's hospital room. The doctors had admitted her and were waiting for the results of her tests to come back. Thankfully none of them had protested my insistence on staying by her side. They agreed that it might help her wake up to feel me beside her. I was glad that they did because I was ready to go to battle if they gave me a hard time.

I was so sure of what I needed to do when I'd sent Jace to get Eva's journal. But now the feel of it in my hands was so dirty. The weight of devastation the pages held radiated from it, sending an immediate depression in a wave. It was no wonder she'd stayed trapped inside the binding of it for so long. How hard it must have been to dig out from it.

My hands shook, teetering on the brink of unclipping the heart-shaped brass clasp, knowing a wave of grief would spill out into me once I did.

It would be one thing if it were my own misery, but this was hers. I was finally going to take the last step, and I was going to do it without her. Though that broke my heart a little more, my girl needed my strength. She needed me to know it all when I finally looked into her eyes again. And the eyes of her family. I threaded my fingers with hers and brought the back of her hand to my lips, breathing through flared nostrils to contain the burn crippling my throat.

Then—

I closed my eyes and twisted the clip.

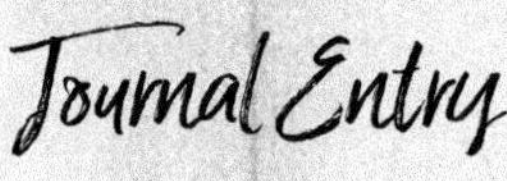

EVA 14 YEARS OLD

I just threw up.

That should have been the biggest moment of my life, and I immediately ran to the bathroom and lost everything in my stomach.

Somehow, it kinda feels like I lost a little bit of me, too. Like I watched who I was flush down the toilet before I walked back into my bedroom a different girl than who had woken up under my purple comforter this morning. I want to feel okay, but I don't. I want to be happy, but I'm not. I want to believe that was normal, but my skin feels itchy and crawly. I know he said everybody does this, that it was supposed to feel good, but my insides felt all slimy the whole time. Like I was constantly holding down vomit just to get through it. I wanted to peel off my own skin to get it out from under him I only agreed to a kiss, but he took so much more, and now I'm scared . . . I'm scared I'll never get it back.

I never want to do that again. Not with him or anybody else. I feel like I could throw up again every time I think about his hands on me. His . . . thing inside of me. And . . .

I hurt.

It hurts. Really bad.

Why do people do this?

Great, now I'm crying again.

I don't want to see my family after this.

And my sister . . .

I can't ever let Abby know. I can't ever let any of them know. That much I'm sure of. But the rest of this is so confusing. I just thank God that never has to happen again. I don't think I could stomach it.

And when does the hurt stop?

I'M GONNA BE SICK.

My breathing seemed to come in waves as I moved my eyes from her journal, focusing on deep, calming breaths to try to stop myself from losing it. Hearing her words right after the first time she was raped did things to me that I couldn't even begin to rationalize. Unhinged something incredibly animalistic and inhumane. So much so that the thought of what I could do to Damon was scaring the piss out of me. I didn't recognize my own thoughts as they skated around in my head mixed with images that I was ashamed to admit.

She was a child. Lonely, confused, alone.

So alone.

My heart cracked open in my chest, creating an ache for her that was insurmountable. I mashed my forehead to the worn out page and sucked in a deep breath.

Beep.

Drip.

Journal Entry

EVA 15 YEARS OLD

He came to see me again tonight. Each time he comes into my room, I hope it's to apologize. I hope he's realized what he does to me and wants my forgiveness. To take it back.

But all he does is take some more. Walks away with a new piece of me that I didn't even know I had left. I wonder when he'll realize that nothing remains but tiny fragments. Or if he'll ever care. He doesn't seem to mind the lifeless body that lies beneath him. Acts as though he's on the ride of a lifetime rather than a one-way ticket to hell.

He doesn't see the pile of dust that I'm left in. Doesn't offer the broom to clean it up when he's zipping up his pants and thanking me before he walks back out the same door he entered. The one that used to keep me safe—tucked in and warm. And now just holds me hostage.

Because I did this. I said yes. And now . . .

I can never say no.

I DRAPED ONE OF MY legs over Eva's thighs wanting to wrap her in security, my enormous body aligned with her tiny frame the best it could be while I twirled a lock of her golden hair.

I needed a break.

A rock lodged in my chest, reading her words. Through my tears, my struggles, I sat with her in those pages—next to her in her room, beside her on her roof, in her yard, under her trees. I followed her, trailing, living in her words, devastated at her fate. Knowing I had to help her through this was all I had to keep me from getting sick because I'd almost chucked a bunch of times. Or sought out his murder. *Either way . . .*

The metal rail along the side of this hard mattress kept digging into my back, but I didn't care. I needed to be as close to her as possible. Needed her to feel the warmth of my body. She was so still, looked so peaceful even through the cuts and scrapes on her face. Her bottom lip was swollen, a jagged cut splicing the tender flesh, and around her left eye, a purple swell bulged.

I don't know how I didn't kill him.

Even now—staring at her injuries, knowing he was in the same hospital in a room of his own—something was calling to me to slip myself inside and unplug his fucking machines.

But that would make me the same as him.

The different shades of gold in her hair mingled with each other as I wrapped and unwrapped them around my finger. I dropped my chin to her shoulder, my thoughts in a faraway fog, tainted by my exhaustion.

My fingers snagged on a hard clump of hair, and I looked to the iron-colored glob. The entire section was fused in that one spot to the gunky, hardened liquid. Blood. Most likely her own.

Every imaginable worst-case scenario bombarded me, no matter how hard I tried to ignore them. To remain positive. And as I wrapped her inside my strong arms, wanting to be the man she needed, to be her strength and support and guidance home . . .

Everything inside of me broke.

I crumpled into her neck, her body barely moving as I meshed into her side, hoping, praying she would feel my love and wake the fuck up.

Beep.

Drip.

"Angel, if you can hear me, I love you so much. Come back to me, please." My voice split with that final plea as I splintered to fucking dust beside her. I cradled her to me as her head fell back into the hard hospital pillow. I couldn't let myself lose it. She needed me to be strong for her right now.

My chest tightened, pulling into the center, as the smell—the room, the familiarity soaked in—bringing with it . . . fear.

What if she pushes me away again when she wakes up like the last time?

My eyes fell to the wooden rolling cart beside her bed, the same kind she had discarded her necklace on months ago. I remembered the pit that sent a sour taste into the back of my throat when I had found it lying there. Though it rested safely in my pocket now, I dreaded the same outcome, knowing how she normally handled these situations, and prayed she was different this time.

I pushed the unease aside and sat up straighter on the unforgiving hospital bed. I'd show her that she had nothing to run from anymore. The secret that had locked her away for so long would now be the truth would set her free.

Journal Entry

EVA 16 YEARS OLD

I fucking hate him. My insides ache with disgust. Sweet Sixteen had never tasted so bitter. This was when I was supposed to say goodbye to my adolescence, but that ship was pirated years ago. Everyone wishing me congratulations, telling me how pretty I am. What a beautiful woman I'm becoming.

Beautiful.

What a filthy fucking word. I'm so ugly inside. So ruined and wrecked. So warped that my own self can't stand to be in my body. I wake up sweating, clawing at myself all night long.

Maybe I'll extinguish all sixteen candles. Blow them out for good and watch from hell as the smoke billows in their wake . . . up to heaven . . . in my place.

OH, NO, BABY.

I crumbled. I fucking lost it into my palm, sobbing like a pussy on the bed beside her, imagining the state of mind she had to have been in to want to take her life. For her to think that was her only way out of this. I had always known it was bad, but I never imagined it was *that* bad. My poor little Angel. My poor girl. I combed my fingers through her hair, pulled her limp body to mine and held her close, trying to make her feel, wherever she was. Let her know that she wasn't alone. She never would be again. My tears soaked into her hair, my eyes aching, head pounding, but I had to go on. I needed to know it all.

To feel what she had felt.

To die alongside her.

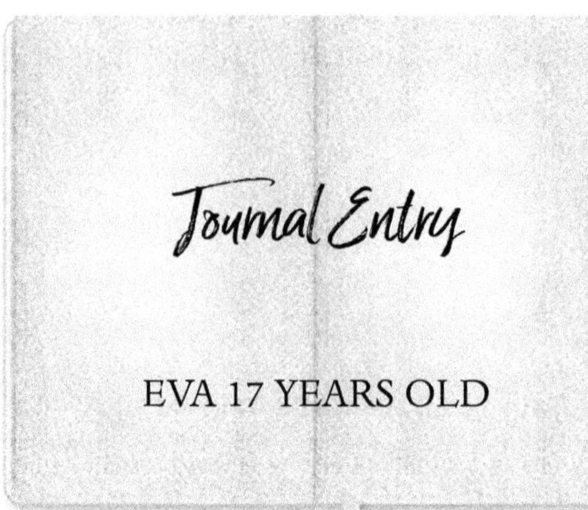

Broken.

Where once I was whole, I fear I never will be again.

Once happy—I now tunnel through sadness.

Alone.

Today was bad.

Jace found me on the bathroom floor passed out in a pool of vomit after Damon's latest "visit."

Once I was cleaned up and sober, he broke me down to the last bit, and I finally cracked and told him what's been happening all these years. When I refused to tell anyone and told him he couldn't either, he got so mad, I was sure I'd made a mistake. But in his Jacely way, he reassured me. Told me it would be okay and we'd figure it out.

Then we came up with a plan. We're going away to college together. I'll have to find a way to get him in because that boy is not about school, but I'll do it. I'm excited. For the first time in a long time, I feel like there might be hope. Or at least maybe some air.

THE STERILE ALCOHOL SMELL WAS clogging my throat. Hospitals always reeked of urine mixed with alcohol, laced with misery. I tried to ignore the burn as I stared down at the honeycomb blanket covering Angel and me. The scent seemed to drift away, but the blanket did little to take away the chill I felt as I took in her still body. My jaw clamped down as I fought anger at the sight of my poor Angel.

The CT scan had shown a bleed on her brain. A bleed on her fucking *brain. That beautiful mind.*

I couldn't even wrap my head around it. The doctors were closely monitoring it, but if a good amount of blood didn't retract today, they were going to talk about possibly making a hole in her skull and draining some out to relieve the pressure. My chest tightened around the notion. Thoughts of her strapped down to some table while someone drilled into her shook me senseless, so I refused to go there. I needed to be strong right now. All I could do was pray it wouldn't happen—that by some miracle, the bleeding would go away on its own. But the fact that she still hadn't woken was scaring the fuck out of me.

I took her hand in mine, brushing my thumb over the cuts on her knuckles, evidence of the fight she'd given that motherfucker before he had taken her out. Such a pussy he was, waiting until she was distracted.

Her cuts were beginning to scab, but I knew her internal wounds, the ones marked on her soul, would be fresh once she—*if* she woke up. Doctors always had to warn you of the worst case scenario, and the thought of that possibility sent a shivering heat up my spine. So instead, I focused on her eyelashes, willing them to flutter, to twitch, to . . . anything.

I curled into her, the ache in my back nearing unbearable, but I refused to move from her side. After hours of sharing the room with her parents, avoiding their questions that were piled high, I was grateful for a moment alone with her while they went for some air and coffee. The answers they sought all lay in this bed with me—wordless.

Abby was scarce, briefly coming to check on her sister and leaving without spending much time in the same room as me. Jace kept vigil but mostly stayed by the door, giving me privacy with her. And I . . . I was never leaving her side again.

"Bl—Blake?" her brokenly beautiful voice croaked.

A pang cricked my neck as I shot up. I blinked, unbelieving as I searched her half-opened, glossy eyes. "Baby?" I rushed to take her face between my hands, my eyes ping-ponging around her features to be sure I wasn't imagining this.

"Wh-what happened?" She lazily fell into my touch, her hands coming up to feel around the tender areas of her head. Her eyes pinched in a wince.

I scrambled, grabbing the call button for the nurse and pushing on it like a lunatic. "You're really awake," I said as more of a statement to myself, still not believing my eyes. I prayed this wasn't a fluke and she wouldn't fall back into a motionless slumber.

All she could do was stare at me like a deer caught in headlights. I could see all of the questions swirling as she tried to piece together past events. Pushing her fingertips into her temples, she squished her eyes shut.

I took her shaking hands in my own, brushing my fingertips along her cheek. "Just relax. I don't want you to get worked up. Let them look you over first, and then I'll explain everything."

Her shoulders melted downward, and she leaned into me. Her lids began to drift closed, and my heart lurched in my chest. I cupped the sides of her face in a panic. "Angel?" I examined her features.

"I'm okay," she replied lazily, her eyes slightly rolling as she sought out mine again.

"You're going to be okay." I wasn't sure who I was reassuring, her or myself. But it didn't matter because she was—she *would* be.

I pulled her to my chest. Her arms wrapped around me feebly and I gently kissed her scalp, feeling a calm wash over me. Resting my chin on top of her head, I looked up at the ceiling. With the blow of a breath, I sent a silent prayer up to whoever was listening in thanks for bringing my girl back to me. As long as she was all right, we could do anything. Beat anything. Now that I knew the truth, I would make it my mission to get her justice. I just had to get her well first.

A moment later, a white coat barged into the room, followed by two nurses. "Evangelina, it's nice to finally see you awake." The skin at the corners of the middle-aged doctor's eyes crinkled with friendliness. Though he seemed like he wanted to give the impression that he was unalarmed, I could see the urgency to examine her in his swift movements to her bedside as he snatched her clipboard and began inspecting monitors.

Eva's eyes moved to the doctor, but her grip around my waist tightened. Nervous, erratic beats thumped from the center of her chest, brushing against my arm.

"You're fine," I whispered assurances in her ear. I would give her every ounce of strength that I had—all she was lacking—to get her through this.

She nodded, loosening her hold. I shifted on the bed to sit beside her, lacing her fingers with mine mostly for her support, but for mine as well.

"How do you feel?" the doctor asked while nurses pushed buttons on boxes, checking numbers and counts.

"My head hurts." Eva felt around in her hair again. The uncertainty was back in her eyes, although she wasn't focusing on anything specific. Just seemed to be lost in a world somewhere. The weight of her questions sat in the deep lines between her eyes as she seemed to search the back of her brain for answers. Part of me wished she'd forget all of it so she could be rid of it for good. The other part wanted her to remember it all. We would need it for ammo.

The doctor seemed pleased with her counts, and any remaining alarm hidden in his posture melted with the final swish of his pen to the paper. "Yes, well it appears you took quite a hit, though no one could seem to tell us what happened." He glanced at me from the corner of his eye.

The line between her eyes grew even deeper as she pulled from her partial-trance to focus on the doctor. He tilted his nose downward and gazed at Eva over the top of his designer frames. "Do you remember anything?" Cracked and dry, her lips were set in a confused circle, and she seemed as though she were genuinely straining.

"Can she have a minute before the interrogation, doc? She only just woke up. Maybe you should just check her out and back off for a few." I traced the back of her hand with my thumb. My jaw was set so tight it was beginning to ache. No one was going to push her or make her uncomfortable. I'd make sure of that.

The doctor regarded me briefly before punching a few buttons on a machine and turning back to Eva. "Take some time." He patted her hand. "Your vitals look good. Relax and see if anything comes to you. I'll be back in a bit to check on you."

Eva's attention fell to the blanket covering her lap, her free hand coming up to twist a lock of hair that lay over her shoulder. When they caught on a knot, her fingers stilled. Her gaze drifted down, her mouth puckering before she dropped her hand.

Suddenly, it was just her and me in the room. I was certain that would change soon. Word would spread quickly that she was awake, and her loved ones would flood in, so I needed to say this fast before we lost our privacy.

"Angel." I turned toward her, but she didn't seem to hear me as she picked at the end of her hair. I took her chin between my fingers and eased her gaze to mine. When she looked up, the indent between her eyes was deep with worry. A pink hue crept onto the apples of her cheeks as a gloss began to film her green irises.

Her dry lips parted, and she whispered, "You know." It was said as a statement.

My shoulders rolled forward, my spine crumbling as I framed her face with my hands. I was quick to keep her grounded, to keep her with me so that she didn't switch to a dark place. "I know."

All the words I'd seen written by her hand. All the hurt—all the pain rushed over me like a tidal wave bringing a grate of nausea. I swallowed it down, knowing she needed me now more than ever. Needed my strength to fill in her gaps and keep her whole.

Her breathing bunched in her chest, halted by the new reality that sat on top of us like an elephant. Her gaze bounced around my features as she gauged where I was at and how much I knew.

Before she could draw some far-fetched conclusion, I jumped in again. "I know it all, and I'm not going anywhere. Except maybe to his room to end his fucking life for good." A tic broke out in my jaw as a new rage rocked me. Rage at seeing the fright etched into her face. Fury at wondering how many times she'd looked like that as a fucking wolf circled her with no one to save her. Reading her words, I felt her emptiness. The isolation. The destitution. It felt like I was lying on the floor of a hopeless pit, covered in dirt. Knowing I was long forgotten with no one to rescue me.

But I finally got it. Got *her*. Got her *why*. Her reasoning for all the times she had pushed me away. But it wasn't going to happen again. Not now. Not fucking ever.

"I'm here," I reassured her again, knowing she would need to hear it over and over to truly make her understand. A tear tumbled over her bottom lid as her chest began a heavy rise and fall, anxiety filling it like a balloon. I cupped her face, brushing my thumbs along her cheekbones, spreading the moisture. Combing my fingers through her hair, I held her gaze. "I'm here, Angel. *Forever*. For You. For it all."

I gave her a small smirk, reciting words I'd said to her over and over, except this time they held the weight of the world. "I told you—whatever you need." I swallowed deep, feeling the worry etched on my own face. Fearing the same result as the time I had spoken those words in the past when she had walked away from me for good. This time she would walk into my arms forever. I was making damn sure of it.

A sob cracked her throat, and her lids drifted closed, her head falling deeper into my palm as she covered my hands with hers.

"Give it to me, baby. Let go of it."

She crumbled into me, her ribs bucking and hiccuping. I rubbed circles on her back, and she melted further. Wanting her to feel nothing but protected, I pulled her into my lap, careful not to disturb all of the tubes raged through me, dancing amongst my darkness, sending a glittering light into my pores.

She answered my call with an urgency of her own, hopefully hearing all of my unspoken words, solidifying a bond that I knew would withstand any obstacle. I drew back and placed a full kiss flush on her lips, then dropped my forehead to hers again. A smile spread my face just as the sound of her mother's voice broke through our moment.

"She's up? Eva?" There was a pause as I left one more chaste kiss on Eva's lips, then pushed some encouragement into her with my expression before moving to her side so her mom could get a good look at her face.

"Oh, thank God." The worry deflated from her voice in a crackling euphoria, the heaviness melting from the words as she sank to envelop her daughter in her arms. Tears rained down her face as she sobbed into Eva's neck. Eva's father, Joe, stood behind his wife with a red nose, moisture pooling in his swollen eyes.

Her mother drew back to take Eva's face in her trembling hands, inspecting her. "Are you okay? How do you feel? What do you need?"

"I'm fine, Mom." She smiled, her gaze skirting away to find the blanket. "A little sore, and my head aches, but I have a good doctor." She moved our joined hands to her lap, smirking at me with the insinuation that I'd been taking care of her.

Her mother's gaze fell to the action, and her lips pulled into a hard line as she straightened her spine, running the back of her hand sharply below her nose with a sniffle.

My spirits sank. While Eva was out, her parents and I had gotten into it. They'd demanded answers, and I'd refused to give them. Not without her. I now understood why Jace had kept her secret for so long and I wasn't about to betray that. It was her story to tell, and she'd do it. When *she* was ready. I could see where they were coming from. Especially when their other daughter was freaking out over what I had done to her fiancé. I hoped more than anything that this would all end soon, but I wasn't about to push her.

Eva's face buckled a little as she took in the look of distaste on her mother's pursed lips. Then her gaze drifted to mine as she searched for the answer of what had gone on in her absence.

and wires poking out of her as I held her to my chest. The blue-green hospital gown lying across her thighs was a dingy reminder of all she had endured.

I hushed her, rocking, holding, supporting all of it. Absorbing her heartache, sheltering her abuse.

With a choked cry, a sound escaped her that I would swear was close to a laugh. I peeled myself from her, confused. Though the pain was still there, a hint of a smile danced in the water in her eyes. She laughed again, and I wasn't certain it wasn't sarcastic. I had hoped she wasn't losing it.

"I had a dream once. I was carrying all these heavy bags, stumbling under the weight. You appeared, and I dropped them at your feet. I remember the feeling of the burden leaving me. It's ironic, that's kind of what you're doing now." She finally focused on me then, a calm settling over her that resembled acceptance rather than defeat. As the muscles in her cheeks relaxed, she wasn't giving *in* to the fact that she had no choice but for me to know. She was *agreeing* to be okay with it.

A warmth took hold of my core, grateful that we were finally on the same page. Where everything was out in the open, and where we were *both* okay with that. Her expression was the most serene it had been since the moment I'd met her, and I knew then we were entering yet another stage of our relationship. And when her delicate fingers slipped into my palm, joining our hands, a burst of new life entered my veins. Of future years and open-ended happiness. It was a sign of no barriers, no lies, and no secrets.

I felt her soul wash over mine, and mine over hers to cleanse it and rid her of the shame from her past. Knowing this wouldn't be easy, I laced our fingers and brought our knotted hands up to each side of her face. I closed my eyes and dropped my forehead to hers, rolling side to side as I attempted to tamp down my heaving chest. I wanted to reassure her with everything that made me up that she would be okay now. I would never let her down. But I couldn't find words as heavy, as powerful, as meaningful as what I felt at that moment. So I let my lips speak the words my tongue couldn't.

As they slid over hers, mingling with her warmth, I inhaled her exhale, taking another piece of her inside of me. In a heated rush, she

I dropped my line of sight to the waffle blanket, not wanting to be the reason for any hard feelings between Eva and her parents.

"What's going on?" Eva's voice was slow, unsteady.

Her dad dropped a kiss on the top of her head. "We were worried about you, lovebug."

Eva's eyes roamed each of our faces, pink prickling her cheeks as she fidgeted to sit up straighter. She winced. "That's not it. What's going on? Tell me."

"We're all just concerned. Wondering what happened. That's all." Joe slid his arm around his wife's shoulder and held on tight.

Eva's mouth opened to respond, but before she could, Abby's high-pitched voice floated into the room. "Damon's awa—" The end of the word hung unspoken as she froze and took in her sister sitting upright, fully conscious herself. Abby straightened her spine, gulping down a ball of nerves as her eyebrows puckered.

Questions.

Answers.

Truths.

Anguish.

Every emotion seemed to float between them as they focused on one another.

As though she had learned all she needed to know in that gaze, Abby crossed her arms over her chest and swapped the weight on her feet with a shrug, clearly uncomfortable although she was trying to portray some kind of stuck-up strength, probably thinking she could intimidate the truth from Eva.

"Well, I guess now *everyone* can answer all our questions." Tears welled in her eyes, seeming to send the moisture straight to Eva's as well.

I covered Eva's hand with my own, lending her support. "Abby, your sister has been through a lot. She just woke up. Why don't you back off a bit?"

"No." Although Eva's gaze was downcast, her eyebrows drawn into a painful center as though she were breaking, the strength in her voice was unmistakable.

A flutter whipped around in my chest, and I wondered if she was really ready. If now was the best time—while she was so fragile, so confused. "Baby?"

After a slight pause, Eva sighed, her gaze dragging to her mom's, the weight of it sending her mother's hand to cover her gasp. With a tear-filled sparkle, her line of sight drifted to Abby, who looked faint, like she had stopped breathing. The circle of Eva's lips parted and words I never thought I'd hear floated between them.

"I'm ready."

EVA

~ And in the light, the truth shall lead you home.

THE AIR FEELS HEAVY.

Tingles paraded along my flesh.

Am I getting enough oxygen?

Blake squeezed the edges of my fingers, reminding me he was by my side, allowing me to draw from his strength. After years of building up a wall so high, convincing myself it would keep me safe, it felt good to allow someone else to shoulder some burden. To give into it. *Finally.*

The ice in my sister's green stare sent a shiver down my spine. *She hates me.*

"*Eva*?" The weight of my mom's questions sat in my name like a torpedo ready to launch. I hadn't even been awake ten minutes, and my world was about to change. It was time to unload the boulder I'd been carrying for far too long. I only hoped it didn't roll back and crush me in the process.

The noise from the hall lulled to silence, and my gaze drifted over as Jace turned and stood in front of the now-closed door. Appreciative, I silently thanked him. He blew me a kiss before clasping one hand in the other and giving me an encouraging nod. I closed my eyes and blew a slow breath through a pinhole between my lips, releasing whatever negative judgment still sat within me. When the last grain of self-hatred floated on that breeze, I opened my eyes and met my family's waiting gazes.

The water building in those familiar eyes told me my hesitation spoke as loudly as my words would.

"Eva, *what's* going on?" The lines of worry cut deep on my mom's forehead, the pinch between her eyebrows showcasing her pain. She didn't even know yet, and already I could tell her heart was crumbling.

An ache consumed my chest as I dreaded the agony I was about to cause her—cause this whole family. Once I said the words, she would know for certain—and she could never *not* know again. My mother was about to find out that the *baby* part of her baby girl had been stolen way too soon.

How devastating.

Tragic.

Life-changing.

Aware that I had shielded her from that burden for as long as I had provided some comfort. Solace washed over me briefly, a sense of serenity that I'd sheltered her from this for all of these years, and for the first time ever, I felt I had made the right decision in doing so. Unloading my burden was sure to explode bits of grief into all of the people I loved, slipping their own load to bear beneath their skin, but I couldn't think of such things, or I would never go through with it.

It was time to end my nightmare.

I didn't look at any of them, kept my line of sight trained on some blurry faraway place, where snippets of my story floated about in space, moving in and out of focus. Blake squeezed my hand once more, and the first of my words dropped like a rock from my lips.

"I believed him."

I faintly registered a sharp intake of air, but I wasn't sure who it came from, and I didn't dare stop. My insides felt as though they were being bashed with stones, my gut swirling with fright, nauseous and unyielding. I attempted to tamp it all down, to move past the flight of angry butterflies whipping through my core. The next words were uncertain as I lost a bit of the nerve I had built up.

"It was innocent enough, I thought. The first time he—" My throat tightened, and I tried clearing it, my eyes still swimming in a hazy mist. "The first time Da—" Fear of his name, of the truth, the lies, the filth and betrayal that they would slay at me halted my tongue. I squeezed my eyes shut, my face pulling into a pinch as I found the courage.

"Damon," I spit out the disgusting taste of that name, "approached me, I believed what he said." My upper lip twitched into a curl as I recalled the dip in my bed that fateful day, the look in his eye as he stared at my chest a bit too long. I remembered the confusion. "He was so close to us. I never thought he'd hurt me." A small sarcastic laugh escaped me in a *hmph*, the memory fizzing into the washed out fog before me.

A strangled cry was swallowed down, and the hazy, gray hues snapped to a focused picture as my gaze swung to Abby in a far corner of the room. Her hand was clamped over her mouth, her posture feeble as her head swished back and forth in disbelief. My eyes burned with an ache as I tried to keep them dry, looking at the horror etched in my sister's green eyes. Knowing it was because of me cut deep and weakened my strength. If I thought too much about it, I wouldn't continue, so I looked away and finished the rest.

"It was only the beginning of the hurt . . ." I pinched my eyes shut for a beat, feeling the pressure on my chest escalate like I was sinking. "The scratch at the belly of the Titanic." I gulped. "The water began to seep in at that point in a slow drawn out nightmare. As much as I prayed it would stop, it just kept rushing in, suffocating me until it took it all, drowning me." I simultaneously leveled my breathing, and my gaze so there would be no misinterpretation. "After that first time—he never *stopped* hurting me. Each time he came to my room, he'd leave with another piece of me. He'd take a little more until eventually there was *nothing left*."

"Oh, god." My mother clutched at her chest and started to weep.

A shuddered breath hiccuped from my chest while I gathered a bit more strength, trying to pull out from under the weight of the memory. My father caught my mother's shoulders with his hands, his own eyes brimming with tears. A look of confusion mixed with anger brewed on his face.

"But, how . . . why wouldn't you tell us?"

How could I tell them? "Because I . . . He . . ." I hung my head. "I agreed to it the first time—kind of," I rushed to add. "I didn't think you'd believe me." My voice cracked. "I thought you'd be mad."

Their faces crumpled, that final declaration taking the last bit of restraint. The flowery world that had painted their existence was now tarnished in a coat of tar lying at the foot of my mother's cries. Abby fled from the room in hysterics, knocking Jace in the shoulder on the way out. His spine sharpened as his gaze followed her and then fell back to me.

"Let her go," I instructed, being pulled tightly into Blake's side.

He kissed the top of my head, whispering, "I'm so proud of you. You're so brave."

I closed my eyes and wrapped my mind around those words, letting them soothe the open wound in my heart as I looked at the pain ripping into the people I loved most. In less than a week, Abby was supposed to be flitting around her engagement party—champagne in hand, euphoric and celebratory. Instead, she was getting the biggest bomb of her life dropped on her. I wasn't sure she'd ever speak to me again. The hovering gloom was squashing the liberation I thought I would feel unloading this.

"I just don't understand." My mom's voice strangled in her tears. "How did we miss this?"

I pushed thoughts of Abby aside, knowing my mom would need the attention of my answers. "He was calculated about it. Quiet. And . . . you love him. You *always* loved him. He puts on a good show."

My mom wailed, her head dropping into the blanket covering my lap. Blake's fingers dug into my side, reminding me that he was hearing this story from my mouth for the first time as well. This couldn't have been easy for him. I kept my focus on my parents, but grazed a soothing thumb along the back of Blake's hand, never more thankful for the support he was giving me.

"Don't beat yourselves up over it. You couldn't have known." I rubbed circles over my mother's back, trying to soothe the race whipping through her.

Red bumps paraded along the skin of my father's neck and cheeks, his eyes bulging in a watery rage. "I'll kill him," he seethed through bared teeth, no doubt finally absorbing all that had gone on. He was always so passive and easy going. I couldn't remember any other time in my life he'd looked so enraged. "All these years. Right under our goddamn noses."

"I can't!" My mom sat up, violently rocking.

I smoothed my hand down her arm. "Shhh. It's not your fault. I'm okay." All eyes were on me as I tucked a strand of hair behind my ear and nodded, reassuring myself just as much as I was them. "I'm finally okay."

My voice cracked as liberation flooded in, the weight that had sat on my chest for so long finally breaking into a million shards in an explosion of happy. Of acceptance. My rib cage expanded as I drew in a giant gulp of air, letting the lightest oxygen I had ever felt filter in. Reliving this secret from my past was the final piece of my healing. When you're bogged down with burden, even the air feels different as it travels through your lungs—thick and unsatisfying. Regardless of what happened from this point forward, I was free. I could never change the past or what had happened to me, and I was okay with that. It made me who I was, and I was pretty kick-ass.

JACE'S FINGERS COMBED THROUGH MY hair, comforting me on this unforgiving hospital bed as I relived my story once again, looking into Jessie and Sandra's glossed-over eyes. Doctor Christianson had been right when she had instructed me to tell anyone who would listen. The more I told it, the freer I felt. The less dirty. Each time I recited some of the hellish details, it made me realize even more that none of it was my fault. I didn't know how I had convinced myself for so long that it was, but the mind does funny things when there's a parasite infesting it.

My friends were draped all around me, supporting me in a big love-bubble. Though my body ached all over, my heart was full. Never far away, Blake sat at the end of the bed, grazing his thumb along my toe as his whole hand enveloped my foot. That one touch lending all the support I could ever need. And now that I had my parents and friends behind me as well, everything was starting to feel like it was finally coming together.

Except for those eyes. I couldn't get Abby's green eyes out of my head. The hurt. The anguish. No one had heard from her, and her phone had been going straight to voicemail for hours now. I prayed she was okay.

I prayed she wasn't with *him*.

"Knock, knock." A soft tapping of a knuckle accompanied by Drew's voice floated into the room. Victoria lingered, close on his heels.

A smile spread across my face. I hadn't seen either of them since before the fight. "Took you long enough. Where've you been?" I sat up straighter.

"Someone had to handle business for you guys." He smiled. To most, the twinkle in his eye would look happy, but I saw the distance in it. I knew him.

Jessie hopped down from the bed. "Next shift."

"I'm almost out of here, you guys. My last CT scan looked much better. I don't even have many beepy things anymore. I think it's safe to head back home now. No sense in all of us waiting around here."

"You sure?" Sandra asked, pushing her arms through her denim jacket and flipping her hair out of the back.

I nodded. "Positive. I'll be home in a couple days, I'm sure. Don't hold yourselves up. I have plenty of babysitters." I rolled my eyes with a playful smirk. I loved the fact that I had so many people behind me now. Now that I had it, it was almost hard to recall how empty and alone I'd been before.

How did I survive like that for so long?

I hadn't noticed how warm my foot felt until the heat of Blake's hand was gone as he stood. My eyes trailed up the tense lines of his body to the hard-set of his jaw. He shoved his hands into his pockets, his sinewy muscles twitching and bunching from the restraint. Everyone else must have noticed as well because they hurried their goodbyes.

"Call us if you need anything," Jessie threw back as they shouldered past Drew in the doorway. I could see the wheels spinning in his head as his eyes never left Blake's movements.

Jace kissed the top of my head. "See ya, baby girl. Love."

"Love," I replied, out of habit. My focus was trained on the other two men in my life, knowing both well enough to know something was about to go down.

As soon as it was only us, Blake jabbed an accusatory finger at Drew. "You knew," he squared off. "You knew it was him, and you knew he was in the house with her. This could've all been avoided if you'd told me. *Did* something." Vibrations rang off his body like a bell. He was on the balls of his feet, ready to lurch.

Drew's hands flew up in defense, his voice pleading as he tried to rein Blake in. "I tried, man. It wasn't like that."

"*Tried* my dick. You did nothing!" he bellowed.

Victoria flinched, the smile melting from her face with her retreating step. It sent the monitor that *was* still attached to me beeping in a hurried rhythm, though no one else seemed to notice.

Drew's eyebrows met in a sharp V, hurt etched on his forehead. "She begged me. Hell, she fucking fought me in your bathroom and made me *promise* not to say anything!" He threw his arm out to me, even though his eyes stayed trained on Blake.

I knew he was already calculating Blake's body language, gauging whether or not he needed to go into attack-mode, and it scared the hell out of me. There was no way I was letting the two of them fight. Enough was enough.

"Guys—"

I was quickly cut off by the growl ripping from Blake's chest. He took a step toward Drew, causing Victoria to back up another. "I don't give a fuck *what* she said. When the guy that's been *raping* her is in my fucking house—*with* her, you tell me!" His voice ricocheted off the walls. "I shook his hand. Welcomed him into my home!"

I swung my legs off the bed as quickly as I could, my adrenaline an anesthetic to the pain. "Stop fighting!" Everyone ignored my plea as the two guys each took another step toward one another.

"Do you think I didn't want to tell you? That I didn't want to kill him?" Drew yelled, his face turning a bright crimson. "Me of all people. You *know* I'd never let anything happen to her!"

"But it did!" Blake returned. "It *did* happen to her, and you could've stopped it!" He jabbed a finger, nearly poking Drew on the chest.

"Guys!" I tried once more, my heart racing at an unbearable pace.

"How is it any different from what you did, huh? *You* kept her secret and silently guarded her, right? Jace, too?" The fire in Drew's eyes and the truth in his words brought the full-flame shooting from Blake's to a simmer. "Look, we're all guilty of doing what we thought was best to protect her. Sometimes it's right, and sometimes it's wrong. You can't crucify me for that, man." He hung his head, the weight of his own guilt sagging his shoulders in a slump. Blake didn't respond, just sank further into his own thoughts as his posture weakened.

Drew continued, calmer. "I watched him all night. All fucking night, even after you guys went to sleep. I relaxed a little knowing she was with you, but I never took my eyes off him. The fucker passed out in the den, and I must've dozed off. I tried, man. I fucking tried."

My insides were in turmoil. Happy moments of feeling so free were slowly being tugged away by the guilt these two hung over themselves when it was all me. *I* was the one who had made them make the decisions that they had. Unable to take this a second longer, I slid my hand over Blake's crumbling shoulder and squeezed. In a soft voice, I pleaded, "*Please*. Stop. Don't attack each other. It's neither of your faults, and you both know it."

Blake's eyes skirted to mine and then back to Drew's feet, before drifting up to his face. He scrubbed his jaw, deflating. "Sorry, man. I didn't mean to throw all that on you."

"Nah, don't apologize. It ain't like I'm not already beating my own ass over it." The corner of Drew's mouth slanted up. "Anyway, I came to let you know you're all clear. Cops took one look at the neck of the broken bottle on the floor by all that blood and took down all of our statements—that you acted in self-defense after he attacked you. Apparently, the fucker was coming after you and wasn't going to stop at just Eva." His eyes brightened as he took in the shock on our faces. "Just make sure your stories match." He winked.

"Wow." Blake exhaled. "You did that . . . for me? And I just sat here and slammed you for not being a friend." He tugged a rough hand through his hair, then hooked his thumbs into his jeans. "I'm an ass. I'm sorry, man. I owe you. *We* owe you," he corrected. "Thanks."

"So, um . . . we good?" Drew looked hopeful, his eyebrows raising with the corners of his mouth.

"We're good." Blake held out his hand to shake Drew's before pulling him in for a hug. "But you're still not sleeping with my sister," he added with a tilt to his lips and a side-eye.

"Blake!" Victoria cried, her cheeks blooming like a rose. "Seriously?"

Blake chuckled. "Seriously."

Victoria rolled her eyes. "I'm ignoring you." With her chin raised, she moved closer to me, her hand reaching out to pet the side of my head, combing her fingers through my hair. "How are you?" Her finger snagged on a knot, reminding me of its state and all that I'd been through. She winced, whispering, "Sorry."

I waved her off, tucking that piece behind my ear. "It's fine. I'm okay." I edged toward my bed.

Blake began to follow when Victoria spoke once again. "Actually, Blake . . ."

Blake stopped and turned to meet his sister. She wrung her fingers together, fidgeting as though she couldn't make herself say what she needed to. "Spit it out, Tori," he demanded.

"Dad's at the house." She cringed, her eyes both apologetic and sympathetic. "I held him off as long as I could and tried to make him understand, but he wants to see you there."

Pinpricks marched along my weakened body as a wave of anxiety rocked me to the bed, my legs turning to jelly. I wanted to be with Blake, to help him handle what was sure to come, but I knew they would never let me leave yet. The idea of him facing that man on his own and me trapped here, wondering what was happening, made me sick. Especially since it was all my fault.

Blake dropped beside me like a weight, his hand covering my knee as realization swam over his face. Neither one of us had contemplated this part. He worked his jaw, his eyes in a disturbed faraway state, no doubt formulating the words he would use. Finally, he squeezed my knee, then gave it a pat, and looked up at Drew. "Can you hang with her for a bit while I go handle things at the house?"

"Course," Drew replied.

Blake nodded and turned to me with bright eyes. His deep swallow gave away that the confidence he was trying to exude was merely that—a show, most likely for my benefit. "I won't be long. I'm just gonna go get this over with."

"Blake . . ." I covered his hand with my own, unsure of what to say since I knew I was paralyzed to help him in this situation.

He pressed a warm kiss to my cheek. "Worry about the stuff you have to worry about. Don't you think twice about this. I'm good." He stood and rubbed his hands along his thighs.

Victoria laced arms with her brother. "I'm coming with you."

Blake looked down at her, an appreciative smile spreading. "Thanks."

Once they were gone, Drew dropped into the place Blake just vacated.

"So . . ." he began.

"So," I finished.

He looked at me from the corner of his eye. "Get some good shots in?"

A smile broke across my face, and I fell into him, a relaxed calm swooping in to replace the lurking tension. "I did. I had a good teacher." I laughed, the gloom of my reality finally lifting to let in some light. "You were right, though. The shots you don't see coming are no joke. We'll have to work a little more on those." I rubbed the side of my head.

Before the overlying weight could return to the conversation, another white-coat entered the room, pushing a wheelchair. It came to a stop beside my bed. "Time for another CT scan."

"Fun times." I winked, slipping into the chair. "We'll catch up later," I called to Drew.

"Later, Sunshine," he replied with a wink.

The hall was a flurry of activity. Beeping things, nurse-call voices, phones, people pushing patients, rolling blood pressure cuffs, wheeling gurneys. My mode of transportation created a soft breeze along my bare arms, brushing along my cheeks and rustling my hair. I took it all in, feeling a little ashamed that I kept peeking into the passing rooms, but unable to stop myself all the same. My eyes roamed, ping-ponging from each door until one room stopped them cold.

An image of someone else being helped into a wheelchair whisked by, a familiarity to his physique that I would never forget.

My psyche had been programmed to remember.

Although the breeze persisted and the swift glide beneath me continued to roll, my heart seemed to drop like a weight into my lap. A murmured lull hung on the dryness coating my tongue.

He's so close.

THE FOYER WAS EERILY QUIET as the front door parted from the seam, the light from it shining in a widening ray, highlighting its wrecked state.

He's gonna kill me.

Everything was still as it was when we had all run out with the gurneys. Beer cans, red cups, napkins, scuff marks. It was a crime scene, so I had called off the cleaning crew and then completely forgot to get them back here.

A can skidded across the kitchen floor, and Victoria's grip on my hand tightened. I looked at her. "Why don't you go to your room? Let me talk to him."

The shimmer in her eyes showed her concern, but I wasn't afraid. It was time to finally put an end to all this. With a quick nod, she turned and quietly made her way up the stairs.

"I don't even know what to say about all this." My father's voice propelled me back to the moment.

"Father," I addressed him without meeting his eyes.

A brief pause.

I didn't turn—just heightened my senses, honing in on the sound of his voice getting closer, the click of his expensive shoes taking one step, then two, in my direction. "Y'know, it's a good thing I've had time to myself here before you came back. When I first walked in, I might've killed you on the spot."

I sucked everything inside of me. Any remaining hurt where he was concerned, any sense of wanting to please him or caring if he was disappointed. I turned, readying myself for the disdain I would see dripping from his eyes, but stopped in my tracks when that familiar sentiment was missing. Something bordering what I imagined was understanding trickled in instead. Or possibly a knowledge of something I wasn't yet privy to.

Another click of his heel as he stopped in front of me, slipping his hands into the pockets of his overpriced slacks. His expression was so unreadable, years of not wanting to show his hand evident in the smooth curve of his forehead as he lifted his chin to me. "There are cameras all over this house, did you know that?"

All I could do was swallow, my mind banging back and forth between the years of parties we'd had in this house, all the times I'd thought he'd never known.

He smirked. "Never think there's *anything* you'll do that I won't know about. *Anything*." The drive in that last word started a race in my heart, wondering what else he knew.

I looked at the floor, relaxing my posture. "Listen, Dad, I'm sorry about the house. I'll get it cleaned up, I always—"

"I don't care about the house." My father cut me off, making my eyes snap to meet his, which were still a bit rough around the edges. He deflated a fraction. "It's just a house," he added, softer, and for the first time in my life, I saw a father standing before me rather than a tyrant.

My knees wobbled, and my nerves weakened from all I had been through in the last couple of days. Years of hurt had trained me to look at him like stone rather than flesh. I wasn't sure how to approach this new version of him, and I didn't know if I had the strength left to figure it out.

The tense lines he always held in his hardened exterior melted, the concrete face softening. "I know."

"You know . . ." The question lingered on my tongue.

"I can see the footage from the cameras anytime I want. Modern technology." A small smirk danced in the corner of his mouth. I cocked my head to the side at the foreign gesture.

"They record," he stated.

Like the sun pokes through parting clouds after a storm, a light emerged, slowly illuminating what he was saying. The slant of his lips told me that my father, always good at reading people, must have picked up on my enlightenment. "You have a tape of him assaulting her?" My voice was weak, barely cracking the surface as a prickling of hope bloomed that she finally had proof.

With the clearing of his throat, my dad adjusted his weight. "No, I don't."

My shoulders slouched, all of the tension they had been harboring sliding from them to the floor as I dragged my hands through my hair.

"The authorities do." His sure-of-himself tone, the tone I had always despised, snapped my gaze back to his. I couldn't remember a time, other than this, that I was happy to hear it or that it was for my benefit.

But as quickly as it came, puffing out my chest and dancing along my prickly skin, it melted into a pool at my feet. "Wait. If you have a video of that, then you have a video of—"

"You?" His tone piqued. He rocked a little on his heels, lowering his gaze for the first time. "I wish I did, son." He paused before peeking up at me. "I told them the cameras are on timers." His lip twitched, almost jovial.

"We could see you come into the room, but then Damon reached for something, and it switched out to the foyer." He shrugged.

Relief knocked into me, sending me on a wave so high I couldn't stop tears from filling my eyes. "You've got to be shitting me." I raked both of my hands through my hair and fisted them behind my head, looking to the ceiling as I blew out a puff of air.

My father continued. "The cops are on the way to the hospital right now. I've already called Damon's father and told him I have proof that his son is a child rapist." He cocked his eyebrow. "Needless to say, they won't be fighting the charges—not unless he wants the video plastered over every major news station and his name in every paper. Which I can assure you someone of his stature does not." He paused, giving me a chance to absorb all he was saying. "He'll be pleading guilty. And since I know just about every presiding judge, I'd bank on him doing a good amount of time."

My knees hit the tile, the sting to them nothing compared to the burst in my heart.

She'll finally get her justice.

Months of my worry—stomach aches, sleepless nights, broken hearts—barreled into me, knocking me in the chest and then floating away on the thought that she'd finally be free. Once and for all. And all because of . . .

"Thank you," I whispered, dragging my line of sight to the man before me. Without any other thought, I propelled myself at him, wrapping him in the embrace I had dreamed about since I was a child. With my eyes wet and squished shut, I squeezed, feeling profound satisfaction pumping through my veins. Probably shocked at my affectionate display, my father didn't react at first, but after the briefest of pauses, his arms circled me as well.

He clapped me on the back. "I told you, I'll always do what's best for you. I'm a hard son-of-a-bitch, I know, but that doesn't mean I don't love you."

I swiped my hand along my nose. "You'll never understand what you've done for her, and what it means to me."

"You forget this is what I do. Find justice for the speechless. For the weak. You have that little faith in your old man?" A playfulness was in his tone, and I wondered who this man was. But the relevance of what he had just said wasn't lost on me.

I finally got it.

"You're right." The answers floated together, completing the puzzle and bringing with it the clarity I had always longed for. "You may have had an off-way of showing it, but you were always right. This *is* what I'm supposed to do. Help the helpless. Give a voice to all of the broken angels out there."

A smile, so foreign and yet so beautiful, broke out across my father's face. "There's my boy."

BEEP.

Drip.

I wonder what he's dreaming about.

Damon's chest rose and fell in a relaxed rhythm, the calm on his face reminding me of the young boy I once knew. He was in worse shape than me, so most of his monitors were still hooked up. His chart said he had a couple of broken ribs and damage to his, um—I coughed out a laugh—scrotum, so he was probably on pain meds, and plenty of them. Most likely the cause of why he didn't feel my presence at the end of his bed, staring all deranged at the IV machine connected to his veins. Wondering what would happen if I flicked the switch in the opposite direction, or tied the tube. My finger twitched on the footrest before my grip tightened.

He's not worth it.

I had won. There was nothing he could do to me anymore. Small flakes of worry still floated around in the air like filthy little dust motes, but I was about to get rid of them, too.

"Ahem!" I tried to get his attention. When he still didn't budge, I shook the rail and jostled the bed. I had a message to deliver, and I wasn't leaving without getting my point across.

Damon jumped with a start, his glossy eyes zinging around, almost frightened until they focused on me where they transformed into something sinister. They had a different look this time, as though he was done with me. The lust was missing. What stared back at me in its place was evil, seething hatred.

My blood ran cold, my breathing clumped in my chest as the reason why I had come flitted from my mind. Those worry motes eating at my insecurities for a fleeting moment.

Immobilized, he tried to sit up straighter but failed. "The fuck do you want?" he spat.

Stilled in my pursuit, I merely stared.

What did *I want?*

When I didn't answer right away, he added, "Can't stay away, can you?"

I took a deep breath and shook myself free from his hypnotizing scrutiny. I refused to allow him that power anymore. "I came to set some things straight."

Damon's split and cracked lip pulled back over his teeth, and he let out a chuckle before wincing slightly and drawing his arm in to cover his chest. I could tell he was downplaying the pain, most likely not wanting to seem weak to whatever damage was done. "The only record being set straight is in my statement to the cops before they cart off your beloved. You stupid bitch," he muttered.

That one statement was all I needed as fuel to my already building fire. I took one determined step.

Damon's eyes narrowed, the cut through his eyebrow slanting. "I wouldn't come any closer, or I'll put your ass right next to your boyfriend's in jail."

My knuckles turned white with restraint, my blood heating as it swooshed to my head. There was no shot in hell I would ever let him damage Blake's reputation or drag his name through the mud. I leaned forward over the slab of plastic at the edge of the bed, lowering my voice and leveling my eyes. "You listen to me, you sick motherfucker. It's over. The only one going to jail is you. Statements have already been given. Blake acted in self-defense after *you* attacked *him*."

Putting on a show, I covered my chest with my hand. "You nearly killed me and then came at him with the neck of a broken beer bottle. Thankfully, he was able to get the upper hand and take you down." I smiled, triumphant, my chest puffing in satisfaction, and cupped the side of my mouth mockingly with a whisper, "There's a house full of witnesses that saw the whole thing."

Red climbed up his neck, speeding in patchy vines before splattering onto his cheeks. "You little . . ."

Aw, I struck a nerve.

"You didn't think I'd leave it to chance that we'd be caught, did you?" I threw his words back at him. A smirk peppered my face as I watched the recognition wash over his.

Seeing the person who'd violated me for so much of my life, essentially cutting off my mobility, now immobilized and strapped to the bed, I realized that I finally had the control and there was nothing he could do about it. This awareness sent a giddy rush through me.

But before I could get too excited, the red began to recede from his cheeks. "Where's Abby?"

The irony of him asking the one question I had always asked him wasn't lost on me. I felt the blood drain from my face and visibly stiffened, while he relaxed into his hospital grade pillow.

"You forgot that one important piece there, beautiful. Abby's never going to go along with that." A disgusting smile slithered across his face. Abby's name on his lips sending a roll through my stomach.

"Those little blue pills I slip her every now and then work like a charm. Always have."

A chill broke a sweat down the back of my neck. "Stay the hell away from Abby. She's through with you."

Damon scrubbed two fingers along his jaw, cradling his chin. "Did she tell you that? Because as of right now, it seems you don't even know where she is, and . . . you see, as far as I can remember, that pretty, naïve little sister of yours believes every word I say." He smirked again, self-assured and cocky. "Am I wrong—*beautiful*?" He accentuated his pet name for me, rolling the *L* off his tongue. "She's never going to believe you. When are you going to realize that? Or maybe you don't care anymore that your sister knows I fucked your brains out your whole life. That you learned on me. I'd hardly call that rape. I did you a favor."

His smile this time was deliberate, and the gleam in his eye unmistakable as he took what he believed to be a victory. "You're fucked. Once again. Seems I'm always fucking you now, doesn't it? Only this time, I don't even have to touch you to do it."

"You fucking bastard." The familiar voice drained the blood from my face as I spun to find Abby in the doorway. She looked wrecked, her eyes watery and wild, her skin blotchy. "How could you?" she asked quietly, as though she was still unsure. Then her regard of the situation seemed to solidify as she added more forcefully, "How could you! I gave you *everything*—waited for you!"

Waited for you?

My gaze swung to Damon, whose eyes were now popped out of his head as he made every feeble attempt to sit up straighter. "Baby . . ."

"Don't you fucking baby me," she threw back. "How many years did I hold myself back waiting for you—waiting until we were married? You agreed! You wanted that, too!" she screamed.

I stumbled back, her words slapping me into the hard plastic footboard.

No . . .

"What?" The word fell from my lips in a whisper—a faint attempt at speaking through an incoherent fog as another piece of this warped reality floated into place.

"You . . . you're a . . ." I couldn't bear to say the word.

She crossed her arms over her chest as though she was sheltering it. "A virgin? Yes." Her eyes barely flicked to mine. In that brief second, though, the struggle behind them spoke. The betrayal she felt toward me warring with wanting to comfort her sister—the rape victim.

"She came on to me!" Damon yelled, a hoax of desperation swimming in his deceitful eyes as he drew another card from his stack.

"How could you do it?" She advanced toward him. "All those years you made me wait—led me to believe we would share something special together, something sacred. And all the while you were . . ." Abby swallowed down tears, then she lifted a shaky pointer finger at him. "Never come near me again." She lifted her chin and side-stepped to me, sliding her palm into mine. "*Us* again."

I looked down to our interlocked fingers and then up to the firm set of her jaw. Tears threatened to pour over her lower lids. Even though she was trying so desperately to hold them at bay, I could practically feel them searing her throat as she made her declaration.

Damon locked his eyes on her. "This ain't over. *We* aren't over," he promised, the determination in his eyes reaching out across the room to cage her to her place. Let her know he wouldn't be dismissed so easily.

Abby opened her mouth to respond when a sharp tapping bounced off the frame of the door. "Mr. Bradshaw . . ." A clattering followed Damon's name, and Abby and I turned to find two police officers crossing the threshold. My heart raced at the sight of them, likely here to take his statement. I wondered what he would say.

At their approach, Abby and I stumbled aside in unison.

"Ms. Ricci?" The first officer to enter the room addressed me.

How does he know my name?

"Y—Yes?" I stuttered out.

"If you plan on pursuing a restraining order, you should probably leave," he stated plainly.

My eyebrows drew in. I couldn't answer as my sights drifted from them to Damon and back again, the officer's words not making any sense.

Abby tugged at my arm as Damon straightened. "Restraining order? I'm the one who needs the fucking restraining order!"

More backward steps as Abby led us from the room. When my heel stumbled over the threshold, the second officer freed the clasp holding the door open. My line of sight into the room diminished on the soft swish of the door as the first officer drew his handcuffs.

"Mr. Bradshaw, you're under arrest for the assault and sexual abuse of Evangelina Ricci and the assault of Blake Turner. You have the right to remain silent . . ."

The window of sight diminished.

The door clicked into place.

Chapter 78

THE BREEZE FROM THE CLOSING door settled like a blanket over my soul, concluding the longest chapter of my life. Damon's protests lashed like muffled whips, but all I could do was stare at the grains in the wooden slab, my mouth hanging open.

What just happened?

"I don't know," Abby's response broke my time-suspension, and my eyes floated to hers. I hadn't known I'd said that out loud. Her palm grew sweaty—or maybe it was mine, I couldn't tell. Our hands just rested inside one another, neither posing a firm grip, but both lending all the support in the world.

Words traveled between our gazes the way only sisters could communicate—broken hearts and unspoken promises, scattered dreams and star-aligned futures. Her fingers twitched around mine, and I squeezed in response.

"I'm sorry," she finally stated. "I'm sorry I didn't know. You tried . . ." Her lip trembled, and she looked to the floor briefly before looking back to me with glassy eyes. "You tried to tell me, and I wouldn't listen." She broke her hand free of mine then and covered her face, sobbing into her hands. "Why didn't I listen?"

I quickly blanketed her back with support. "Shh . . . don't cry. I'm the one who's sorry. I never should have—"

"Don't! Just . . . don't." Abby sniffled. "Don't start blaming yourself." She peeked up at me. "I was mad at first. Hurt. But then it hit me."

Her eyes solidified on mine. "I know you." She offered a small smile before squaring her shoulders and adding as more of a statement, "I know you. Even if I don't know the whole story yet, I know it wasn't you. So, please." She slipped her hand back into mine. "Please don't say you're sorry."

My gaze fell to our joined hands. To the support my sister was lending me when she herself was breaking into her own pieces. I yanked her to my chest in an embrace, squeezing so tight, trying to hold her together before she could crack into too many fragments, feeling us finally come together after so many years apart. Knowing that, after this—after we healed, after we forgave—we would be all right.

My tears soaked into the crown of her head, hers into the front of my shirt, and we rocked in unison—just like our mama used to do. One rhythm for two girls until my pain became hers, hers becoming mine, our joint heartbreak and heart-healing mingling in a tightly wound bond that we would carry around forever.

Chapter 79

THE LAST CT SCAN SHOWED that all of the blood had receded from my brain, so the doctors were releasing me tonight. "Can't say I'll miss this place." Packing my belongings, I grabbed my birth control, solemnness washing over me before I hobbled out of the bathroom. The feel of the little round cylinder brought a topic to mind that needed to be addressed. My sights landed on my sister, who was folding a shirt on my bed. I flipped the canister over and back again as I slid onto the bed in front of her. Her gaze moved to my hand before traveling to my eyes.

"He told me . . ." I inhaled a shaky breath. "He told me everyone practiced on each other. Friends. Said that you guys did, too." A short, condescending laugh escaped my lips. "Obviously, that was another lie."

Abby took a long swallow. Behind her eyes, I could see her mind reeling as she twisted the shirt in her grasp. "Yes, obviously." Her grip slackened, and she dropped the shirt into her lap. "I just don't know how I could've been so stupid. So blind."

She needed to know the rest of the truth. "He said . . ." My heart tripped in my chest. "The other day he admitted he would slip you something."

Her mouth dropped open as the reality of those words sunk in.

"You would always fall asleep. All the time, but I thought you just liked to nap." Tears welled in my eyes that my sister had fallen victim to Damon as well, in a different capacity. "He said he made sure we wouldn't be caught. So, you see, it wasn't your fault, Abby."

"Oh my God." Abby's words floated on a confused, dazed whisper, her eyelashes fluttering through the onslaught of tears at this new piece of knowledge. It broke my heart to know what this was doing to her. "He said he'd never hurt me. That he'd take care of me forever. And I believed him." Her voice cracked. "He was hurting me the whole time and I didn't even know it."

She straightened. "What made me stupid enough to believe he was actually waiting for me?" She practically snarled, her nose red and shiny with restraint. "And the whole thing was his idea! One hundred times I would've given in, but he was all," she deepened her voice with a disgusted curl to her lip, *"it's going to be so special.* Meanwhile, it was because . . ." She threw her arms out toward me, her words lingering as she caught herself. Abby swallowed hard, her eyes glassed over, a sheen which mirrored itself in mine as my breath caught in my throat.

"I'm sorry. I didn't mean—"

"No, it's okay. It all makes sense now. I'm actually glad . . ." I paused, gathering the right words. "I'm glad he never got to taint you that way. It helps." The corner of my mouth raised in a half-smile.

"Oh, Eva." Abby threw herself onto me, wrapping me in an embrace while sobbing into my shoulder. Instead of shushing her or reiterating reassurances, I let my heartbreak seep into her as well, our tears a hurtful river necessary to carry the sorrow away from us and wash us clean of his filth and betrayal.

When we broke free of our embrace, we were each a mess of tears. We washed our faces, the soap and water spiraling down the drain, taking it all away. In the middle of a hospital bathroom, I felt the cleanest I had ever felt as I shut off the water. My soul felt cleansed. I was so used to feeling dirty inside all the time that it felt like I was walking on air, free of the gunk that usually bogged me down as I exited the bathroom. Abby had gone back to the task of folding clothes, while I juggled what remained of my toiletries in both of my hands.

"Talk to Mom and Dad?" I asked her.

"Yeah. They're still by Blake's helping his dad get a handle on stuff."

Blake's voice drifted in behind me. "Did you ever imagine you'd see the day your parents and mine were hobnobbing?"

A warmth swarmed my chest, a smile spreading as I looked over my shoulder to find him. Comfort always surrounded me the moment he was around. "Not any time soon, at least."

The look of Blake, so strong and powerful sauntering into my room, stopped my heart. He must have cleaned himself up at home because he was sporting a fresh shave, his hair slicked back and away from his face. Dressed in a faded pair of jeans and a black thermal with the sleeves pushed mid-way up his forearms, I wanted to lunge at him. And I might have if every muscle in my body wasn't screaming at me in protest.

"You look delicious." My sights drifted over his chiseled features to the plump lip that was drawing up into a smirk.

"Why thank you," a second voice responded, a familiar face moving in behind Blake to perch on his shoulder. Eric smiled his boyishly triumphant smile, the way he always did after one of his sarcastic chides.

"Wrong sister," I responded, moving into Blake's side and sliding my hand onto his chest.

Abby's eyes, which had been devoid of any signs of life for the entire afternoon, now sparked as she rose to her feet in an almost dreamlike state.

"That's the one I wanted anyway." Eric licked his lips and stood up straighter as his heady eyes locked on Abby before being replaced with a solemn expression. "You good?"

With a tight nod, and a blush to her cheeks, she tucked a strand of hair behind her ear. "I will be."

A smile crawled across Eric's face as he seemed to take her word. He moved to her side and lifted a pair of pants. "Can I help?"

Longing replaced the heartache in Abby's eyes as she nodded, and the biggest smile broke out across my face watching their exchange.

A warmth coated my heart seeing all of the parts of this warped story finally find their closure. I was confident that, in time, my family would heal from all of this and move forward even more solid than we were before. That the scabs on our hearts would eventually dry up and fall off, and in their wake only but a sliver of silvery-shine would remain as a reminder. The tiniest of scars reminding us of the silver lining that lay in the darkness. Of the strength that love holds in the face of evil. That when all seems hopeless and lost, there is always a possibility of a second chance. Much like the silver star that rests at the heart of the dainty, sky blue forget-me-nots—a token I would have from year to year, each time *they* got their second chance. I recalled Audrey Hepburn's quote at the bottom of the flower box Blake had given me, its purpose never holding as much meaning as it did at this moment.

"To plant a garden is to believe in tomorrow."

My eyes slid up to Blake, to *my* second chance, who was already watching me closely. Then I glanced down to watch his smiling mouth descend to blanket mine, taking me away in a sweet, intoxicating kiss. And as he slipped another little piece of himself inside my heart's pocket, I was sure I had my answer to the question I asked myself so long ago when I first fell in love with him. That his heart did, in fact, have pockets as well. And as he collected another of my heartbeats, my soul sang a new song—this one the most memorable yet. Of love and life and living. Of freedom and security and breathing.

We're going to be okay. We're all *going to be okay.*

~ And in the end, the Angels rain down their blessings.

Heaven

I gasp

Air rushes in, sweeping away the fog
And I can finally breathe air that doesn't feel like smog

The murky night is washed away by the day's light
Eyes wide open—a cleansing, freeing
breeze rescues me from my plight

Piece by piece, I float with purpose
As they come together, all of the answers surface

Pieces of me that make up one whole
Pieces of me that finally have a soul

The pieces fix the broken, supply stability to the weak
Scrambling through the darkness, only one face do they seek

To live him is to breathe him
Soaked beneath my skin
Now that I've let him inside
I feel him swimming from within

The light is different on this side
Looking past the shades of gray
Staring toward a future
Gleaming bright with dawn's new day

I've said goodbye to the night

Waved so-long to the pain
Embraced the new and glorious journey
Where I'm free to prance and reign

My love by my side, we walk hand-in-hand
An unbreakable bond, through any weather it withstands

As they united, the pieces fixed the broken
Painted the pretty picture my life is now cloaked in

Gone is the girl with the light missing from her eyes
In its place shines a beacon, calling him forever to my side

For our journey to heaven
Is how we'll spend our remaining days
Me as his Angel
And him all of my sun's rays

Breathe . . .
Live . . .
Laugh.
Love.
Cherish.

Cut the ties that bind and then . . .
Then watch how we flourish

A new beginning
I'll forget not our second chance
A blessing in the darkness
Found by mere happenstance.

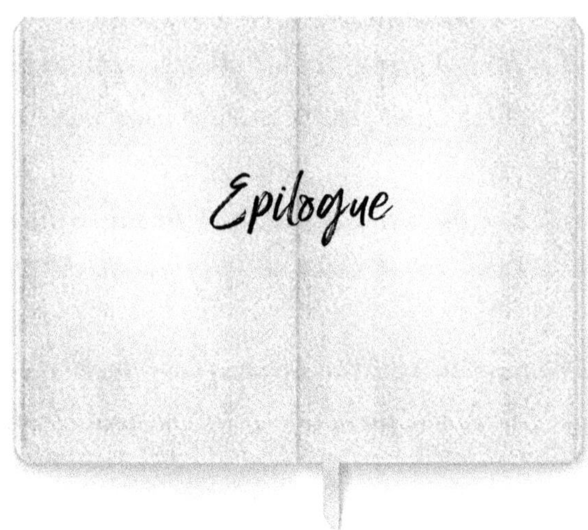

THE SKY WAS THE CLEAREST I had ever seen, a powdery blue hue blanketing the entire expanse with barely a white wisp to be had. A warm breeze trickled through the baby hairs lining my forehead, the steady rhythm of my heart melting into the ground beneath my back, leaving a bit more of me in its soil. I couldn't remember the last time I had breathed so easily. Relaxed so fully.

Strong yet loving fingers slid between my own, aligning lifelines with mine. My head dropped to the side to meet another clear blue—this one my most favorite hue.

"What's going on in that gorgeous head of yours?" Blake's eyes sparkled in the sunlight, the breeze doing its own dance in his hair.

My sights traveled across each of his features as my heart skipped another beat. I guess he would keep collecting those from now on. "I just can't believe we're here."

"Here? At Bertha?" Blake's thumb brushed my palm.

"No, here—in life. No secrets, no stresses. I've never felt so at ease. So content." I rolled up on my side and looked down at him. "Can we do this forever?"

Blake rolled up on his opposite side to meet me. "I'd have to say yes." His smile broadened, bringing with it the dimple I knew I could never live without. "Because forever's already started." His fist came up, and my eyes traveled to it. It slowly opened, and my chain rolled from it to dangle from his fingers.

I shot into a seated position, my hand immediately coming up to blanket my chest. "How did you . . . ? I didn't even notice it was gone."

"I'm very, very sneaky," he said like the butler in *Mr. Deeds*, his eyebrows doing a jig.

"Gimme that." I laughed and reached out playfully to swipe it back from him.

"Uh-uh-uh. Not so fast." He pulled his hand back. "I added a charm." His eyes were locked on mine.

My smile was stuck on huge. "Let me see."

When I plucked it from his grasp, my eyes roamed over each familiar charm—a tree, a camera, a microphone—I continued over them, each one warming my heart a bit more than the last. When my eyes hit the newest charm, they stilled, the burn of tears taking its beauty away in a blur. "Blake," I whispered, entranced in the authenticity of the ring, the reality of what it meant—but he was already up and bent on one knee.

"I love you, Angel. Any day apart is a day I'm not prepared to spend. You're my best friend—my *BFF*." He smiled with a dimple, momentarily lightening the heavy situation in a way only Blake could. "You're my breath when I feel like I'm suffocating, the life in my veins. I *live* and *breathe* you. And I want you to spend the rest of your life living and breathing me, too."

As if in a fog, I rolled to my knees in front of him, me on two, him on one. Tears dripped from my eyes, but I was too in awe to wipe them away as I stared at the man who loved me more than I ever could have loved myself. Who gave me faith, life, the second chance I never thought I'd have.

Blake reached into his hip pocket and pulled something from it, the sun bouncing off its shine like a ray but I couldn't take my eyes off his to focus on it. A choked sob ripped from my throat, and my hand flew up to cover the sound as my knees wobbled.

Blake continued. "You're it for me. For now and forever." Blake's own eyes filled with a mist and he drew in a heavy breath before finishing his proposal.

"Even though I meant it just as much the first time I asked you, this one is a well-thought-out proposal. I want you to take me seriously because it's what's truly in my heart. I know we're young and just starting out, but I want you to wear my ring. The one that matches that charm in our story around your neck. To know without a doubt that's where we're going. That you're mine and I'm yours. Sometimes second chances are forever." Blake focused his eyes deeply on mine so there would be no misinterpretation and repeated words that he spoke so many months ago which now held the weight of so much more.

"*Be with me.* Be my wife. My future. My life and my air."

My chest crashed on top of his as I fell forward, wrapping my arms around his neck. "I love you so much," was all I was able to choke-whisper into his shoulder. His broadness, his comfort, his love enveloped me, blanketed in his scent and my heart burst at the seams knowing I would have this man by my side forever.

He held me while it all sank in before his words trickled through my hair. "Is that a yes?"

I pulled myself back to meet his eyes. The same eyes that had found me in the crowd all those months ago and locked me in with a promise of never letting go. The eyes that had cried with me, loved with me, and begged me not to leave them. The eyes I wanted to be looking into when I finally met my children. There was nothing to consider. My heart had married his the second they met.

"Yes. More yesses than I could ever say—yes."

Our smiles spread simultaneously, then met to mingle together in a sweet, inviting rhythm. So un-rushed, so focused on feeling this moment. On cataloguing it. Blake's fingers crawled up the edges of my face, cradling it while I breathed in as much of him as I could. His sweet taste rode my tongue, sending me soaring on a high I never wanted to come down from. This place I didn't think I would ever reach where no walls remained. The pressure in his kiss bore deeper, and I arched my back to compensate for his urgency.

Blake spoke against my lips, "Mine."

He left a peppered trail amongst my reply. "Yours."

"Forever," he added through his kiss.

"And ever," I spoke around his mouth.

"You're going to be my wife." *Pepper.*

"Yes," I replied, still arched and chasing kisses.

"Say it again." *Kiss.*

"Yes," I repeated.

"One more time." Blake parted our lips and steadied his gaze with mine. "So you never forget." With a sparkle in his eye that seemed to be placed there by the sun, Blake hung on my every breath. His study tactic took my heart and exploded it into millions of fragments, each holding a little slice of him.

I met his stare head-on. "Yes. Forever and ever, yes."

Blake's dimple emerged in a slow, playful plunge, and then disappeared just as fast as his lips crashed back into mine.

Just as a heat began to prickle my spine, moving my pelvis deeper into his, Blake parted our mouths. He searched my eyes as though he were looking deeper into them—into our future together—a smile sweeping across his face lost in what he saw there. He pushed a soft kiss to my lips once more and brushed the edge of his nose to my own before smoothing his thumbs along my cheekbones. His hands slid over my shoulders, down my arms, and finally brought my hands to rest inside of them. With a calculated smoothness, he took my left hand within his own, perching what looked to be a beautiful one carat, round diamond at its edge, its white-gold circle just bordering the pink manicure that sat at my finger's tip. A shiver zinged through him, and he rolled with a cute little jiggle before adjusting his neck and evening himself out.

Every centimeter that ring descended around my finger solidified him to me even more. I think Blake felt it, too, because he stared down at it, the same way I did, with such an unhurried pace as he placed his mark on me once and for all. This was the ring I would wear until I took my dying breath, the life that we would share together already taking shape beneath my skin. When it finally came to rest in its permanent place on my hand, we each sucked in a breath and breathed for the first time.

A long strand of Bertha's hair landed on our joined hands, and our eyes snapped to each other's, slow smiles drawing across each of our faces before we looked up at her in unison. Her mane swayed in the breeze in a rejoicing manner. A calm settled over us and I was sure we had her blessing. As our current state of euphoria melted into the soil, I knew this couldn't have taken place in a better spot. Our story was etched into her bark, lived in her roots, danced through her leaves.

"What the hell is that?" Jace's voice broke my happy bubble. "No one asked for my blessing." I guessed our friends were finally here.

Both of us turned to Jace. He stood with a hip popped and scowl on his face. When a cheesy grin broke across mine, Jace followed suit. "Baby girl, get up here and hug me!" he squealed before pointing down at Blake. "*You* can stay right there on your knees. I like how that looks."

I catapulted myself at him as Blake rose with a red face.

"What's happening?" Abby called over Jace's shoulders, looking over at each of us. When I unraveled my hold on Jace's neck to prop my left hand in front of her face, her eyes widened. "Get out! Oh my god, Eva!" She hugged around Jace's back as the three of us jumped up and down in a ball.

Jace backed up, sending Abby stumbling into Eric's chest, who was never far behind these days. "You know I'm the man of honor, right?" Jace pointed his glare at my sister.

Abby took two steps forward, attacking him. "Bitch, I'll cut you. Don't even."

I laughed, looking back and forth from Abby to Jace. "No fighting. Don't worry, nothing's happening yet, and there's room for each of you at my side when it does."

My smile spread as I looked at my sister. *Abby.* She still had a lengthy road ahead of her, but she had come a long way over the last couple months. The first week or so had been rough. No matter how much of a slimeball Damon was, he'd been her first love and all she knew. Thankfully, things moved rather swiftly in the courts; you'd be surprised what money and power will do. Once the judge had handed Damon a year in prison, and he was safely tucked away, Abby had relaxed a bunch, but I could see something negative loitering beneath her surface, even though she tried to hide it. I was a pro at recognizing the broken, and I would have to keep an eye on it.

Although a year seemed insignificant for all the pain and suffering Damon had caused, I was happy that he got that. Unfortunately, most abusers don't serve much time, if any. That was the harsh reality of this perverted injustice. And it was sad.

My savior came in the form of Judge Turner, something I never saw coming in my wildest dreams. Once he learned of the extent of my story, he was on a mission to make Damon suffer as much as possible and be sure he received the maximum sentence he could. I would forever be grateful that he gave me back my voice. Never again would I have to suffer in silence. Things between Blake and his dad, and I and his dad had completely turned around. Blake was now happy to be walking in his father's footsteps, looking forward to helping all of the victims he could, rather than dreading a life behind a desk. And I couldn't be more proud of his decision. His happiness was all I had ever wanted and to see the determination and drive behind his eyes meant the world to me.

Eric clapped Blake in a man-hug. "Congrats, man. I'm happy for you guys."

"Thanks." Blake beamed at him.

Jace, Eric, and Abby began to make their way toward the rest of our friends who were setting a picnic. Their voices drifted as they chattered about whose role was going to be more important, and I watched them, my heart full and gratified. I was glad Jace looked happy, although, knowing my best friend, I could tell being here without his new love interest was taking a toll on him. Something in me was sure his happy ending wasn't far behind, though. I could feel it. There weren't many that could deny his unsurpassed spirit.

Blake stepped in front of me and reached back over his shoulders. "Hop on." His dimple smiled down.

My eyes skirted to his playful ones, and I took a moment to study my gorgeous fiancé.

Number nine-million-two-hundred-thousand and sixty-seven.

The amount of times my mind would think of him was going to be infinite. He was mine. He looked so content and relaxed like he no longer had a care in the world.

Blake.

There he was. It was the look he was always meant to have. I not only loved it on him, but I loved that *I* was the one ultimately responsible for putting it there. A slow smile drew out along my features as my new reality sunk in for good. Of a life that I would finally be allowed to live, without secrets or worry. With my man at my side and my friends and family surrounding us.

Slipping my palms into Blake's, I hoisted myself up, my gaze catching on the sparkle dancing off my ring finger. I looked up to Bertha one final time, thanking her for her support and guidance, knowing that this memory would remain here and cover up any lingering bad ones. I wrapped my legs around Blake the way I knew he loved, and dropped a kiss to the side of his neck before letting him carry me off into our future—to the group of people who each owned a space in my heart—the same way he had carried me that very first night so long ago and the way I would have him carry me through the rest of my life.

The End
For real this time.

APPROXIMATELY 4 OUT OF 5 of assaults are committed by someone known to the victim. 68% of sexual assaults are not reported to the police. 44% of the victims are under the age of 18.

82% of sexual assaults are perpetrated by a non-stranger

47% of rapists are a friend or acquaintance.

25% are an intimate.

5% are a relative.

Source: *www.rainn.org/statistics*, U.S. Department of Justice, *National Crime Victimization Study: 2009–2013.*

Sexual abuse can happen behind closed doors or in plain sight and can start from the littlest of children to the oldest of adults. It's debilitating and degrading and can cause the most helpless of feelings in the strongest of people.

There is help.

If you are being abused, or suspect someone you know is being abused, please seek help:

Rape, Abuse, and Incest National Network

National Sexual Assault Hotline ~ 1–800–656-HOPE

National Sexual Assault Online Hotline ~ *www.ohl.rainn.org/online/*

Visit *www.rainn.org* to find more information and resources.

TIME'S UP LEGAL DEFENSE FUND WILL provide subsidized legal support to women and men who have experienced sexual harassment, assault, or abuse in the workplace and while in pursuit of their careers. The Fund will ultimately be housed at and administrated by the National Women's Law Center, an established, national women's rights legal organization. A network of lawyers and public relations professionals across the country will work with the Center's Legal Network for Gender Equity to provide assistance to those ready to stand up. Access to prompt and comprehensive legal and communications help will mean empowerment for these individuals and long term growth for our culture and communities as a whole.

The clock has run out on sexual assault, harassment and inequality in the workplace. It's time to do something about it.

No more silence. No more waiting. No more tolerance for discrimination, harassment or abuse.

www.timesupnow.com/

Acknowledgments

DROPS DEAD

I, no doubt, lost pieces of my life with this story. These two left me feeling hollow so many times and swollen with life so many others. They became something I could never have imagined when I was trying to *think up* their story. But, silly me, it was *their* story to tell *me* all along. I just had to listen.

The first people I have to thank is them, Eva and Blake. They left me for a long time in the black space that Eva was left in at the end of Live Me, stranded below Bertha in a dark nothingness. Eva was quiet, not ready yet, and I was so scared that she never would be. I have to thank them for finding me again. For giving me their ending. Their trust. It took my breath away so many times, but they got it out. *I* got it out.

I have to thank God for letting me hear this alternate world that (I'm telling you) DOES exist somewhere and allowing me to tell it to you.

To my family. *To my family.* No, that is not a typo. I need to say that twice, maybe a thousand times. When they pulled on my arms to stop me from working. When they let it slide that although my eyes were on them, my brain wasn't. When they noticed me coming apart and just chose to act like I wasn't. I love you. Thank you, Fred, Christian, and Cienna, for being what drives me. My motivation to be the best that I can be. You are my world, and I wouldn't want to spend a day without you. I can't wait to live our new life together. Hopefully, it will give me time to write many more of these.

To my parents and Allison, you've always supported everything that I do. For that, I will always be grateful (even if none of you have read my work). *Bastids.* LOL. My prayer is that we can all be together again one day, the way that it should be. My heart's just not the same.

To Tracy, you read my work over and over and love it just the same each time that you do. Thank you for typing this whole book! You were my savior, and I can't thank you enough. I'm so glad we get to live closer and spend more time together now.

Barbara Wolfe, the girl who will always do whatever I need to make this story right. Edit. Read. Re-read. Anything. You're my everything. I can't wait to be by your side on your new journey and officially meet our child!

BL Berry, you're one of the real ones. Thank you for your endless help and support. Your knowledge of all things and your passion for sharing all that you've learned is inspiring. You're a true friend. I love you.

Mo!!! Where would I be without my Mo? Probably in a ball in the corner, holding an iPad with a square sticking out of it, rocking and crying with no cash bag. I love you fierce, girl. You're the light in my day and my left and right hands. I thank you for so much more than I can type.

Heather Carver, thank you for being as stubborn as you are. For loving these two enough to put your foot down and demand it be done differently for them. For helping me get it right even when you hated it. I love you. You've lived this story as much as I did. Now on to the next!

Jena Mason Campbell, girlfriend!! As much as I want to kick your coolie for not finishing, your touch and your work on the beginning of this book was the most priceless piece. You stomped and whined and "just no'ed" me to death until it was perfect. And it's your keen eye and unrelenting demand for realism that made it what it is. I will love you forever, and I am more proud of you and more in awe of your talent than you will ever know (Ahem, PLUG—Fiona Cole).

Kelly Siskind, we did it! But, did you ever think you'd see the day? Thank you for your hours and YEARS of hashings and what-if-ing. You're mine forever.

To Danielle Kelly, Tina Lynne, Shannon Mummey, and Stacia Lynette, thank you guys for jumping in and SAVING my ass when I was at the end of my rope with worry for this book. Your encouraging words and tears for my babies meant the world. You guys put so much of your hearts into your reading, and I love you all. Thank you for your time and effort and love and hearts.

Kaitie Reister, everyone's biggest fan, you are unmatched. I've never met anyone so genuine and so eager to help. Thank you for reading this prologue and offering your feedback.

To everyone in the group, Books By Celeste, you guys are UNREAL! I love you all so MUCH! The amount of support you have given me always floors me. No matter how disappointed you all were about the release being pushed back, about how long it takes me to complete a novel, you all stuck right by my side, coaching me through to the finish line. I am so grateful and humbled by that. You truly mean more to me than you can ever realize.

Megan Hand, my waterer of my pretty, flowery words. I don't think anyone lives and breathes all the fluff in my work as much as you do. And I love you greatly for it, my twin. Thank you for editing this baby in just the right way, making my pretty prettier and adding your little love touches all over.

Jennifer Roberts-Hall, so much more than an editor. You rocked every piece of the book. You bled it and drank it and loved it and petted it. I can't thank you with enough thank yous. It's you and me forever.

Lauren Watson Perry of Perrywinkle Photography, your ability to catch a moment and make it live in stillness astounds me. Thank you so much for the most perfect photo of the most perfect couple. I see a long and beautiful future for us.

Sommer Stein of Perfect Pear Creative, what I didn't put you through! Your cover brought me to tears. Thank you so much for your patience and for putting up with me. It was so worth it!

Lorie Rebecca, thank you so much for that perfect photo of Angel. You're stunning. It truly brought her *home*.

Julie Deaton of Deaton Author Services, thank you for being so accommodating. Your love for Blake astounds me, and your attention to detail and ability to find even the smallest errors is unsurpassed.

Christine Borgford of Type A Formatting, your willingness to help and be available for me means so much and shows how seriously you take your job. Thank you for always making my books so beautiful, both on screen and on paper.

Linda Russell with Foreward PR & Marketing, thank you for taking my hand and leading me in the right direction. For always being a positive word of encouragement and having my back so that I could finish this book the right way and put out something I'm proud of, no matter how long it took. Thank you for telling the world about my baby.

To the superstar bloggers out there, you guys do so much, and your only motivation is your love for books and the craft and the stories. You do it all selflessly and lovingly and shouty, and we love you just as much as you love us. Thank you for your passion, your love, for your screams, and for simply being you. I heart you.

And lastly, to *you*. If you are reading this sentence, that means you've made it to the end of this very long journey, through the love and through the fire. You waited for me. You didn't lose hope that I would bring you the end of Blake and Angel's story, and I have no words other than thank you. From the bottom of my heart, thank you. You complete me. I hope I've done you proud.

Forget not to live, to breathe, and to love . . .

XO

C

Breathe You Playlist

The Lonely ~ Christina Perri

What If You ~ Joshua Radin

In The End ~ Linkin Park

Alive ~ Sia

Distance ~ Christina Perri

Fight Song ~ Rachel Platten

The Words ~ Christina Perri

Fix You ~ Cold Play

Jumper ~ Third Eye Blind

Stand By You ~ Rachel Platten

Shots ~ LMFAO, Lil Jon

Into You ~ Ariana Grande

Ain't My Fault ~ Zara Larrson

About the Author

CELESTE GRANDE GREW UP LOVING words. From an early age, it was easy for her to open her heart through pen and paper and come away with something poetic. She never thought anything more than releasing her emotions would come of it though. A workaholic that can't keep still, in her 'real' life, she's a Certified Public Accountant who dreams of writing sexy books all day long. When she isn't working, she's reading, writing, mommying and being a wifey to the love of her life. She's newly relocated to the state of Florida, but don't worry, she has taken her pen with her.

www.celestegrande.com
authorcelestegrande@gmail.com
Facebook
Twitter
Instagram

Thank you for purchasing Breathe You ~ a Pieces of Broken Novel. Please consider leaving an honest review.

CPSIA information can be obtained
at www.ICGtesting.com
Printed in the USA
BVHW031436090822
644153BV00008B/355

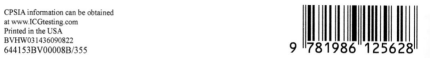

9 781986 125628